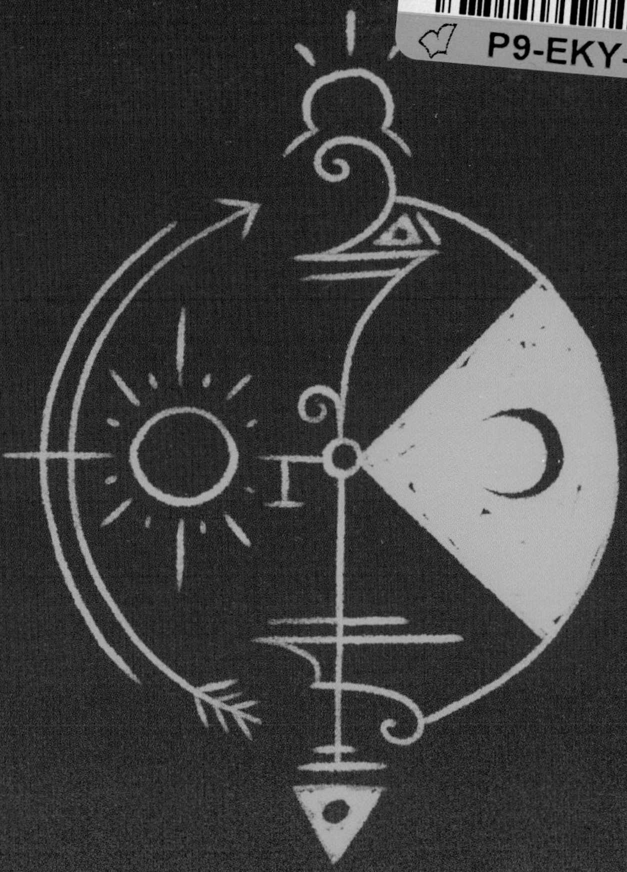

MOLLY KNOX OSTERTAG

THE MIDWINTER WITCH

graphix

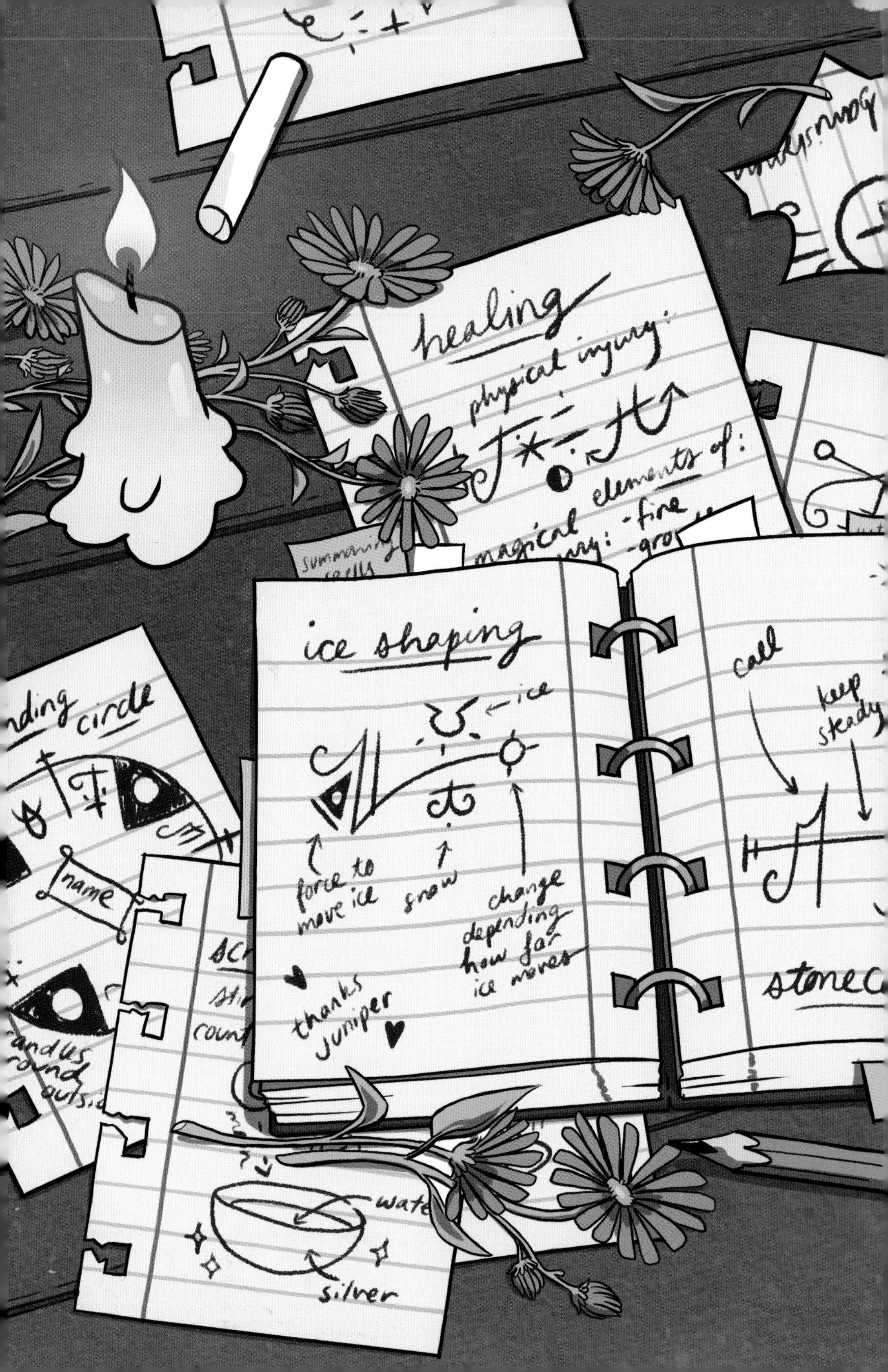
healing
physical injury:
magical elements of:
-fire
-gro
ice shaping
ice
force to move ice
snow
change depending how far ice moves
thanks juniper
call
keep steady
stone
circle
name
candles around outsi
wate
silver

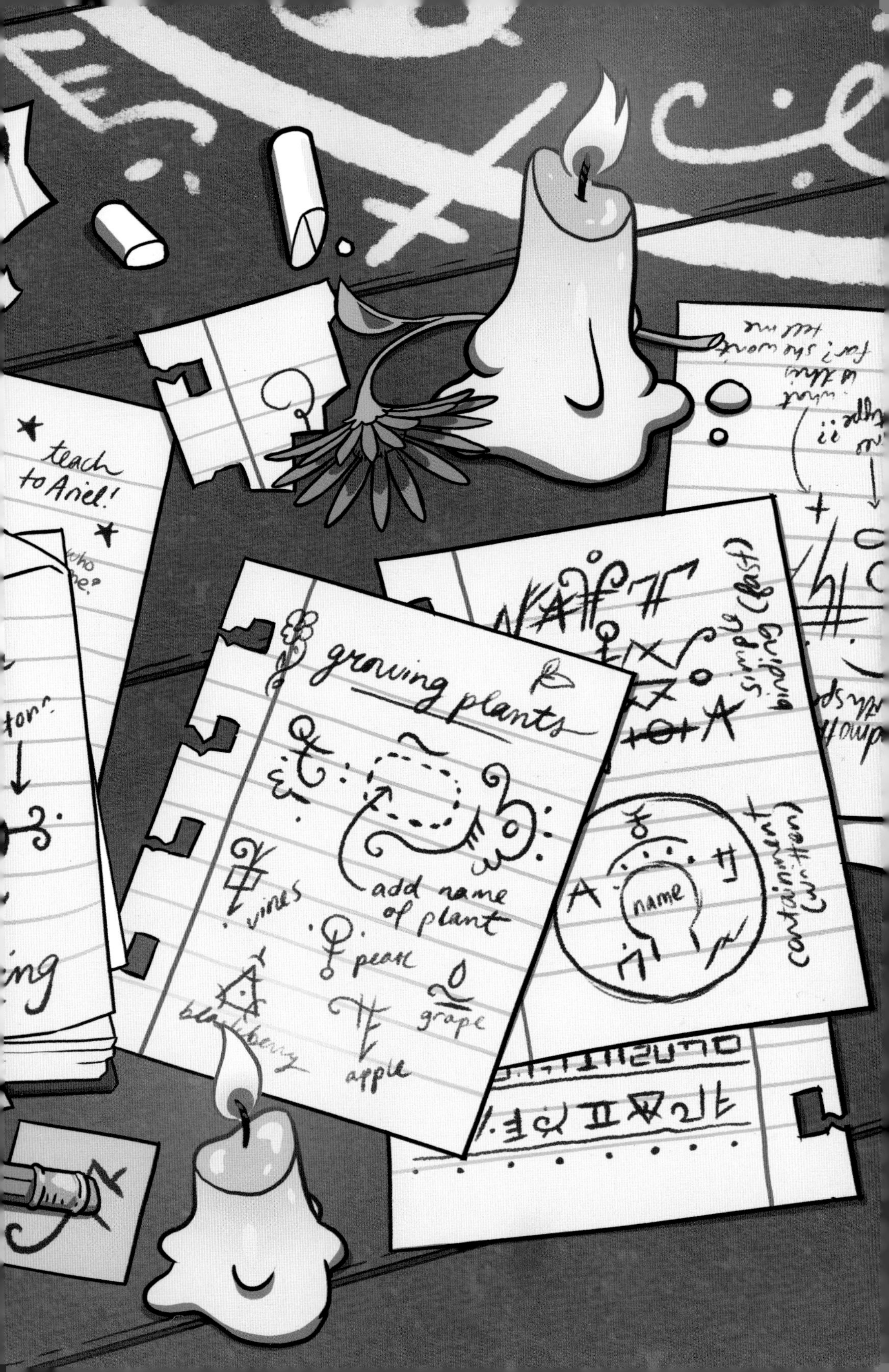

teach to Ariel!
growing plants
add name of plant
vines
pear
grape
blackberry
apple
simple (fast)
binding
name
containment (written)

For witch boys, shifter girls,
and those who are in between.

Library of Congress Control Number Available

ISBN 978-1-338-54056-7 (hardcover)
ISBN 978-1-338-54055-0 (paperback)

10 9 8 7 6 5 4 3 2 1   19 20 21 22 23

Printed in China   62
First edition, November 2019
Edited by Amanda Maciel
Color by Molly Knox Ostertag and Maarta Laiho
Lettering by Molly Knox Ostertag
Additional color by Niki Smith
Author photo © Leslie Ranne
Book design by Molly Knox Ostertag and Phil Falco
Publisher: David Saylor

The way the tales
tell it, magic is a
wild force.

It is the province
of spirits and demons, and
they can use it as easily
as we breathe.

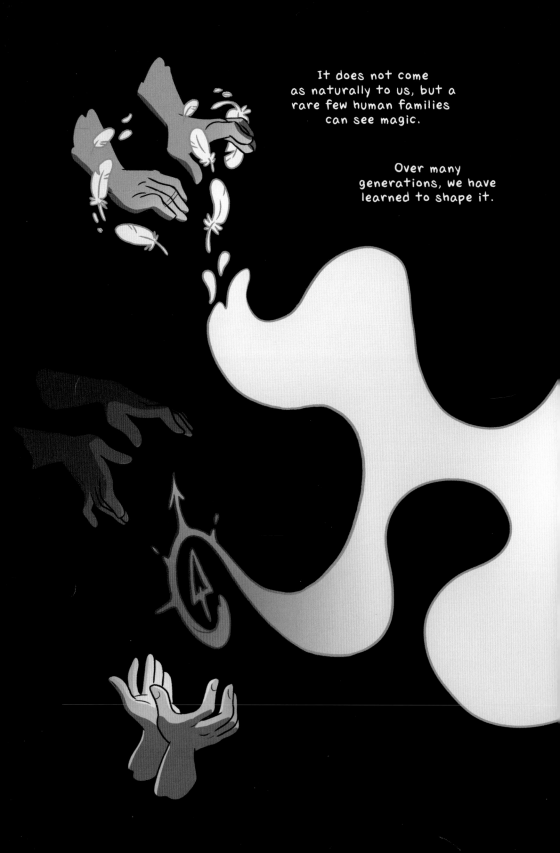

It does not come as naturally to us, but a rare few human families can see magic.

Over many generations, we have learned to shape it.

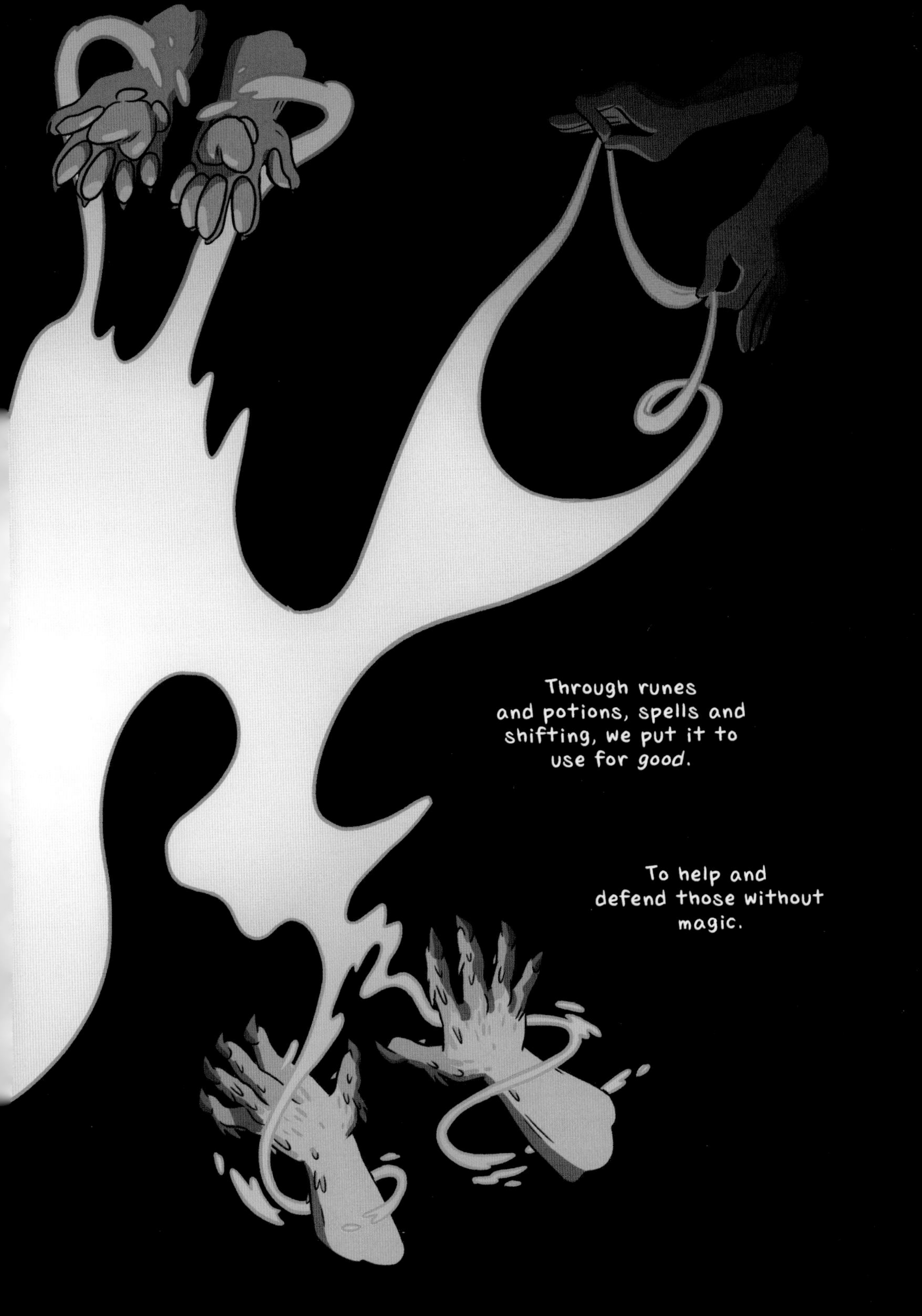
Through runes and potions, spells and shifting, we put it to use for *good*.
To help and defend those without magic.

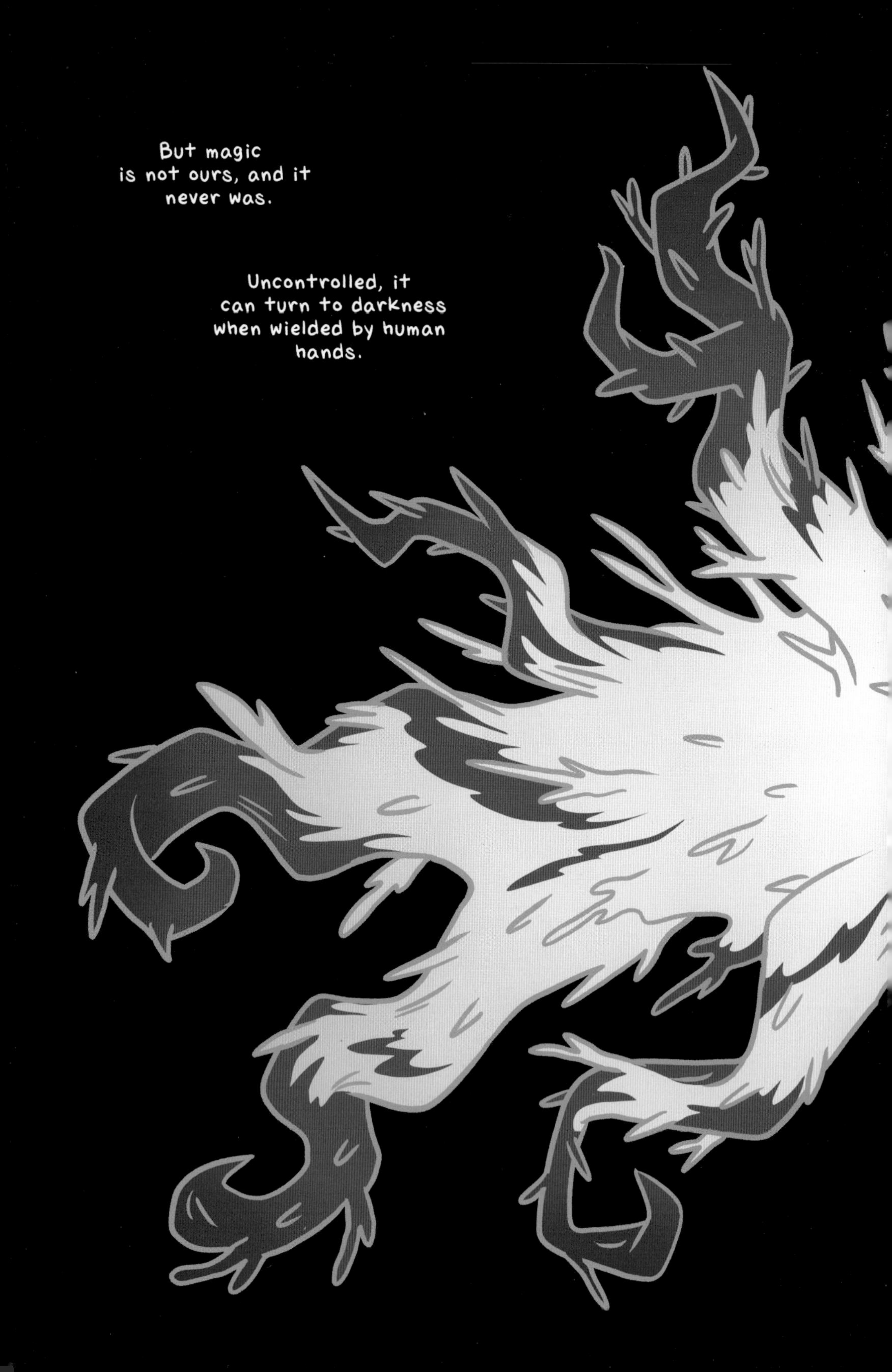
But magic is not ours, and it never was.
Uncontrolled, it can turn to darkness when wielded by human hands.

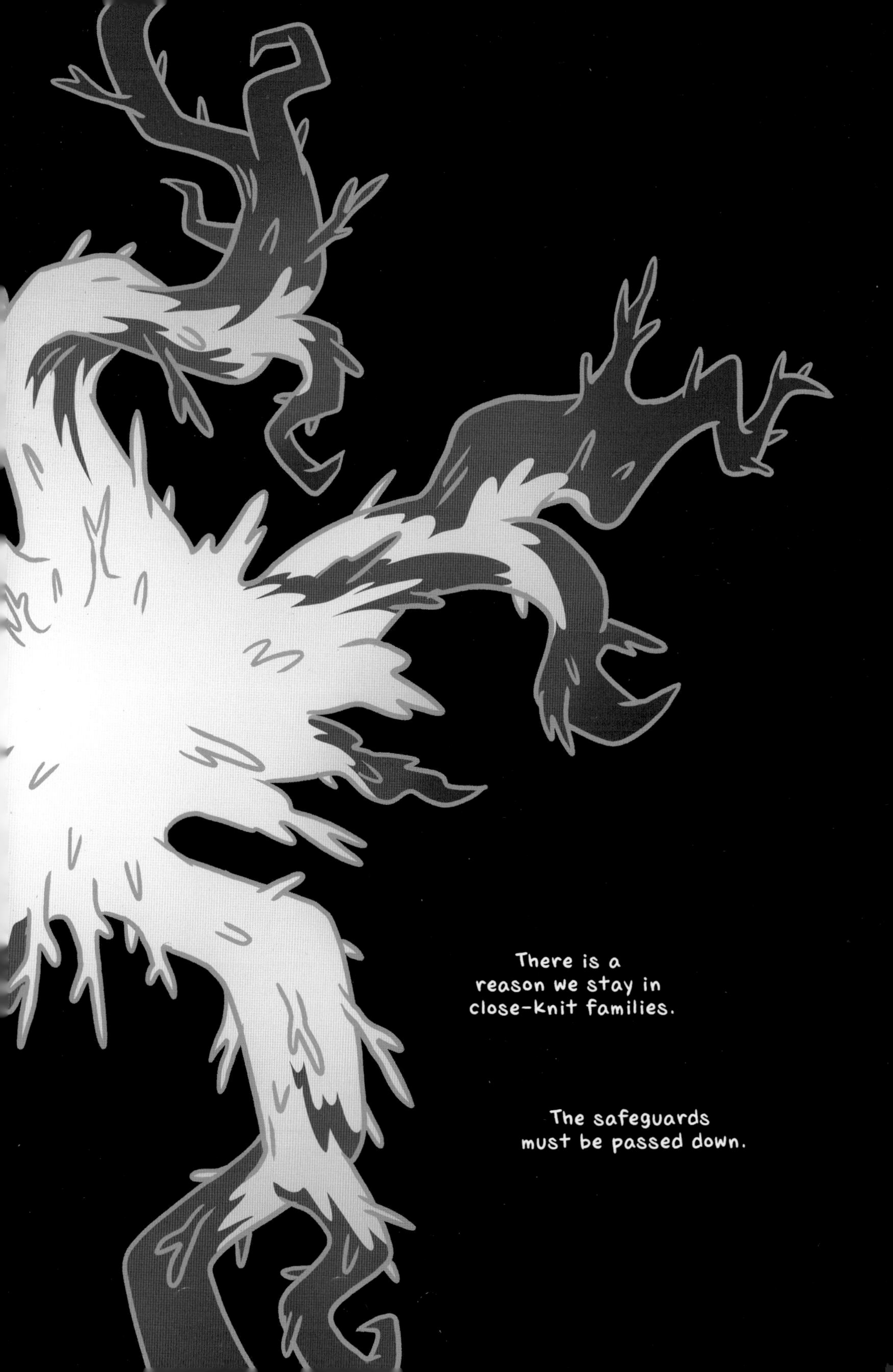
There is a reason we stay in close-knit families.
The safeguards must be passed down.

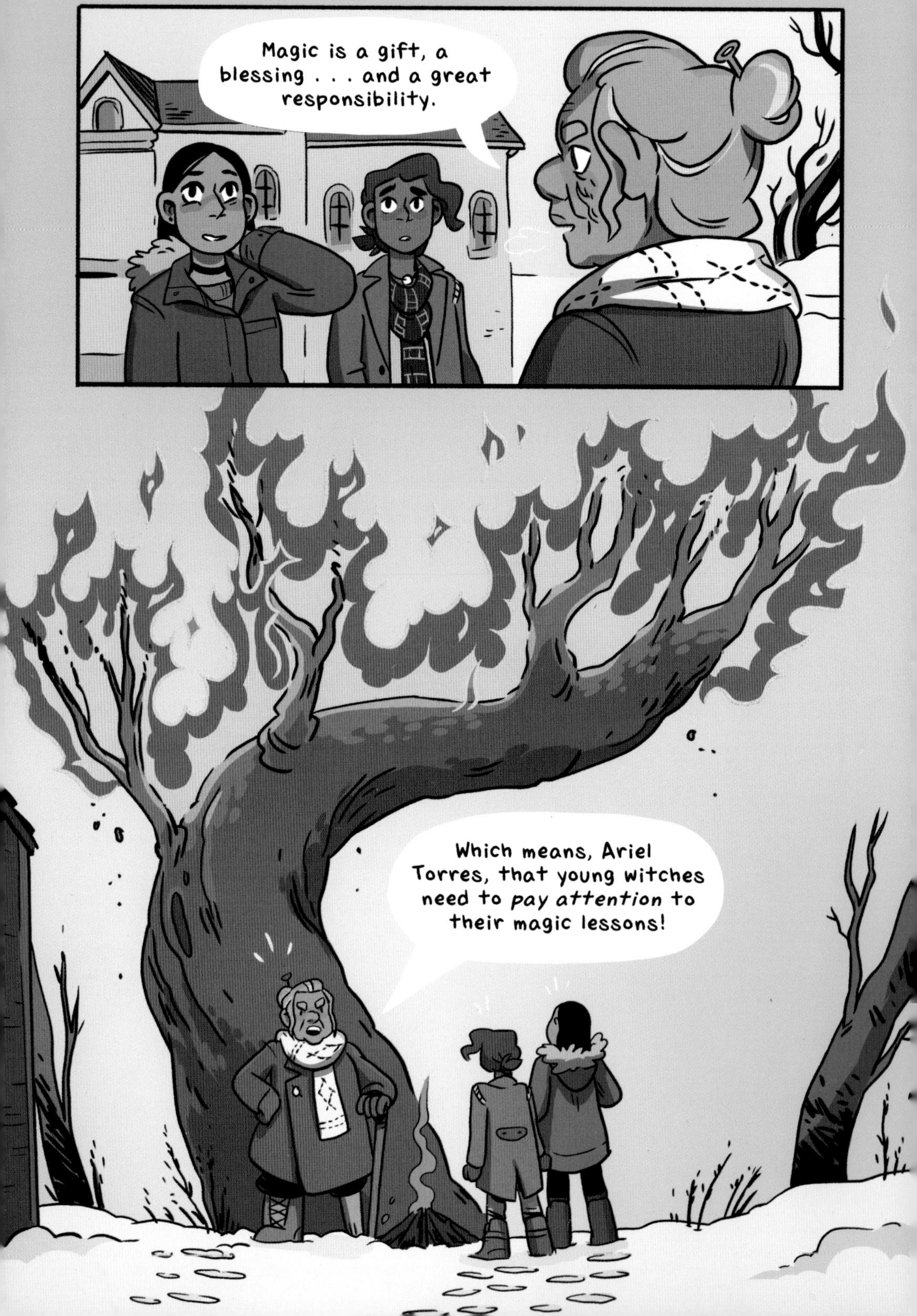
Magic is a gift, a blessing . . . and a great responsibility.
Which means, Ariel Torres, that young witches need to *pay attention* to their magic lessons!

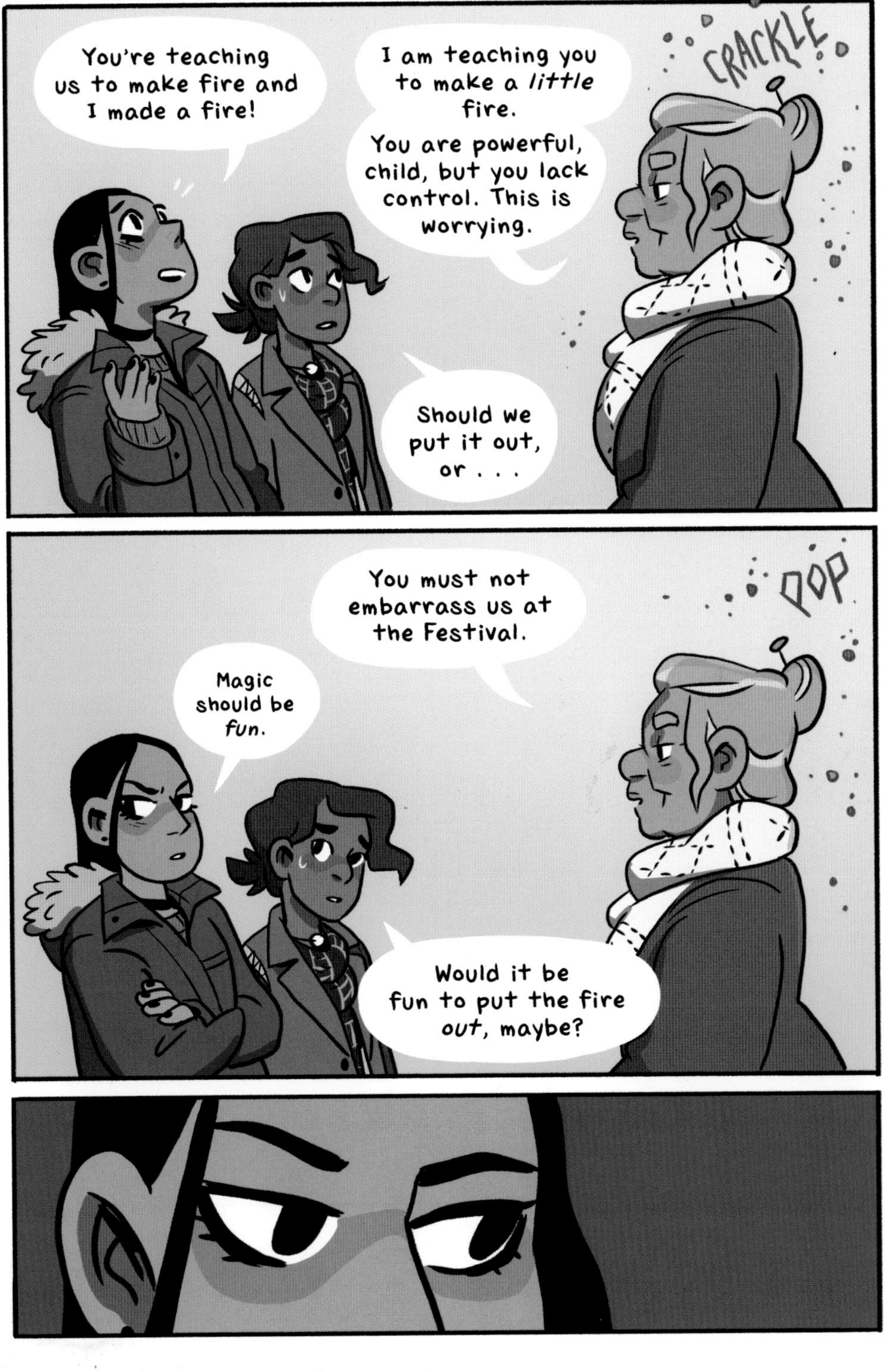

You're teaching us to make fire and I made a fire!
I am teaching you to make a *little* fire.
You are powerful, child, but you lack control. This is worrying.
CRACKLE
Should we put it out, or . . .
You must not embarrass us at the Festival.
POP
Magic should be *fun*.
Would it be fun to put the fire *out*, maybe?

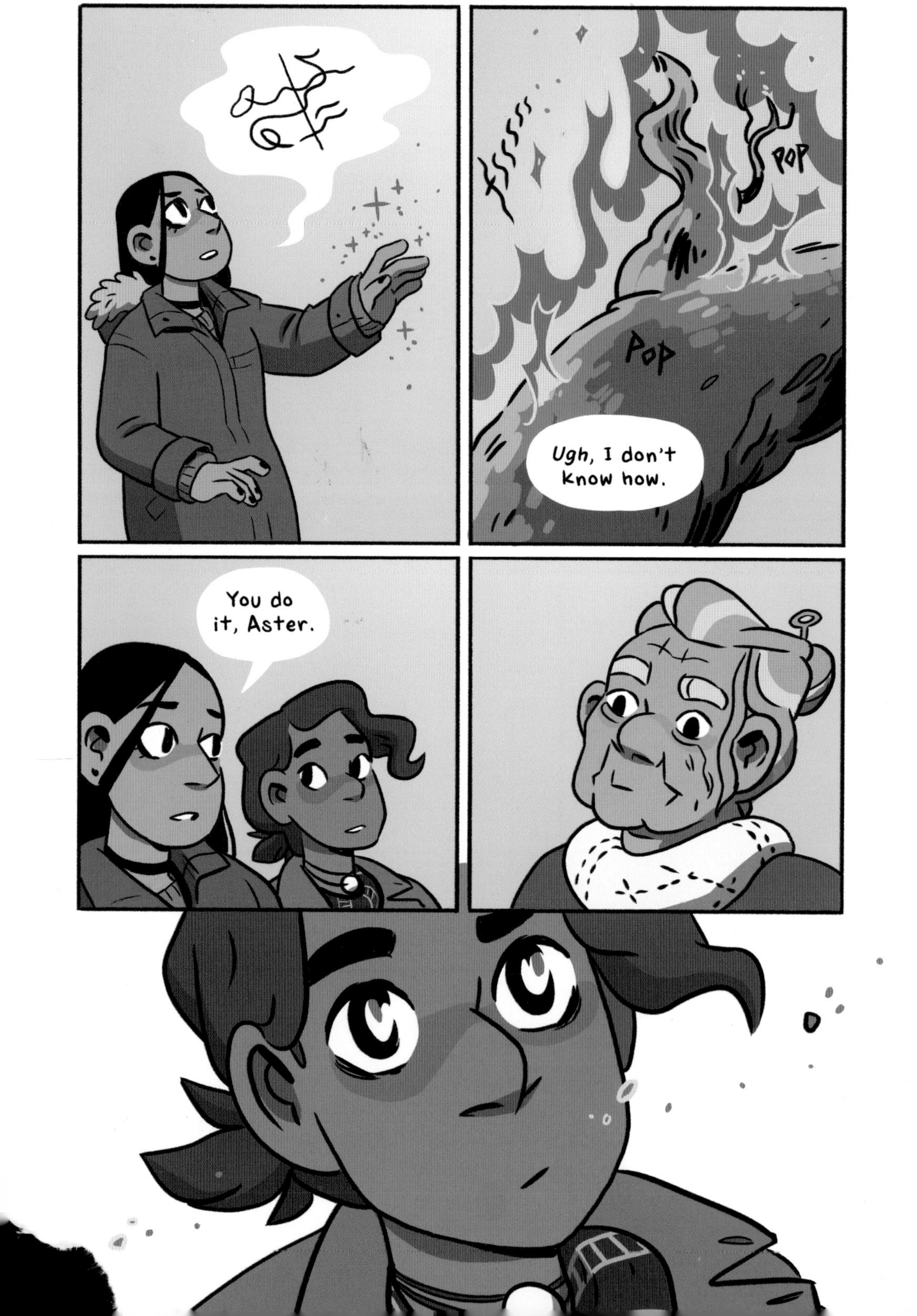

fsssss
POP
POP
Ugh, I don't know how.
You do it, Aster.

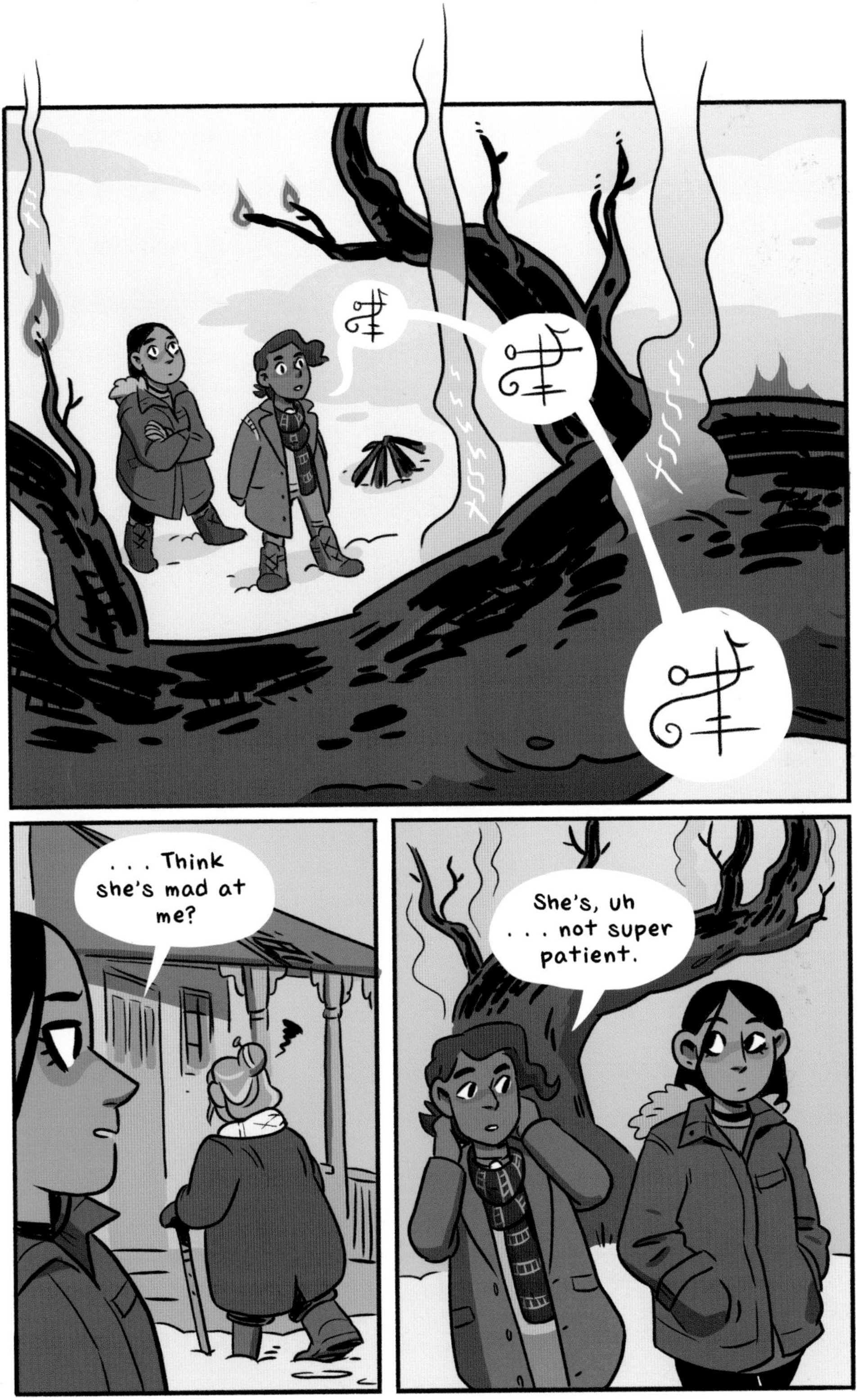

. . . Think she's mad at me?
She's, uh . . . not super patient.

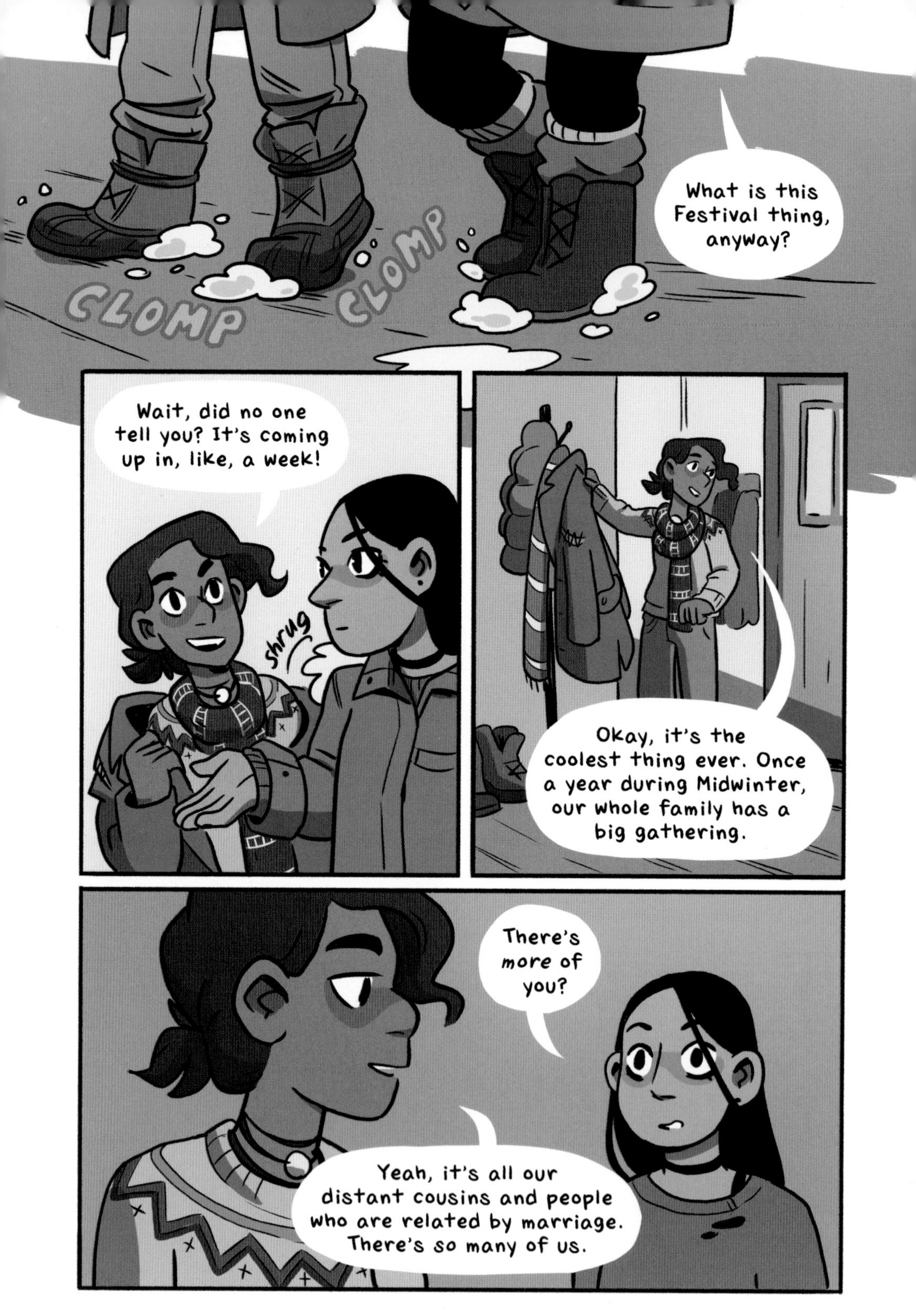
CLOMP
CLOMP
What is this Festival thing, anyway?
Wait, did no one tell you? It's coming up in, like, a week!
shrug
Okay, it's the coolest thing ever. Once a year during Midwinter, our whole family has a big gathering.
There's *more* of you?
Yeah, it's all our distant cousins and people who are related by marriage. There's so many of us.

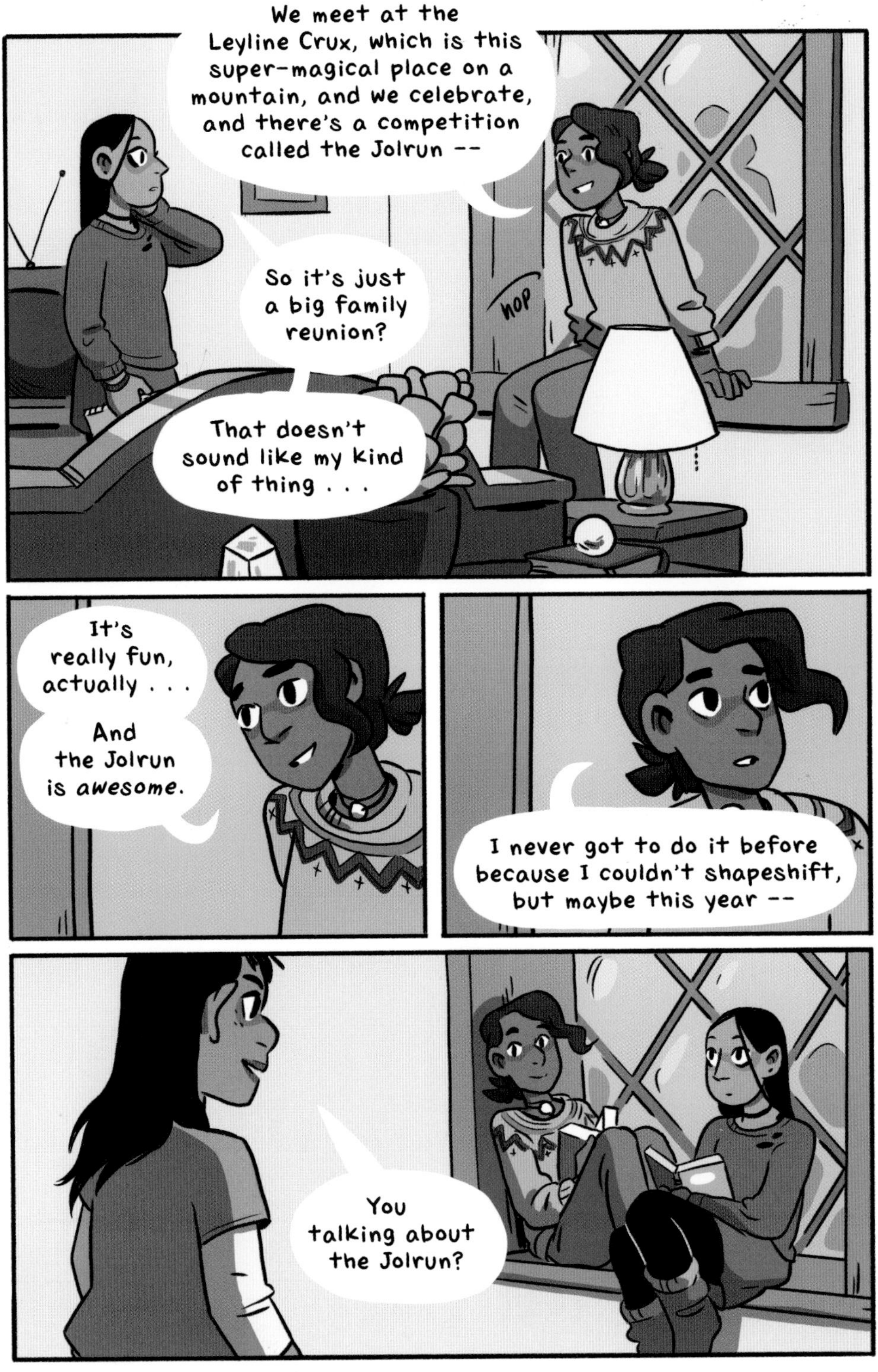
We meet at the Leyline Crux, which is this super-magical place on a mountain, and we celebrate, and there's a competition called the Jolrun --
So it's just a big family reunion?
hop
That doesn't sound like my kind of thing . . .
It's really fun, actually . . .
And the Jolrun is *awesome*.
I never got to do it before because I couldn't shapeshift, but maybe this year --
You talking about the Jolrun?

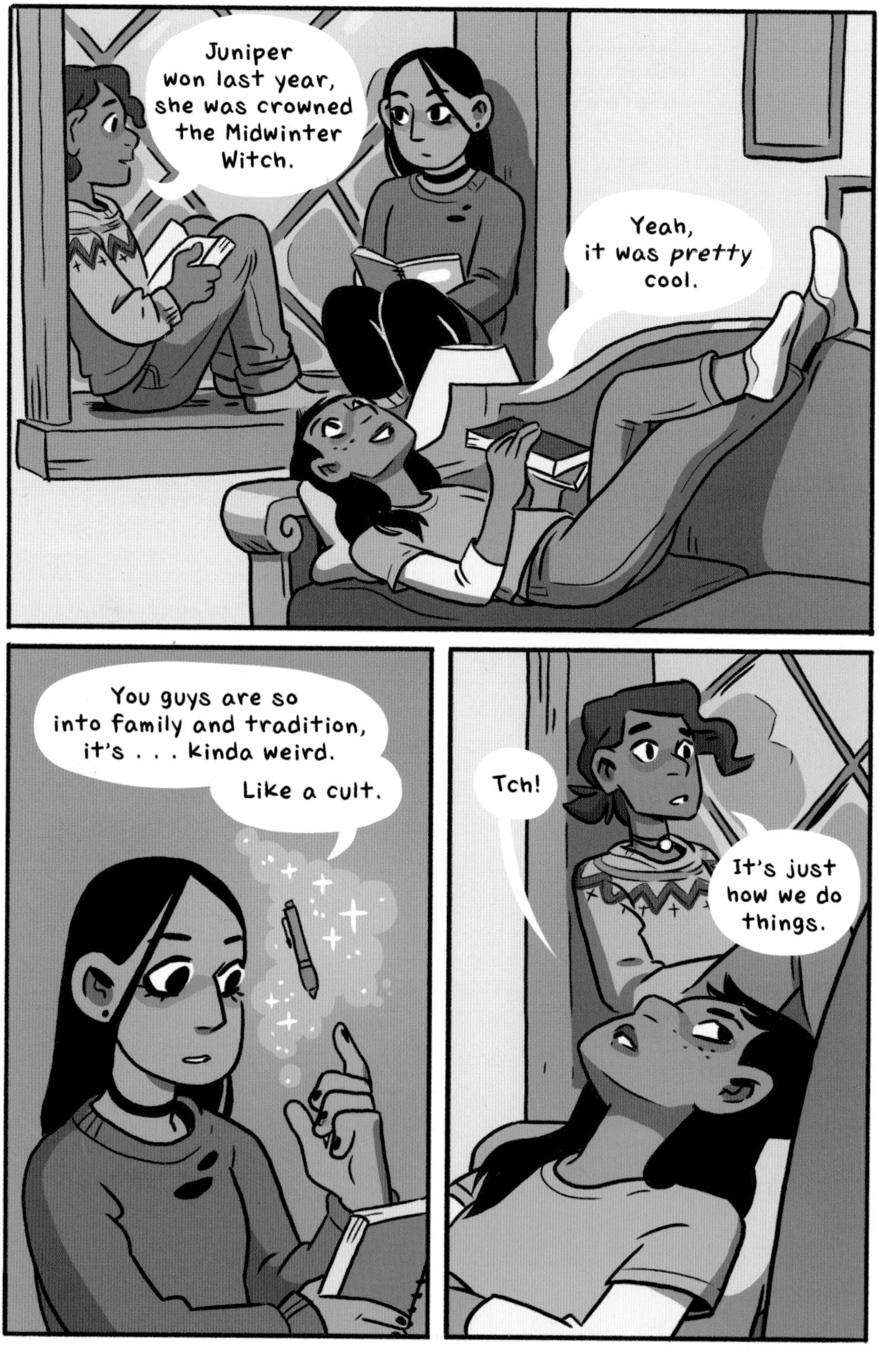
Juniper won last year, she was crowned the Midwinter Witch.
Yeah, it was *pretty* cool.
You guys are so into family and tradition, it's . . . kinda weird.
Like a cult.
Tch!
It's just how we do things.

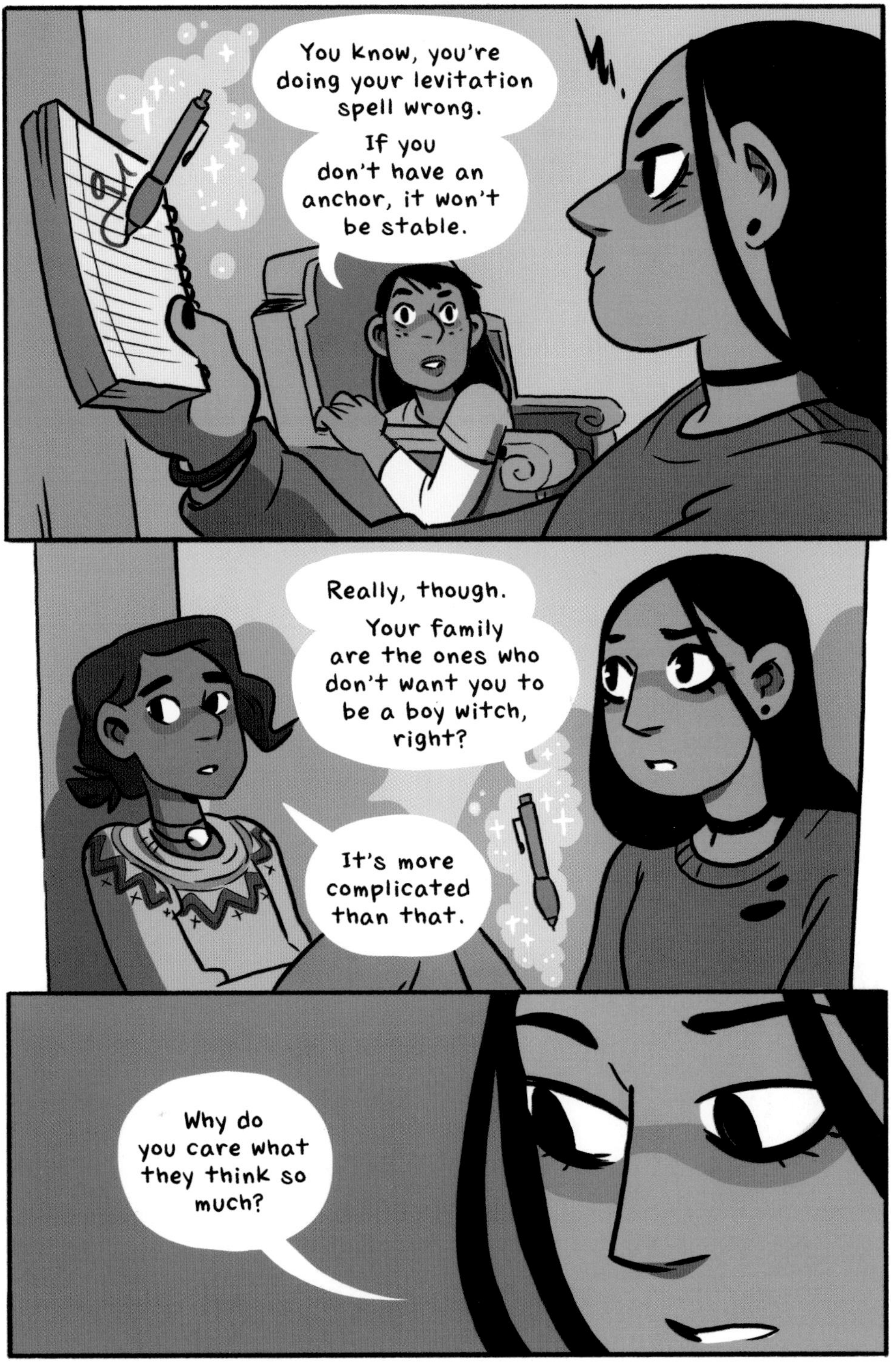
You know, you're doing your levitation spell wrong.
If you don't have an anchor, it won't be stable.
Really, though.
Your family are the ones who don't want you to be a boy witch, right?
It's more complicated than that.
Why do you care what they think so much?

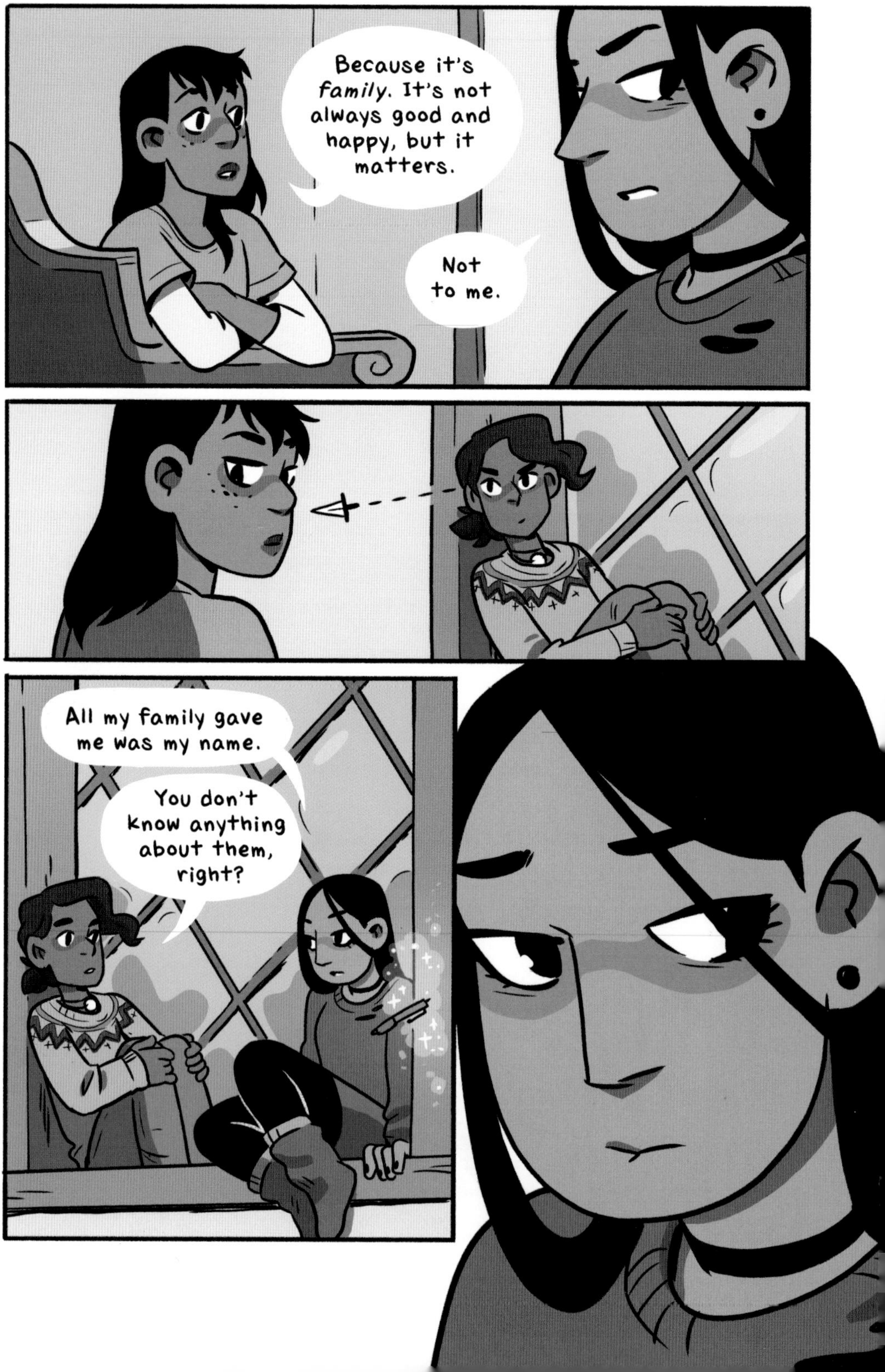
Because it's *family*. It's not always good and happy, but it matters.
Not to me.
All my family gave me was my name.
You don't know anything about them, right?

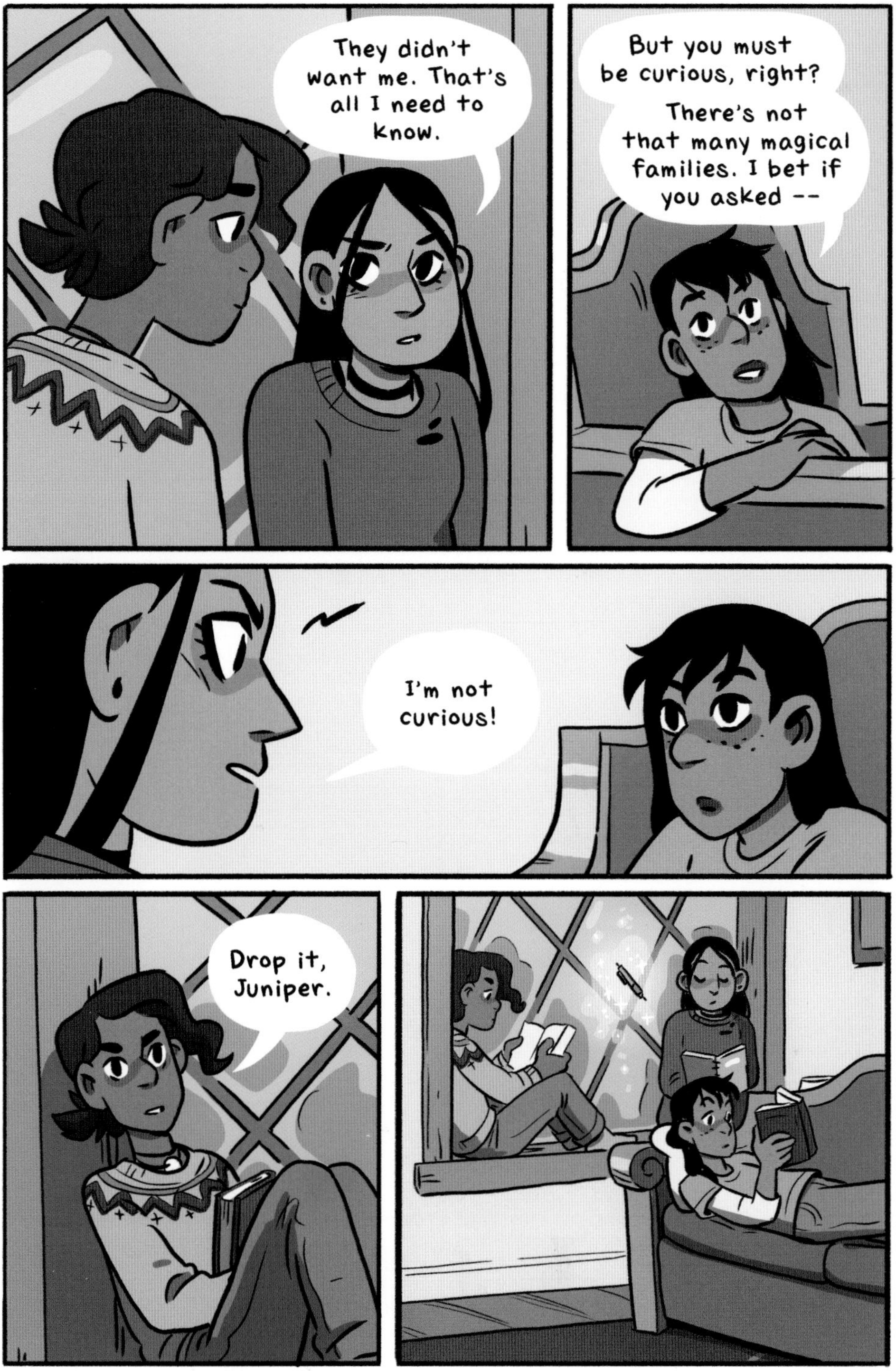
They didn't want me. That's all I need to know.
But you must be curious, right?
There's not that many magical families. I bet if you asked --
I'm not curious!
Drop it, Juniper.

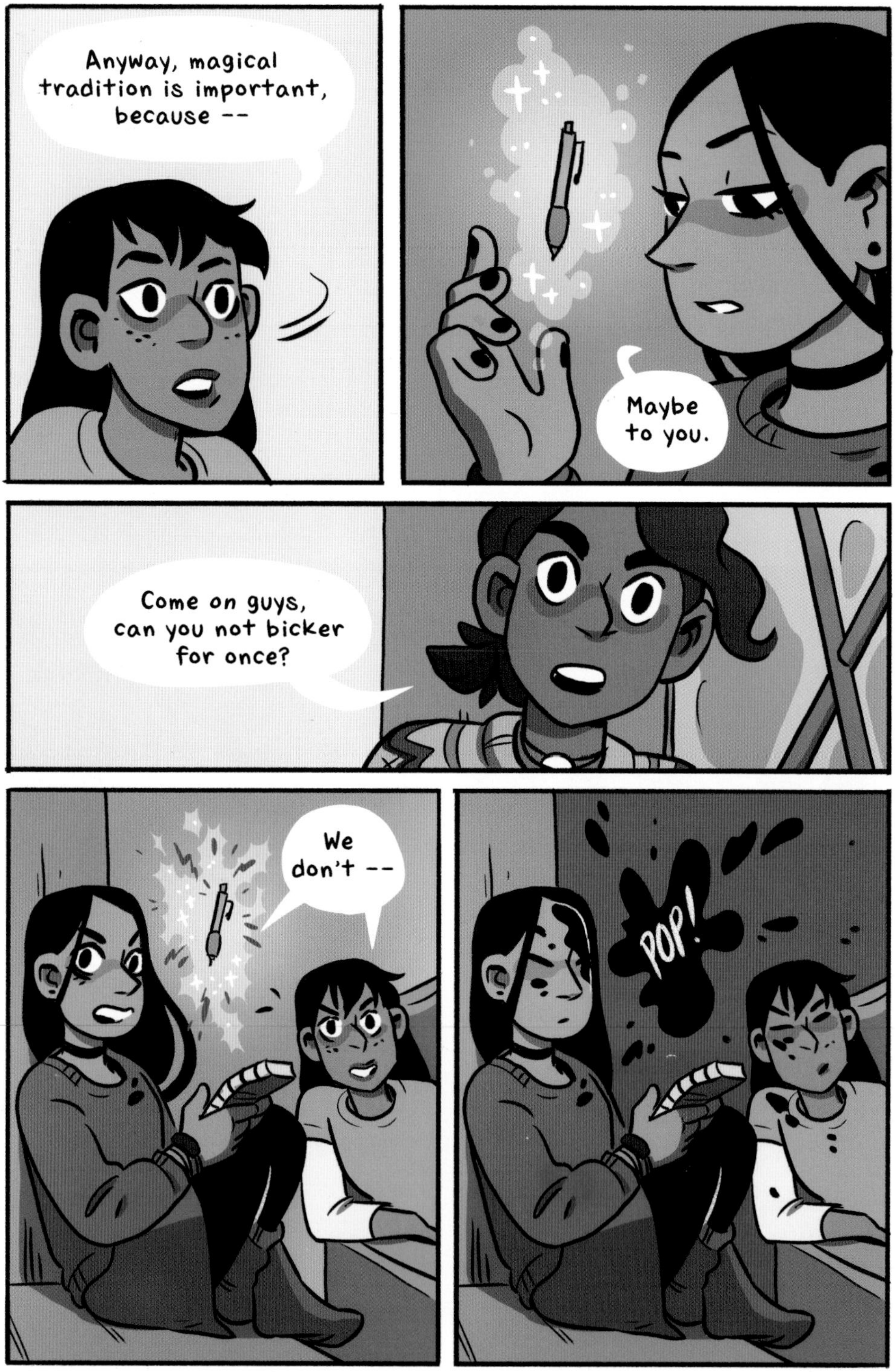

Anyway, magical tradition is important, because --
Maybe to you.
Come on guys, can you not bicker for once?
We don't --
POP!

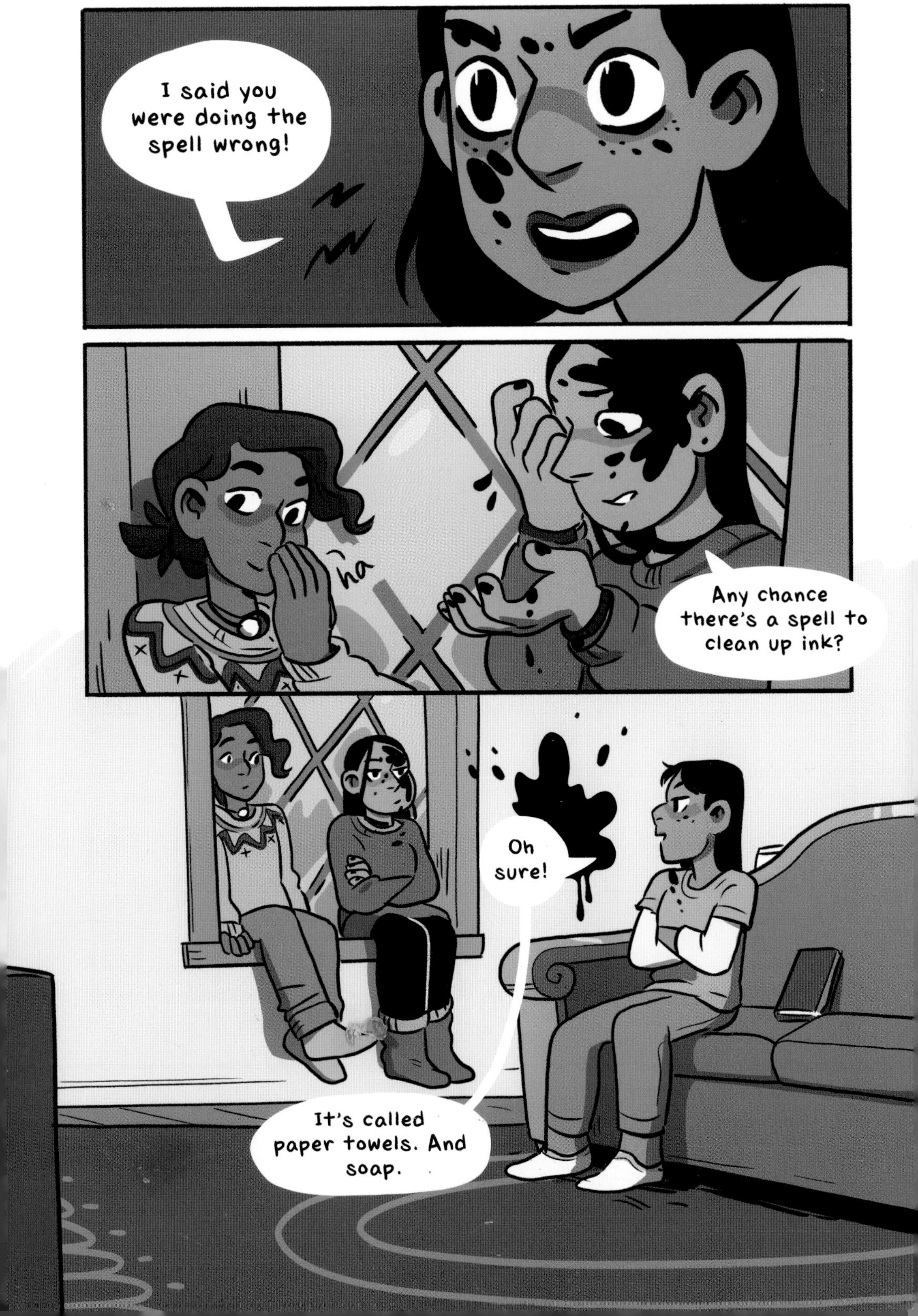
I said you were doing the spell wrong!
ha
Any chance there's a spell to clean up ink?
Oh sure!
It's called paper towels. And soap.

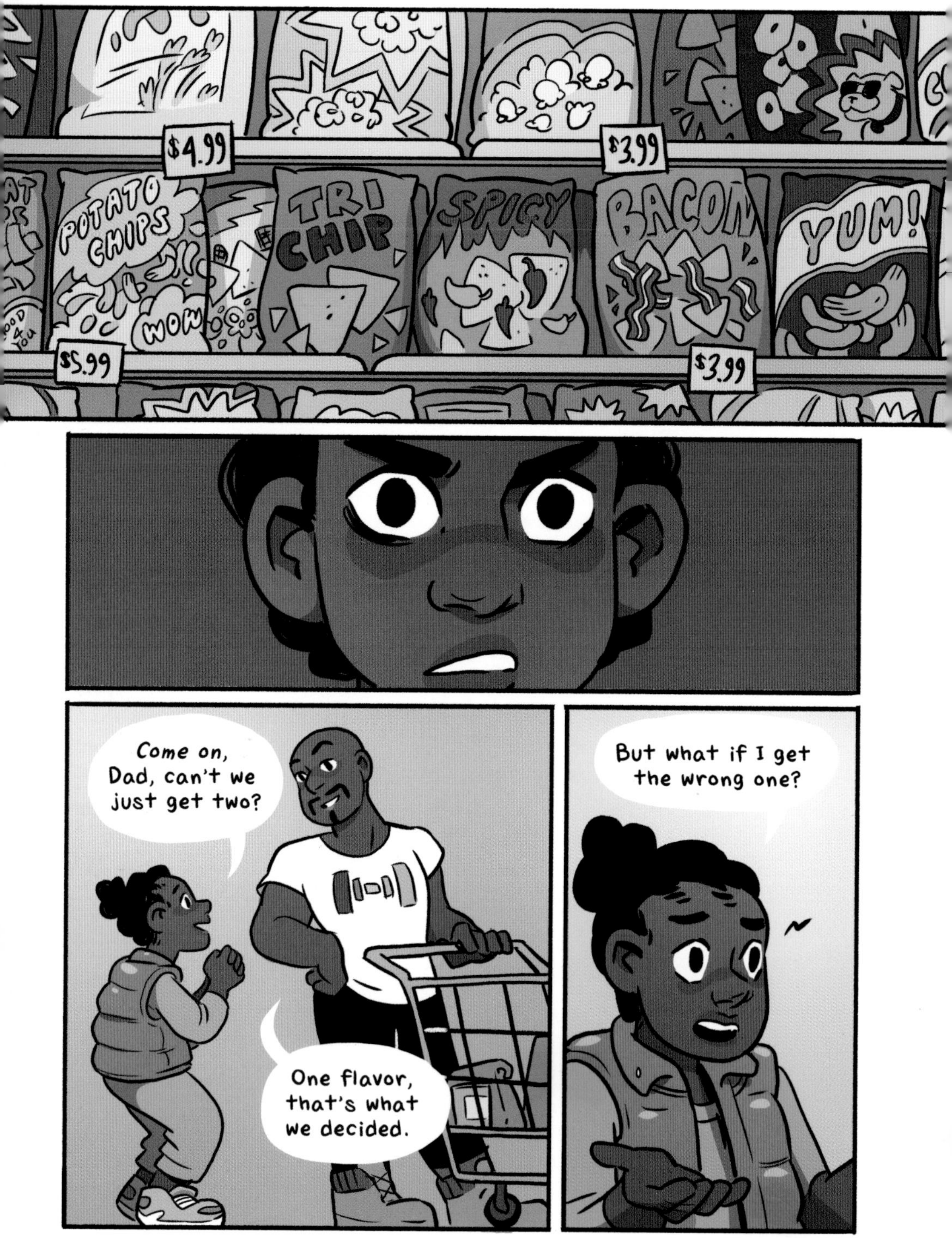
POTATO CHIPS
WOW
TRI CHIP
SPICY
BACON
YUM!
$4.99
$3.99
$5.99
$3.99
Come on, Dad, can't we just get two?
One flavor, that's what we decided.
But what if I get the wrong one?

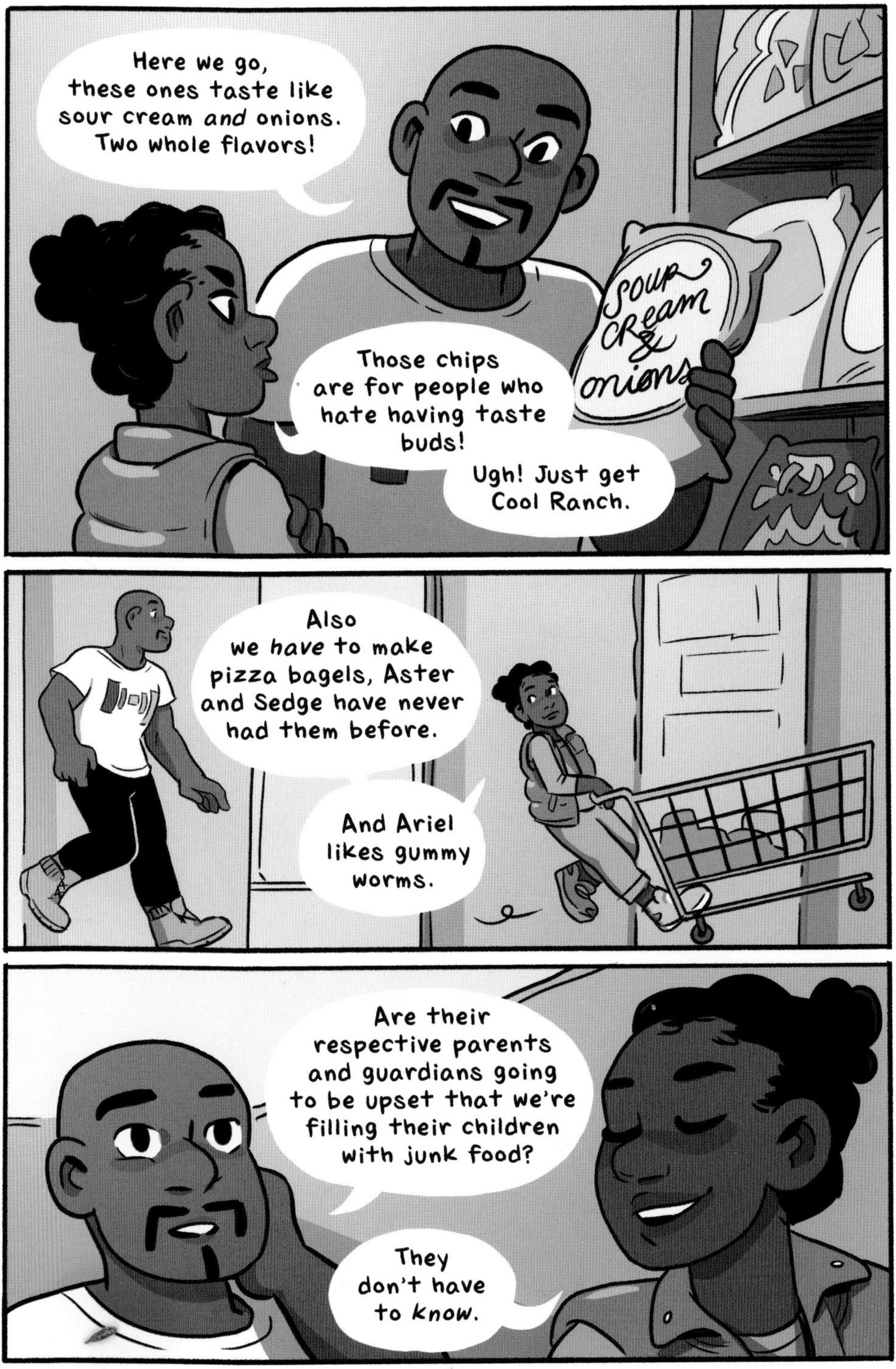
Here we go, these ones taste like sour cream *and* onions. Two whole flavors!
Sour Cream & Onions
Those chips are for people who hate having taste buds!
Ugh! Just get Cool Ranch.
Also we *have* to make pizza bagels, Aster and Sedge have never had them before.
And Ariel likes gummy worms.
Are their respective parents and guardians going to be upset that we're filling their children with junk food?
They don't have to *know*.

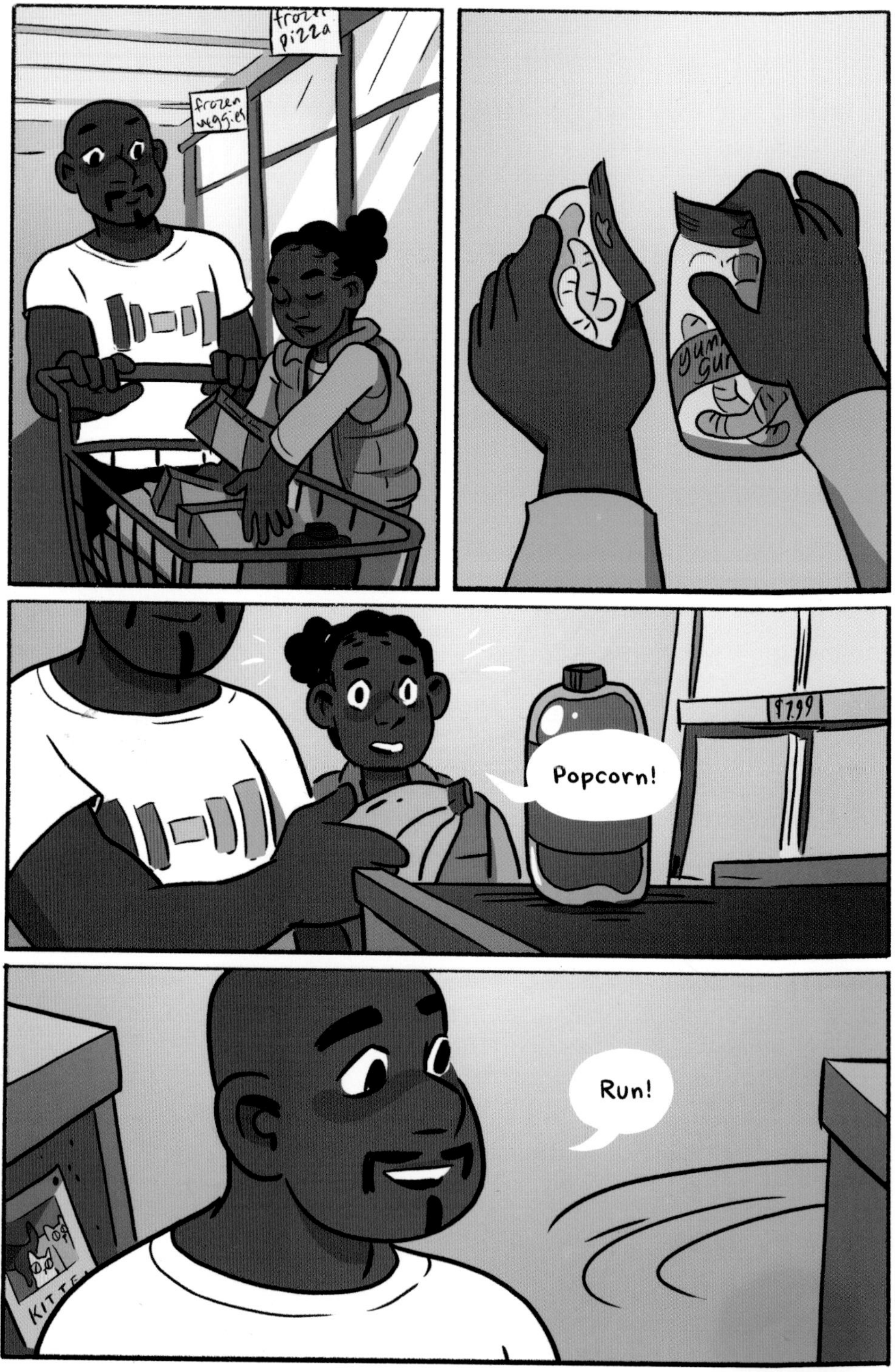
frozen pizza
frozen veggies
Popcorn!
Run!

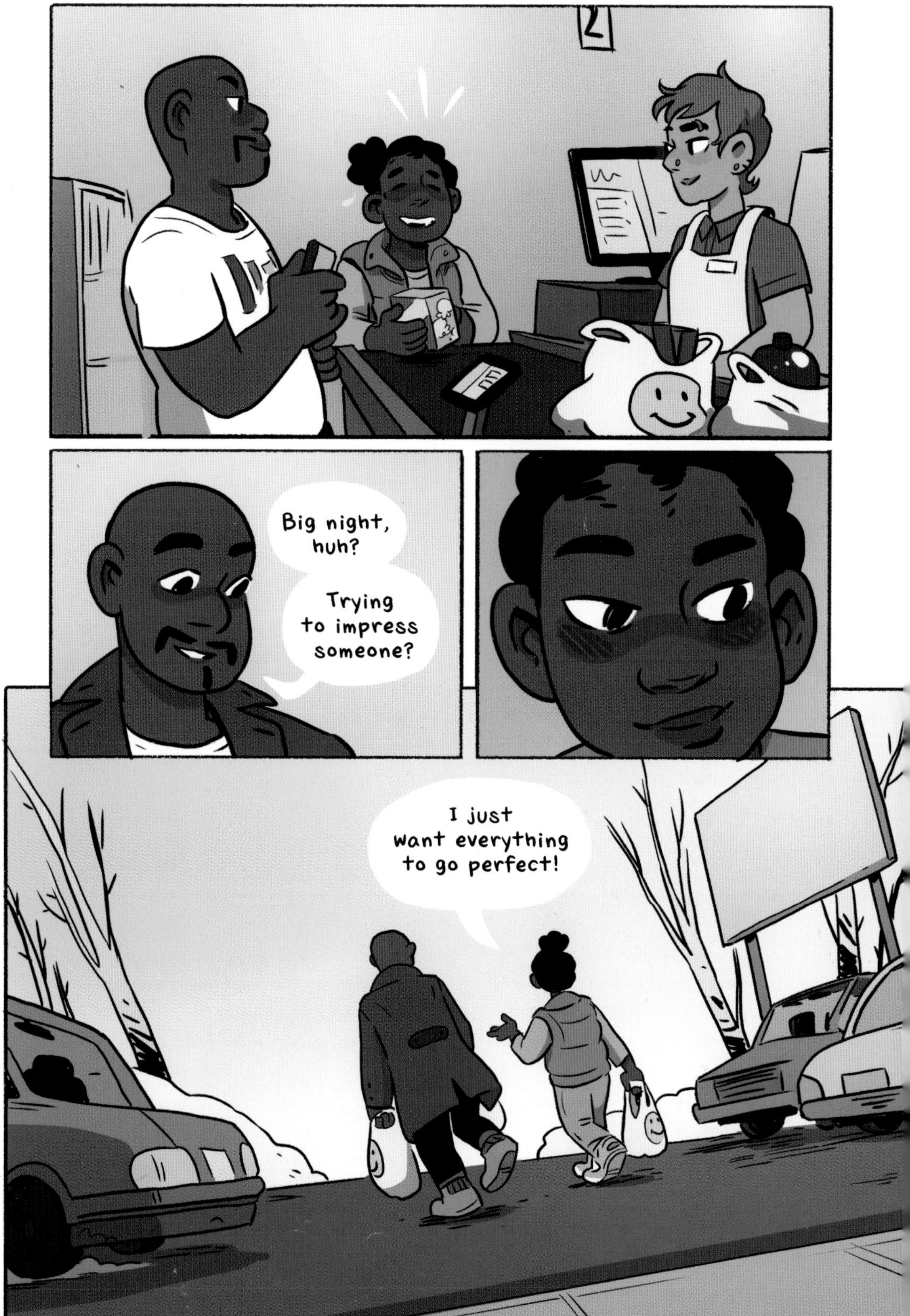
2
Big night, huh?
Trying to impress someone?
I just want everything to go perfect!

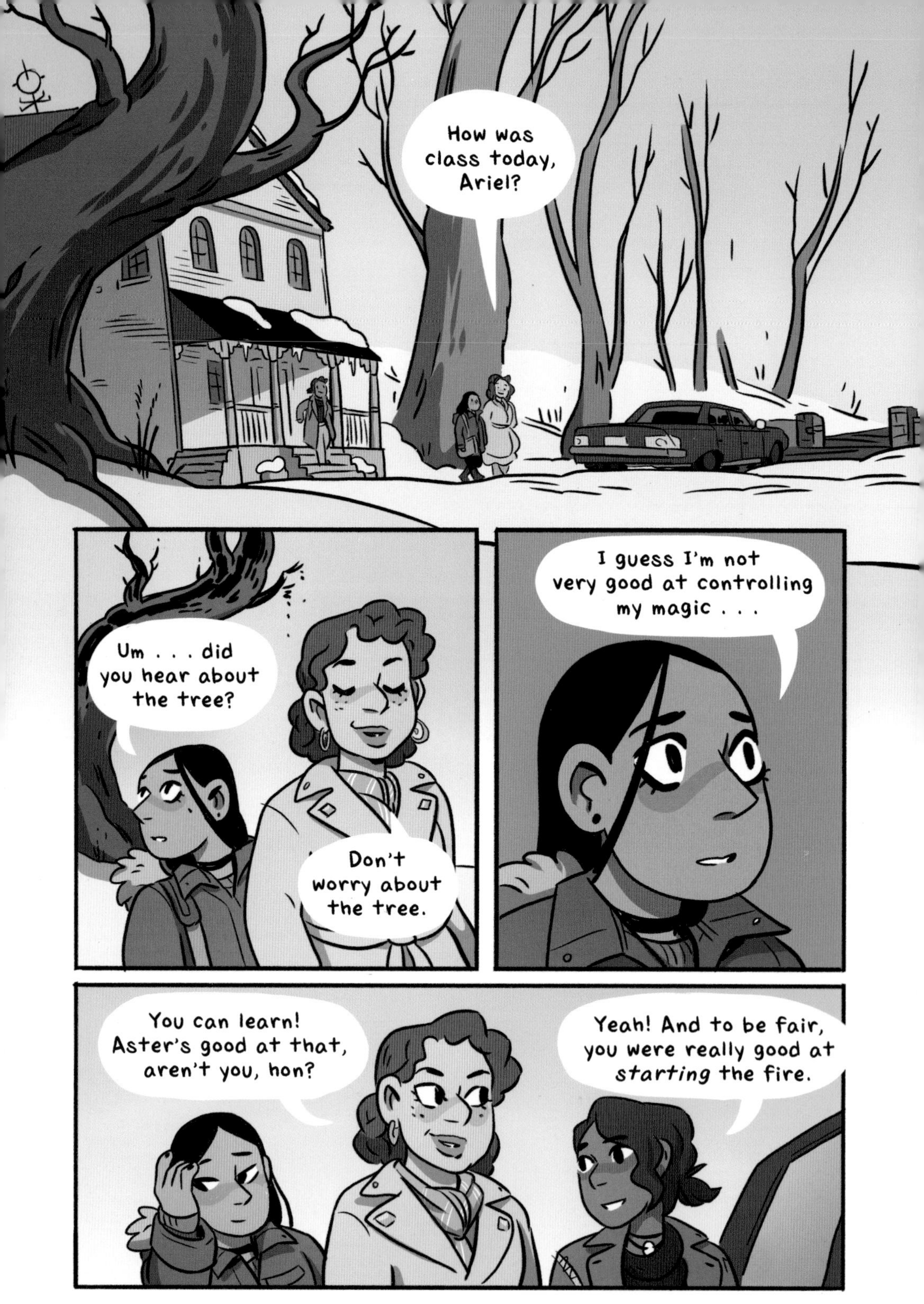
How was class today, Ariel?
Um . . . did you hear about the tree?
Don't worry about the tree.
I guess I'm not very good at controlling my magic . . .
You can learn! Aster's good at that, aren't you, hon?
Yeah! And to be fair, you were really good at *starting* the fire.

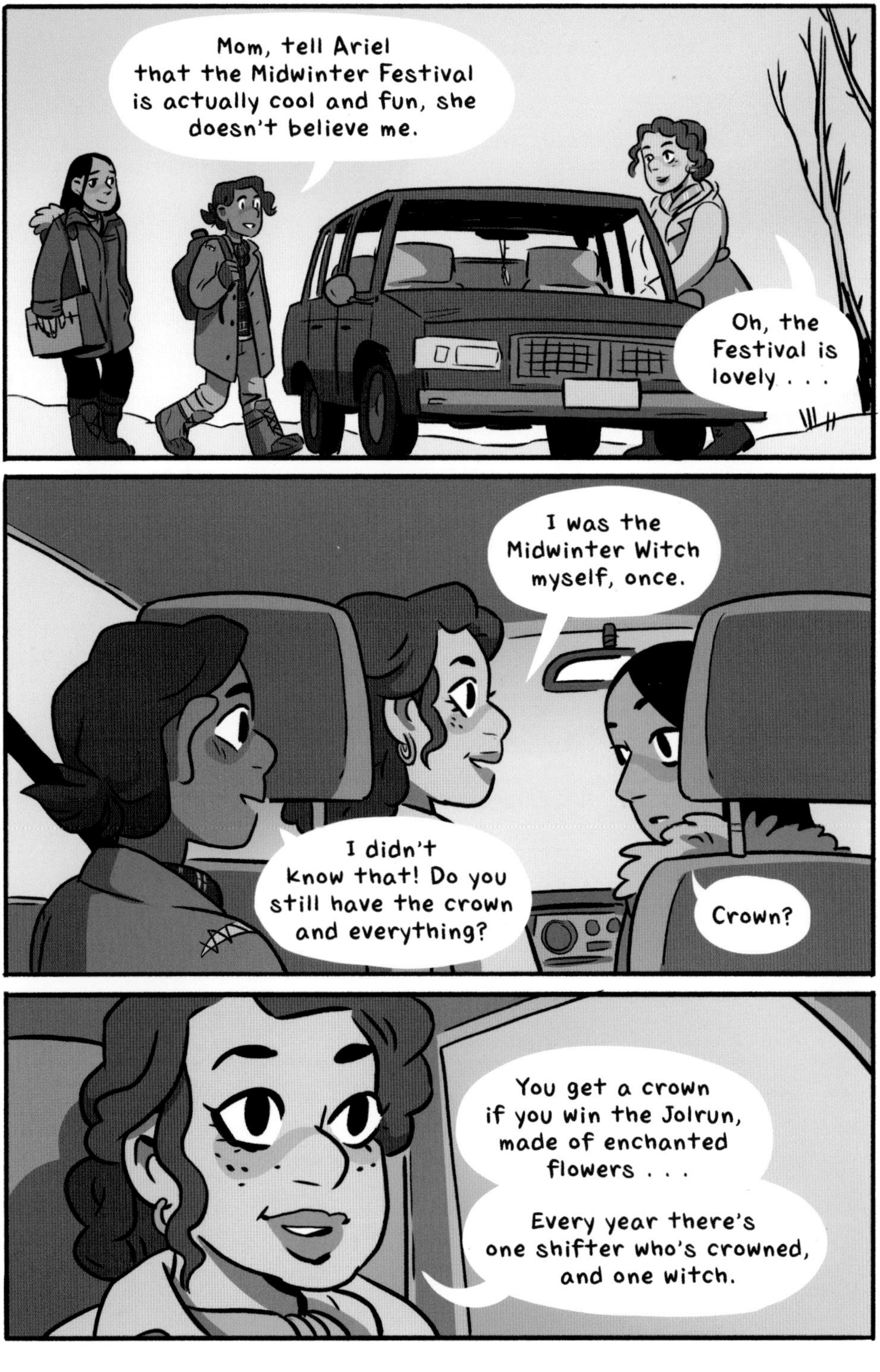
Mom, tell Ariel that the Midwinter Festival is actually cool and fun, she doesn't believe me.
Oh, the Festival is lovely . . .
I was the Midwinter Witch myself, once.
I didn't know that! Do you still have the crown and everything?
Crown?
You get a crown if you win the Jolrun, made of enchanted flowers . . .
Every year there's one shifter who's crowned, and one witch.

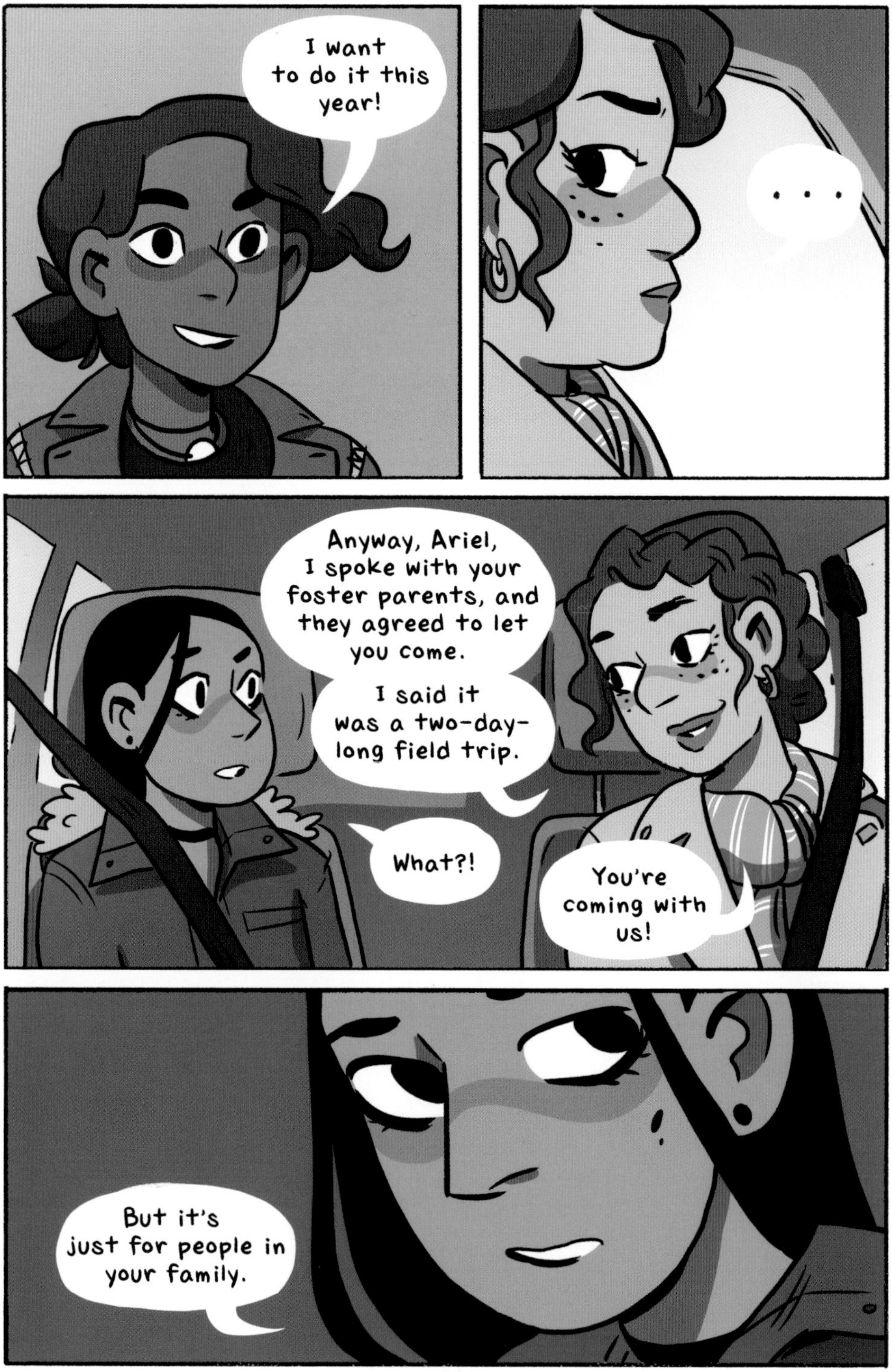
I want to do it this year!
. . .
Anyway, Ariel, I spoke with your foster parents, and they agreed to let you come.
I said it was a two-day-long field trip.
What?!
You're coming with us!
But it's just for people in your family.

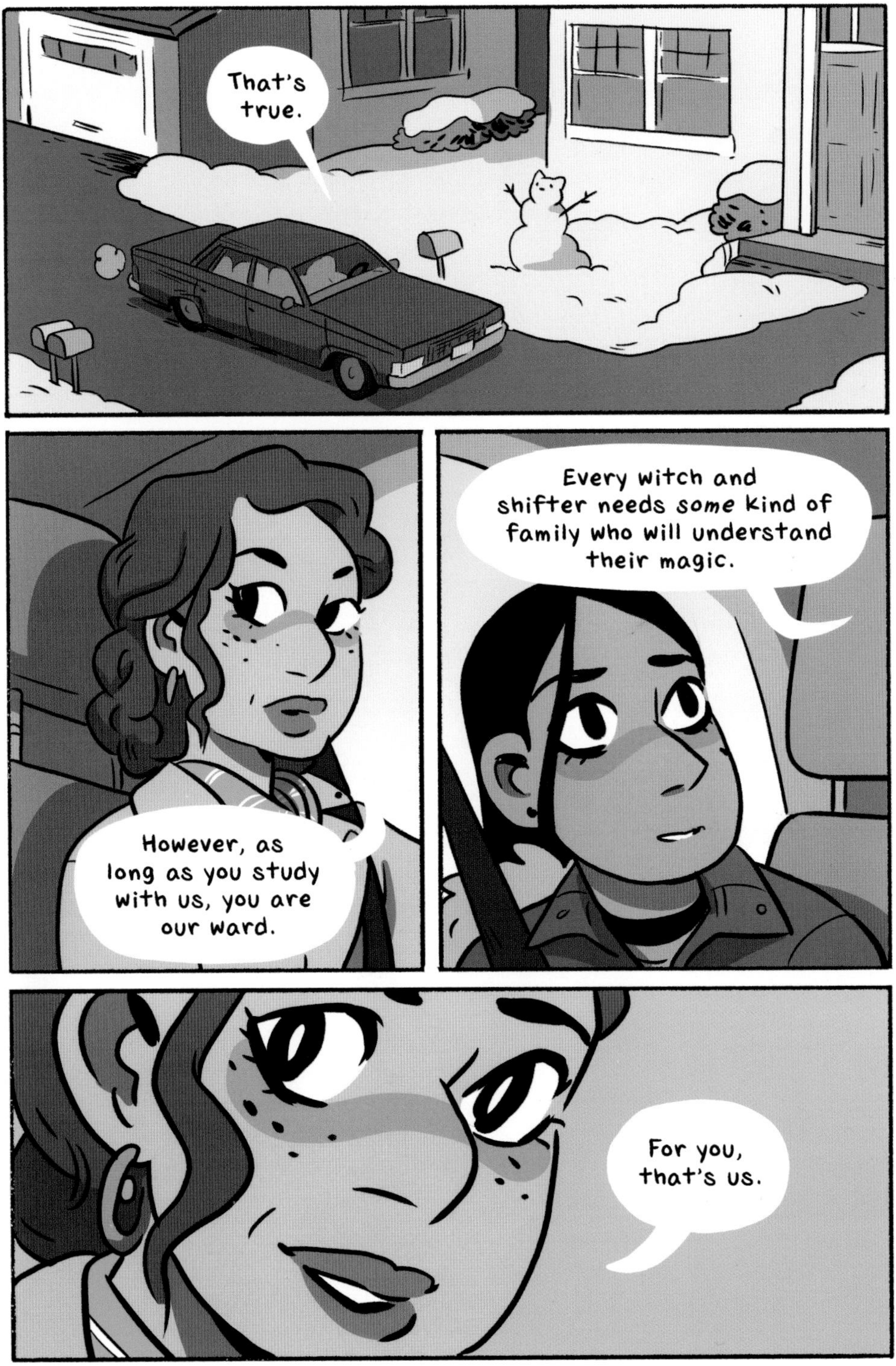
That's true.
However, as long as you study with us, you are our ward.
Every witch and shifter needs *some* kind of family who will understand their magic.
For you, that's us.

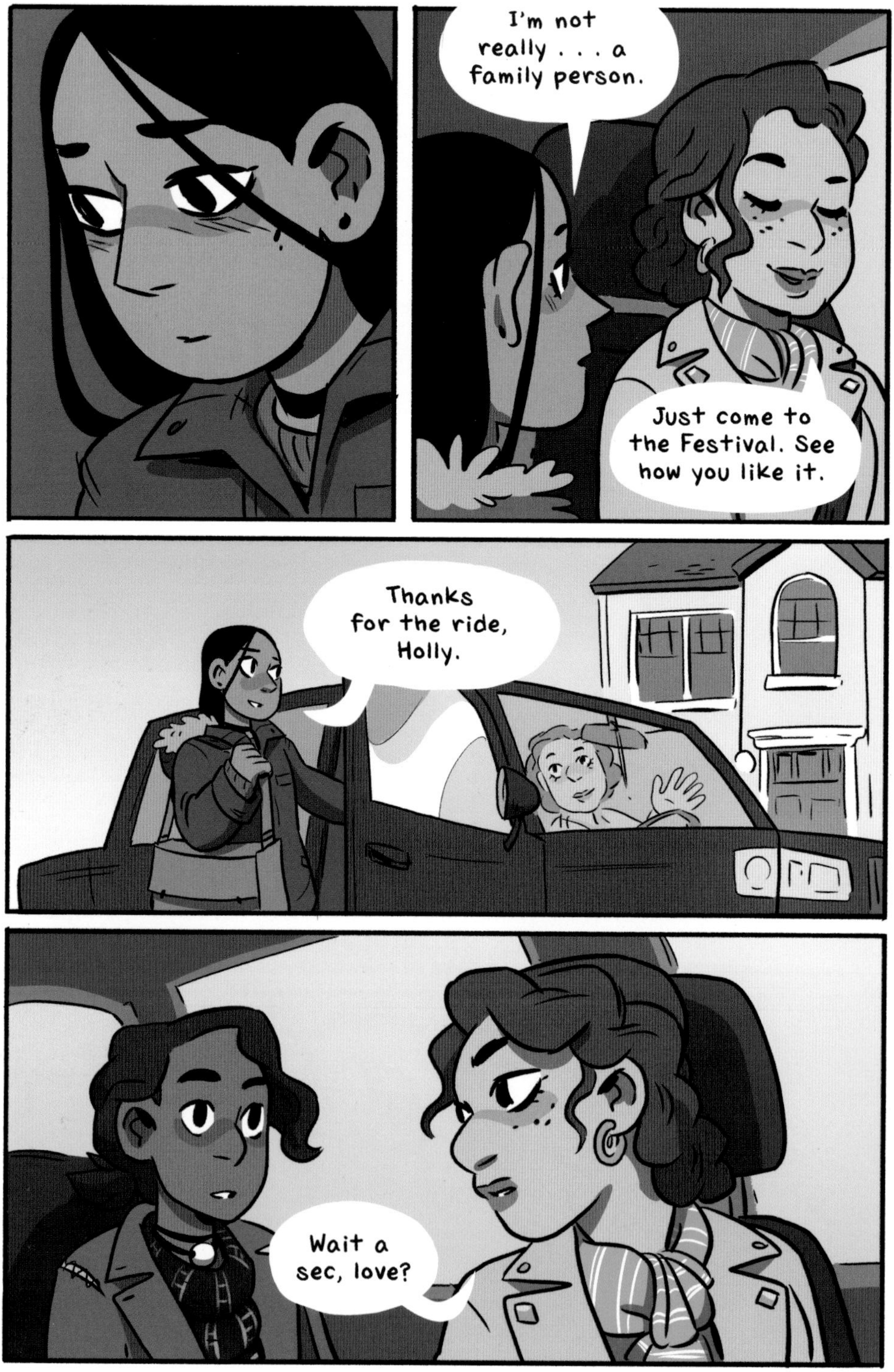
I'm not really . . . a family person.
Just come to the Festival. See how you like it.
Thanks for the ride, Holly.
Wait a sec, love?

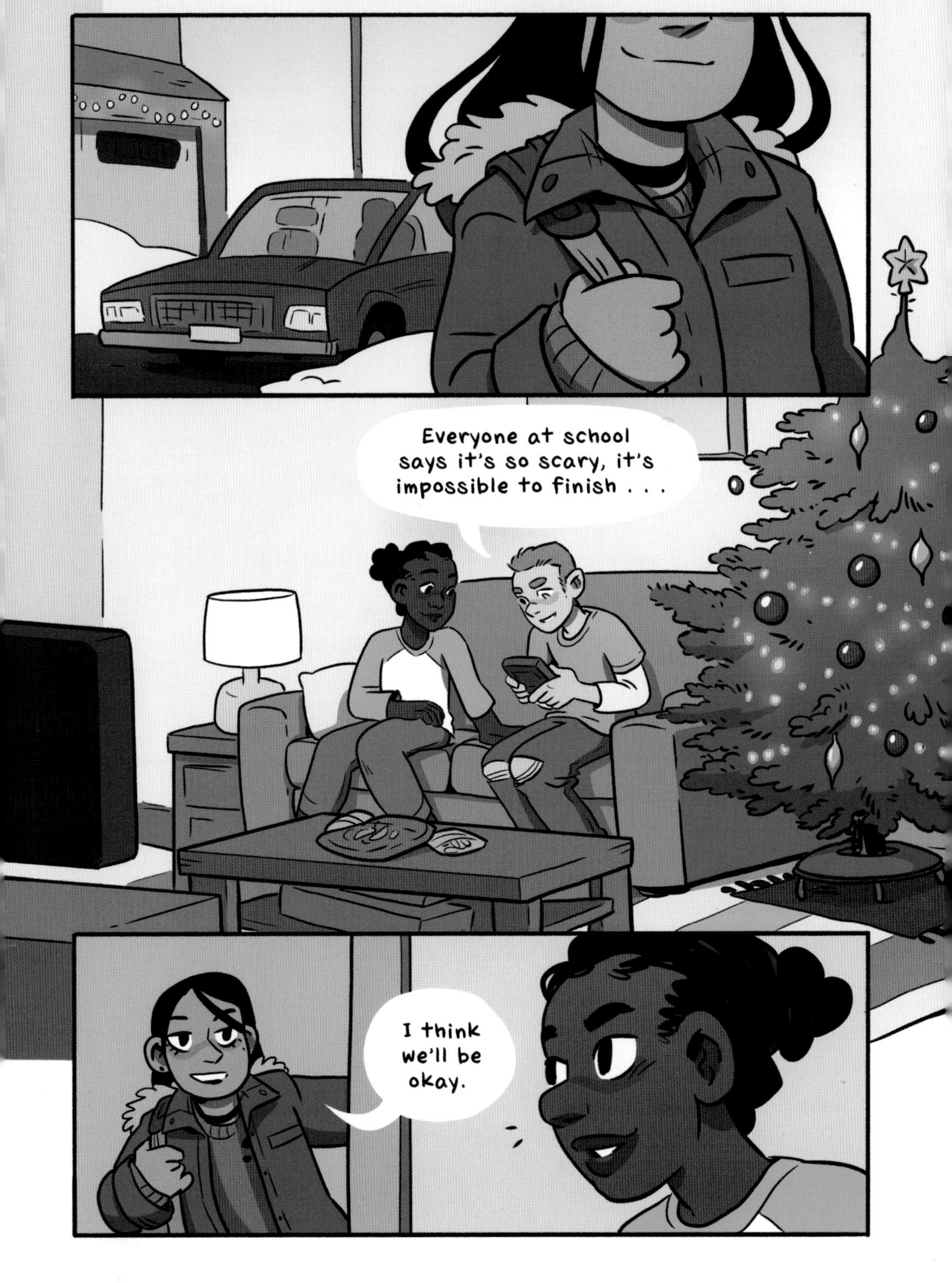
Everyone at school says it's so scary, it's impossible to finish . . .
I think we'll be okay.

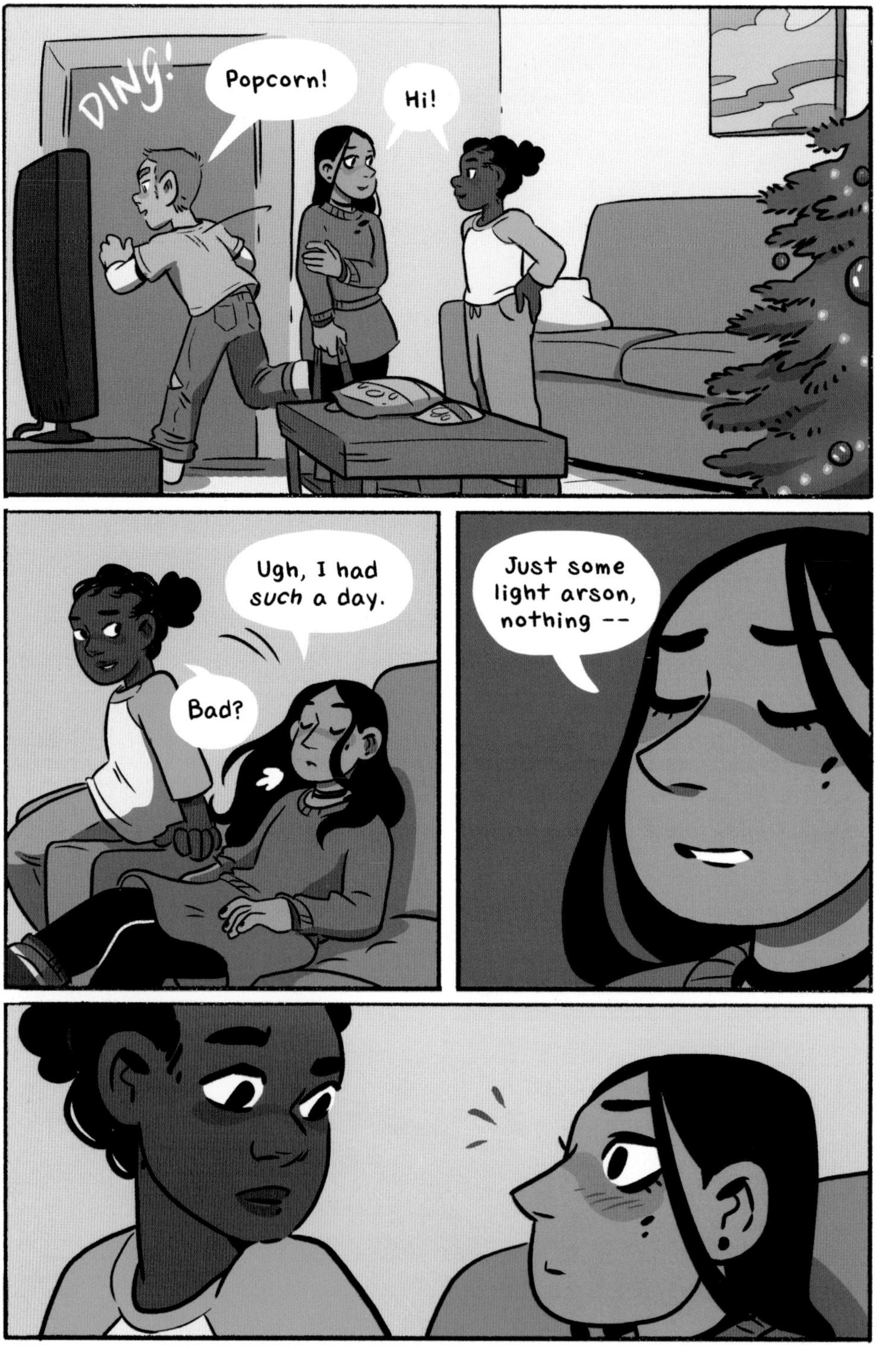
DING!
Popcorn!
Hi!
Ugh, I had *such* a day.
Bad?
Just some light arson, nothing --

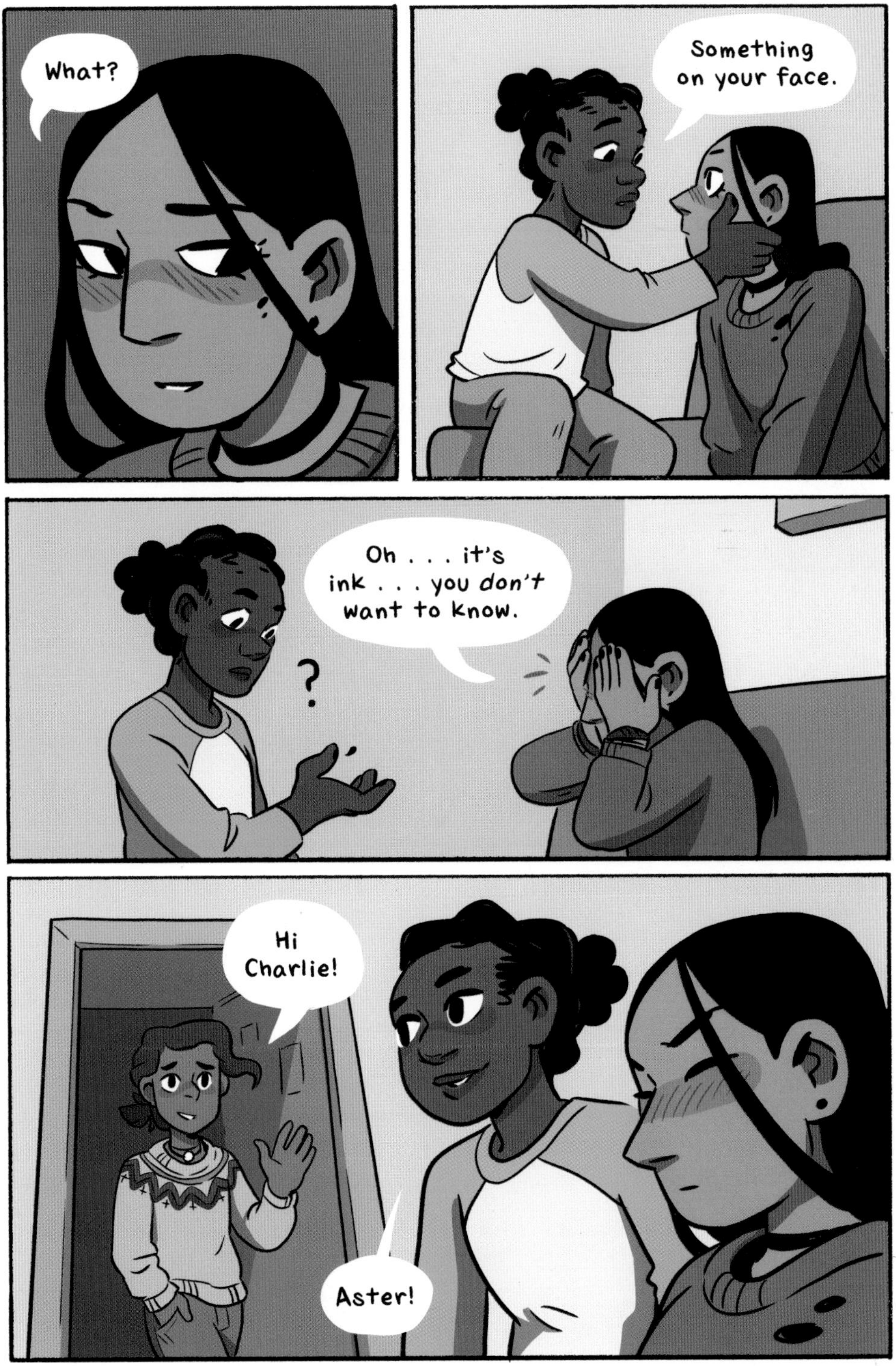
What?
Something on your face.
Oh . . . it's ink . . . you don't want to know.
?
Hi Charlie!
Aster!

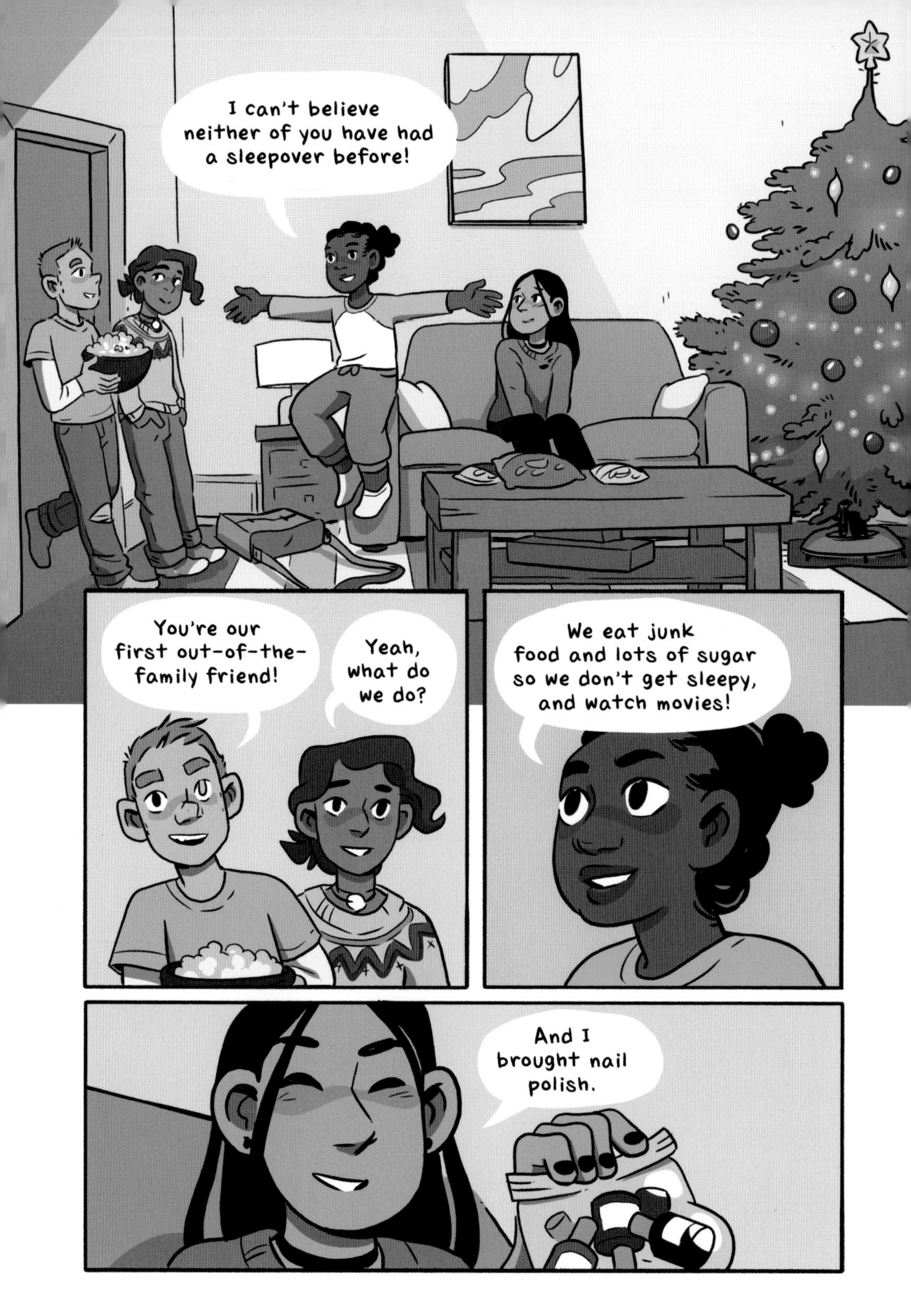
I can't believe neither of you have had a sleepover before!
You're our first out-of-the-family friend!
Yeah, what do we do?
We eat junk food and lots of sugar so we don't get sleepy, and watch movies!
And I brought nail polish.

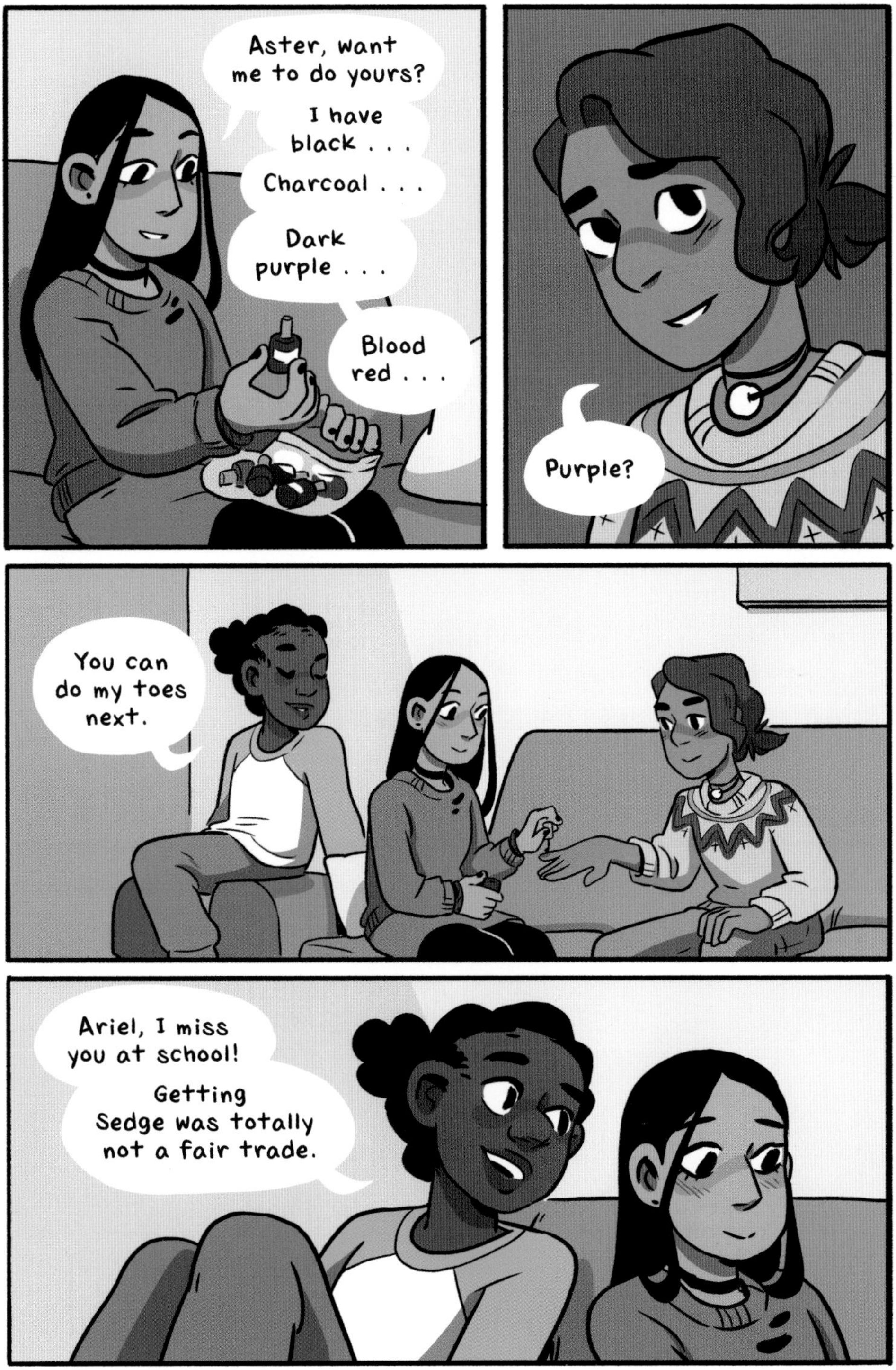
Aster, want me to do yours?
I have black . . .
Charcoal . . .
Dark purple . . .
Blood red . . .
Purple?
You can do my toes next.
Ariel, I miss you at school!
Getting Sedge was totally not a fair trade.

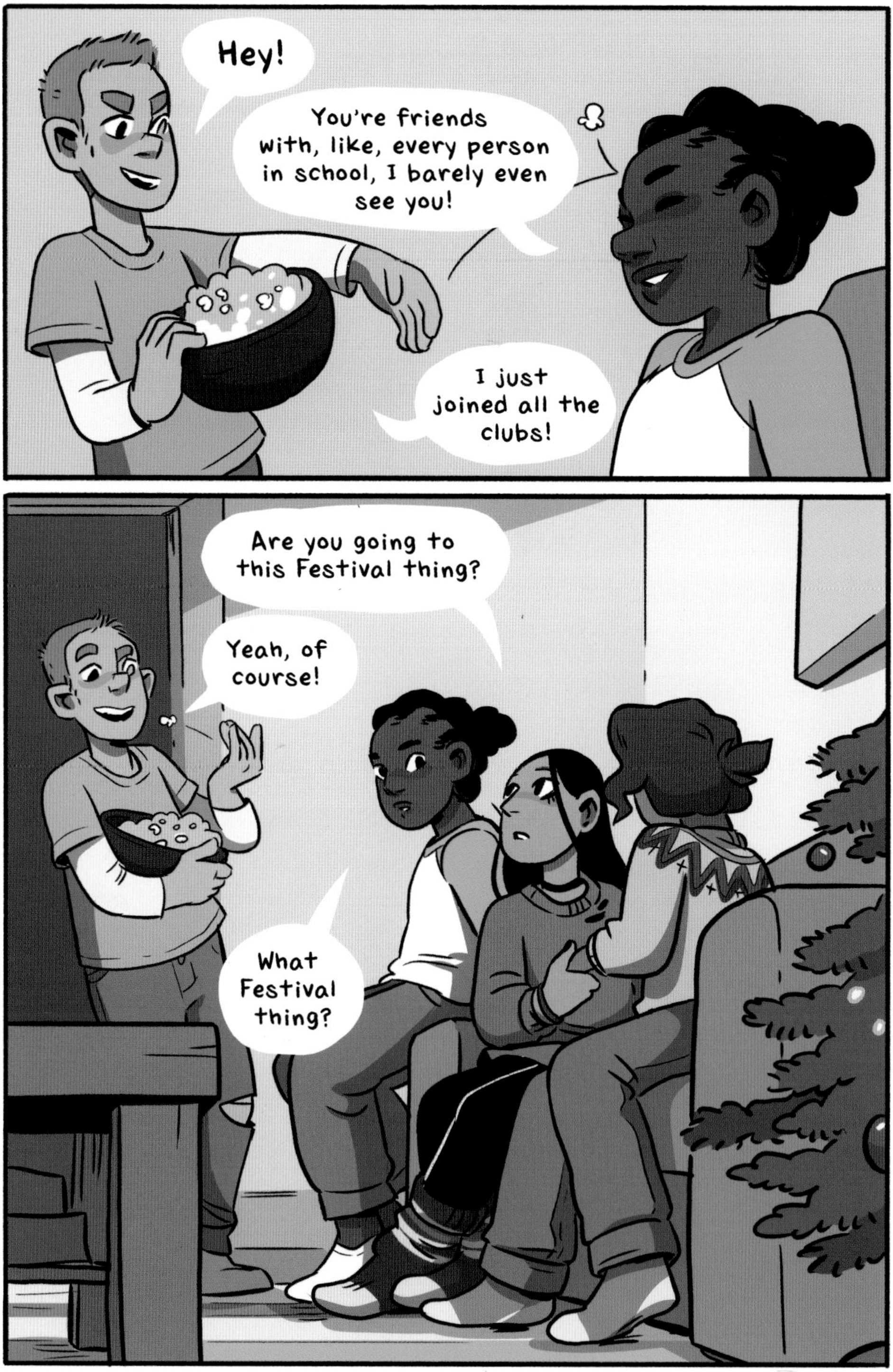
Hey!
You're friends with, like, every person in school, I barely even see you!
I just joined all the clubs!
Are you going to this Festival thing?
Yeah, of course!
What Festival thing?

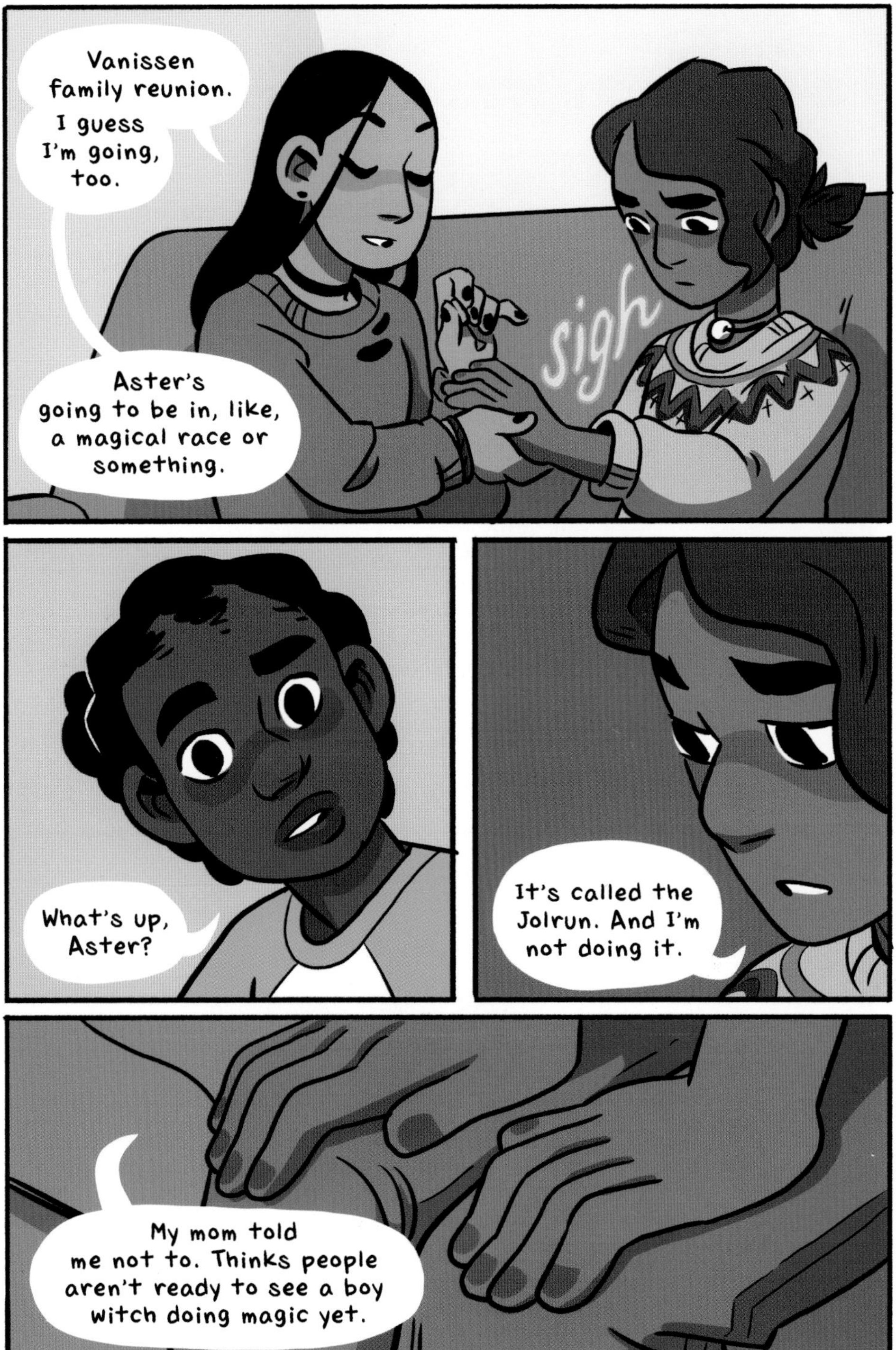
Vanissen family reunion.
I guess I'm going, too.
Aster's going to be in, like, a magical race or something.
sigh
What's up, Aster?
It's called the Jolrun. And I'm not doing it.
My mom told me not to. Thinks people aren't ready to see a boy witch doing magic yet.

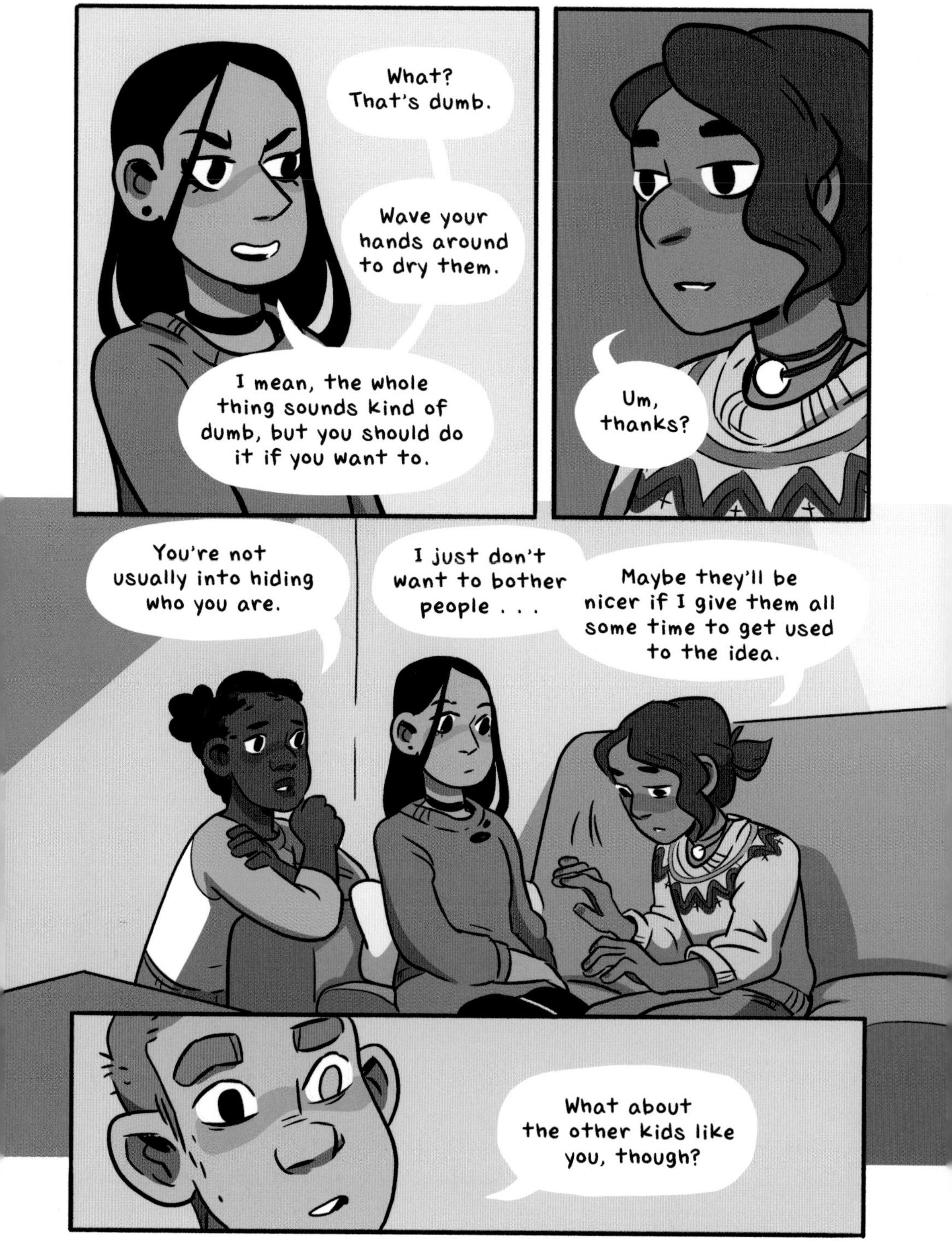
What? That's dumb.
Wave your hands around to dry them.
I mean, the whole thing sounds kind of dumb, but you should do it if you want to.
Um, thanks?
You're not usually into hiding who you are.
I just don't want to bother people . . .
Maybe they'll be nicer if I give them all some time to get used to the idea.
What about the other kids like you, though?

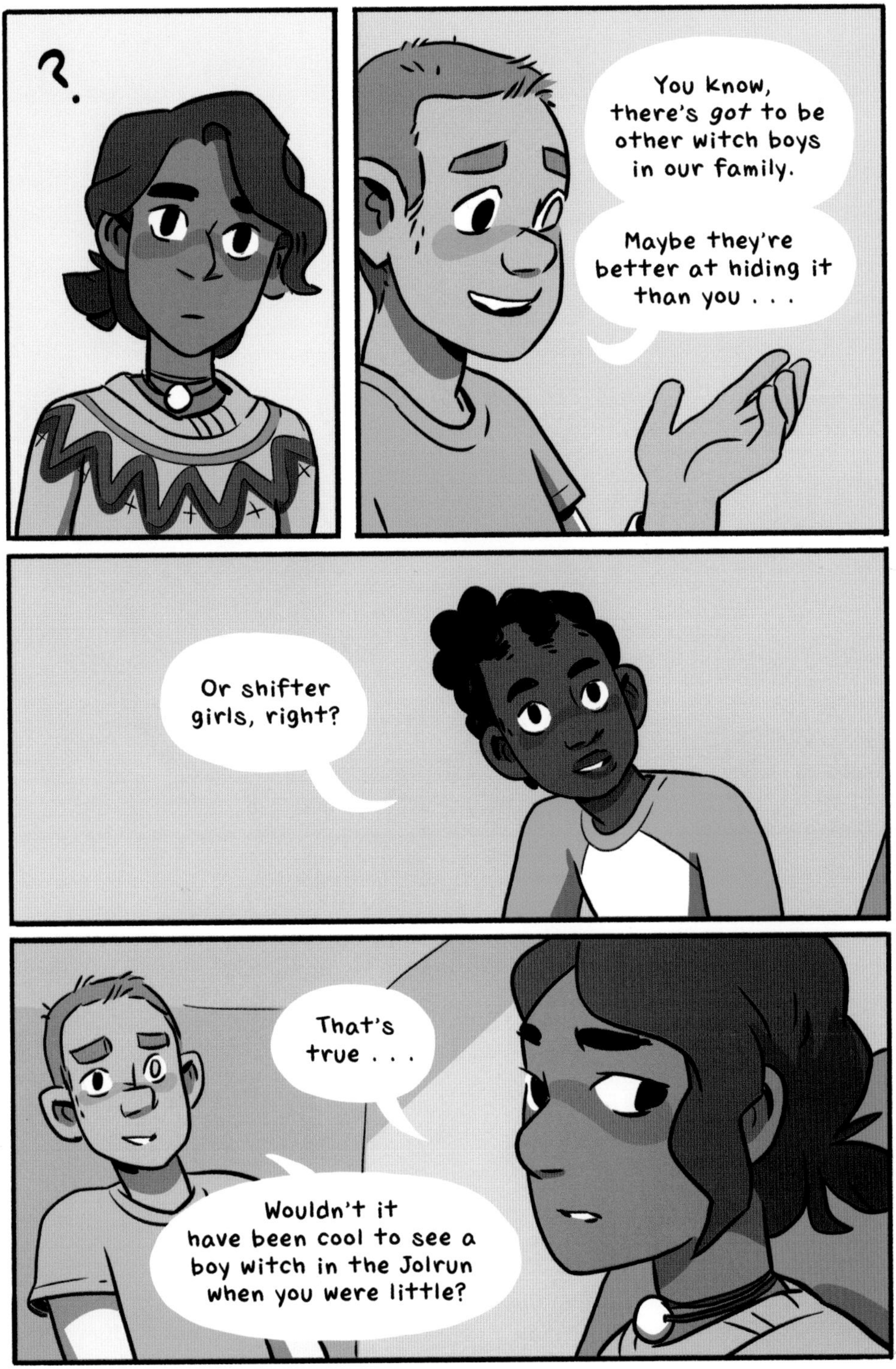
?
You know, there's *got* to be other witch boys in our family.
Maybe they're better at hiding it than you . . .
Or shifter girls, right?
That's true . . .
Wouldn't it have been cool to see a boy witch in the Jolrun when you were little?

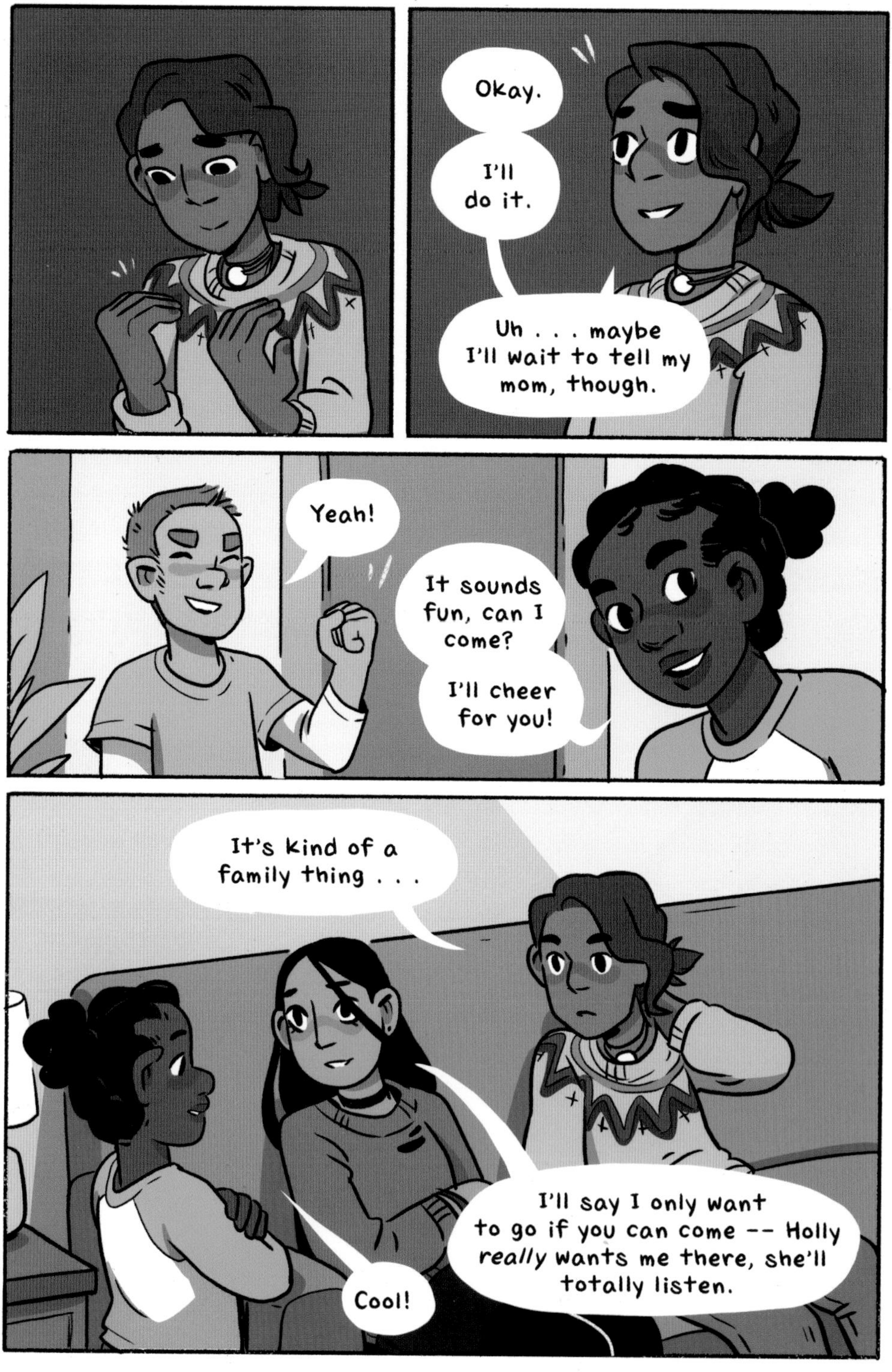
Okay.
I'll do it.
Uh . . . maybe I'll wait to tell my mom, though.
Yeah!
It sounds fun, can I come?
I'll cheer for you!
It's kind of a family thing . . .
I'll say I only want to go if you can come -- Holly *really* wants me there, she'll totally listen.
Cool!

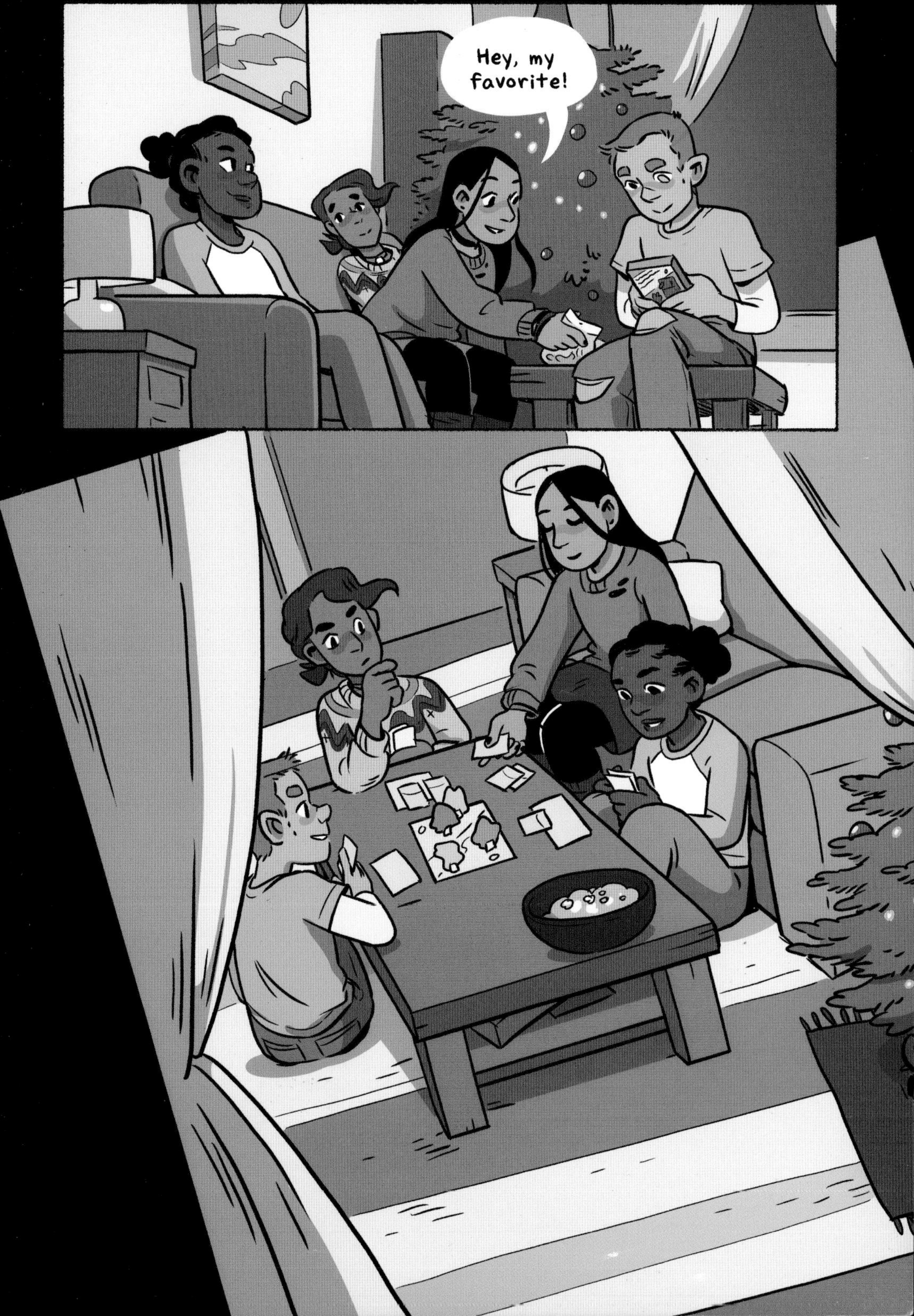
Hey, my favorite!

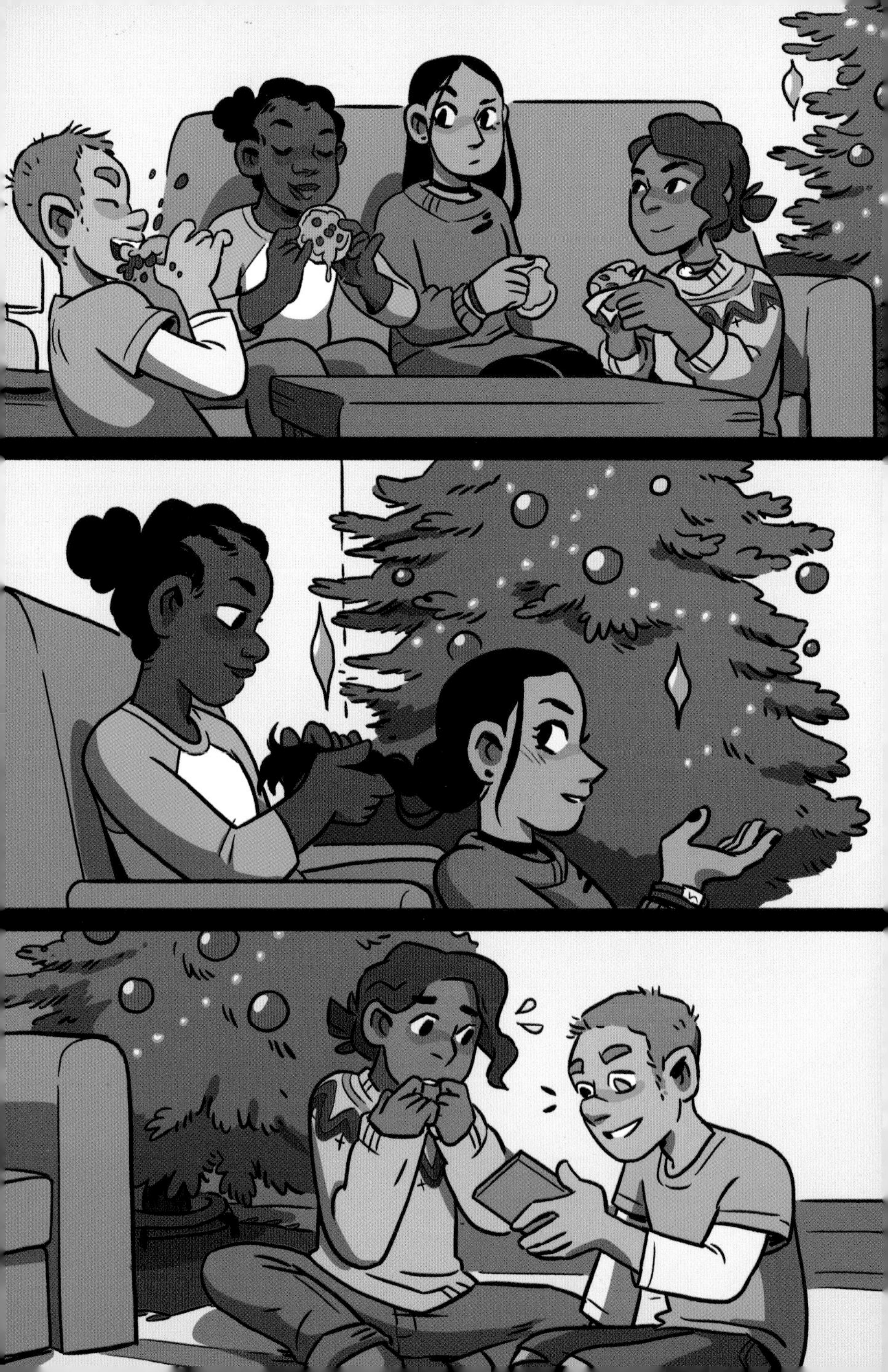

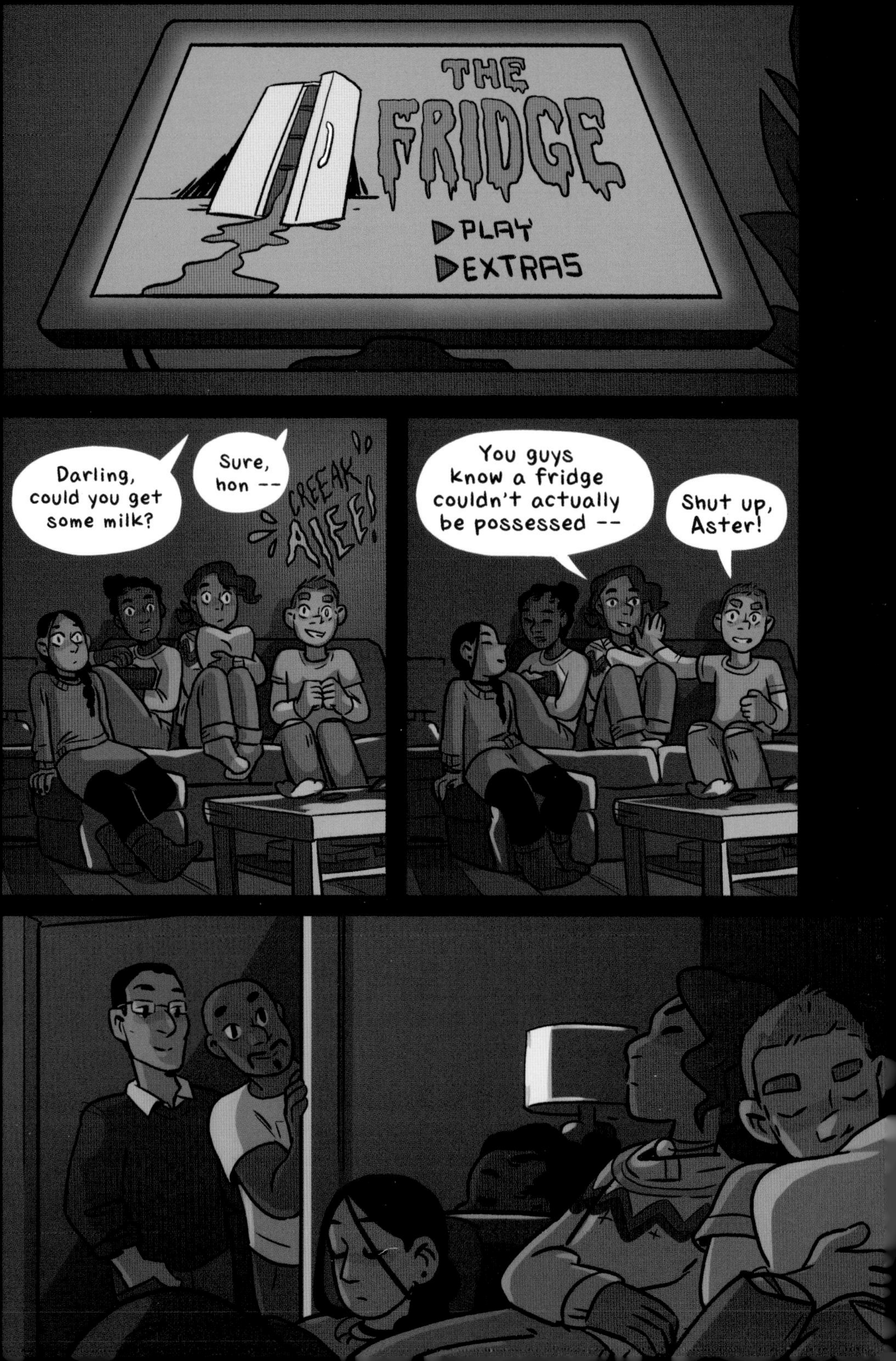
THE FRIDGE
PLAY
EXTRAS
Darling, could you get some milk?
Sure, hon --
CREEAK
AIEE!
You guys know a fridge couldn't actually be possessed --
Shut up, Aster!

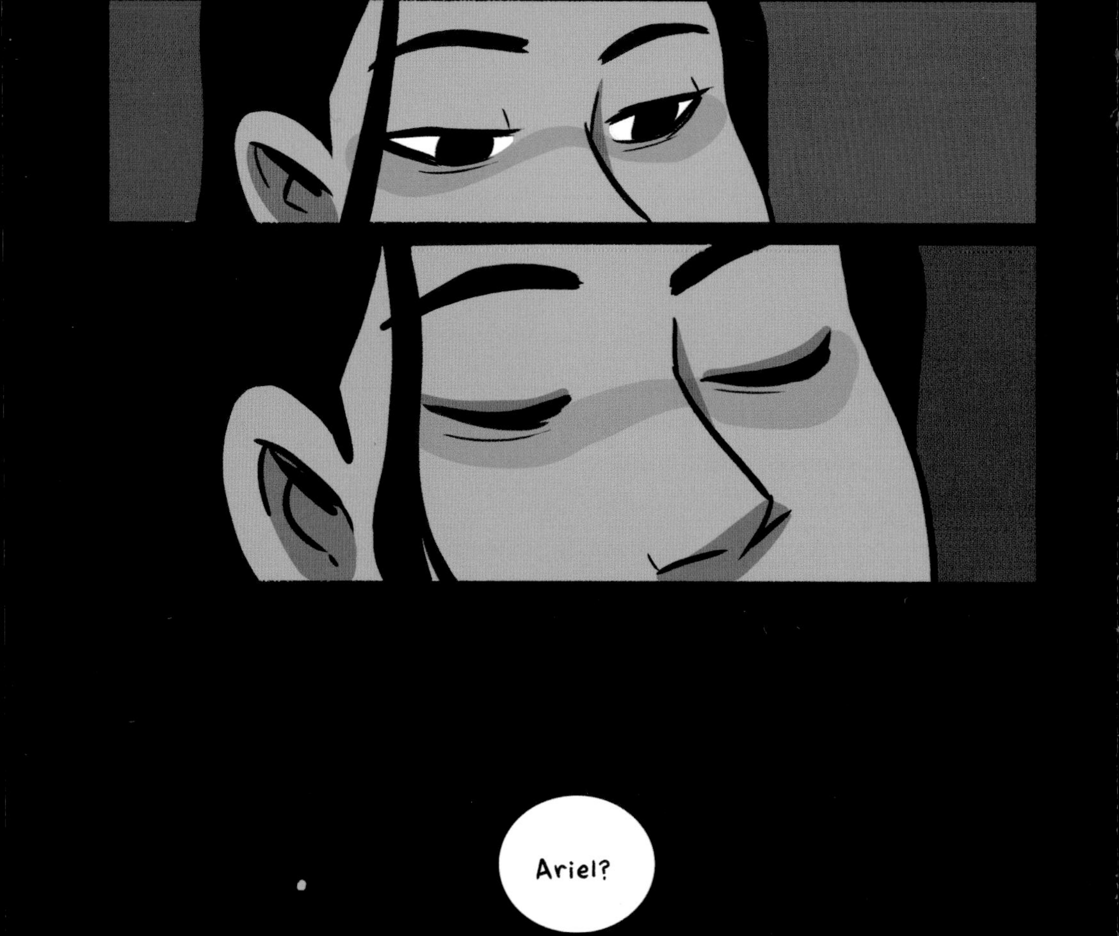
Ariel?

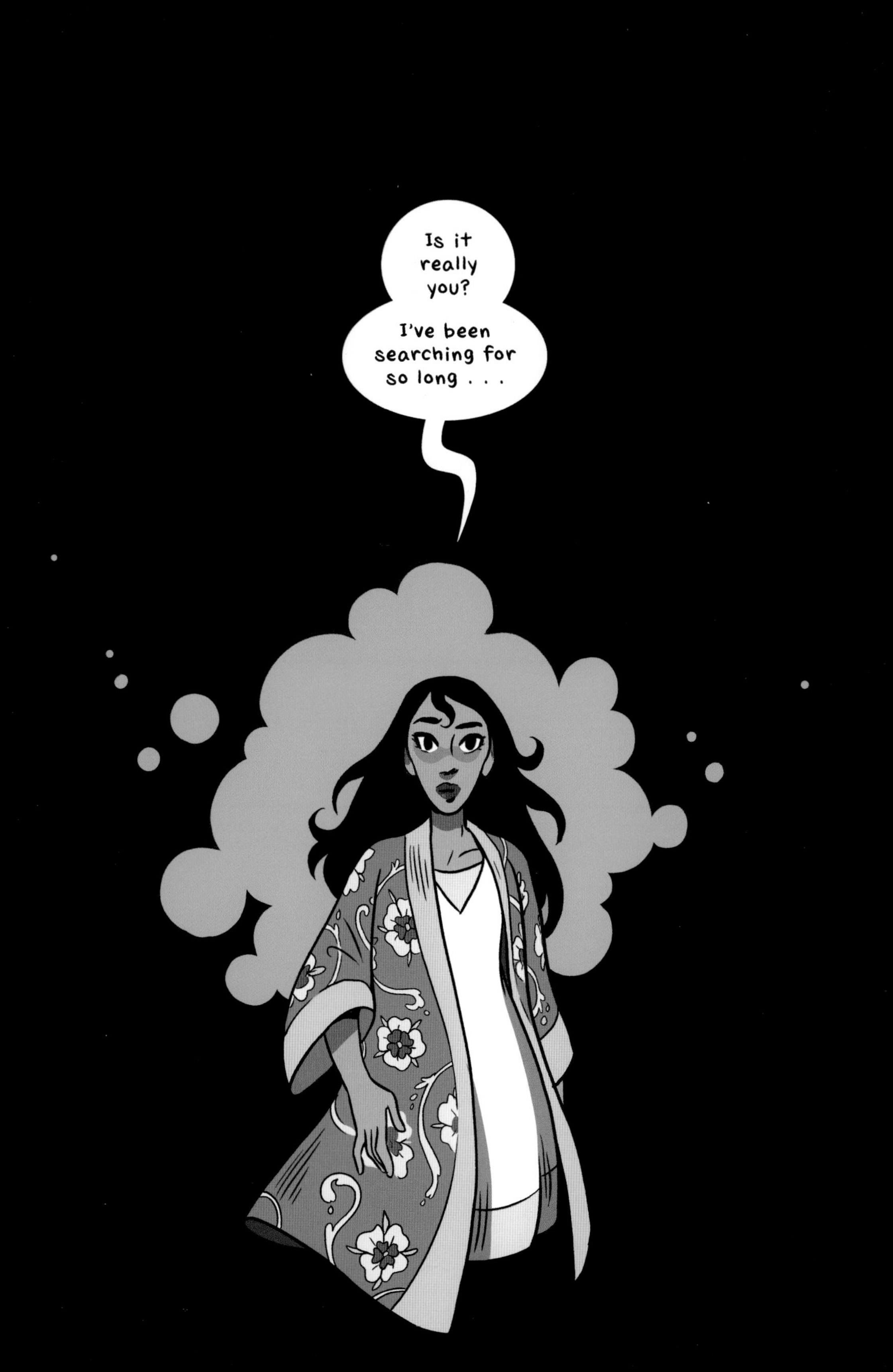
Is it really you?
I've been searching for so long . . .

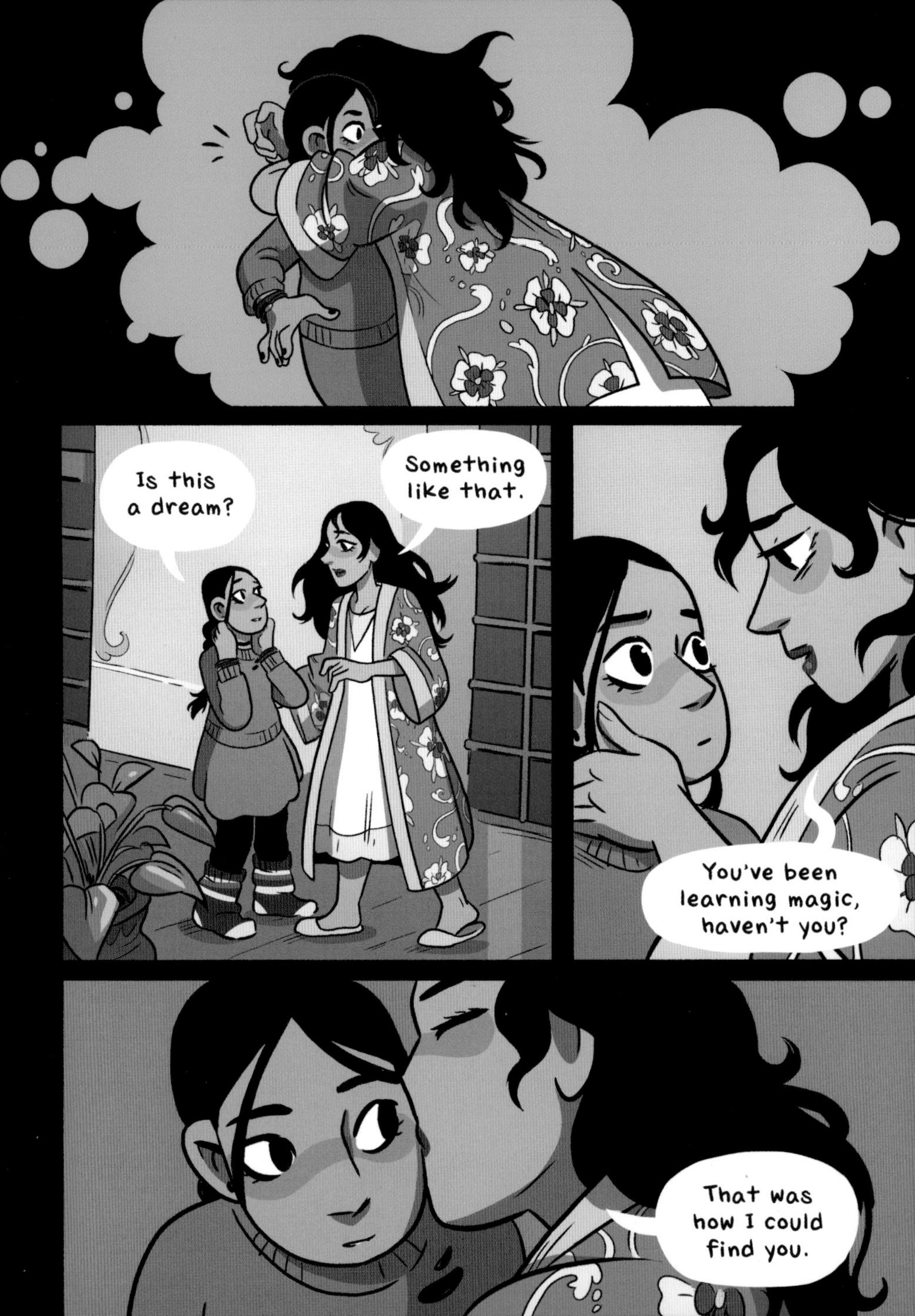
Is this a dream?
Something like that.
You've been learning magic, haven't you?
That was how I could find you.

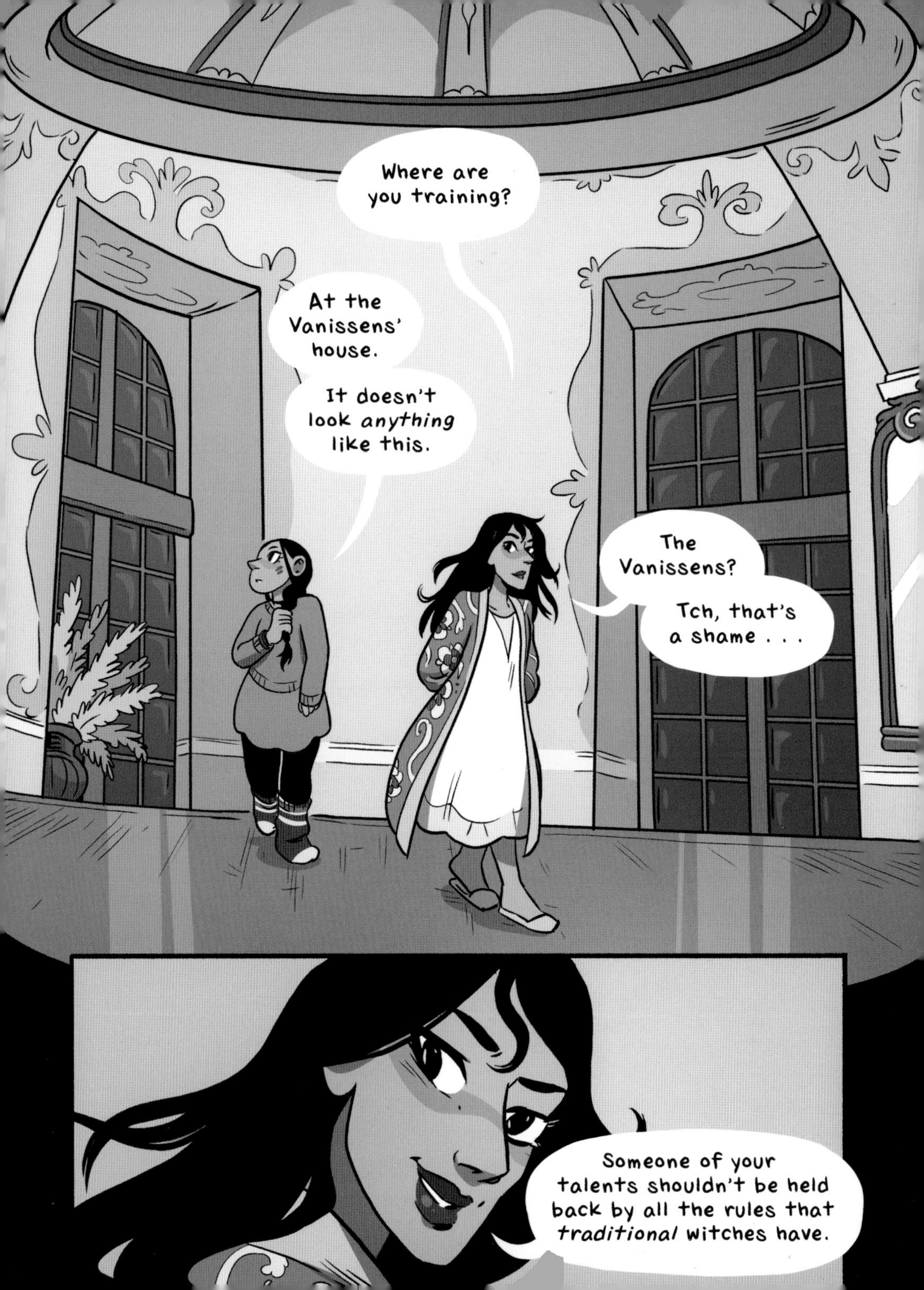
Where are you training?
At the Vanissens' house.
It doesn't look *anything* like this.
The Vanissens?
Tch, that's a shame . . .
Someone of your talents shouldn't be held back by all the rules that *traditional* witches have.

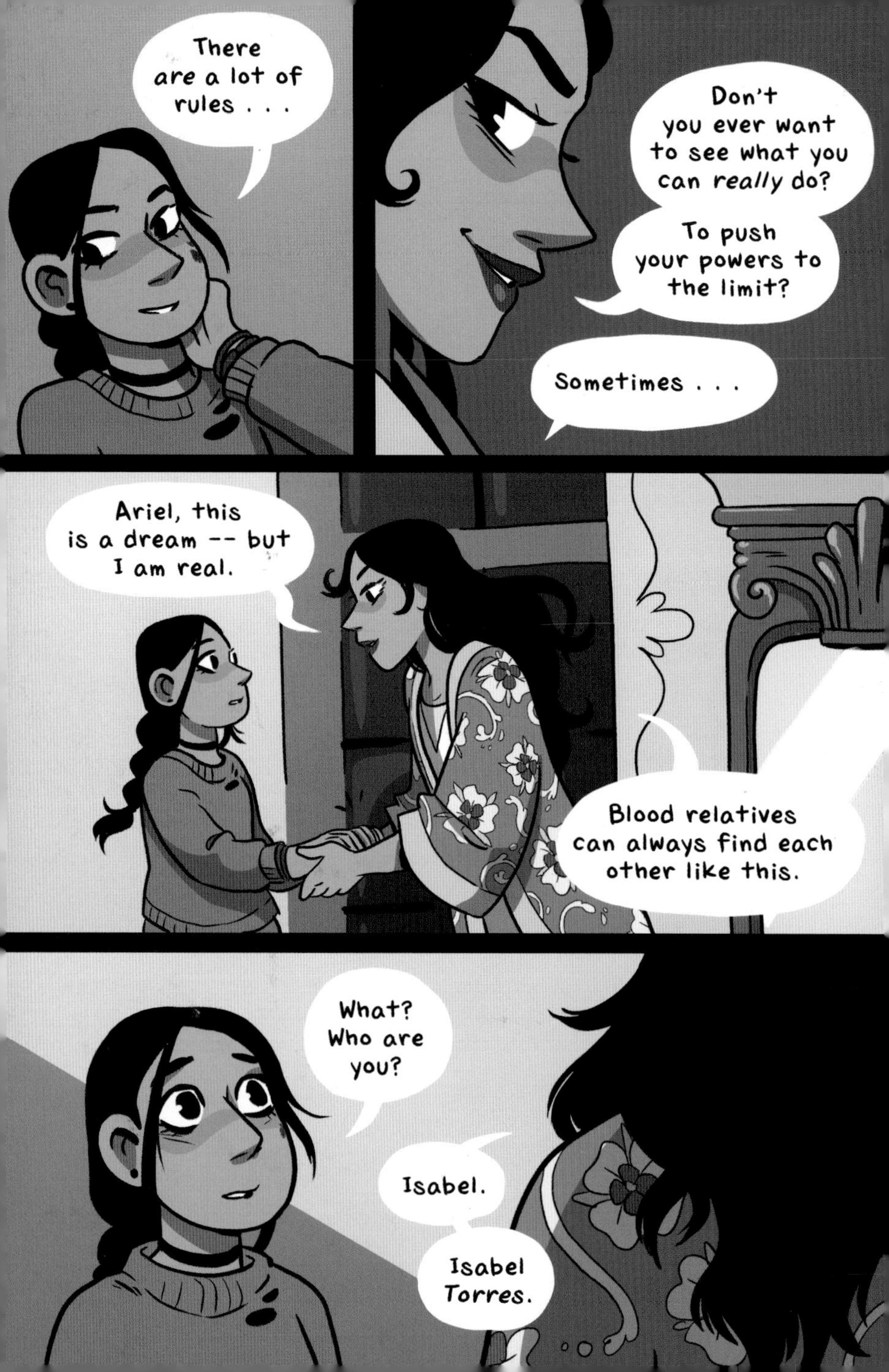
There are a lot of rules . . .
Don't you ever want to see what you can *really* do?
To push your powers to the limit?
Sometimes . . .
Ariel, this is a dream -- but I am real.
Blood relatives can always find each other like this.
What? Who are you?
Isabel.
Isabel Torres.

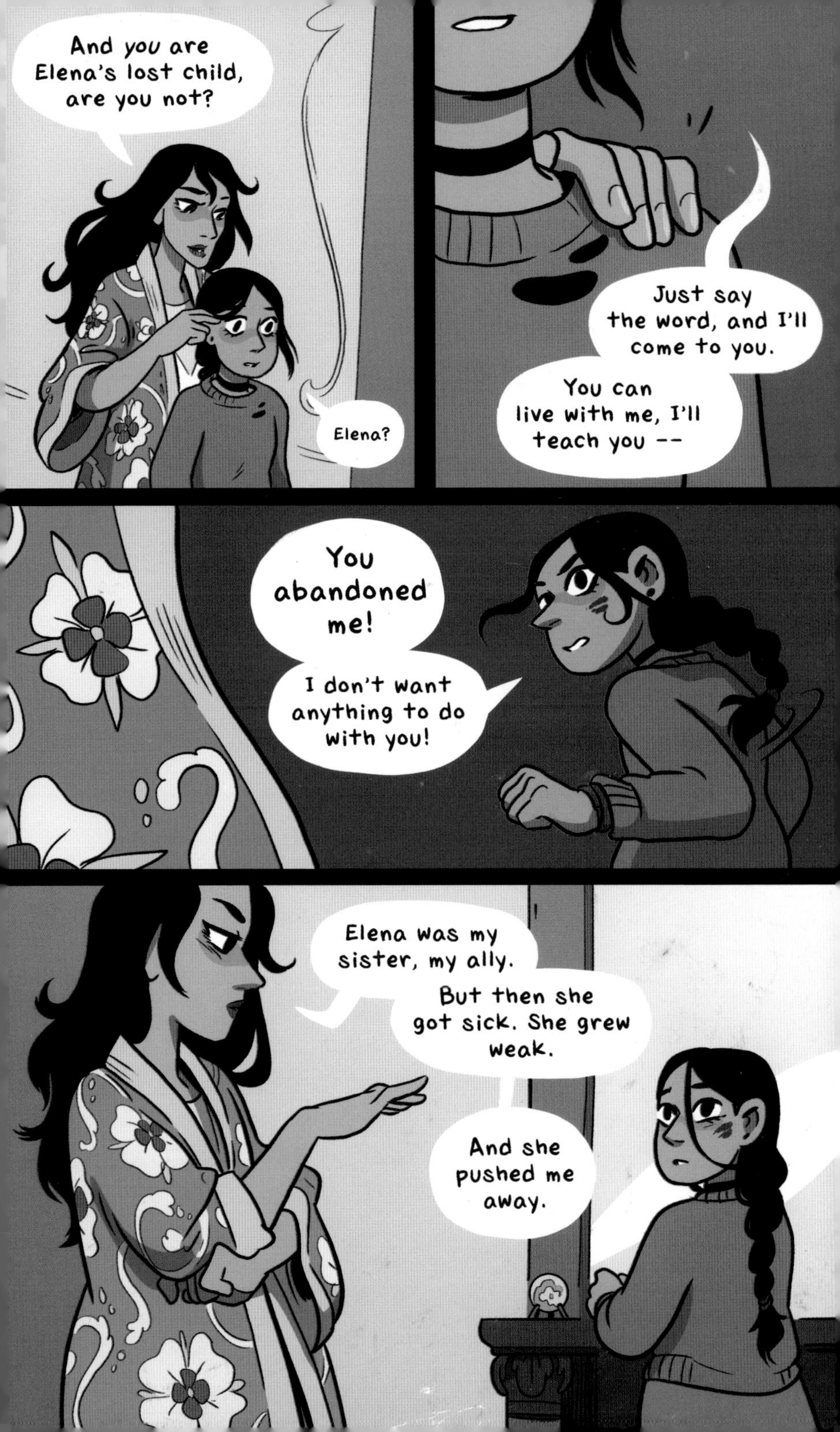
And you are Elena's lost child, are you not?
Elena?
Just say the word, and I'll come to you.
You can live with me, I'll teach you --
You abandoned me!
I don't want anything to do with you!
Elena was my sister, my ally.
But then she got sick. She grew weak.
And she pushed me away.

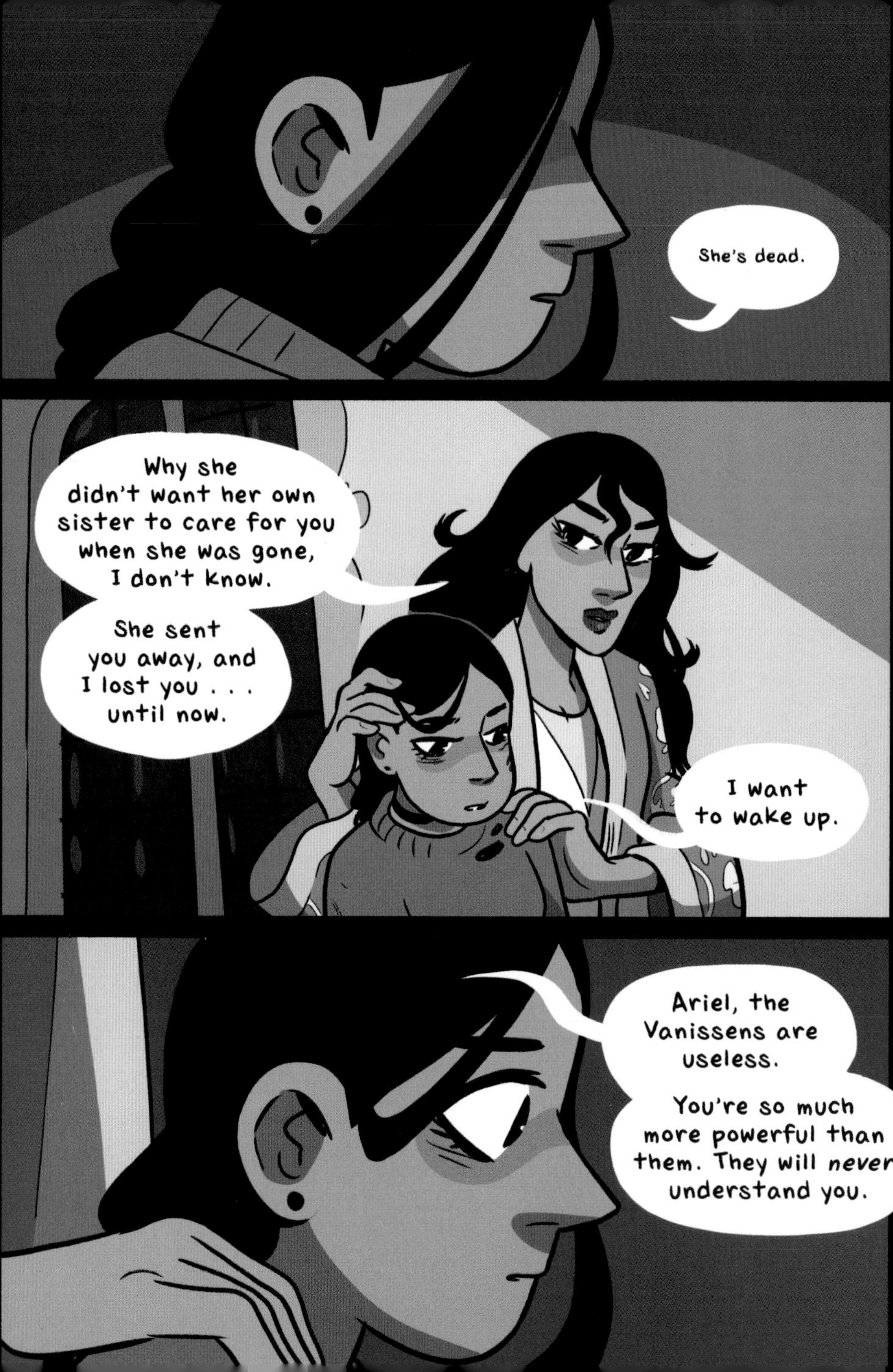
She's dead.
Why she didn't want her own sister to care for you when she was gone, I don't know.
She sent you away, and I lost you . . . until now.
I want to wake up.
Ariel, the Vanissens are useless.
You're so much more powerful than them. They will *never* understand you.

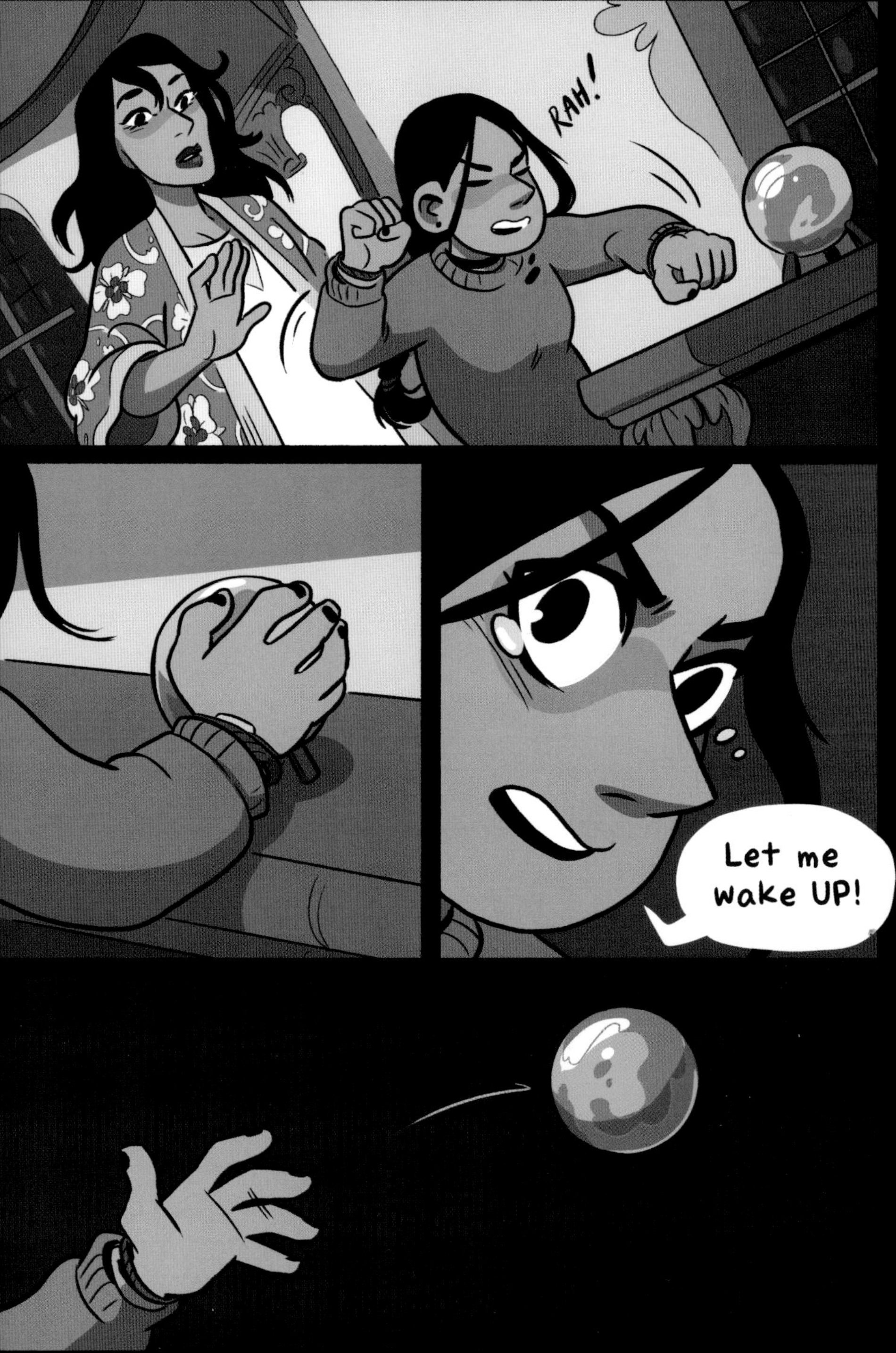
RAH!
Let me wake UP!

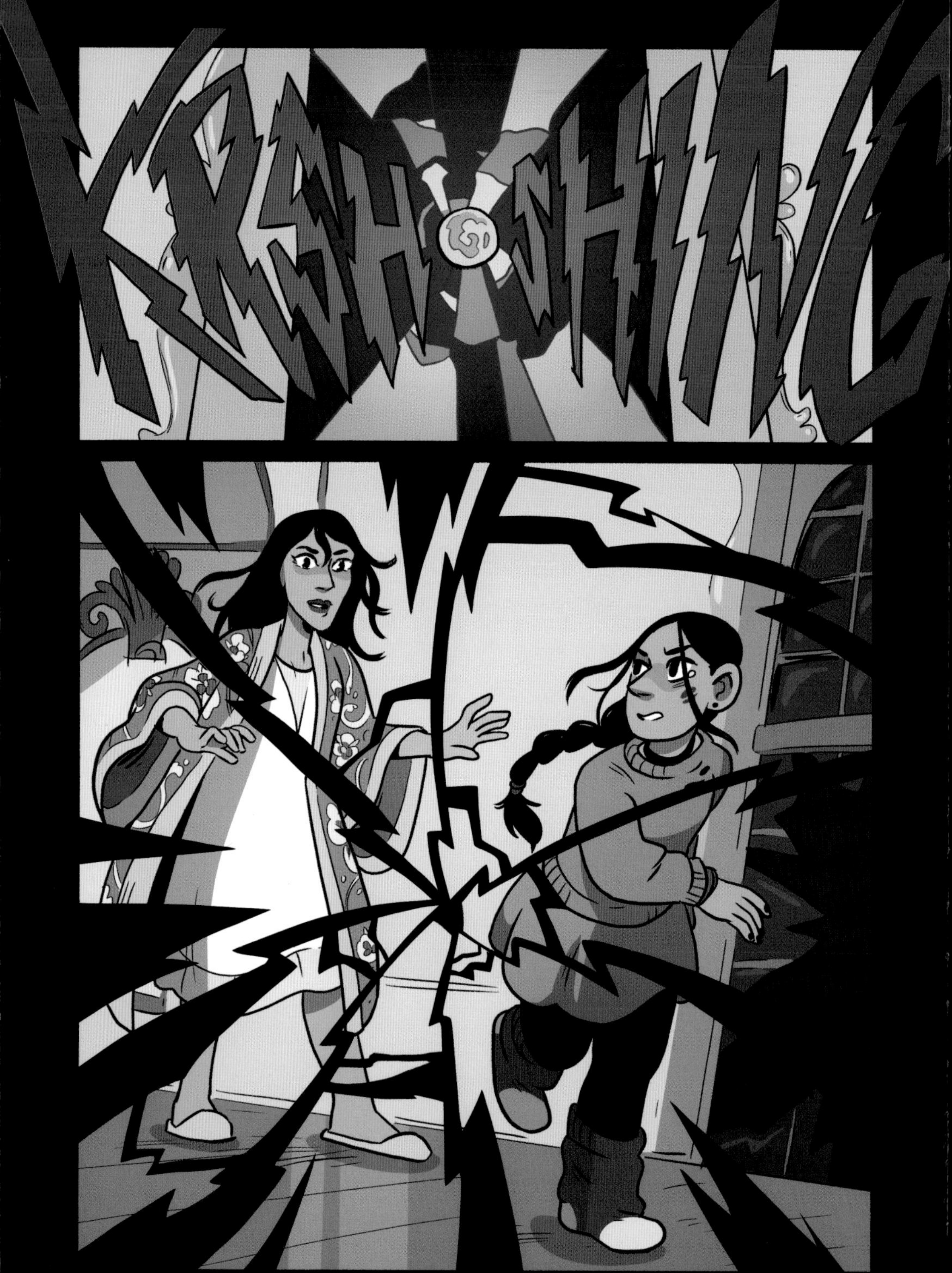

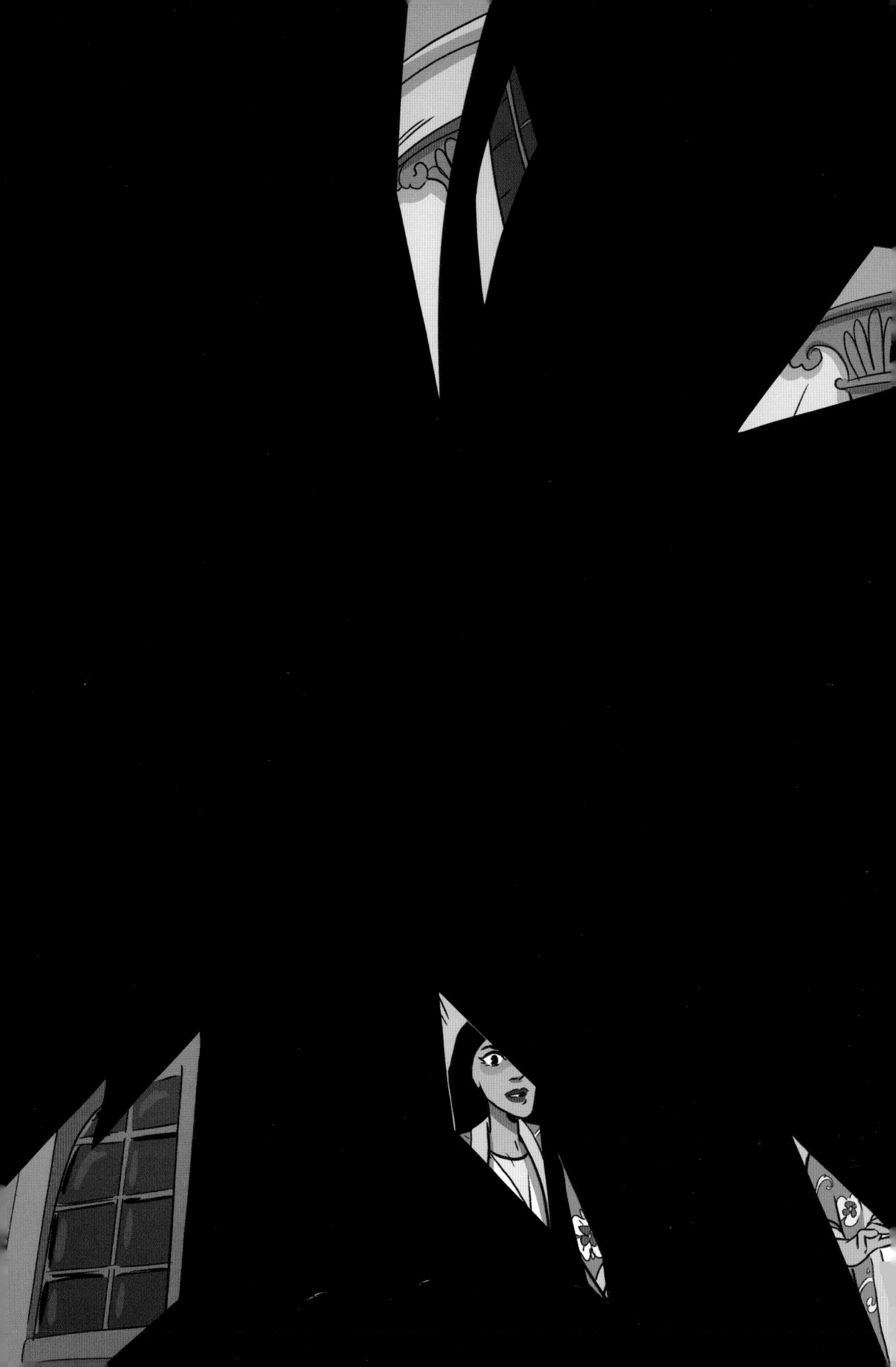

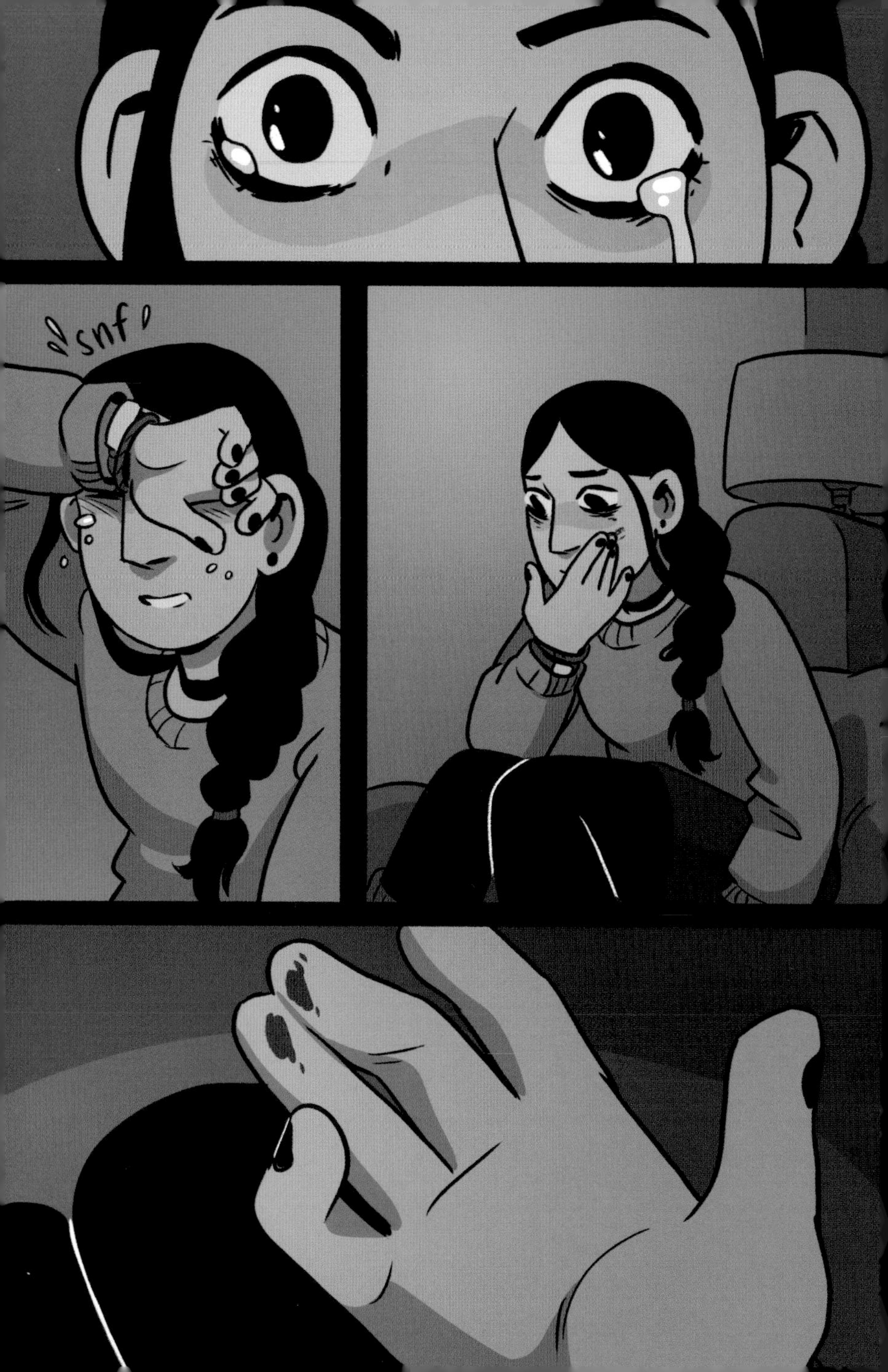
snf

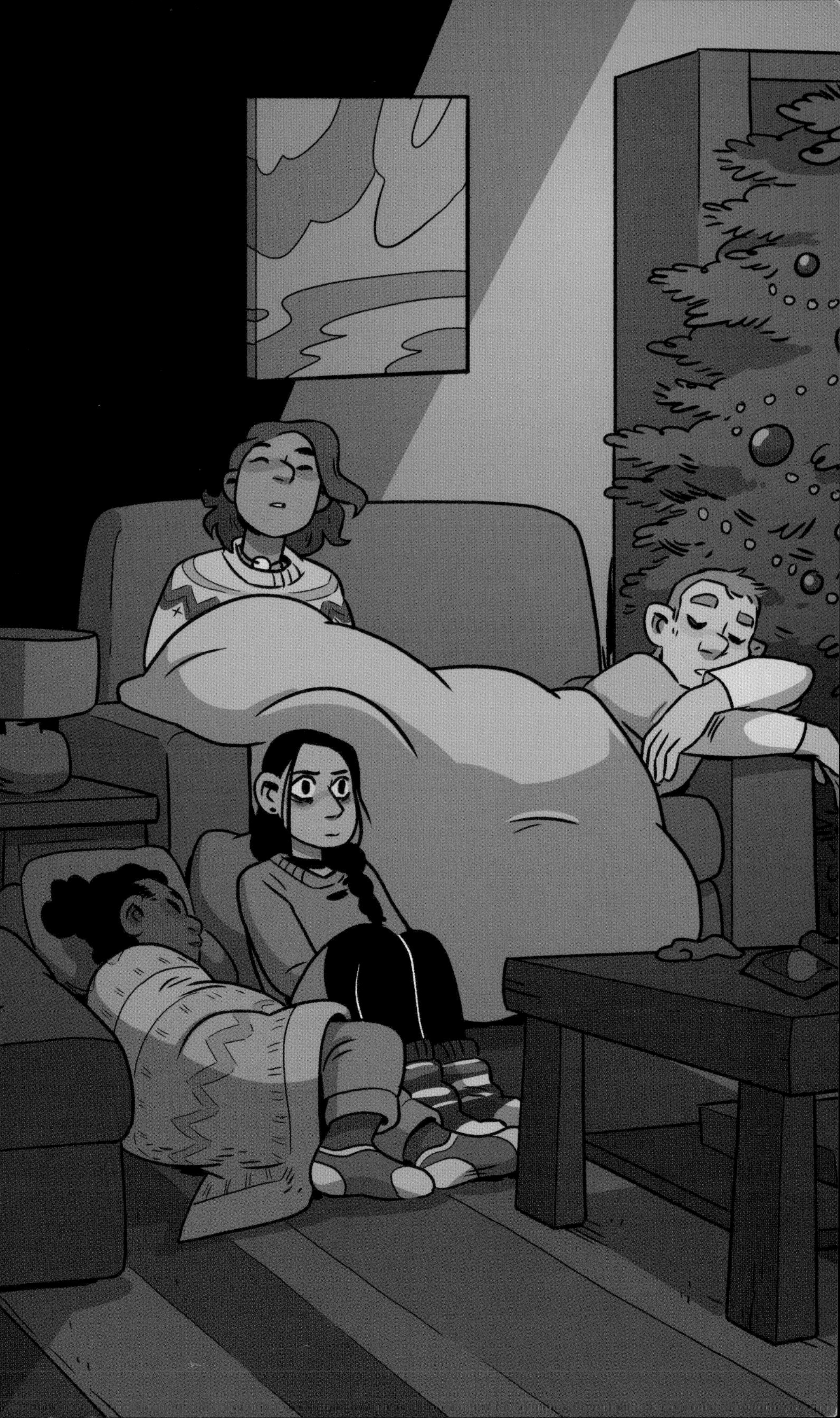

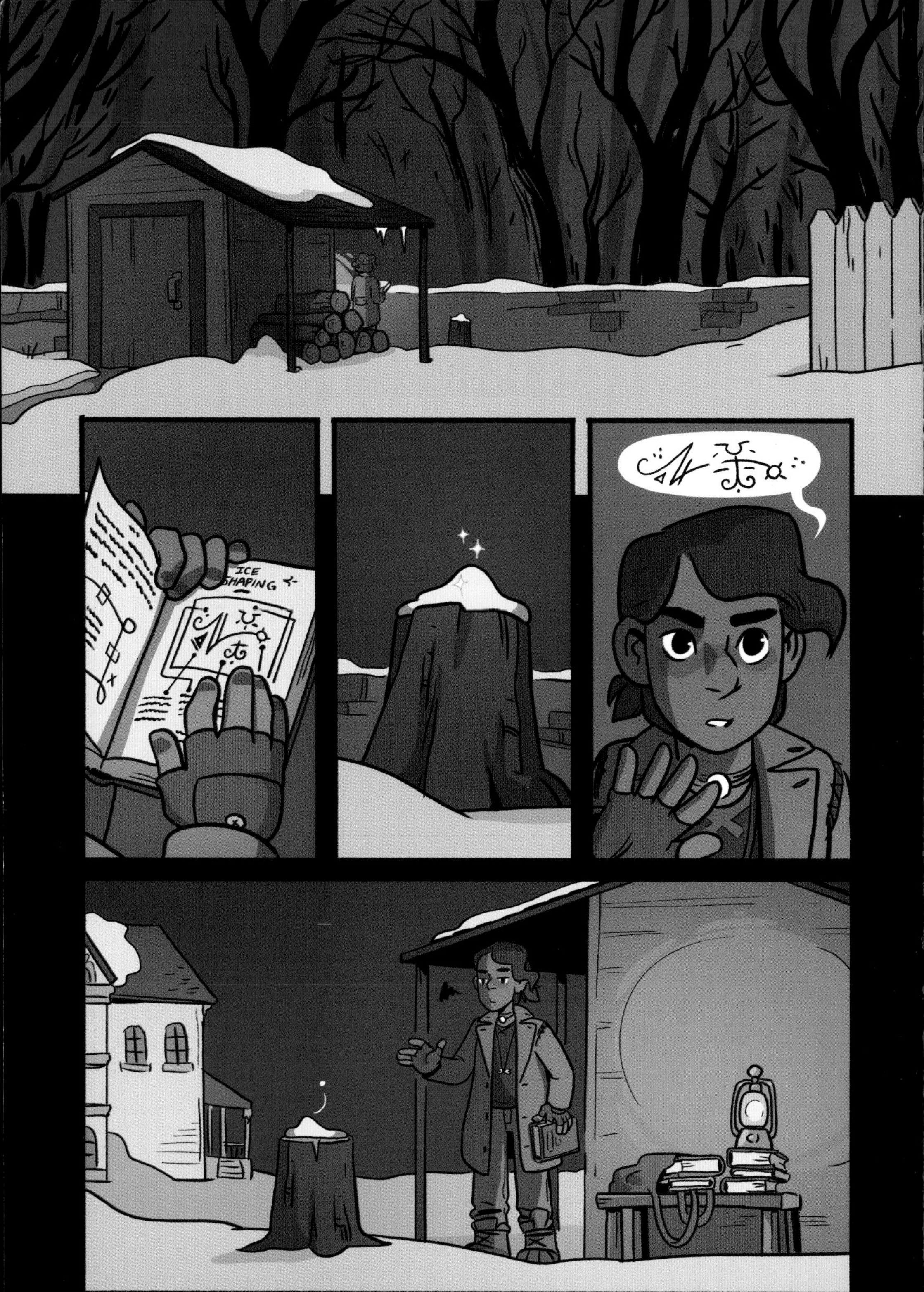
ICE SHAPING

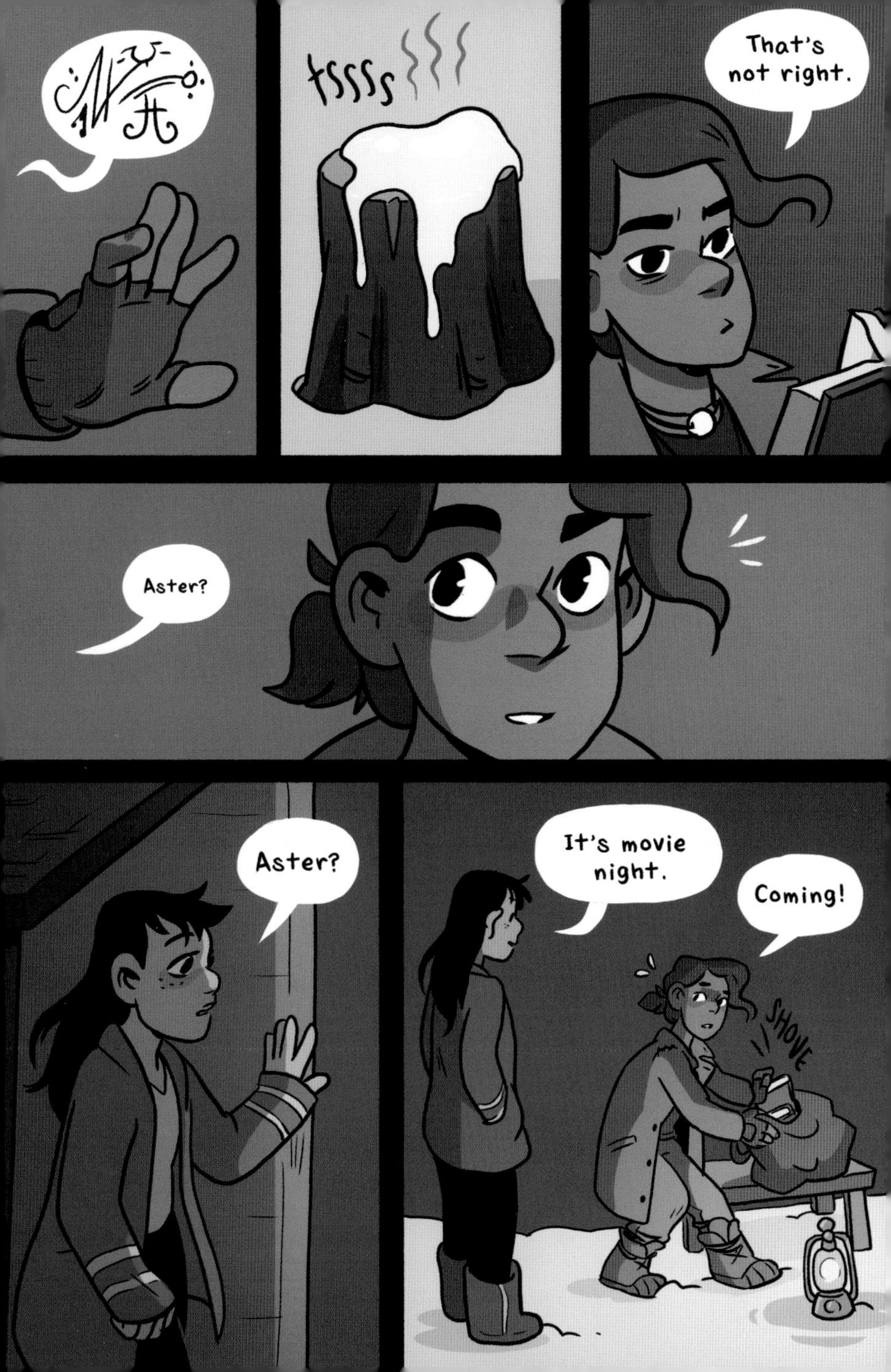
tssss
That's not right.
Aster?
Aster?
It's movie night.
Coming!
SHOVE

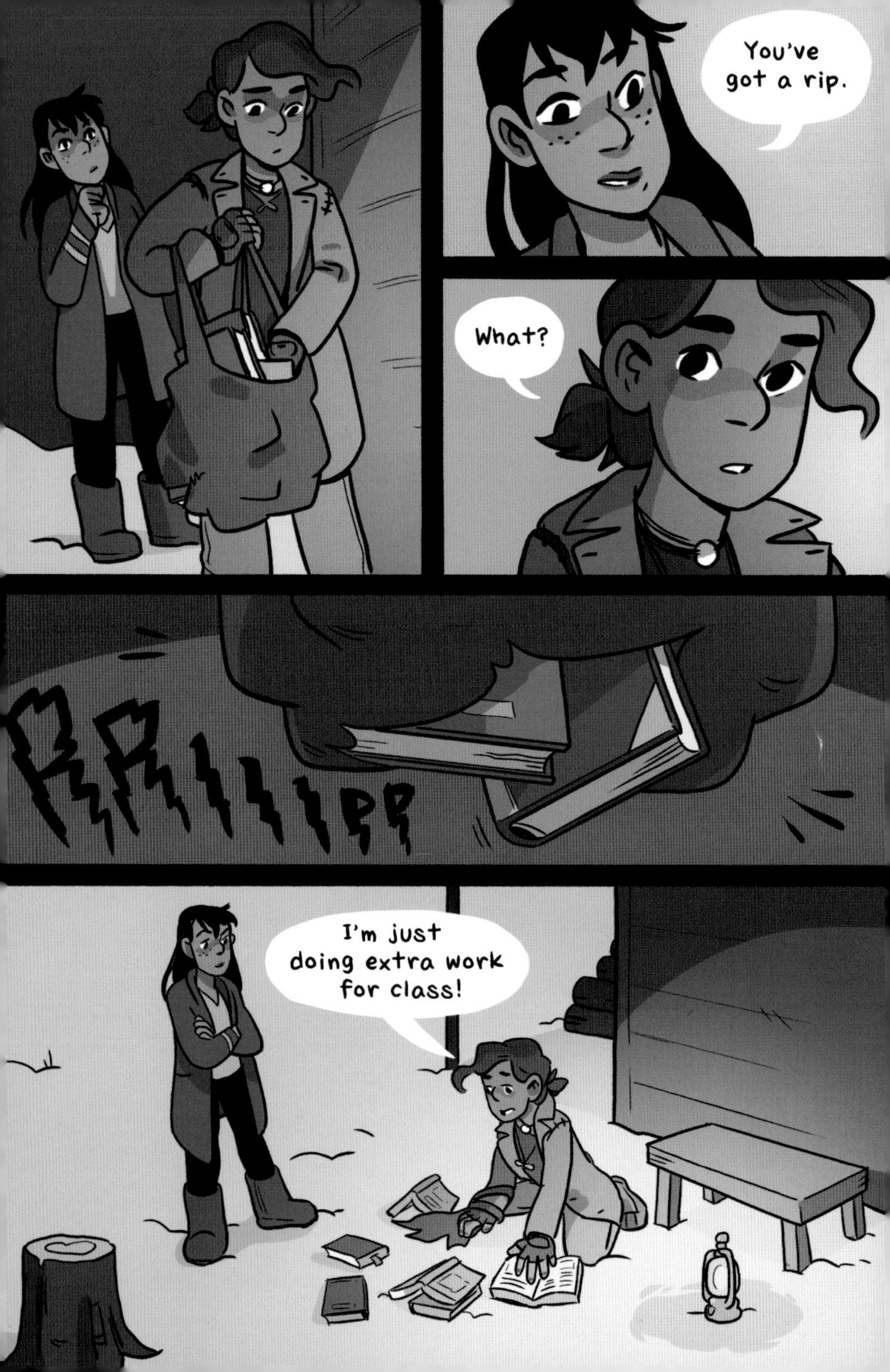
You've got a rip.
What?
RRIIIIIPP
I'm just doing extra work for class!

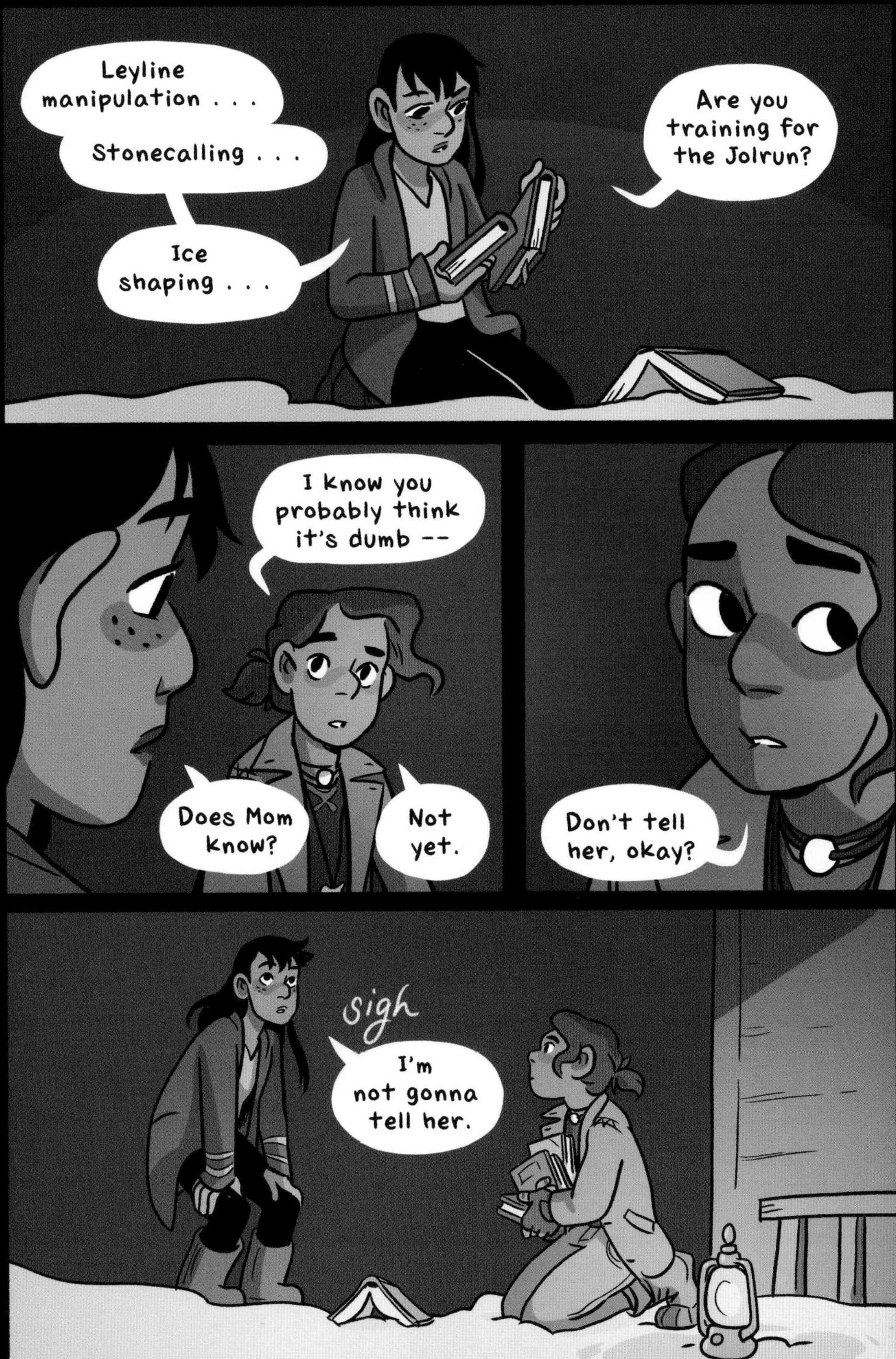

Leyline manipulation . . .
Stonecalling . . .
Ice shaping . . .
Are you training for the Jolrun?
I know you probably think it's dumb --
Does Mom know?
Not yet.
Don't tell her, okay?
sigh
I'm not gonna tell her.

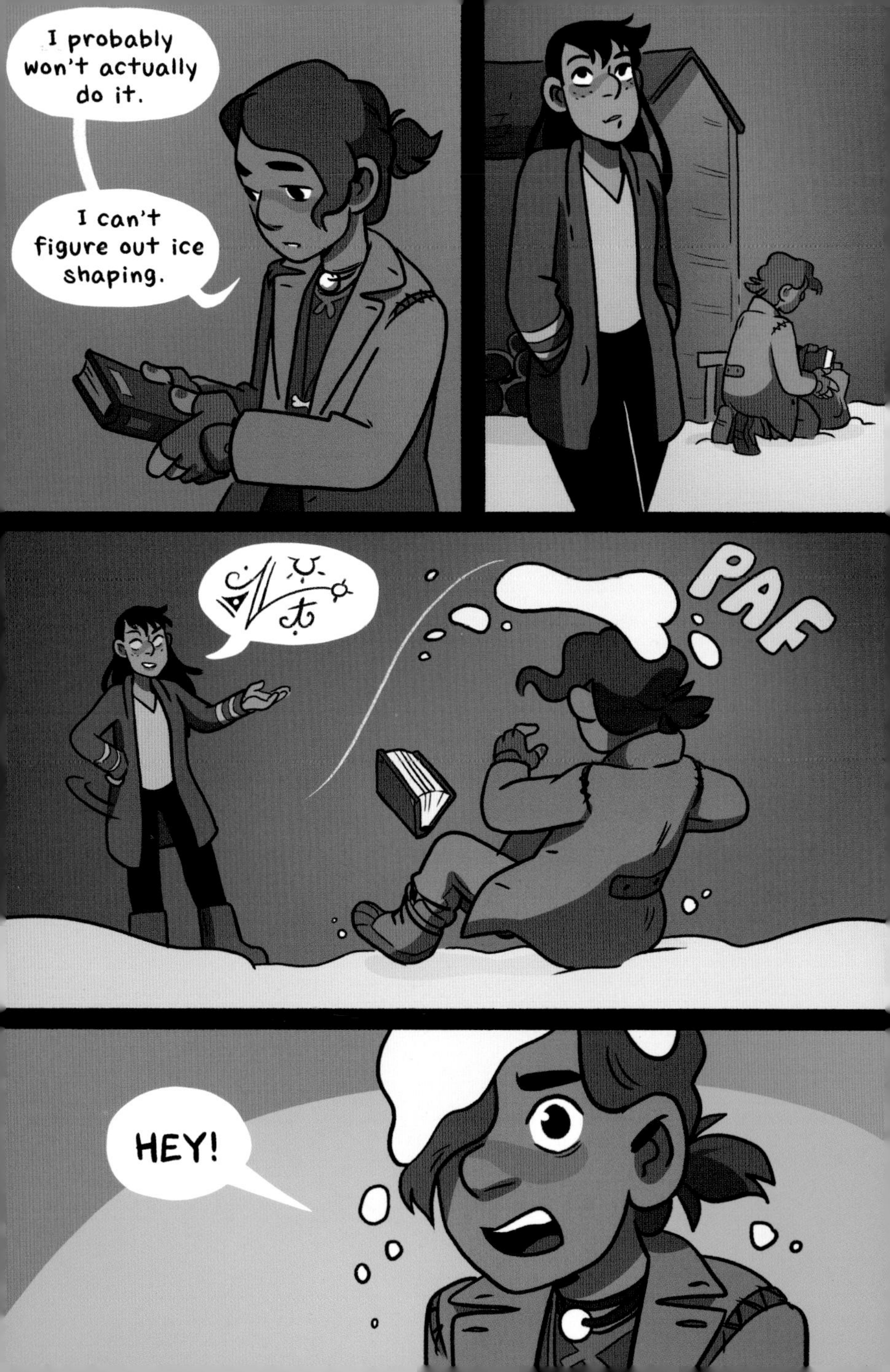
I probably won't actually do it.
I can't figure out ice shaping.
PAF
HEY!

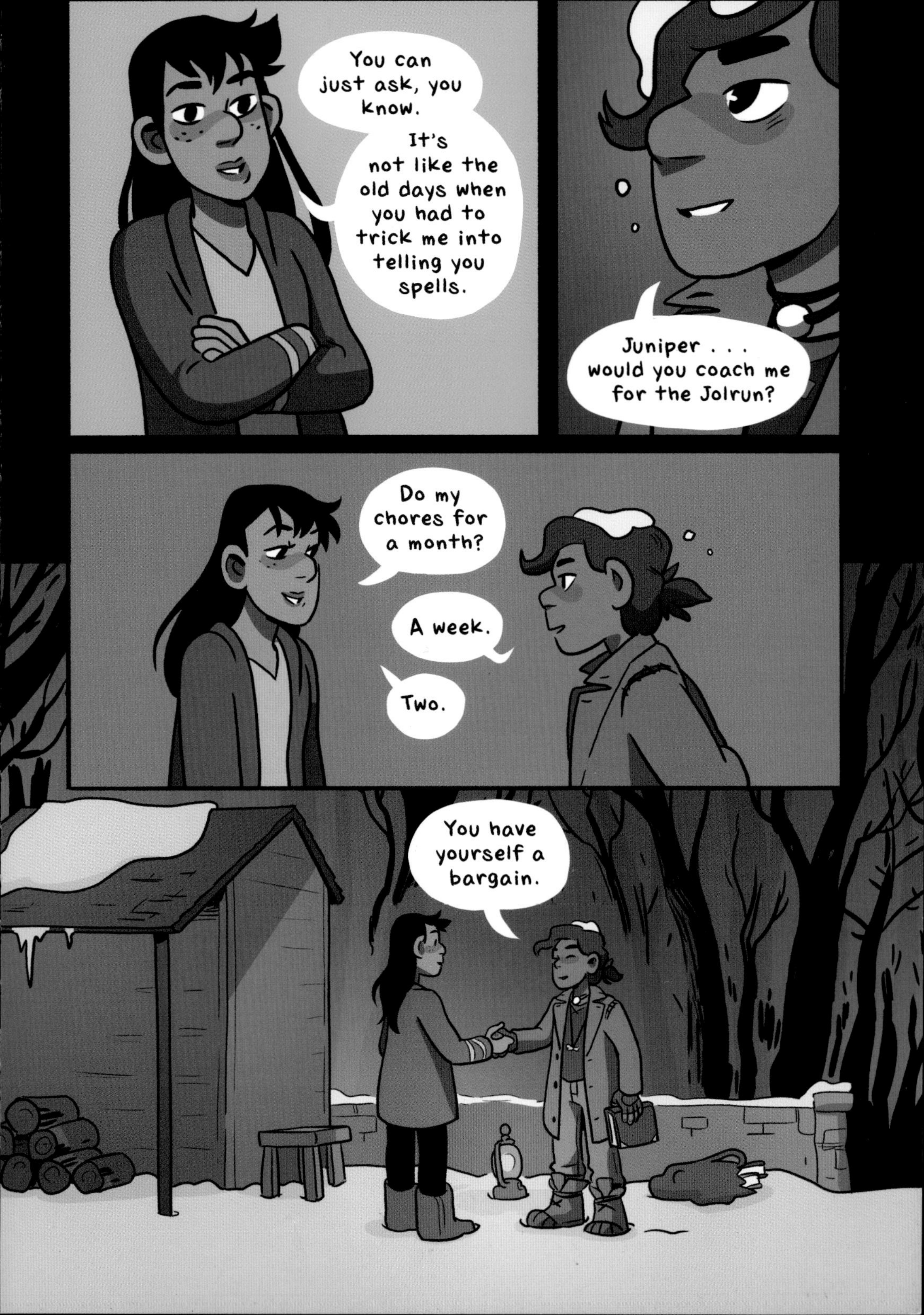
You can just ask, you know.
It's not like the old days when you had to trick me into telling you spells.
Juniper . . . would you coach me for the Jolrun?
Do my chores for a month?
A week.
Two.
You have yourself a bargain.

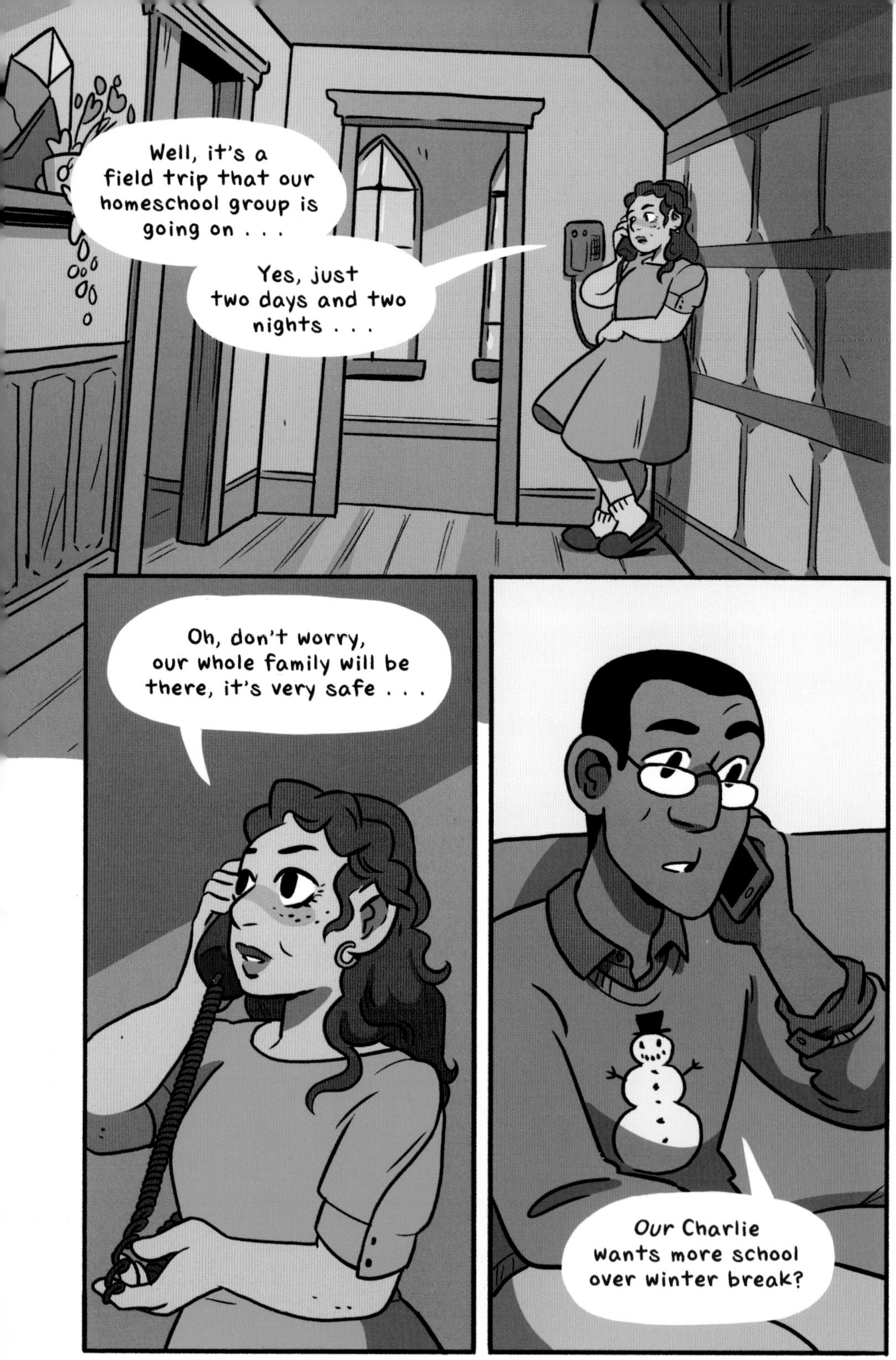
Well, it's a field trip that our homeschool group is going on . . .
Yes, just two days and two nights . . .
Oh, don't worry, our whole family will be there, it's very safe . . .
Our Charlie wants more school over winter break?

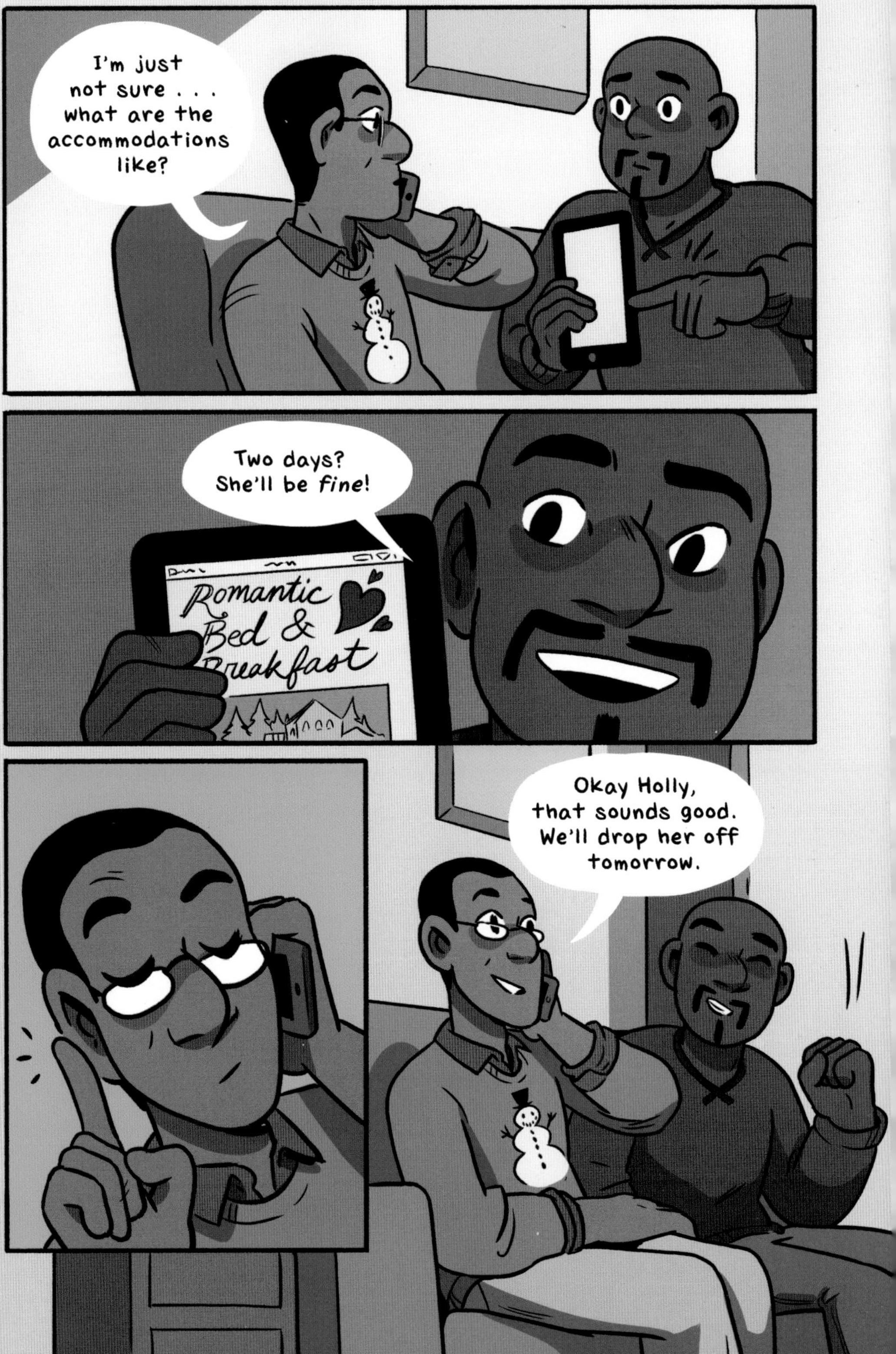
I'm just not sure . . . what are the accommodations like?
Two days? She'll be *fine*!
Romantic Bed & Breakfast
Okay Holly, that sounds good. We'll drop her off tomorrow.

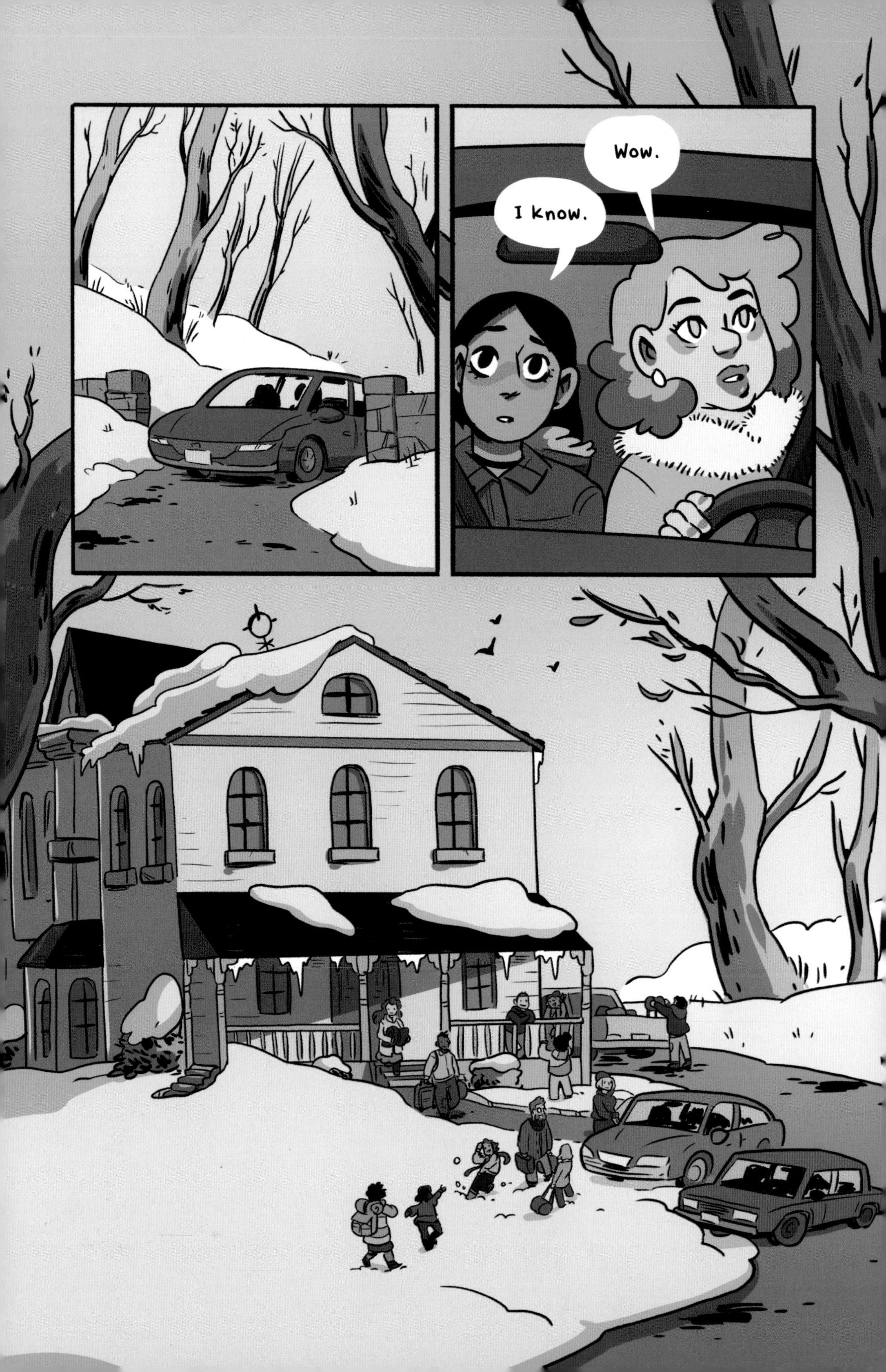
Wow.
I know.

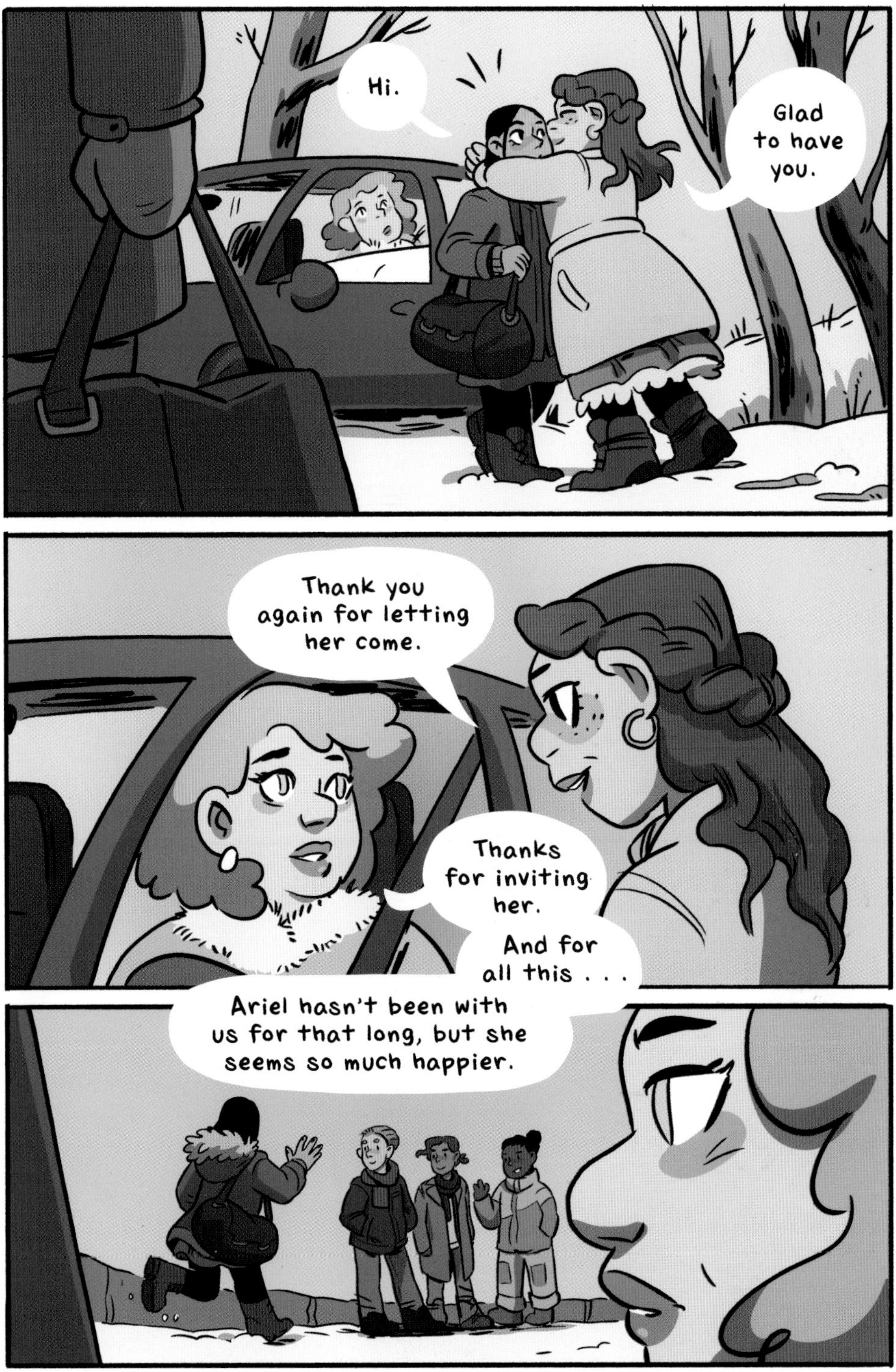
Hi.
Glad to have you.
Thank you again for letting her come.
Thanks for inviting her.
And for all this . . .
Ariel hasn't been with us for that long, but she seems so much happier.

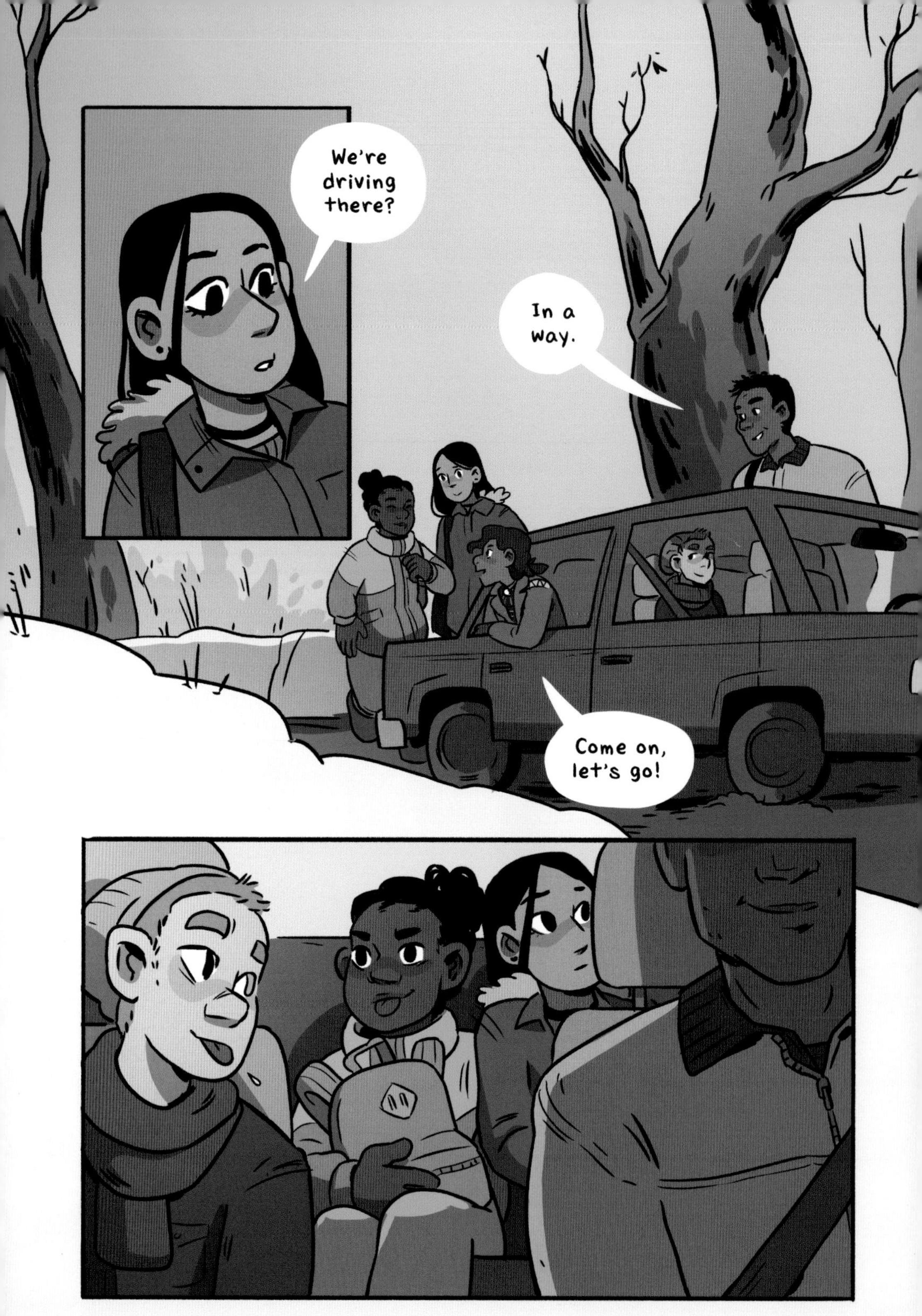
We're driving there?
In a way.
Come on, let's go!

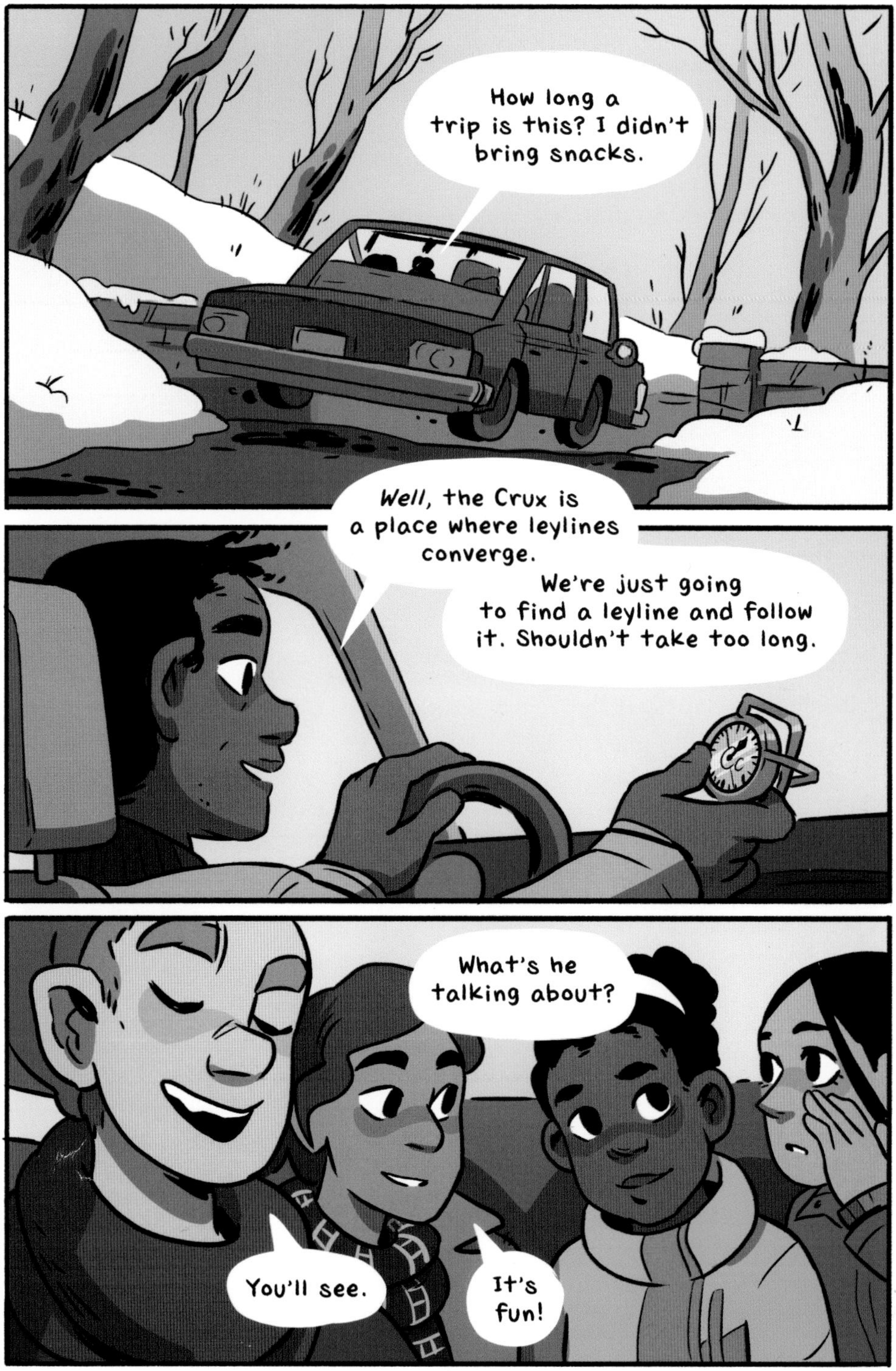
How long a trip is this? I didn't bring snacks.
Well, the Crux is a place where leylines converge.
We're just going to find a leyline and follow it. Shouldn't take too long.
What's he talking about?
You'll see.
It's fun!

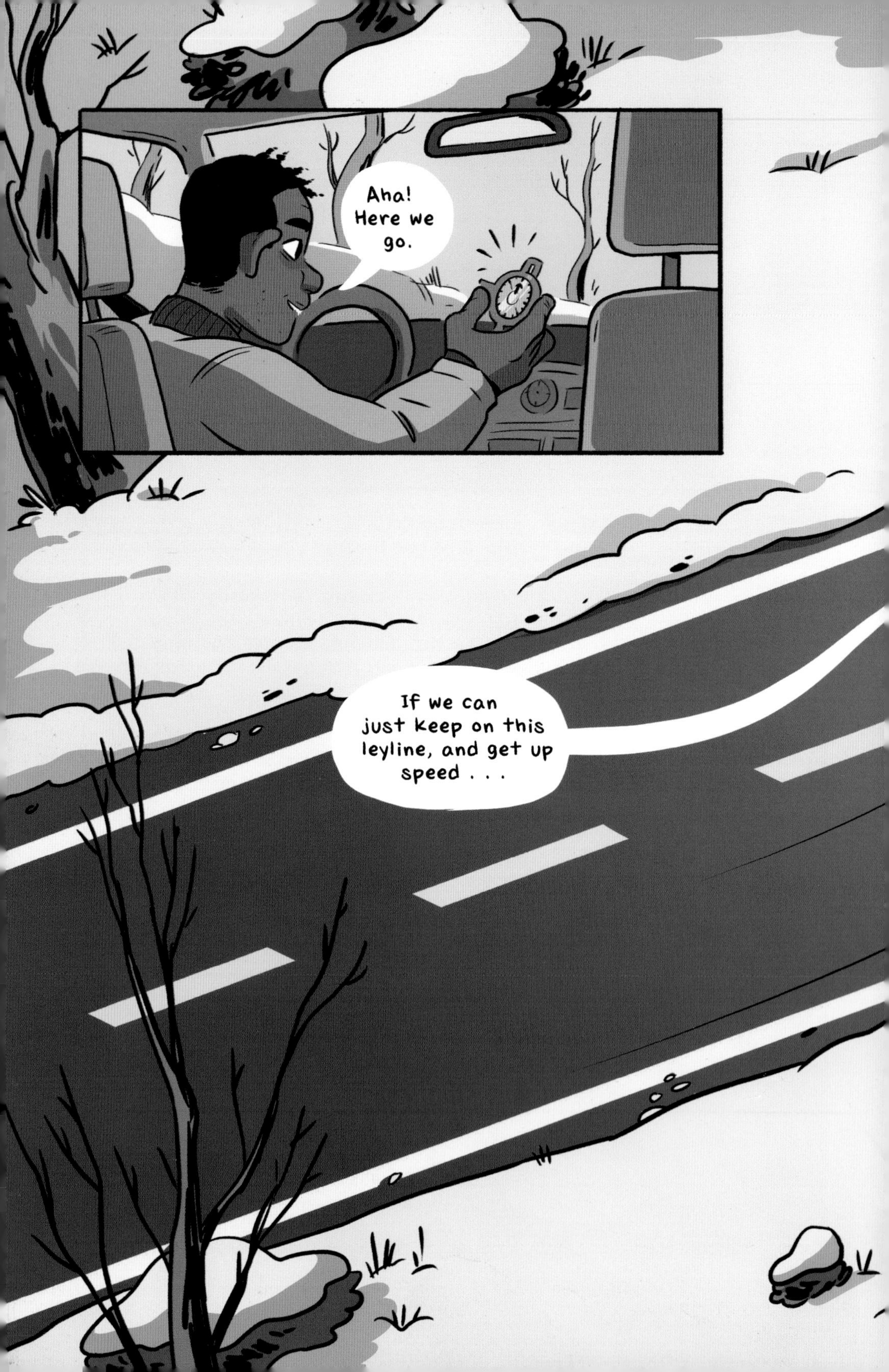
Aha! Here we go.
If we can just keep on this leyline, and get up speed . . .

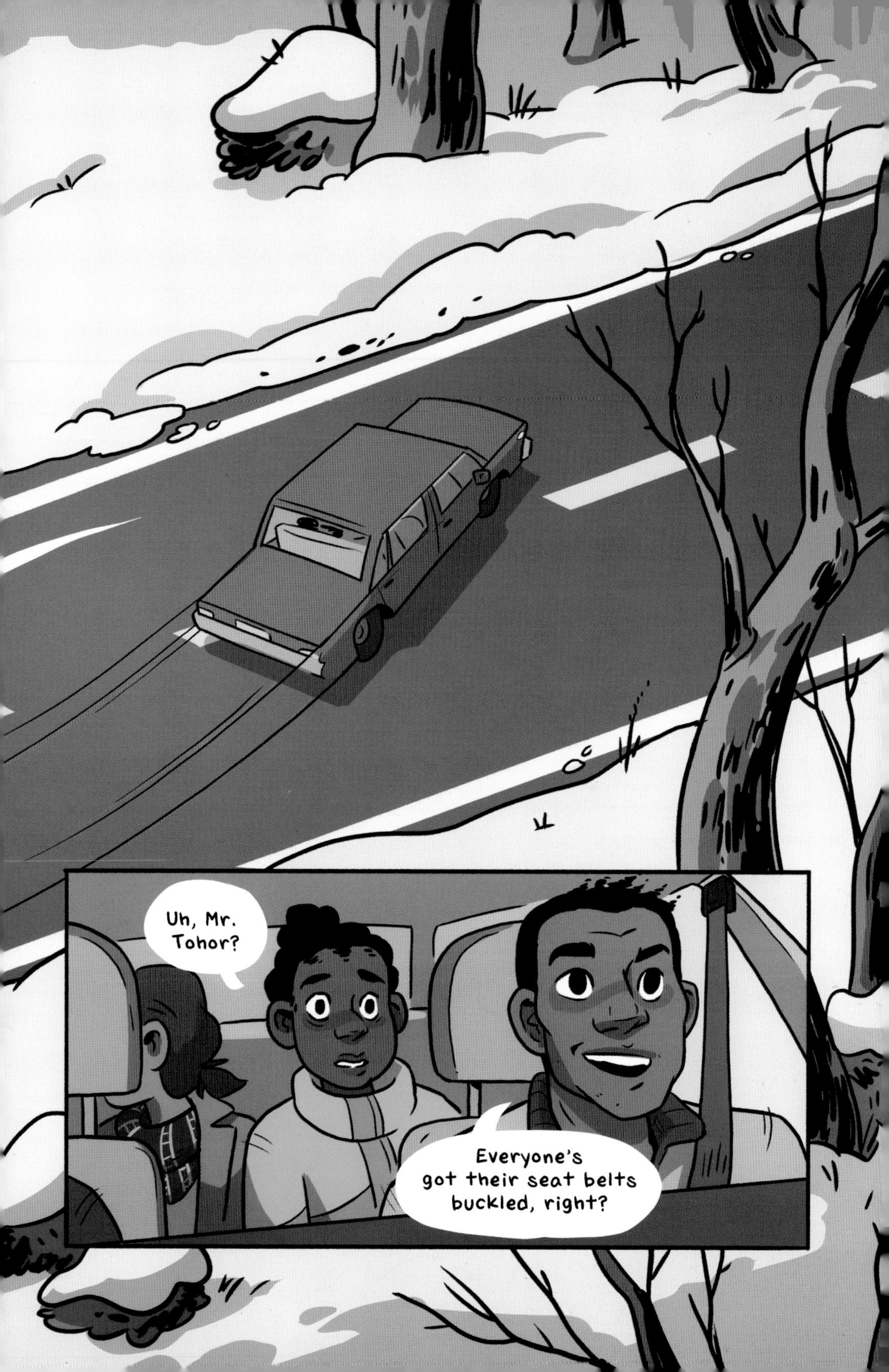
Uh, Mr. Tohor?
Everyone's got their seat belts buckled, right?

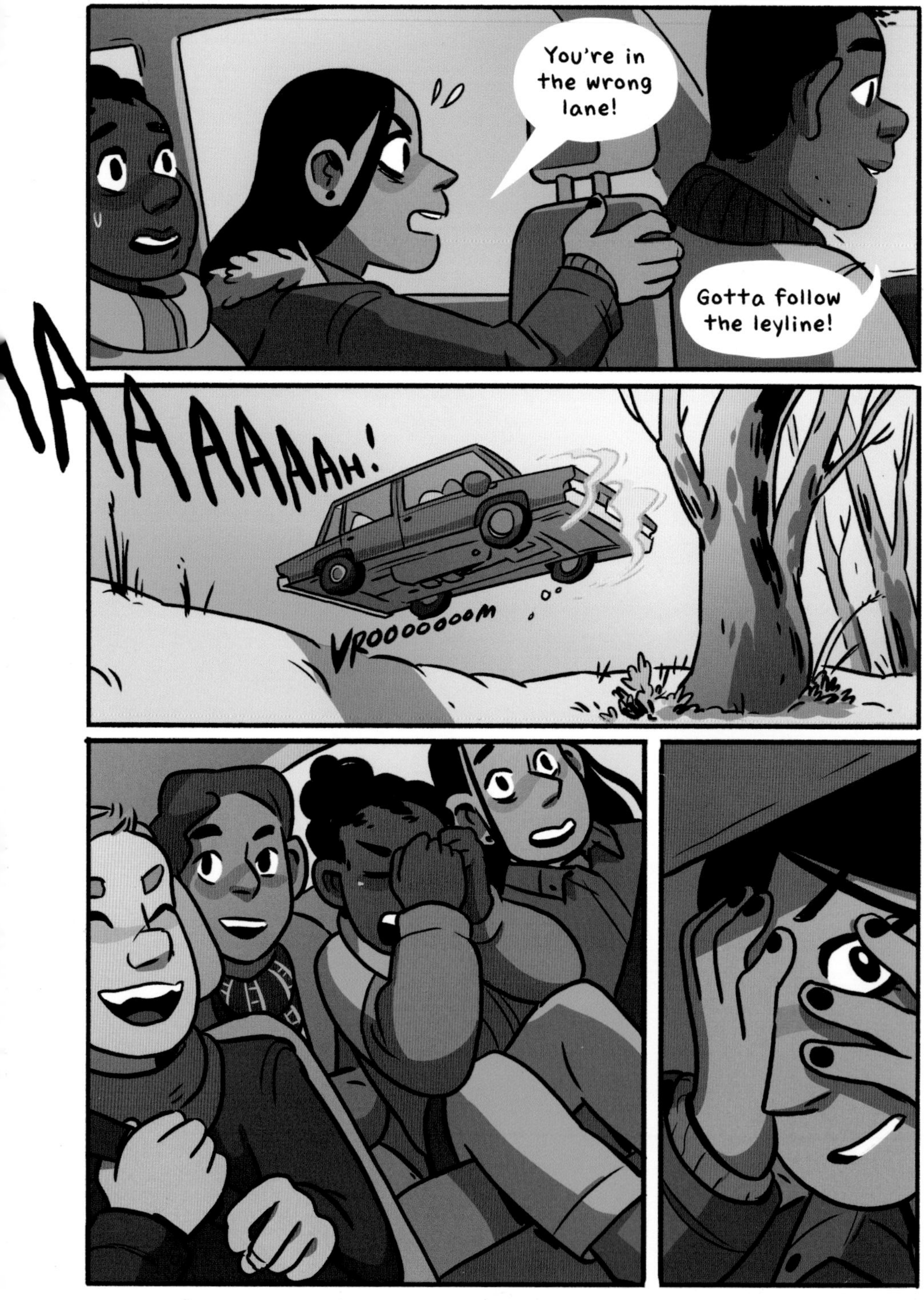
You're in the wrong lane!
Gotta follow the leyline!
AAAAAAAAAAH!
VROOOOOOOM

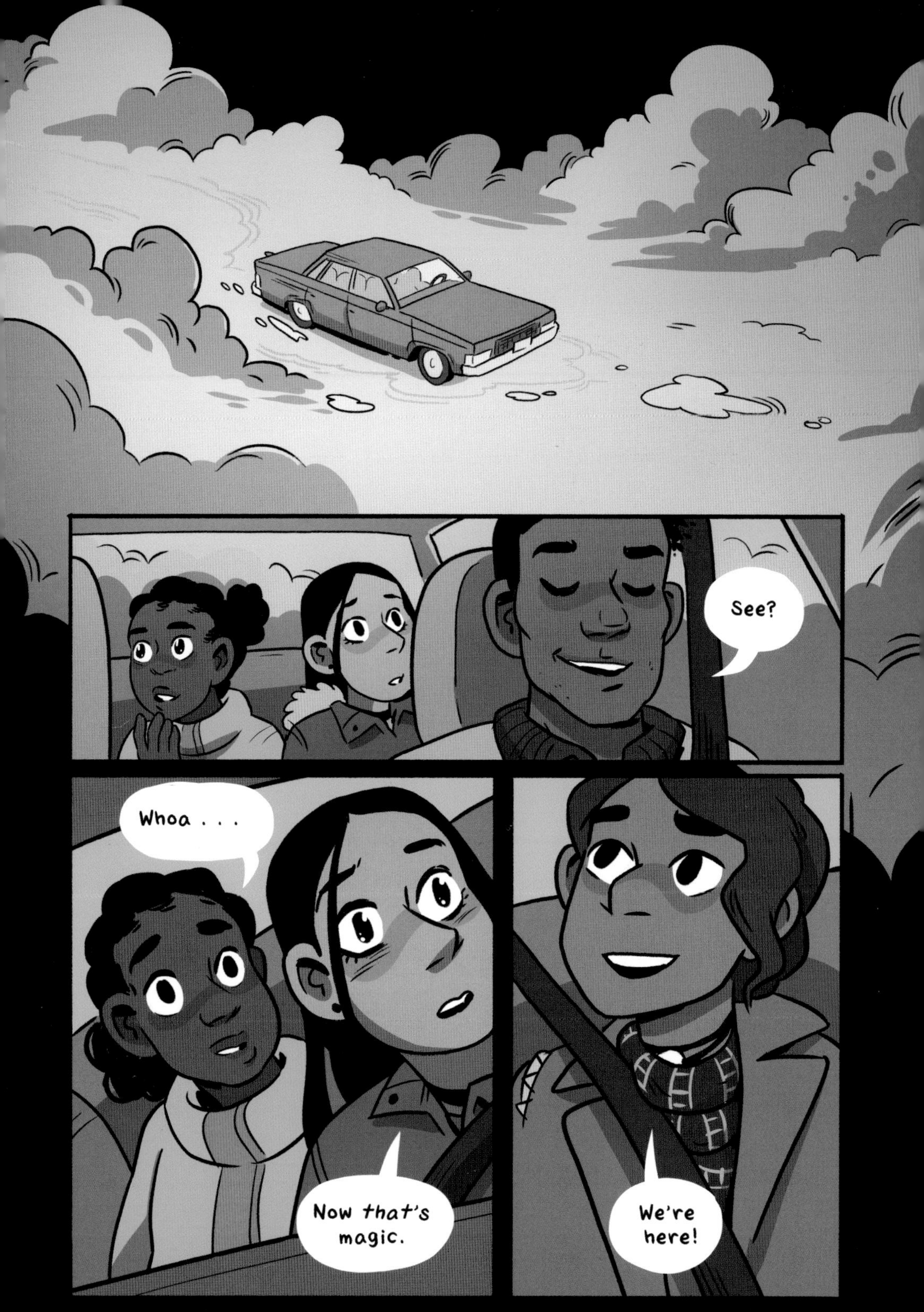
See?
Whoa . . .
Now that's magic.
We're here!

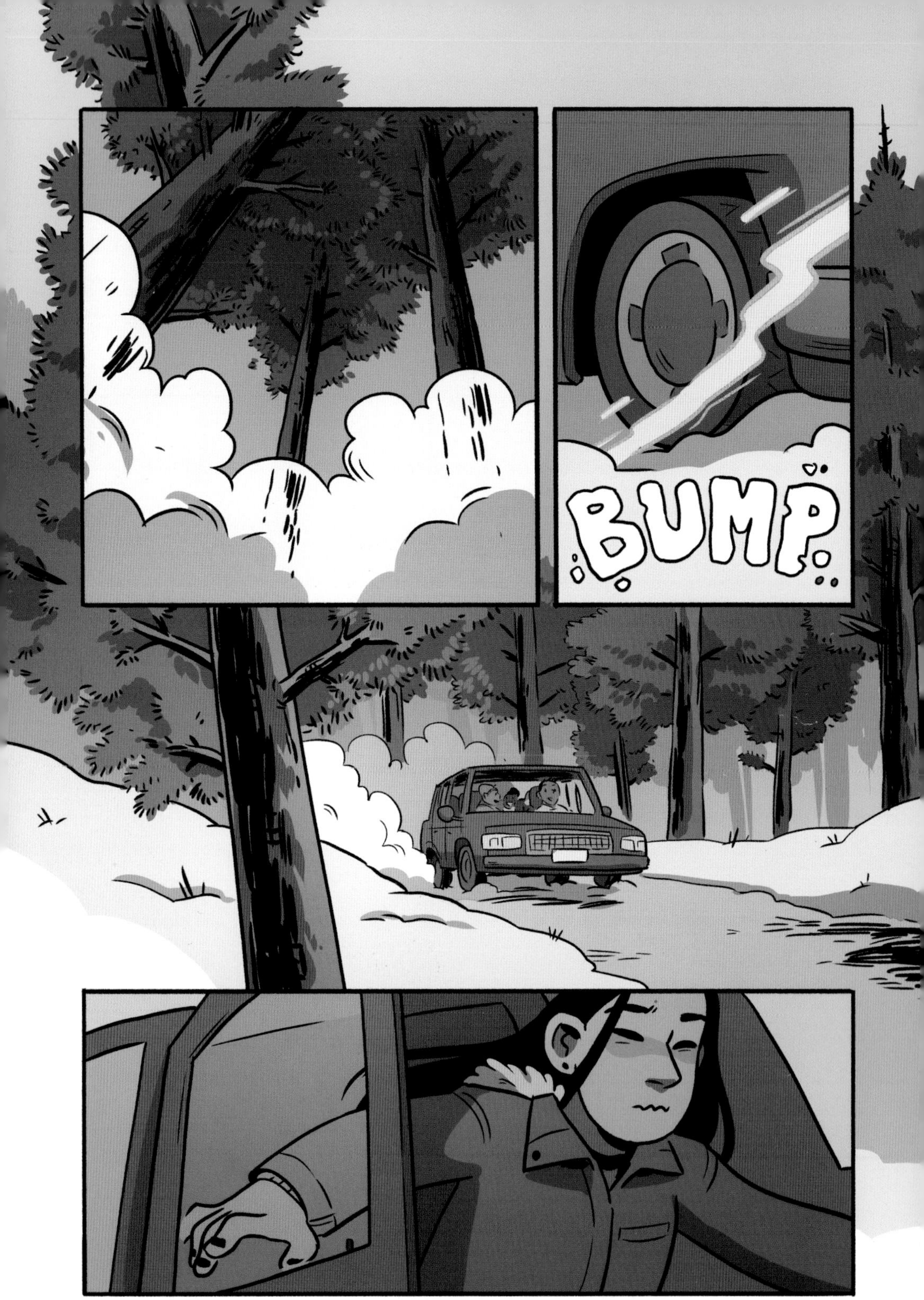
BUMP

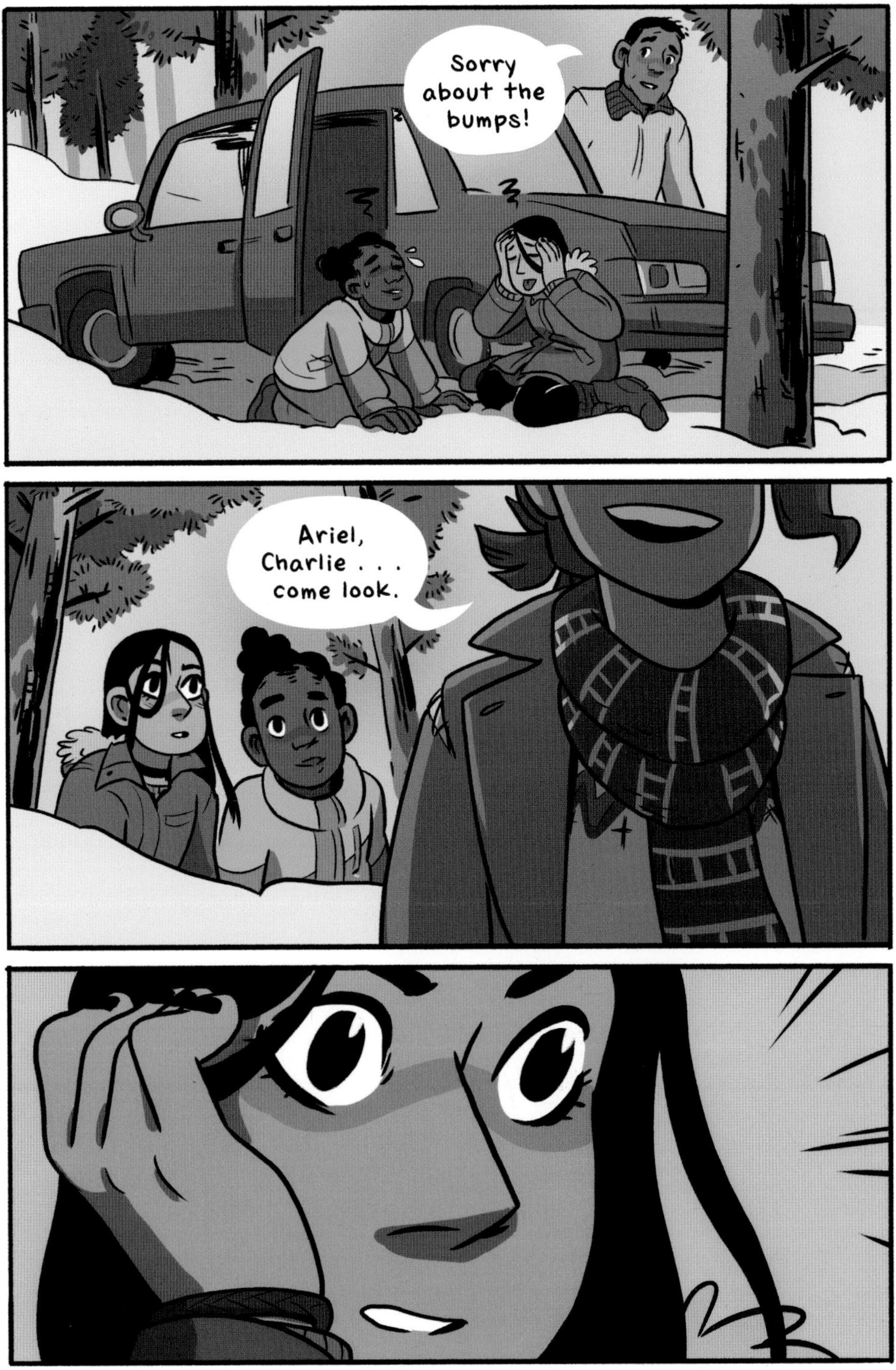
Sorry about the bumps!
Ariel, Charlie . . . come look.

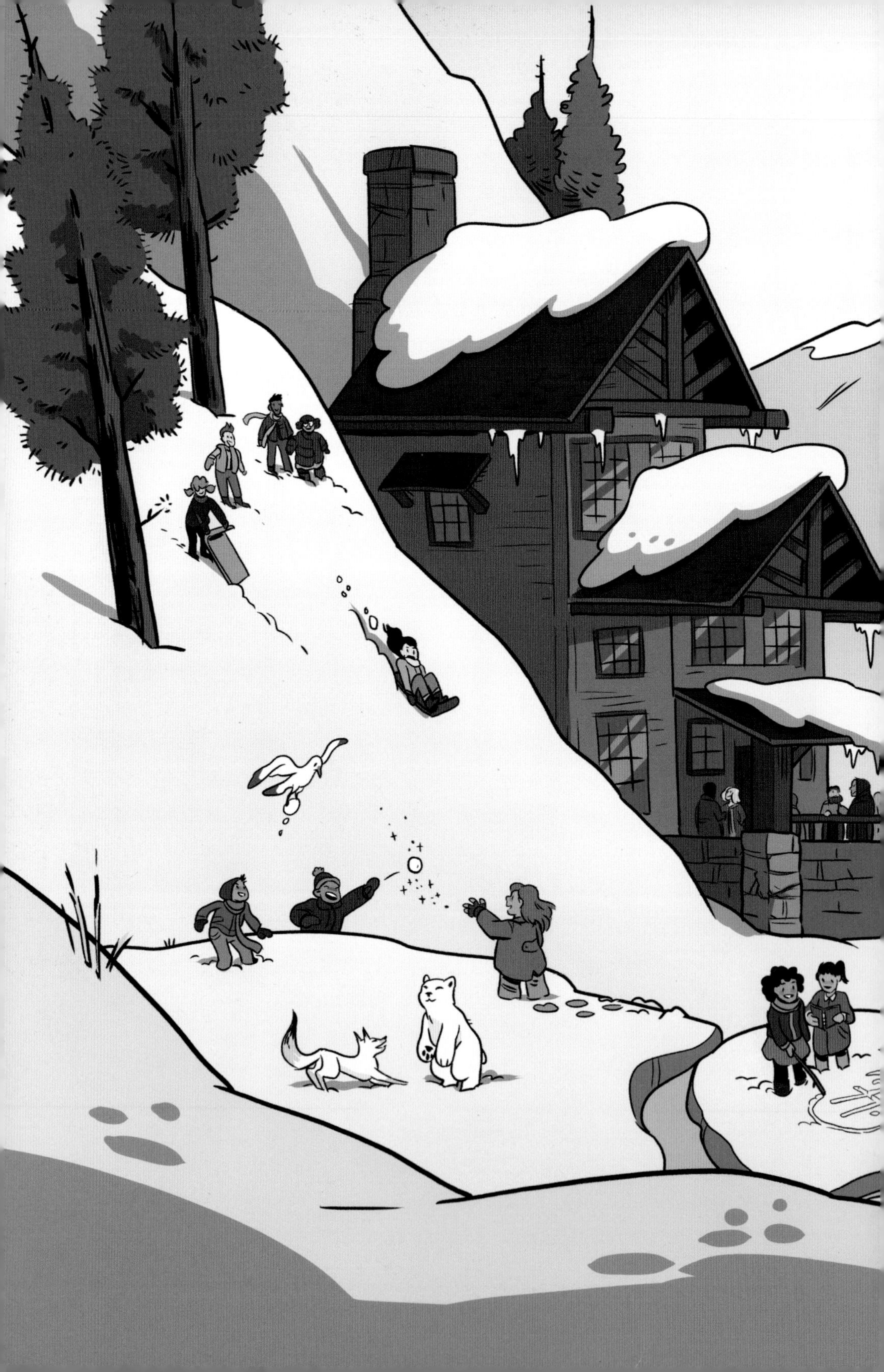

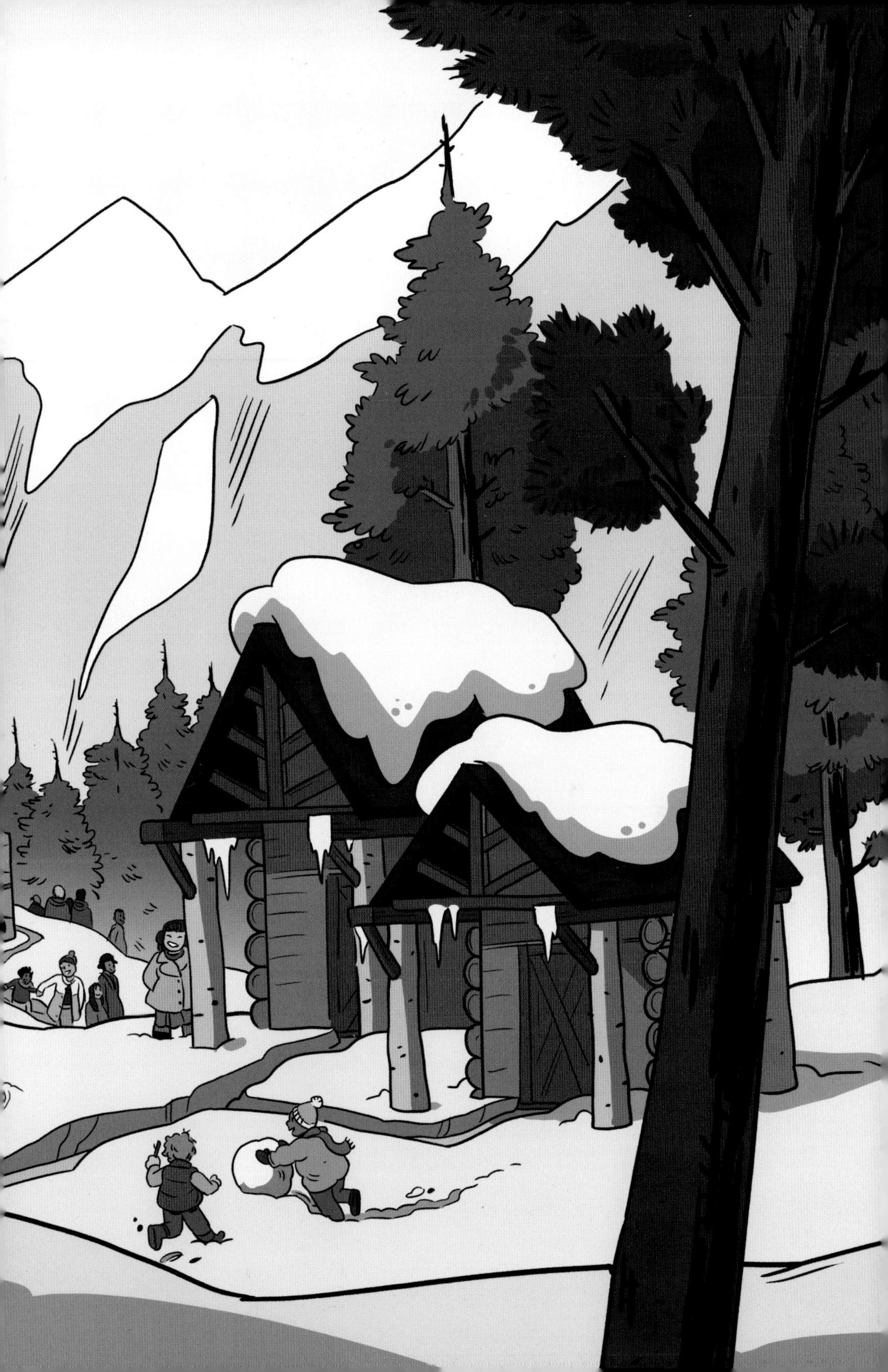

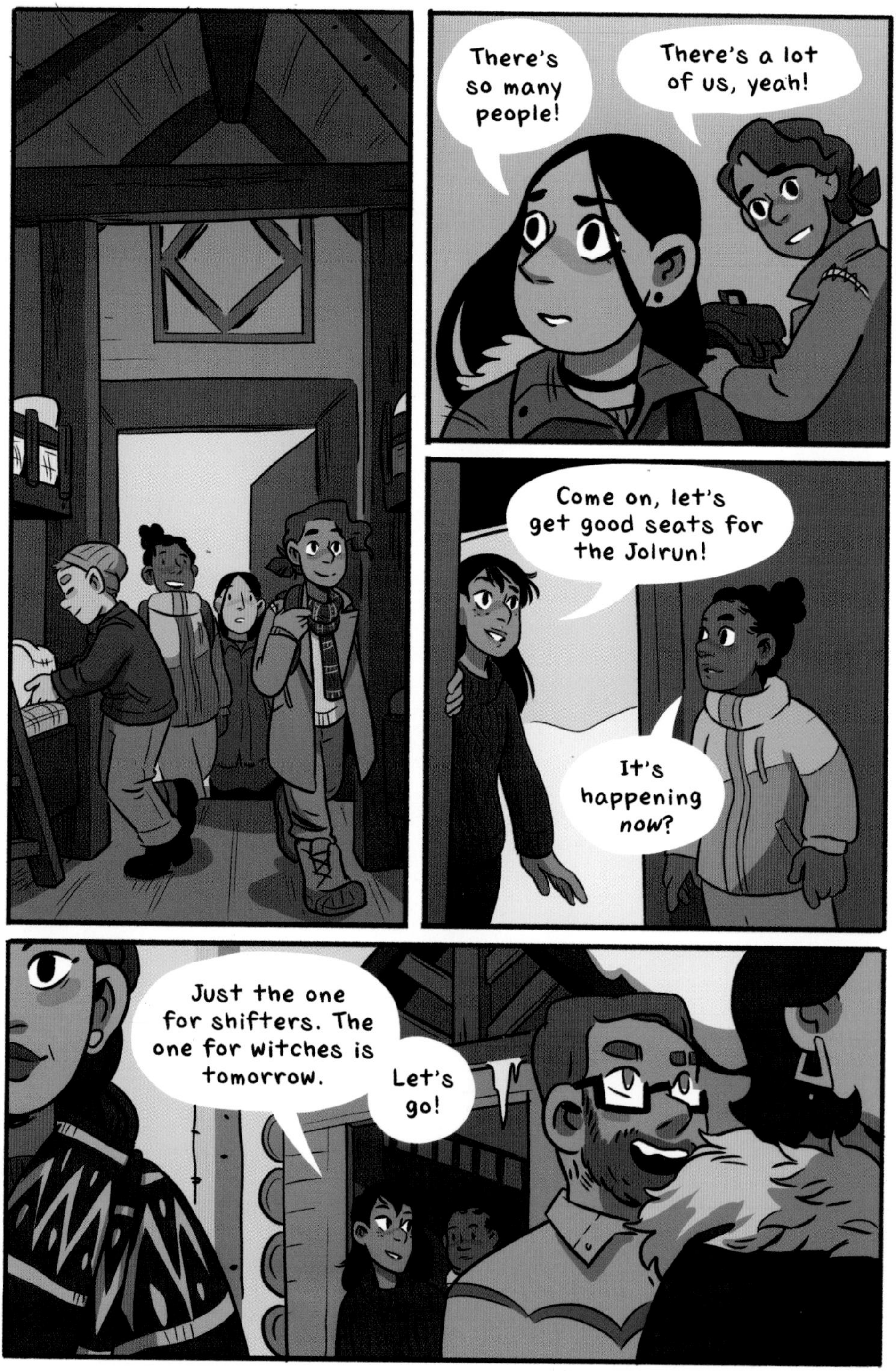
There's so many people!
There's a lot of us, yeah!
Come on, let's get good seats for the Jolrun!
It's happening now?
Just the one for shifters. The one for witches is tomorrow.
Let's go!

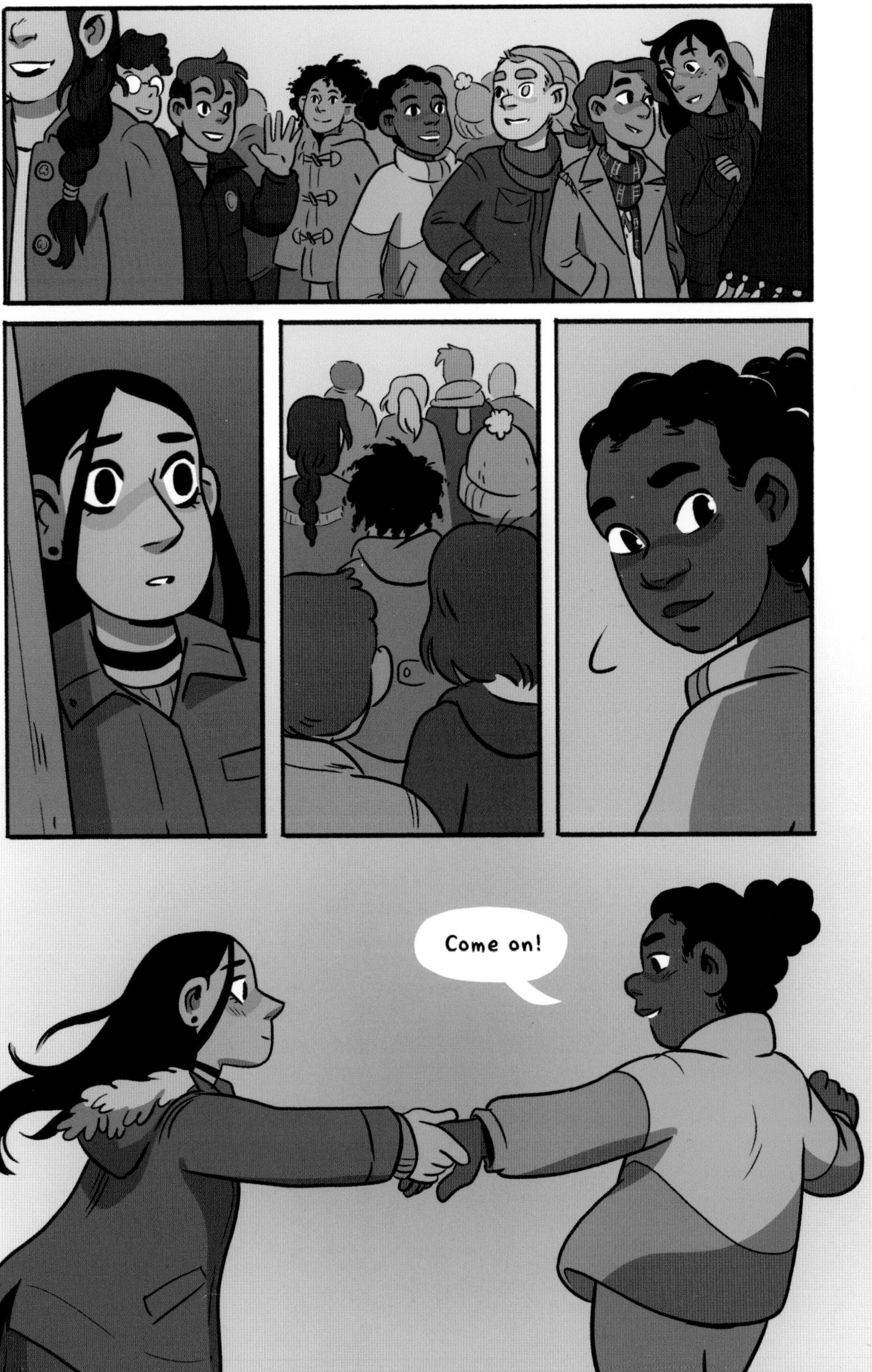
Come on!

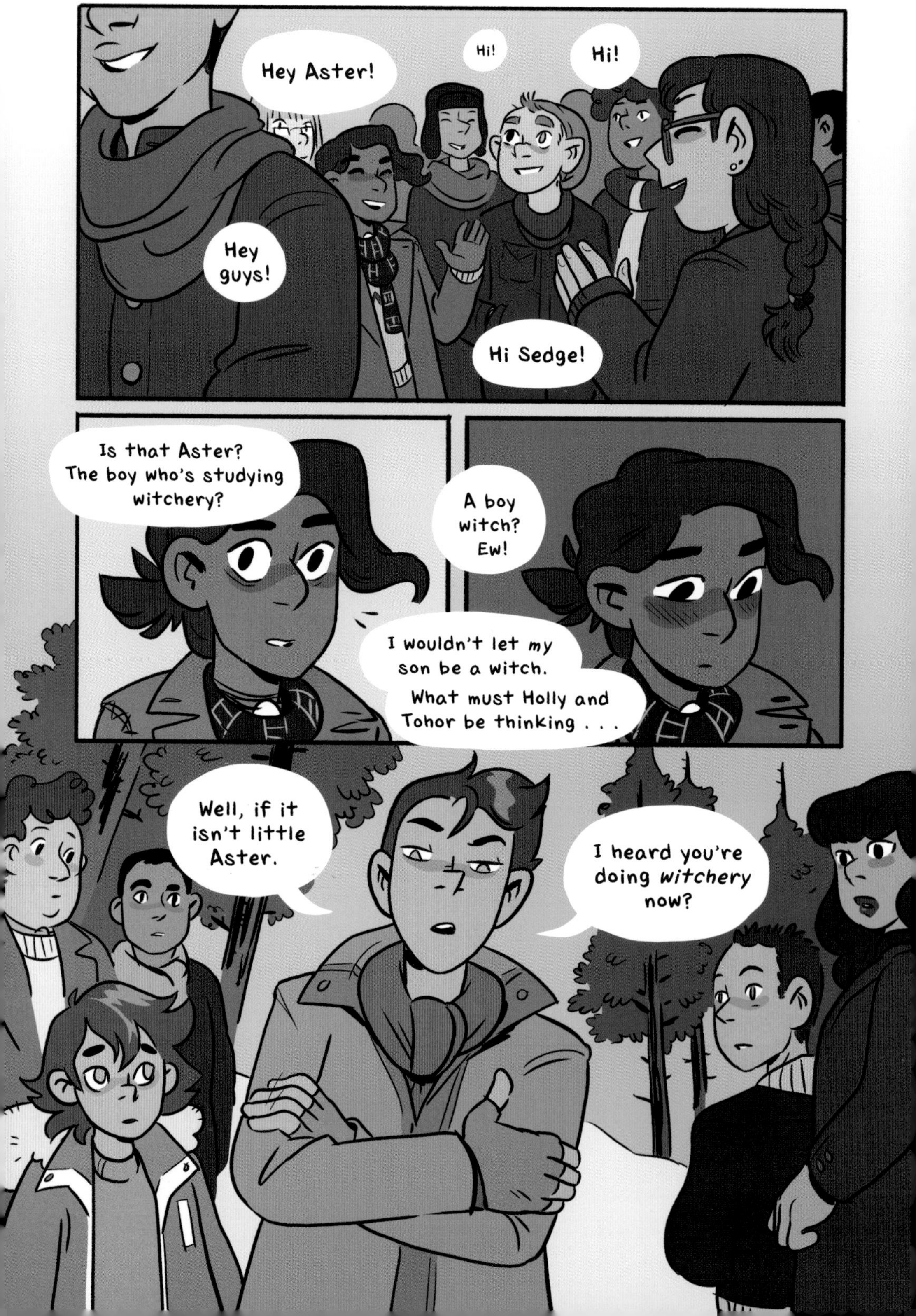
Hey Aster!
Hi!
Hi!
Hey guys!
Hi Sedge!
Is that Aster? The boy who's studying witchery?
A boy witch? Ew!
I wouldn't let *my* son be a witch.
What must Holly and Tohor be thinking . . .
Well, if it isn't little Aster.
I heard you're doing *witchery* now?

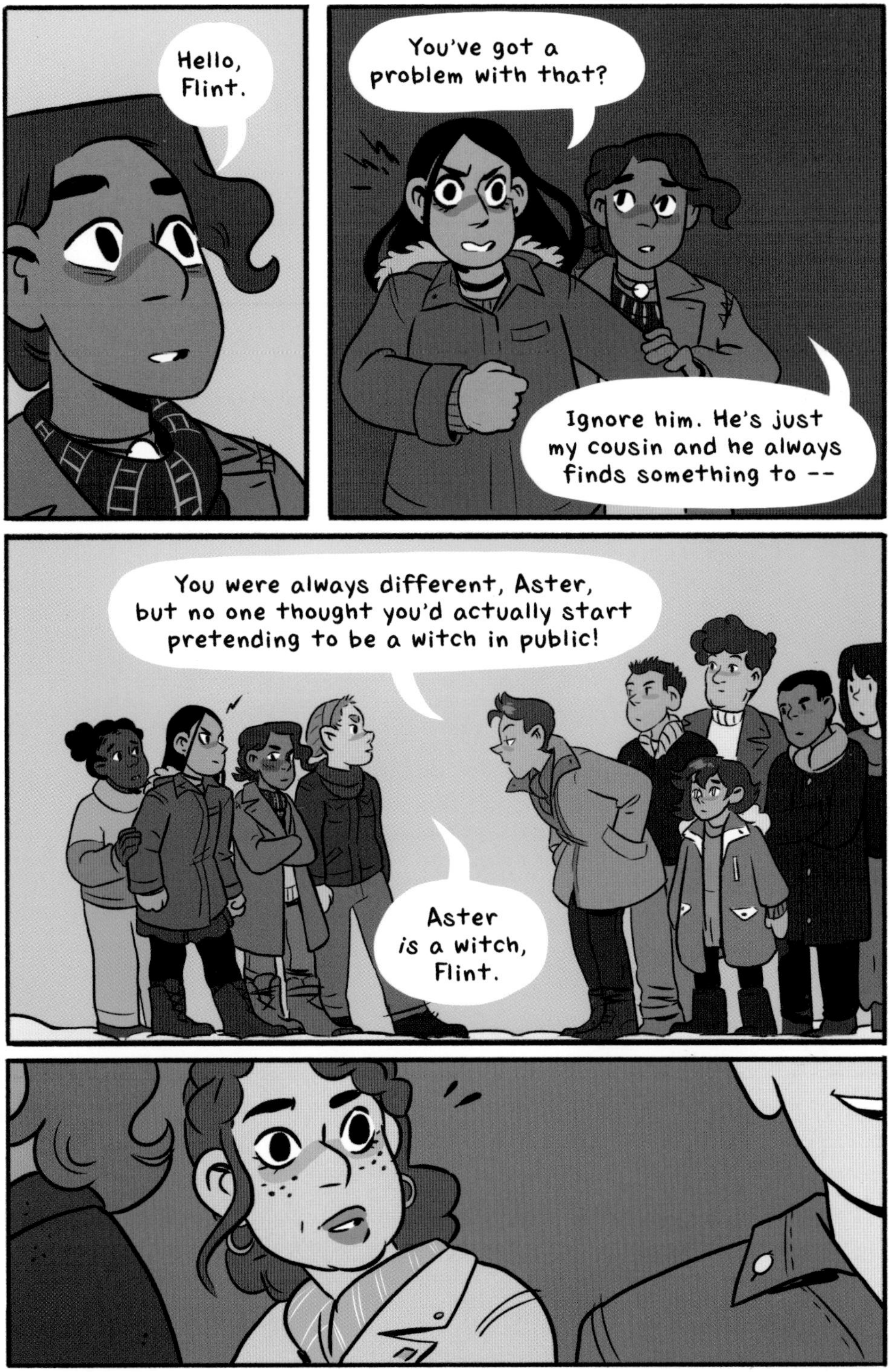
Hello, Flint.
You've got a problem with that?
Ignore him. He's just my cousin and he always finds something to --
You were always different, Aster, but no one thought you'd actually start pretending to be a witch in public!
Aster *is* a witch, Flint.

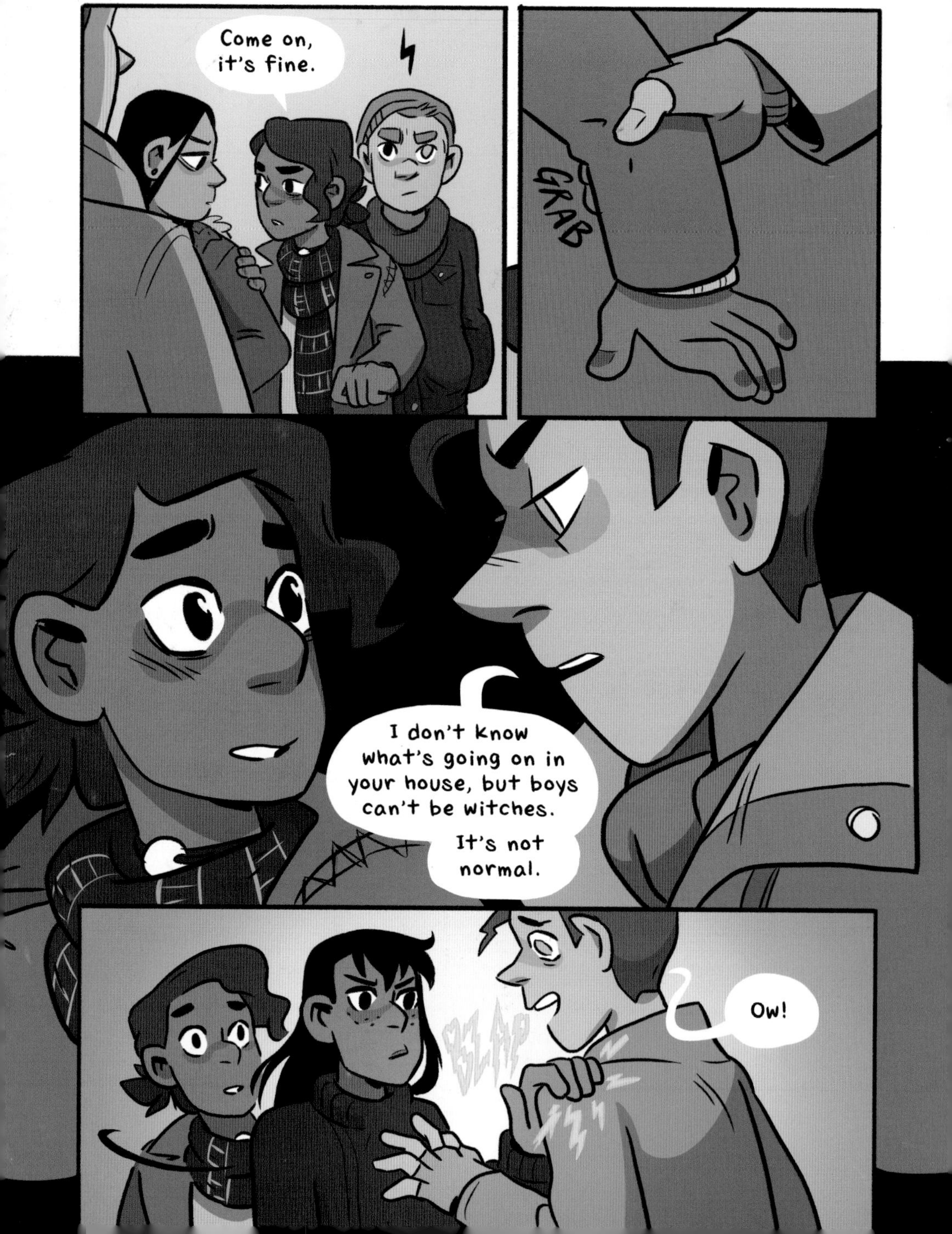
Come on, it's fine.
GRAB
I don't know what's going on in your house, but boys can't be witches.
It's not normal.
Ow!

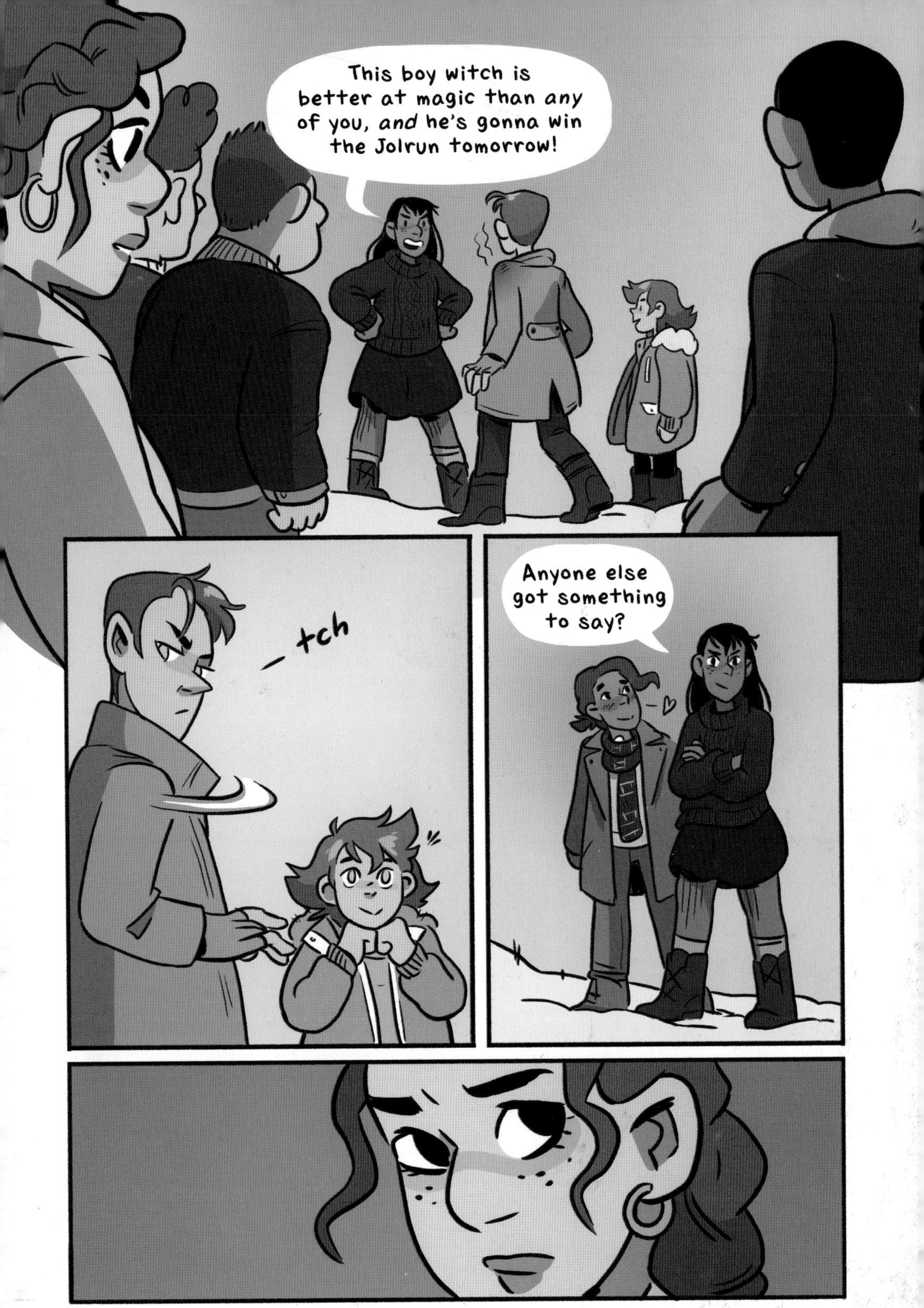
This boy witch is better at magic than any of you, *and* he's gonna win the Jolrun tomorrow!
–tch
Anyone else got something to say?

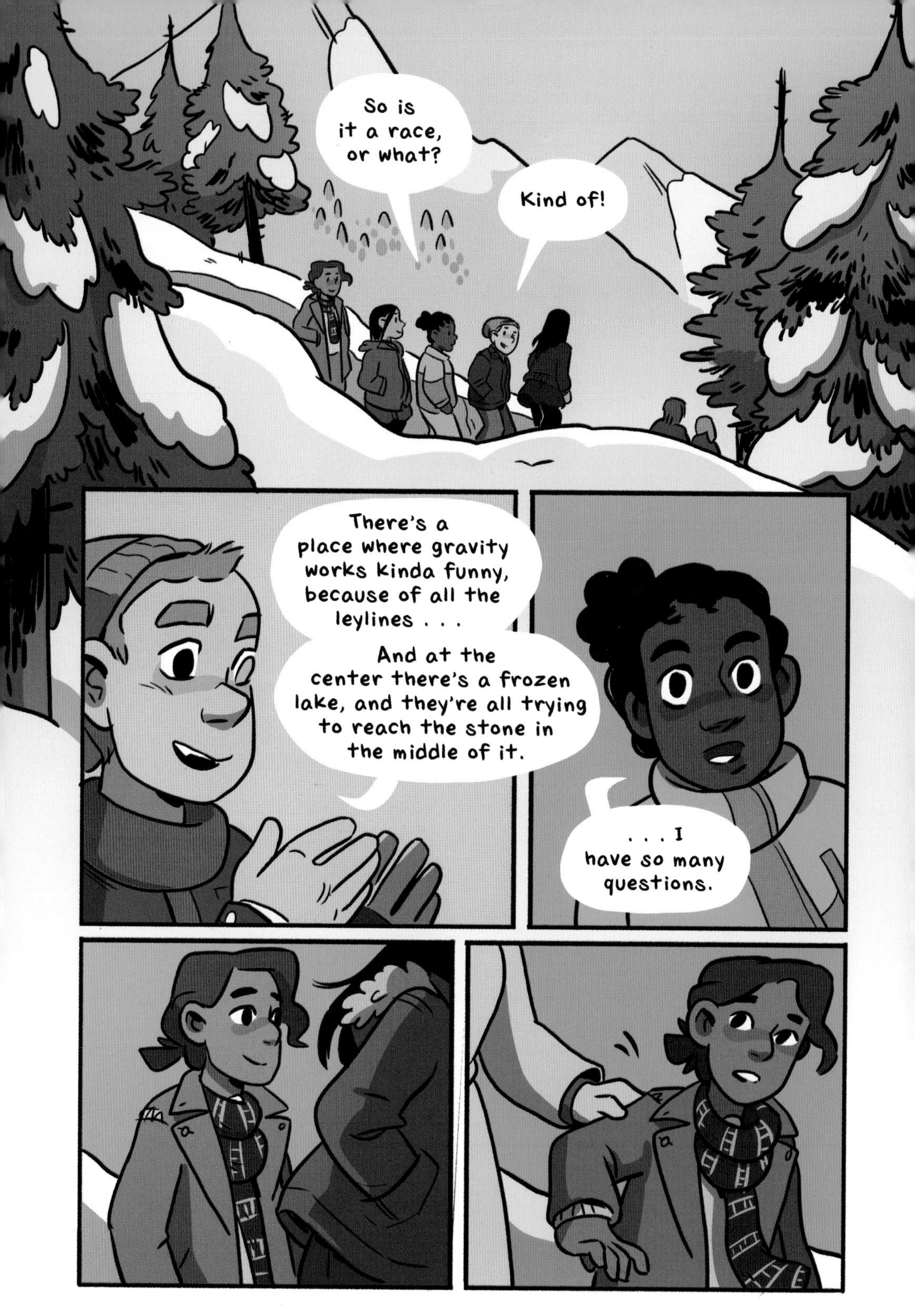
So is it a race, or what?
Kind of!
There's a place where gravity works kinda funny, because of all the leylines . . .
And at the center there's a frozen lake, and they're all trying to reach the stone in the middle of it.
. . . I have so many questions.

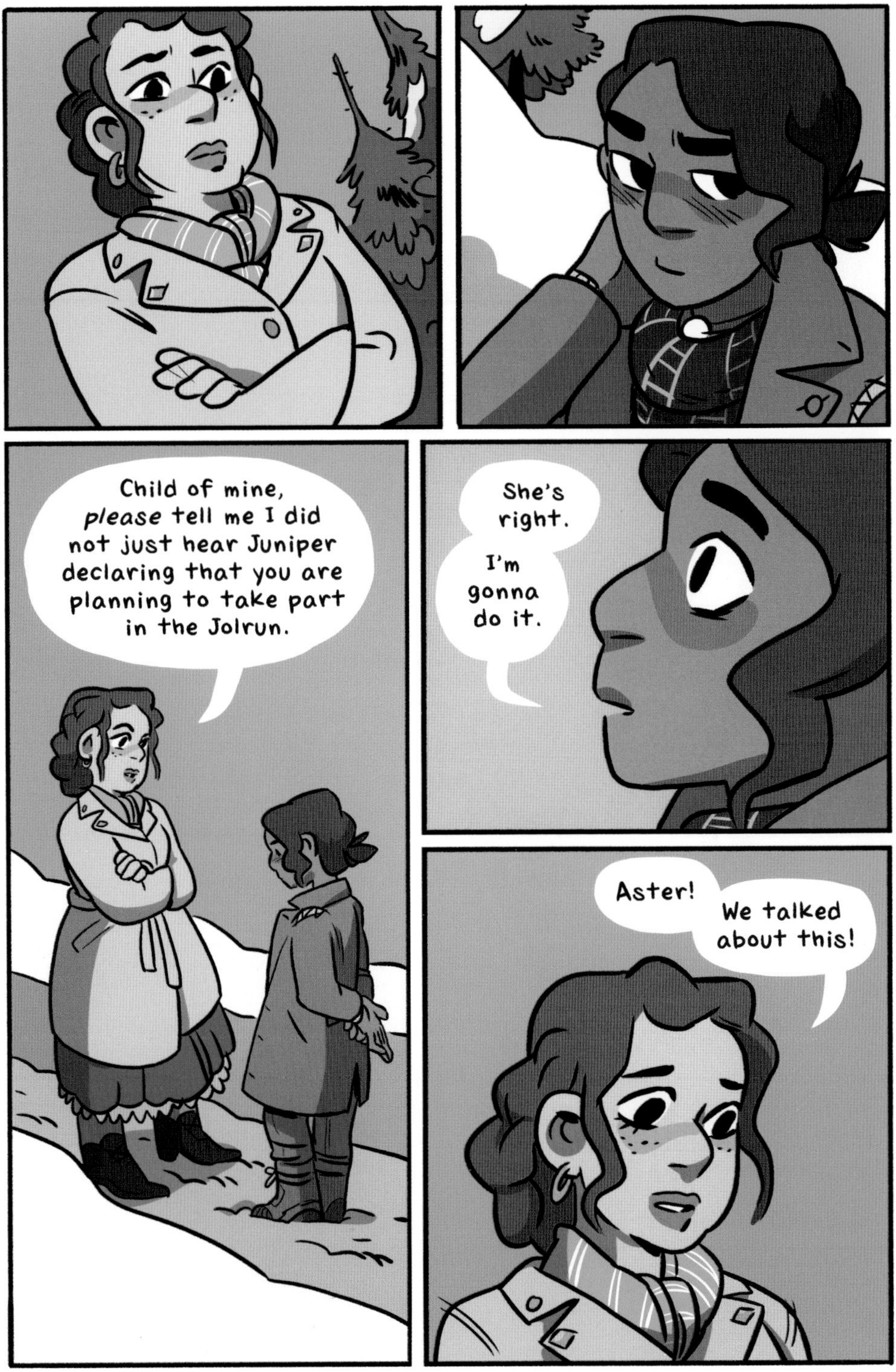
Child of mine, *please* tell me I did not just hear Juniper declaring that you are planning to take part in the Jolrun.
She's right.
I'm gonna do it.
Aster!
We talked about this!

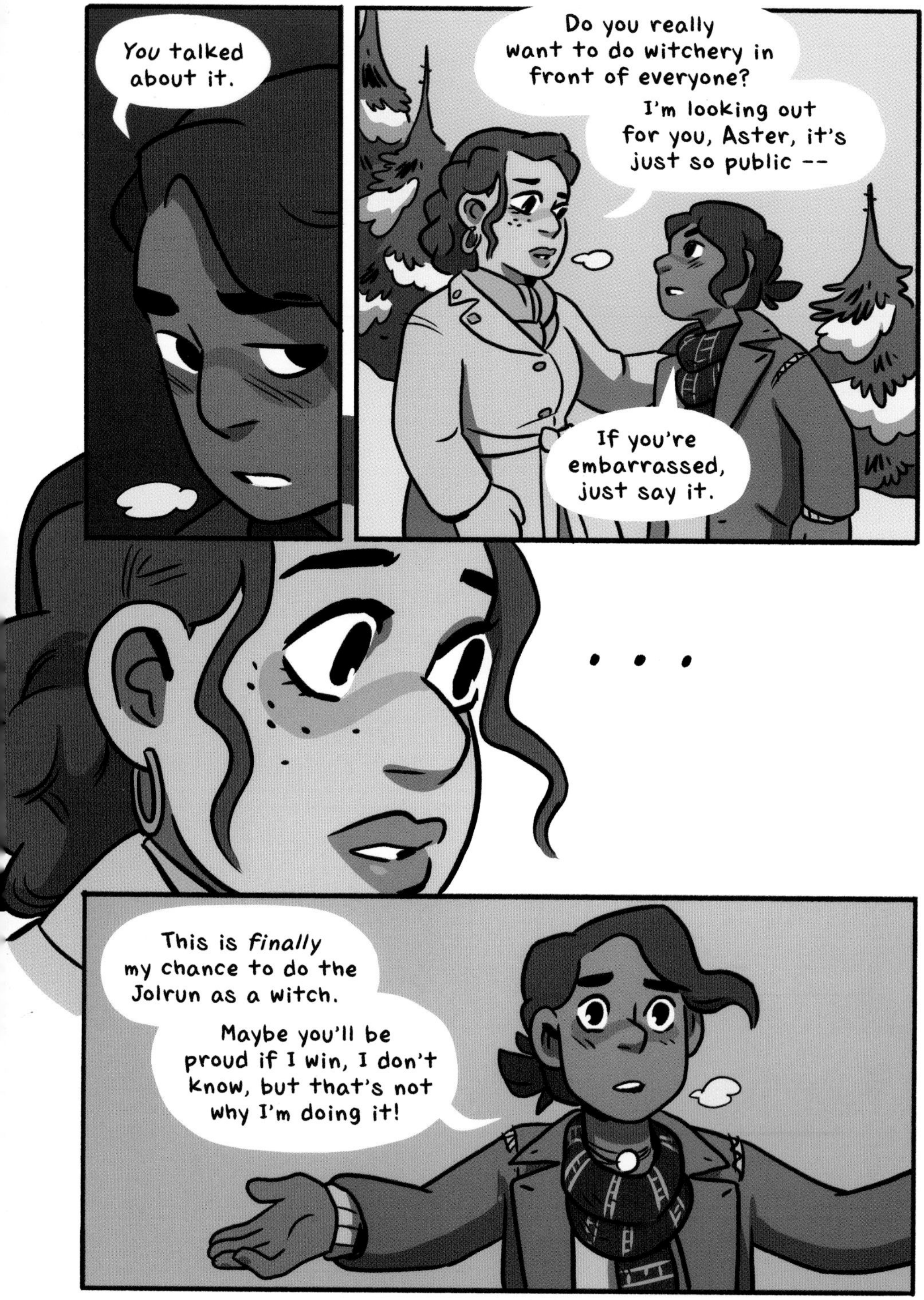
You talked about it.
Do you really want to do witchery in front of everyone?
I'm looking out for you, Aster, it's just so public --
If you're embarrassed, just say it.
. . .
This is *finally* my chance to do the Jolrun as a witch.
Maybe you'll be proud if I win, I don't know, but that's not why I'm doing it!

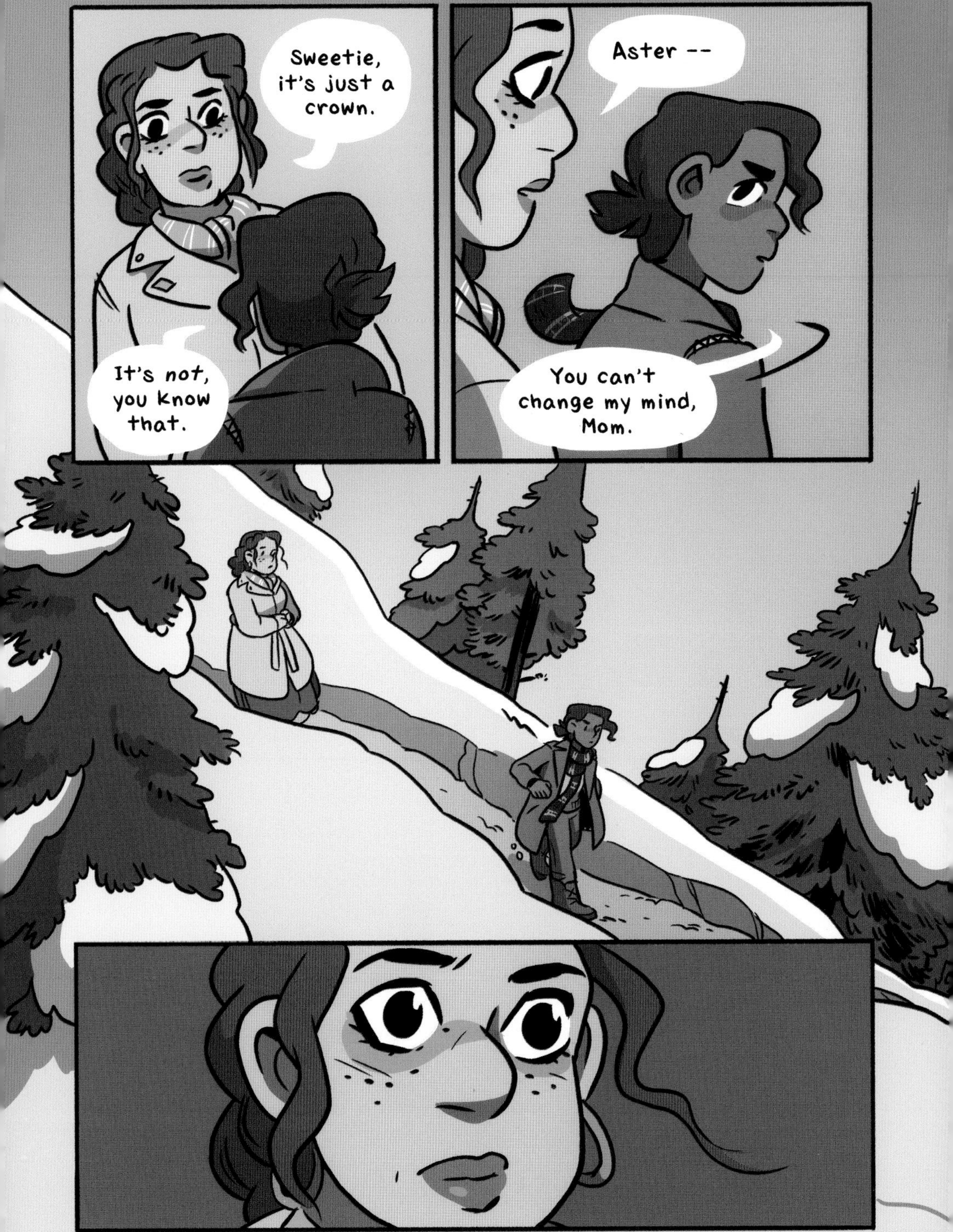
Sweetie, it's just a crown.
It's *not*, you know that.
Aster --
You can't change my mind, Mom.

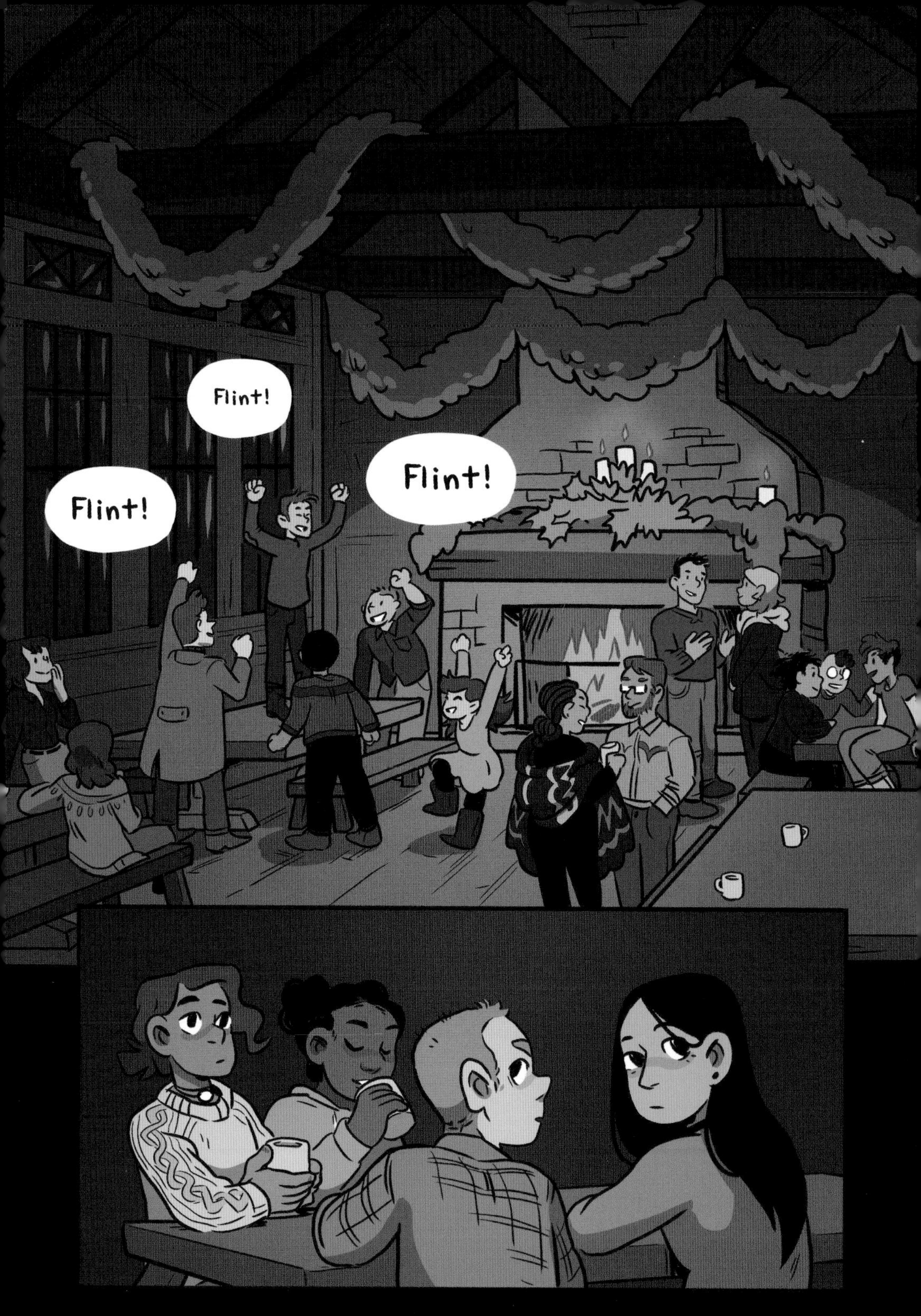
Flint!
Flint!
Flint!

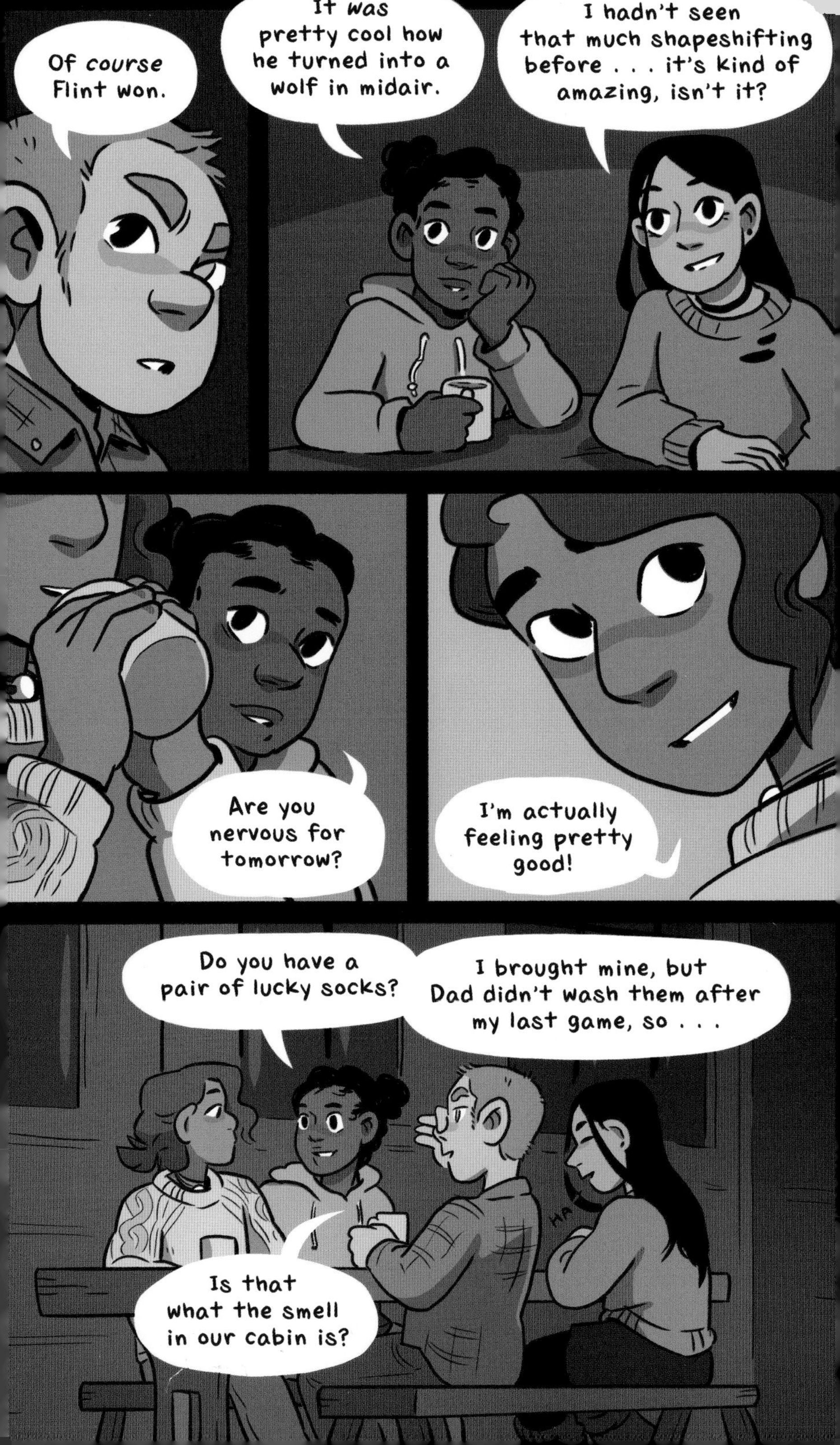
Of course Flint won.
It was pretty cool how he turned into a wolf in midair.
I hadn't seen that much shapeshifting before . . . it's kind of amazing, isn't it?
Are you nervous for tomorrow?
I'm actually feeling pretty good!
Do you have a pair of lucky socks?
I brought mine, but Dad didn't wash them after my last game, so . . .
Is that what the smell in our cabin is?
HA

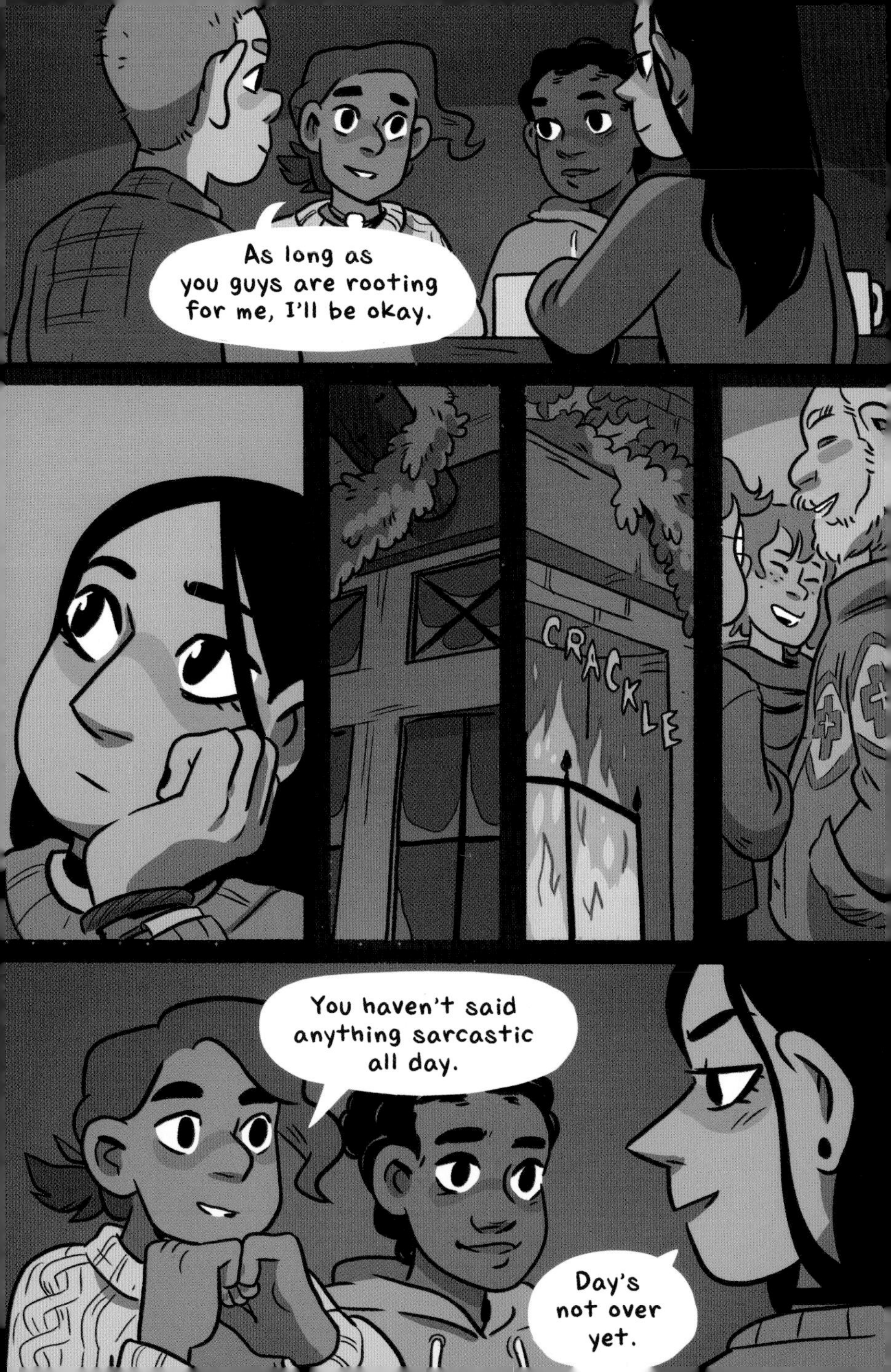
As long as you guys are rooting for me, I'll be okay.
CRACKLE
You haven't said anything sarcastic all day.
Day's not over yet.

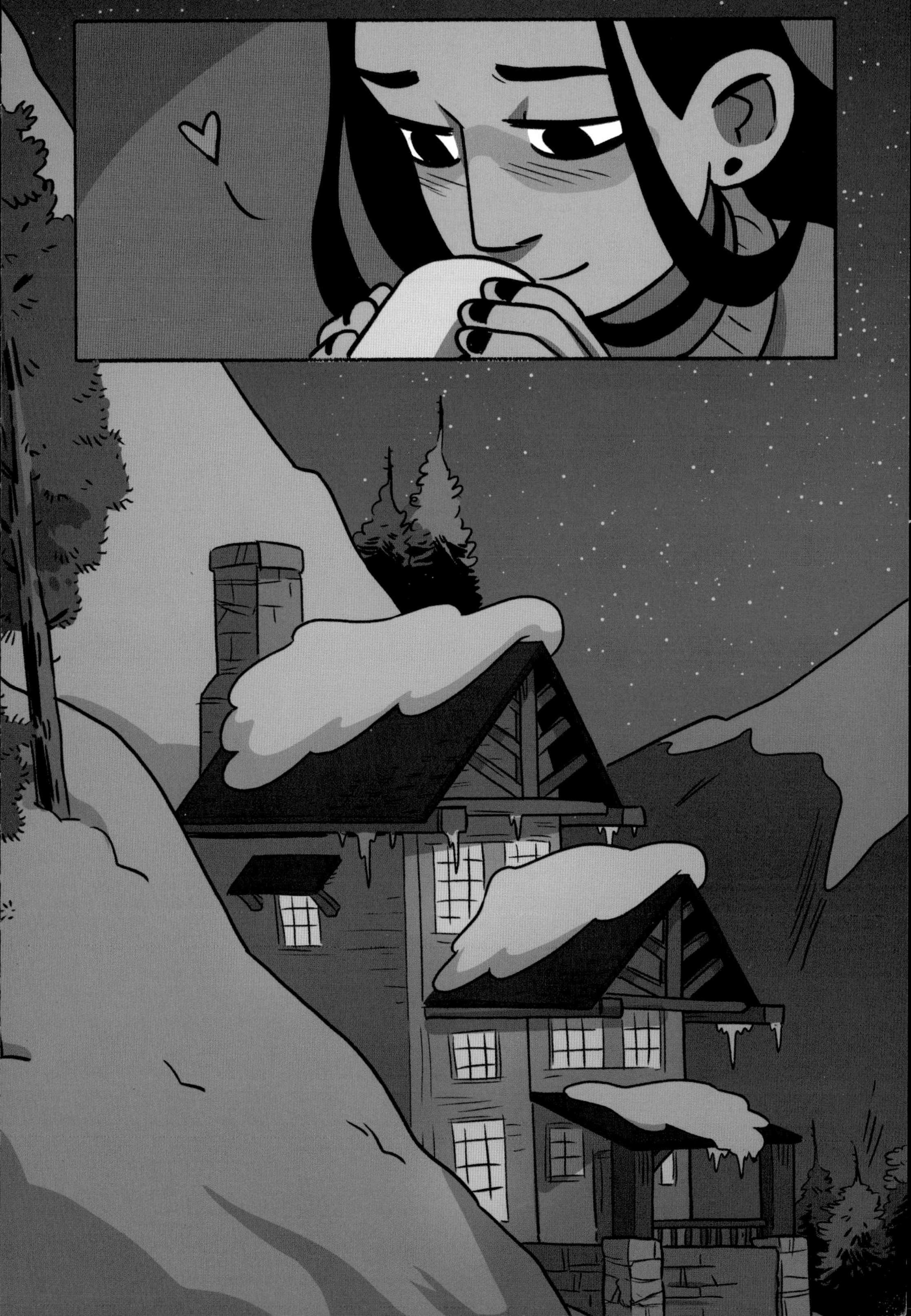

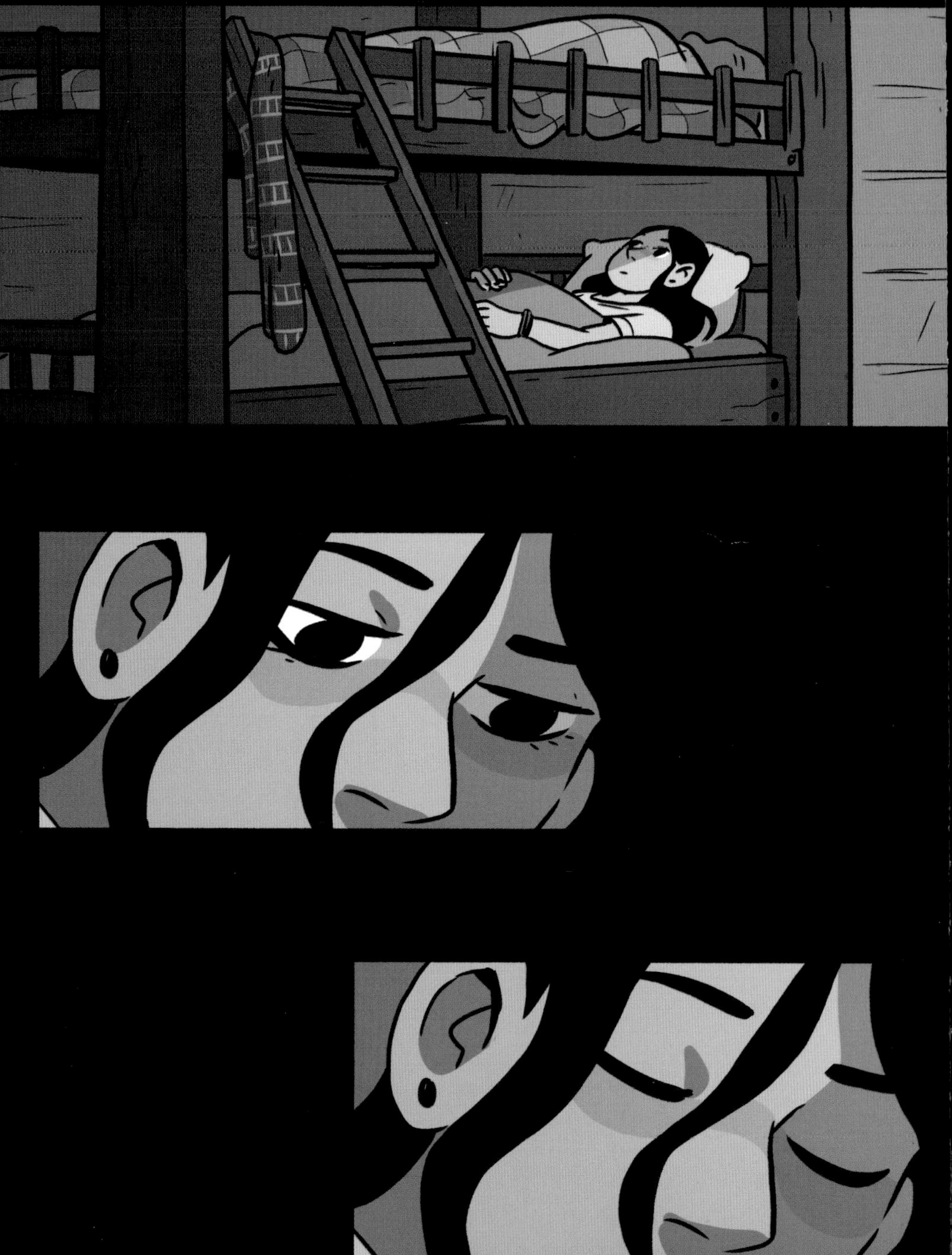

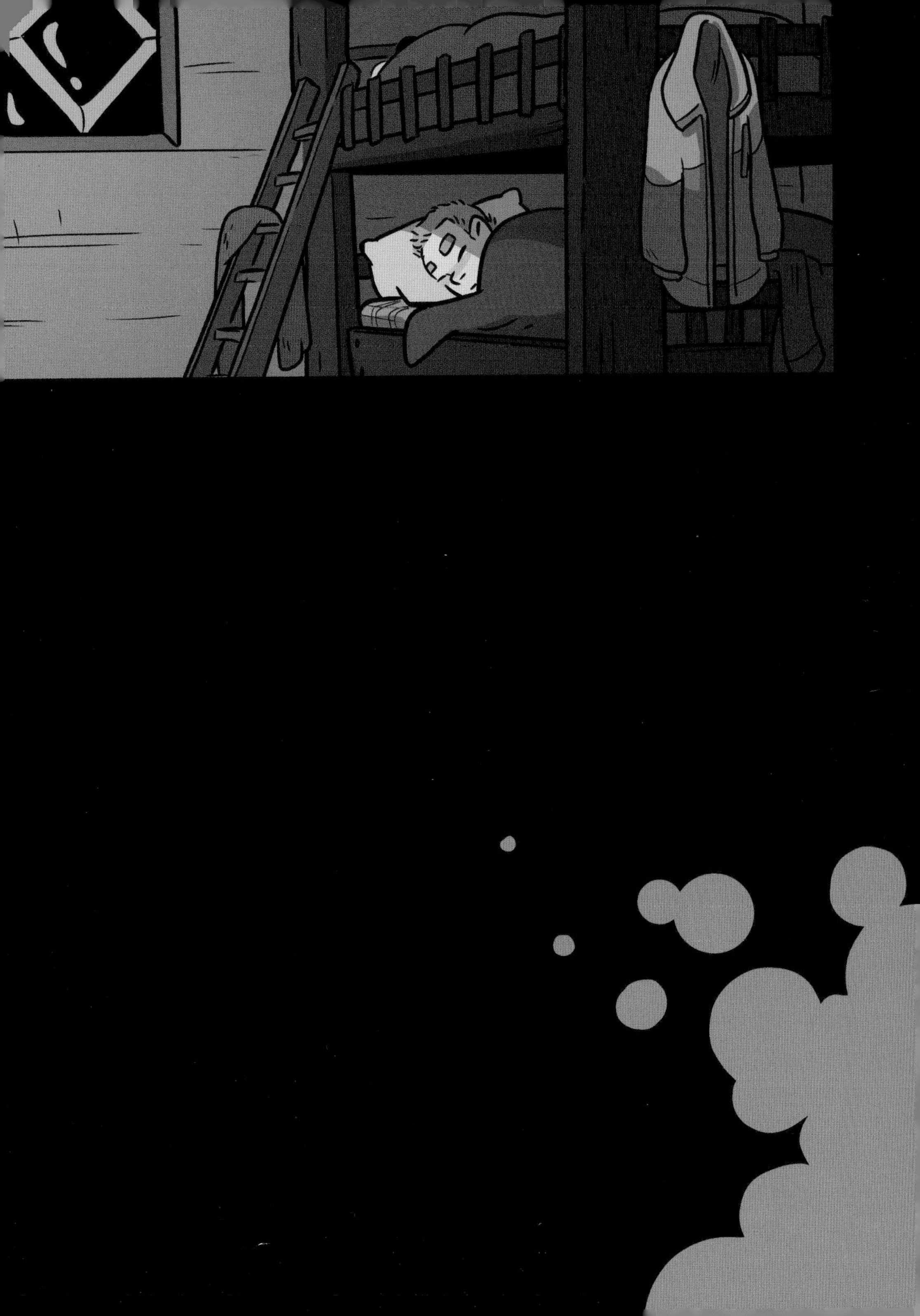

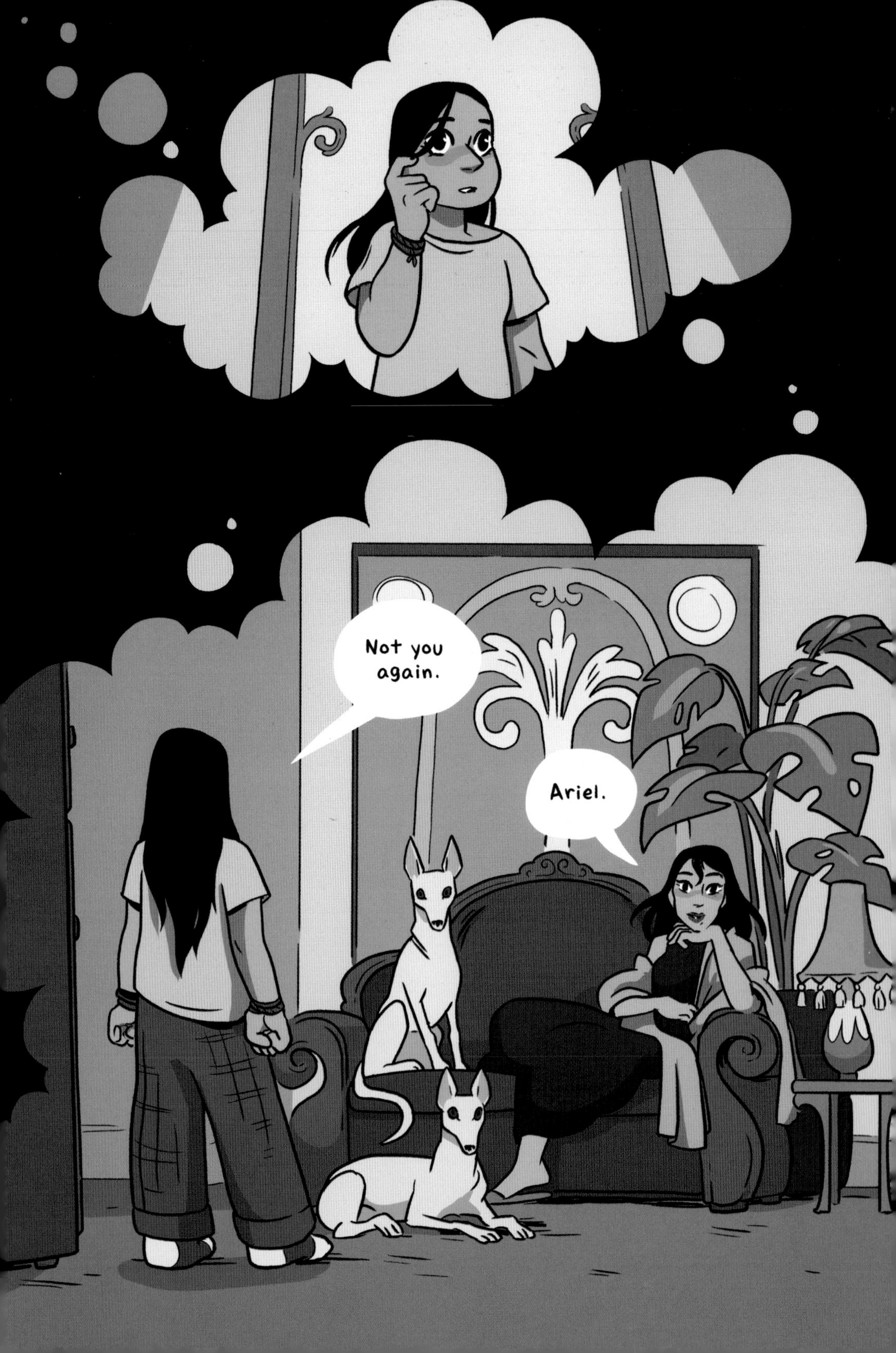
Not you again.
Ariel.

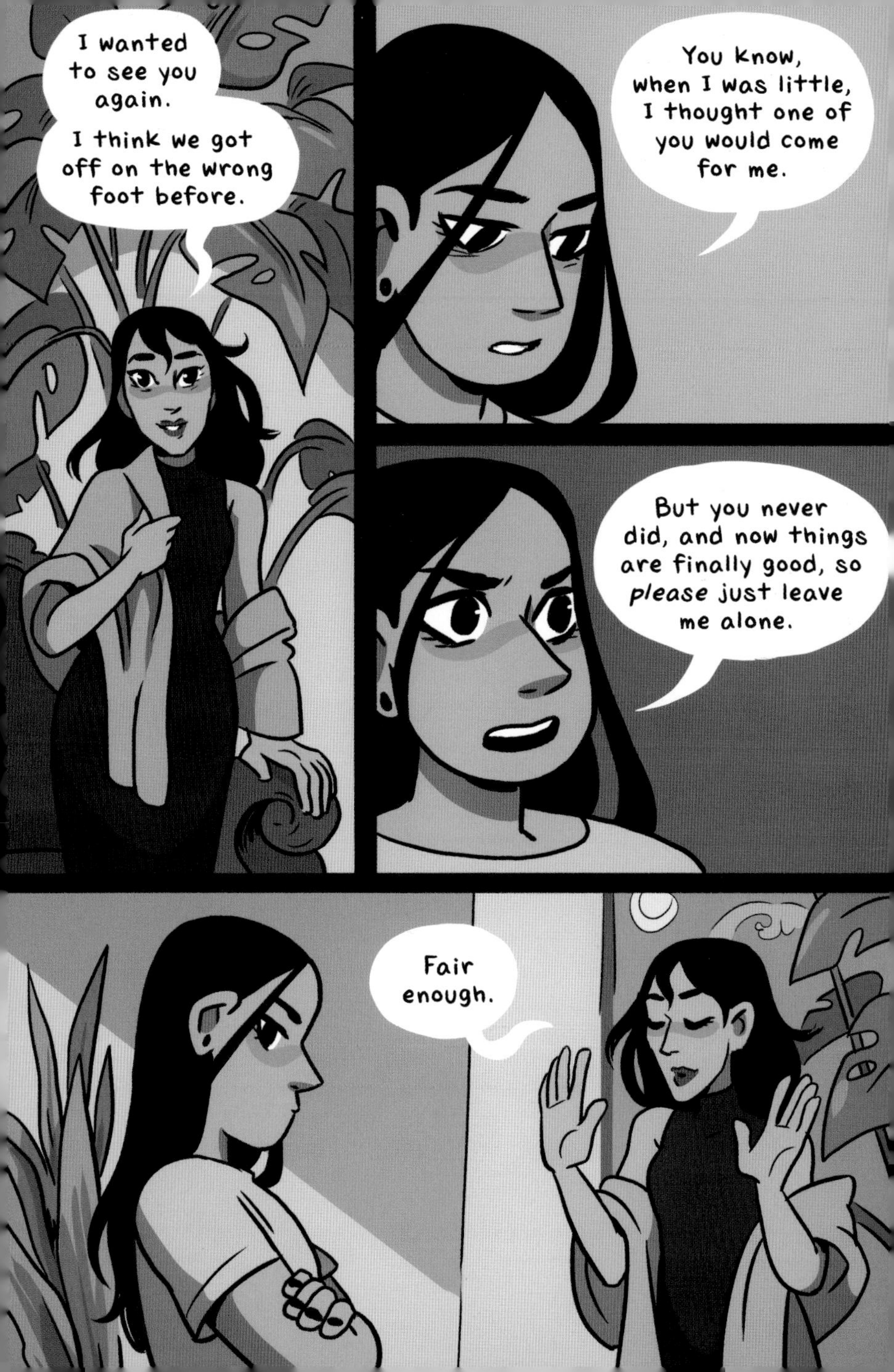
I wanted to see you again.
I think we got off on the wrong foot before.
You know, when I was little, I thought one of you would come for me.
But you never did, and now things are finally good, so *please* just leave me alone.
Fair enough.

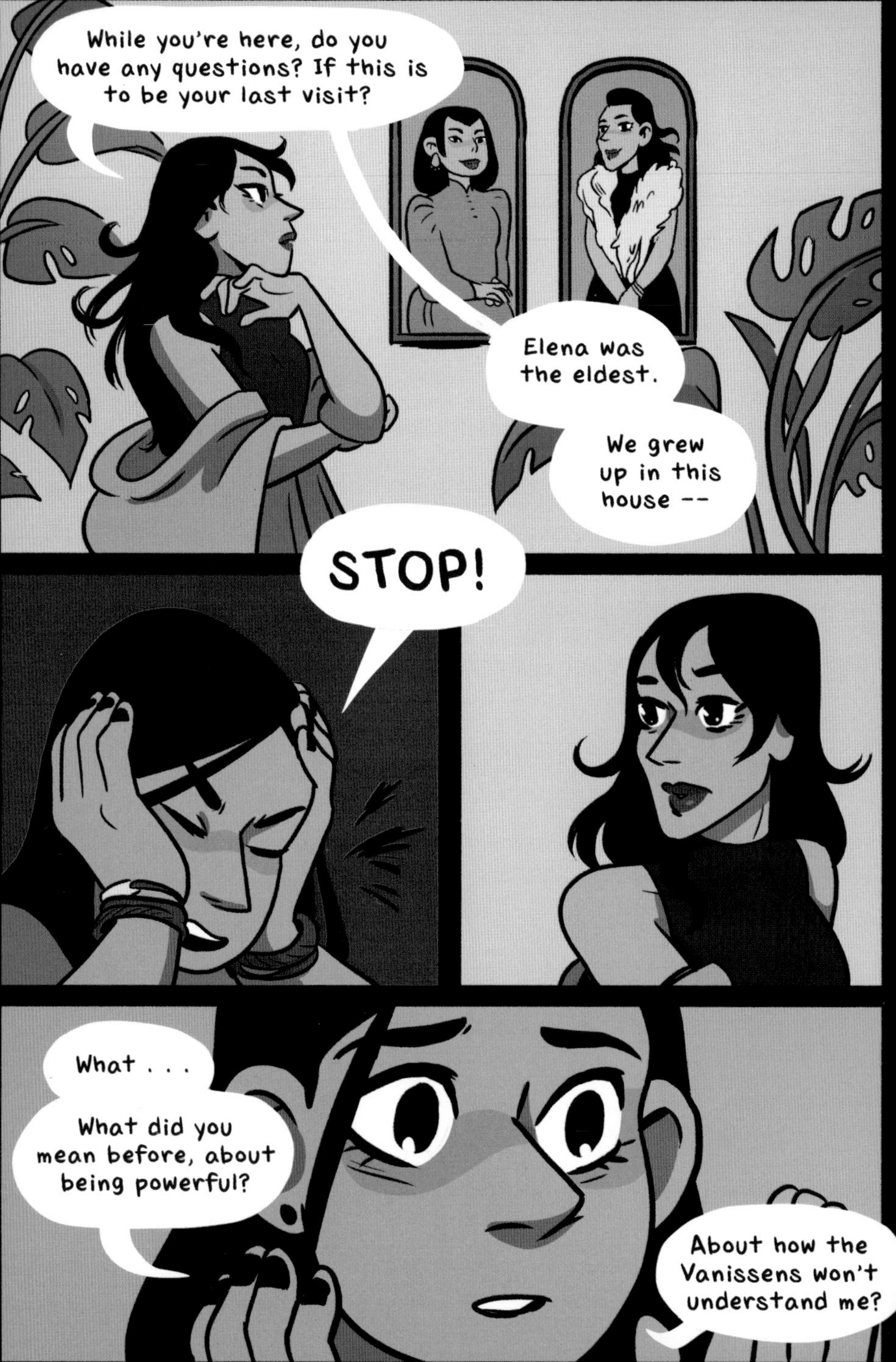
While you're here, do you have any questions? If this is to be your last visit?
Elena was the eldest.
We grew up in this house --
STOP!
What . . .
What did you mean before, about being powerful?
About how the Vanissens won't understand me?

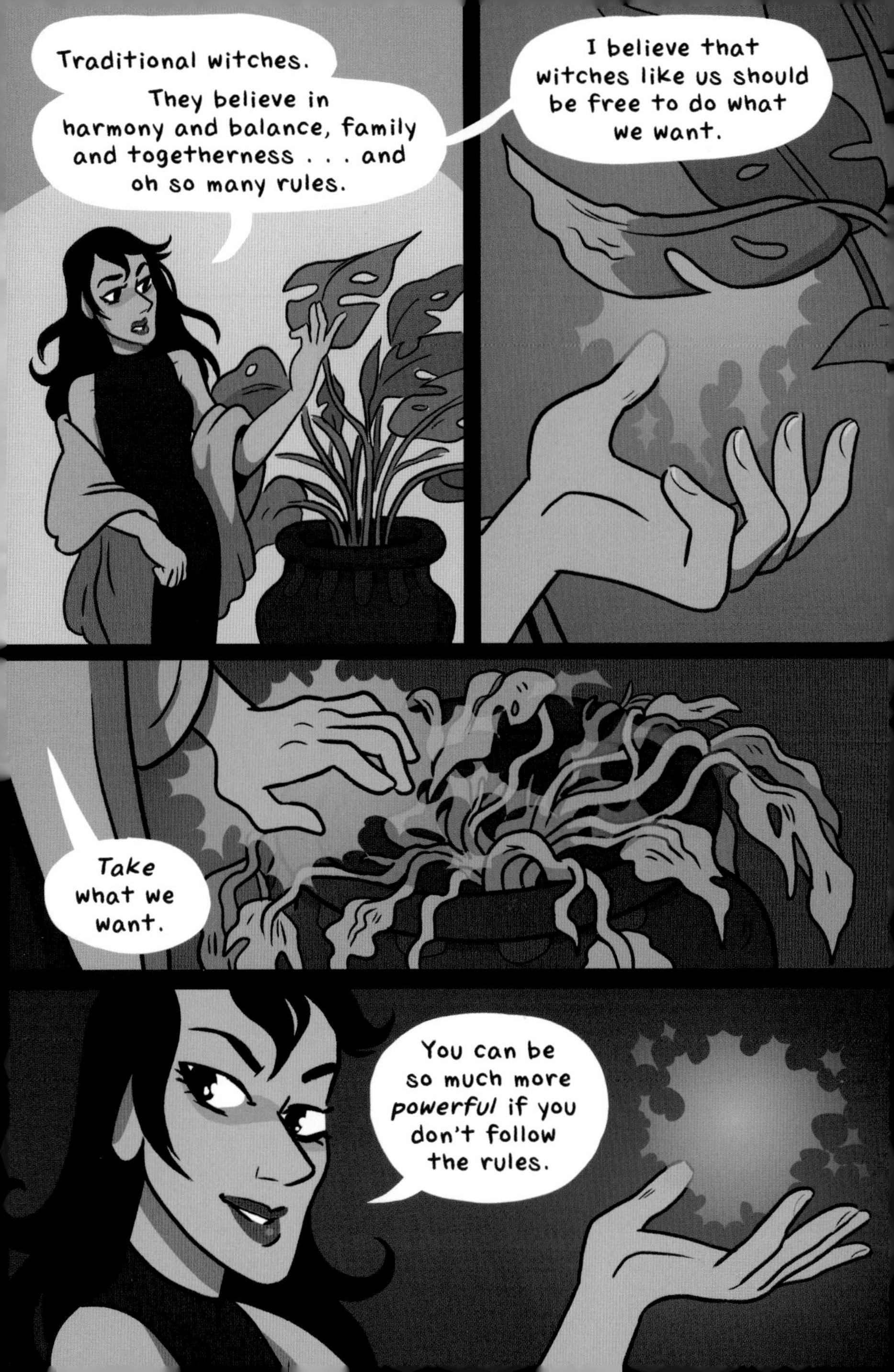

Traditional witches.
They believe in harmony and balance, family and togetherness . . . and oh so many rules.
I believe that witches like us should be free to do what we want.
Take what we want.
You can be so much more *powerful* if you don't follow the rules.

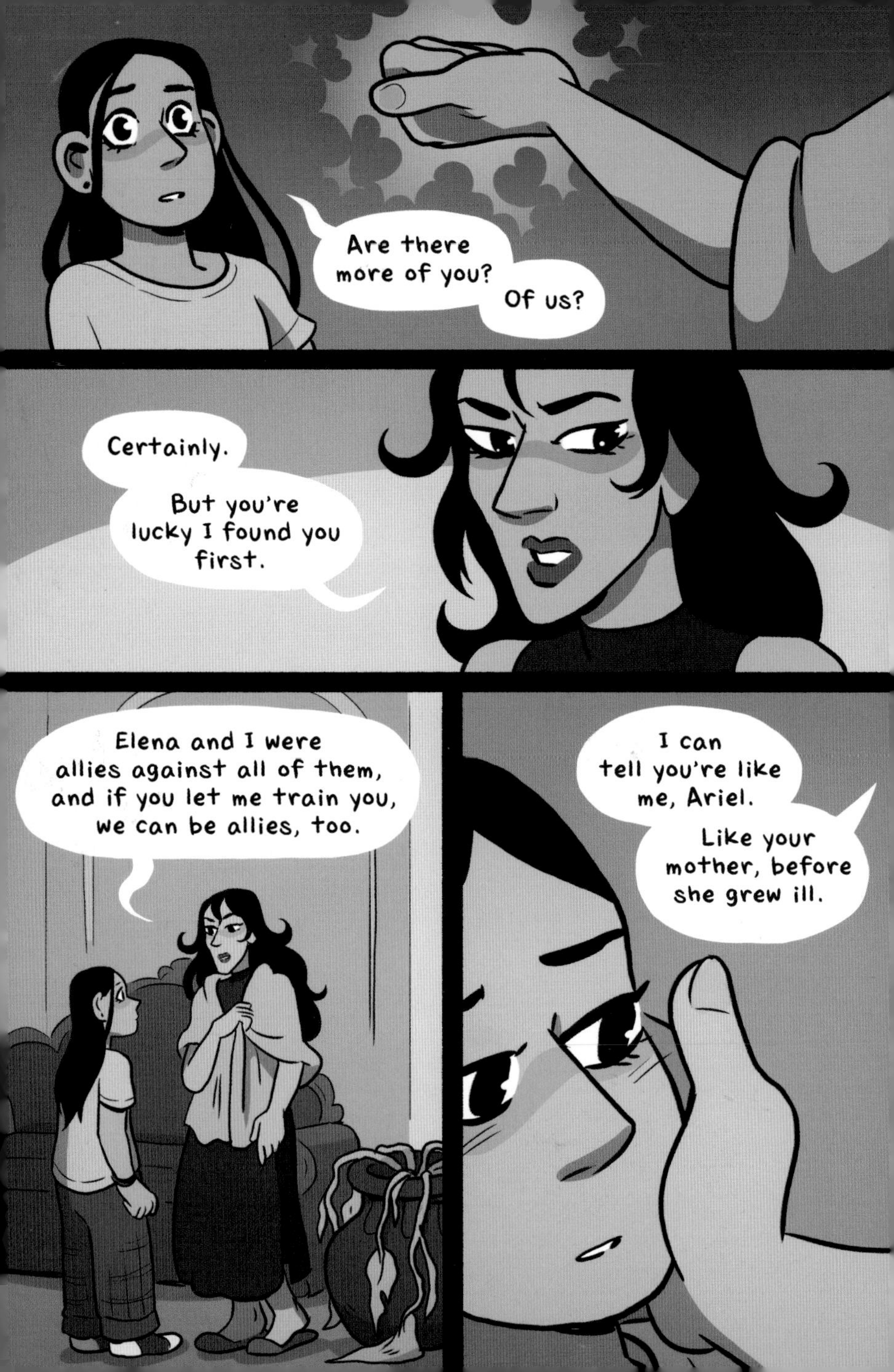
Are there more of you?
Of us?
Certainly.
But you're lucky I found you first.
Elena and I were allies against all of them, and if you let me train you, we can be allies, too.
I can tell you're like me, Ariel.
Like your mother, before she grew ill.

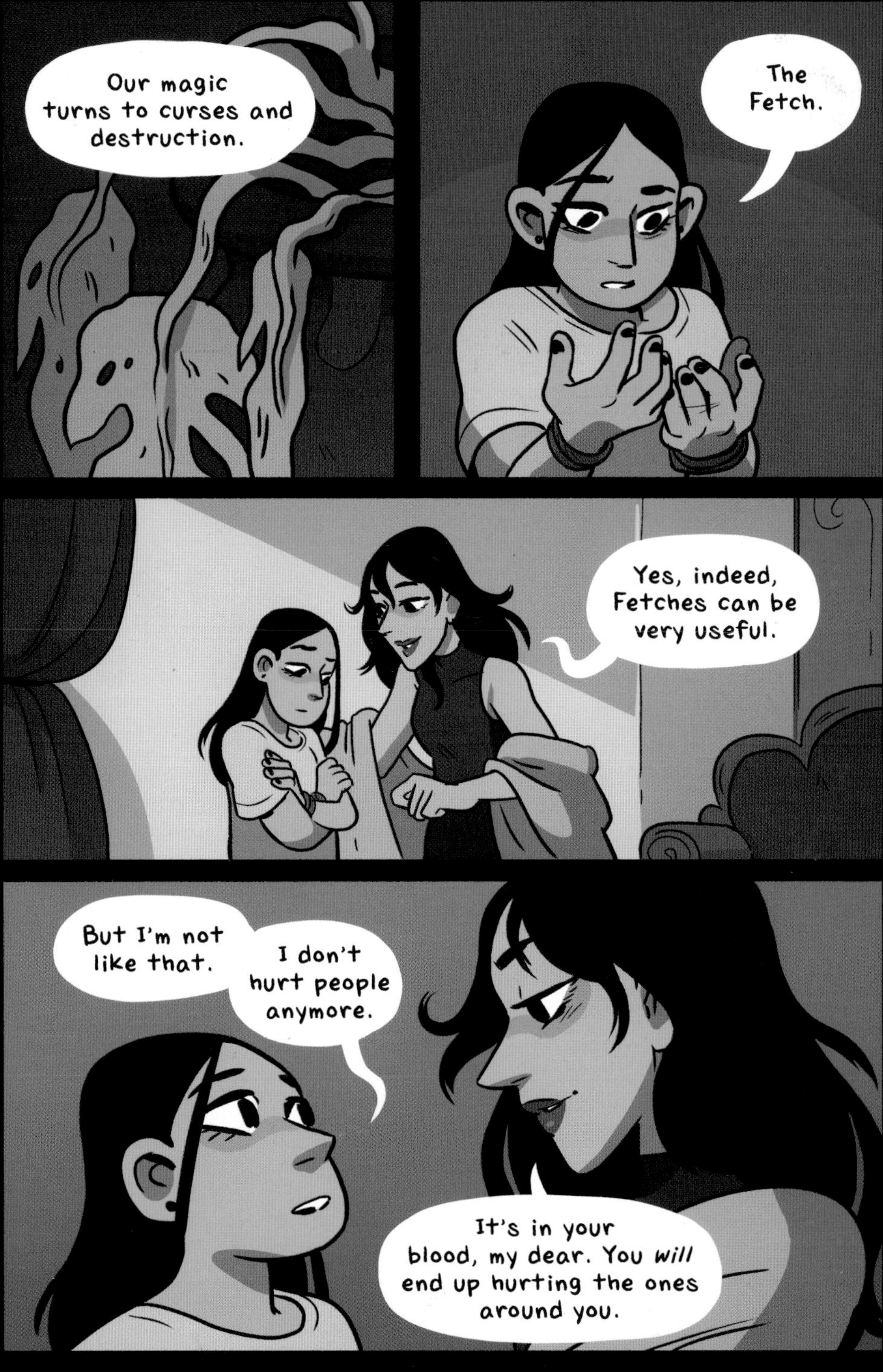
Our magic turns to curses and destruction.
The Fetch.
Yes, indeed, Fetches can be very useful.
But I'm not like that.
I don't hurt people anymore.
It's in your blood, my dear. You *will* end up hurting the ones around you.

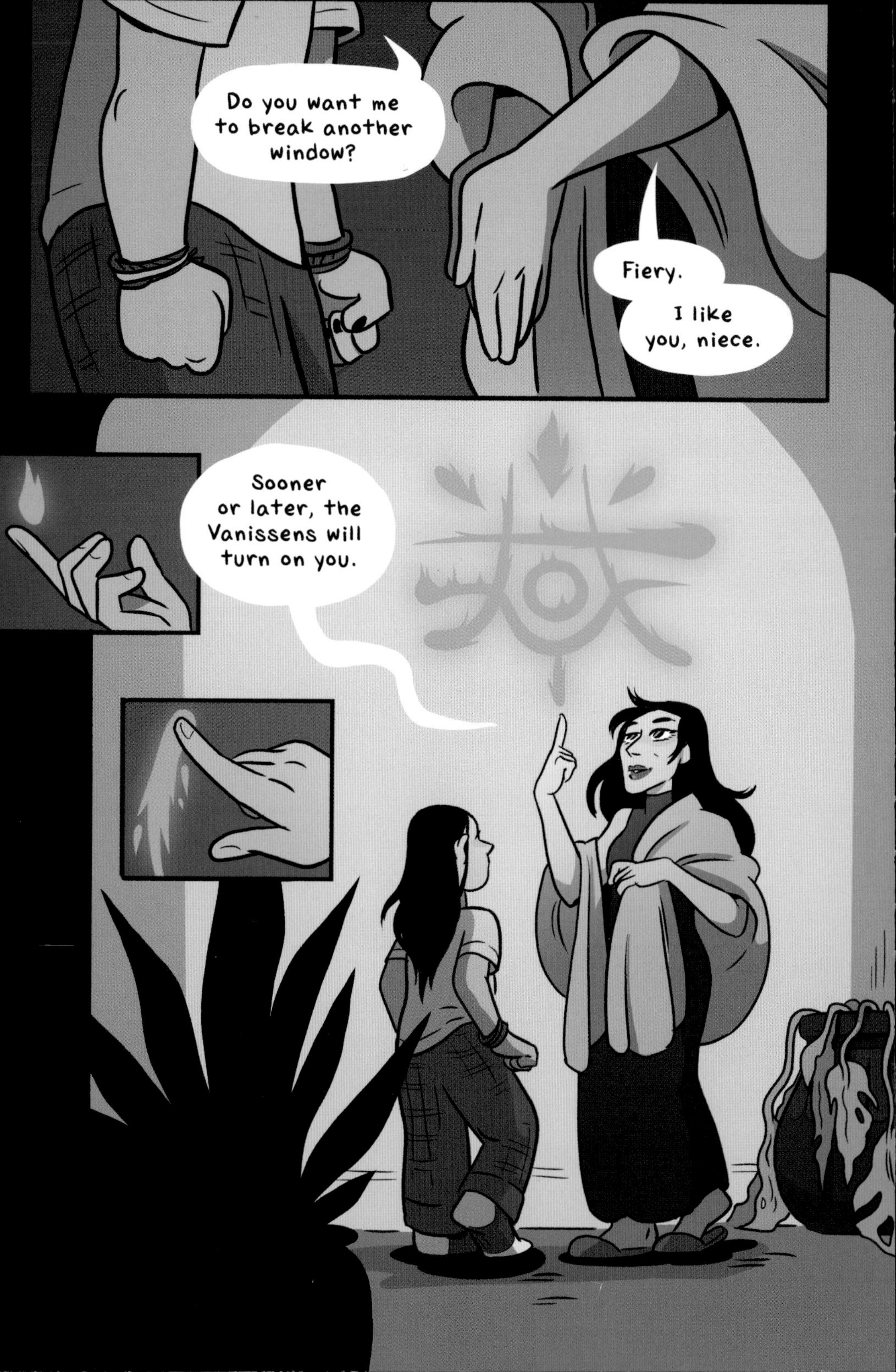
Do you want me to break another window?
Fiery.
I like you, niece.
Sooner or later, the Vanissens will turn on you.

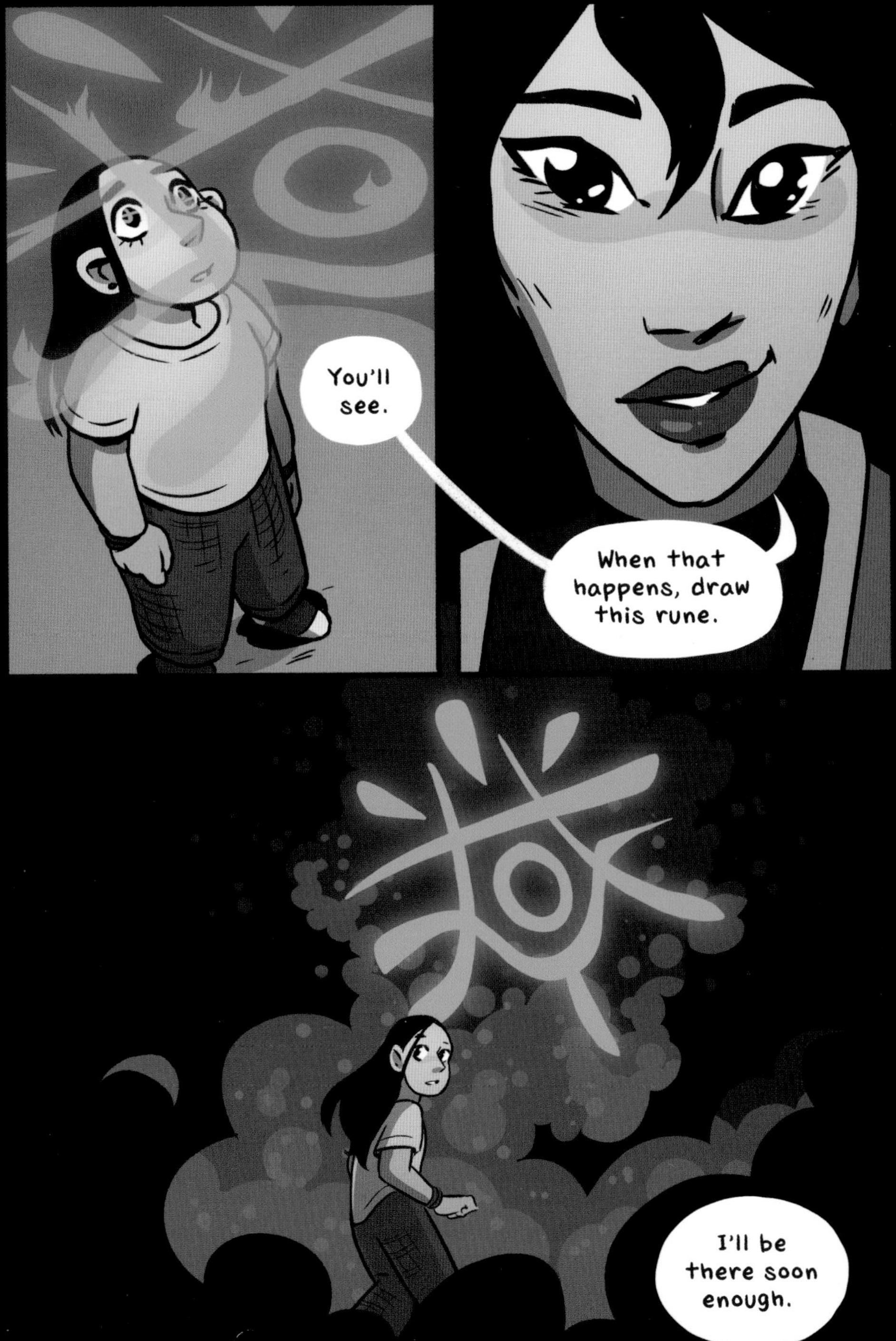
You'll see.
When that happens, draw this rune.
I'll be there soon enough.

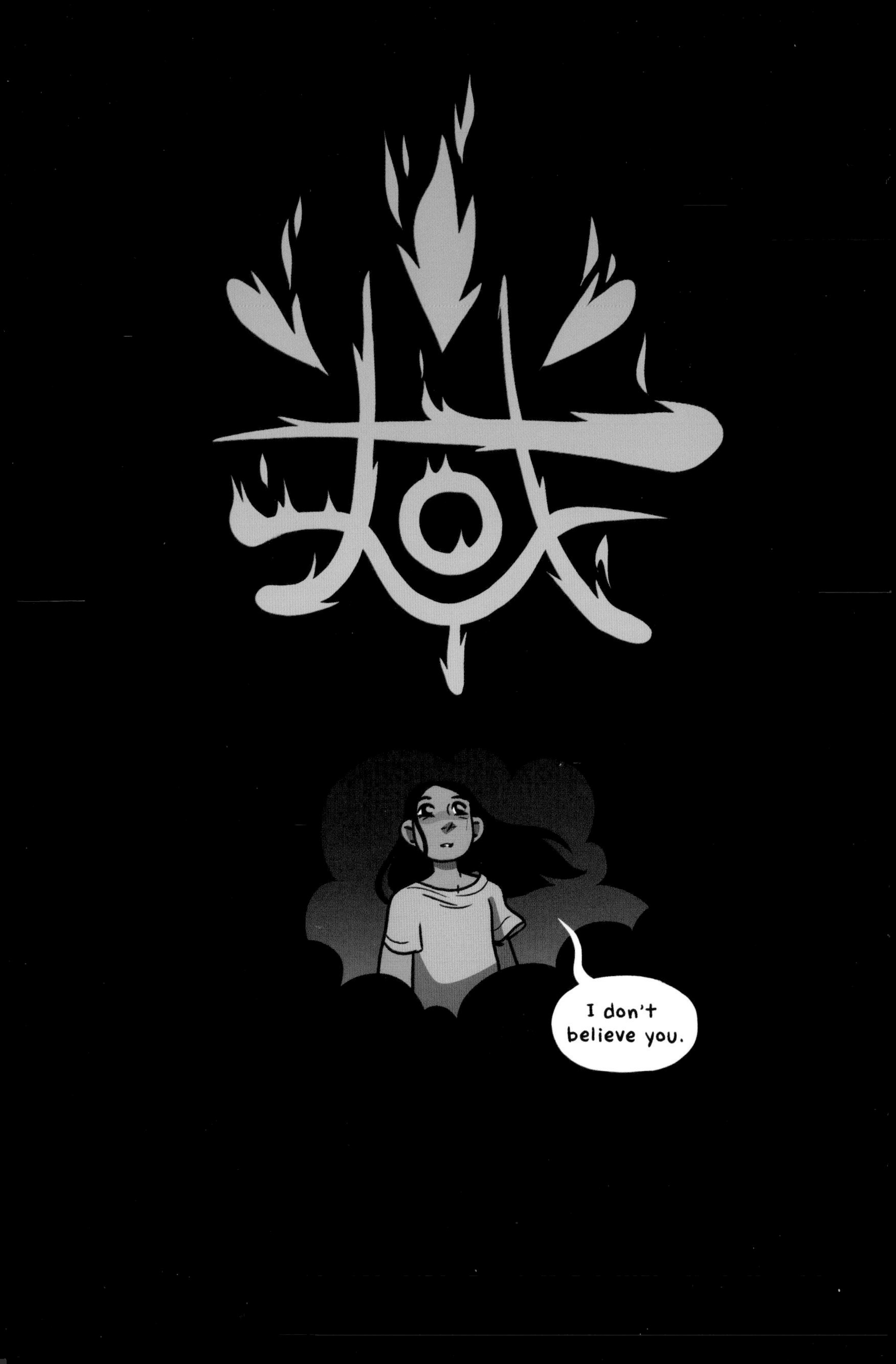
I don't believe you.

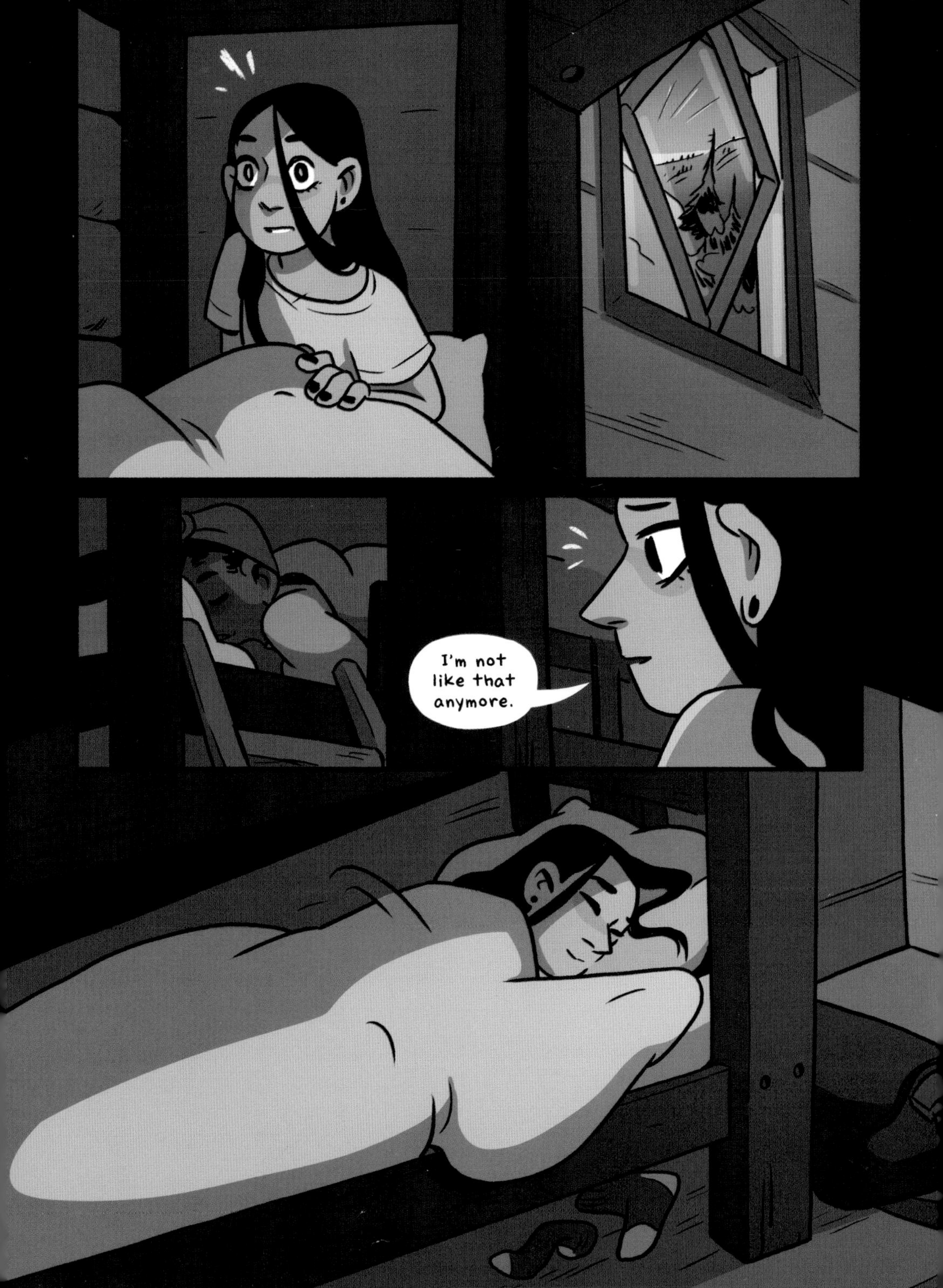
I'm not like that anymore.

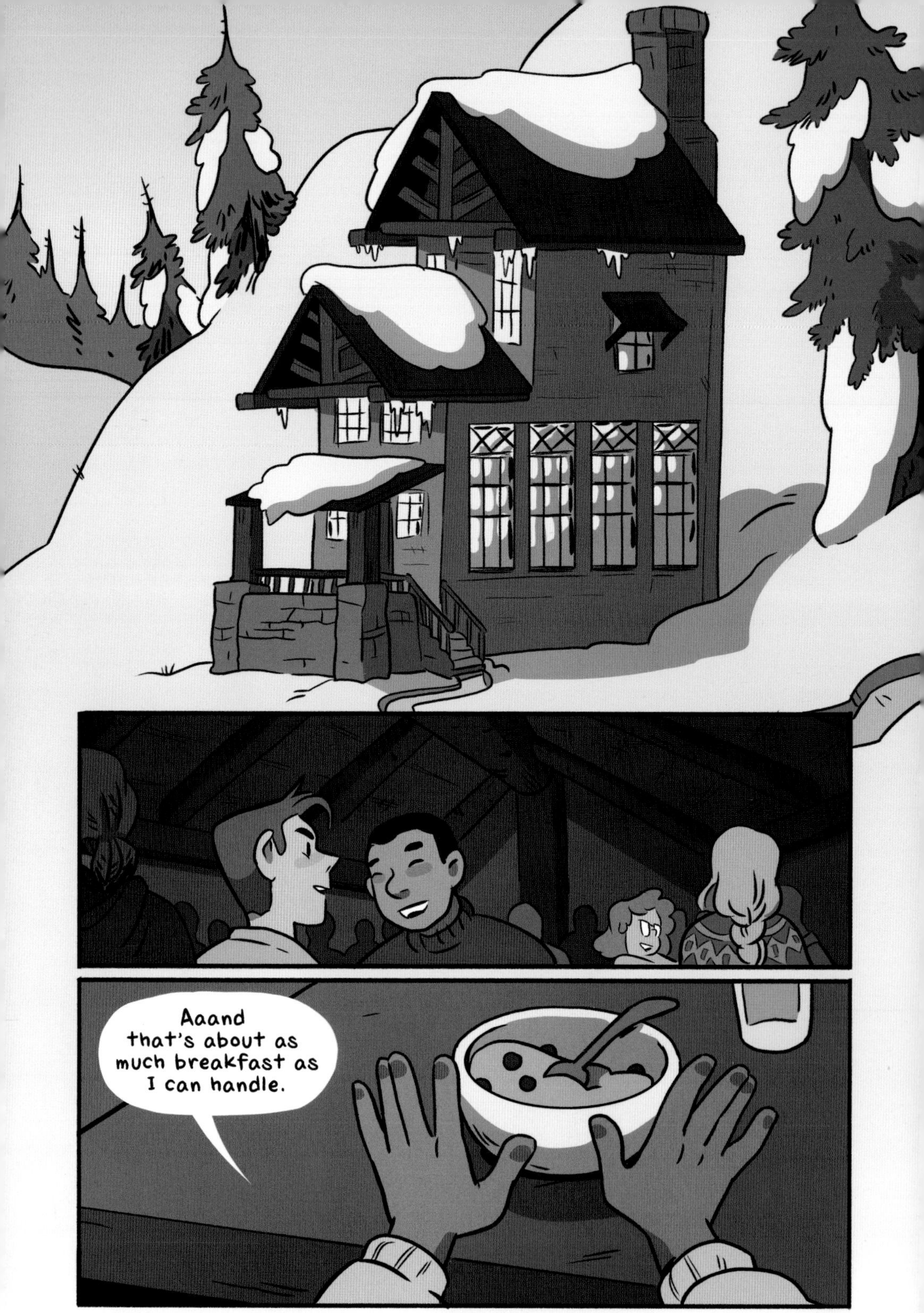
Aaand that's about as much breakfast as I can handle.

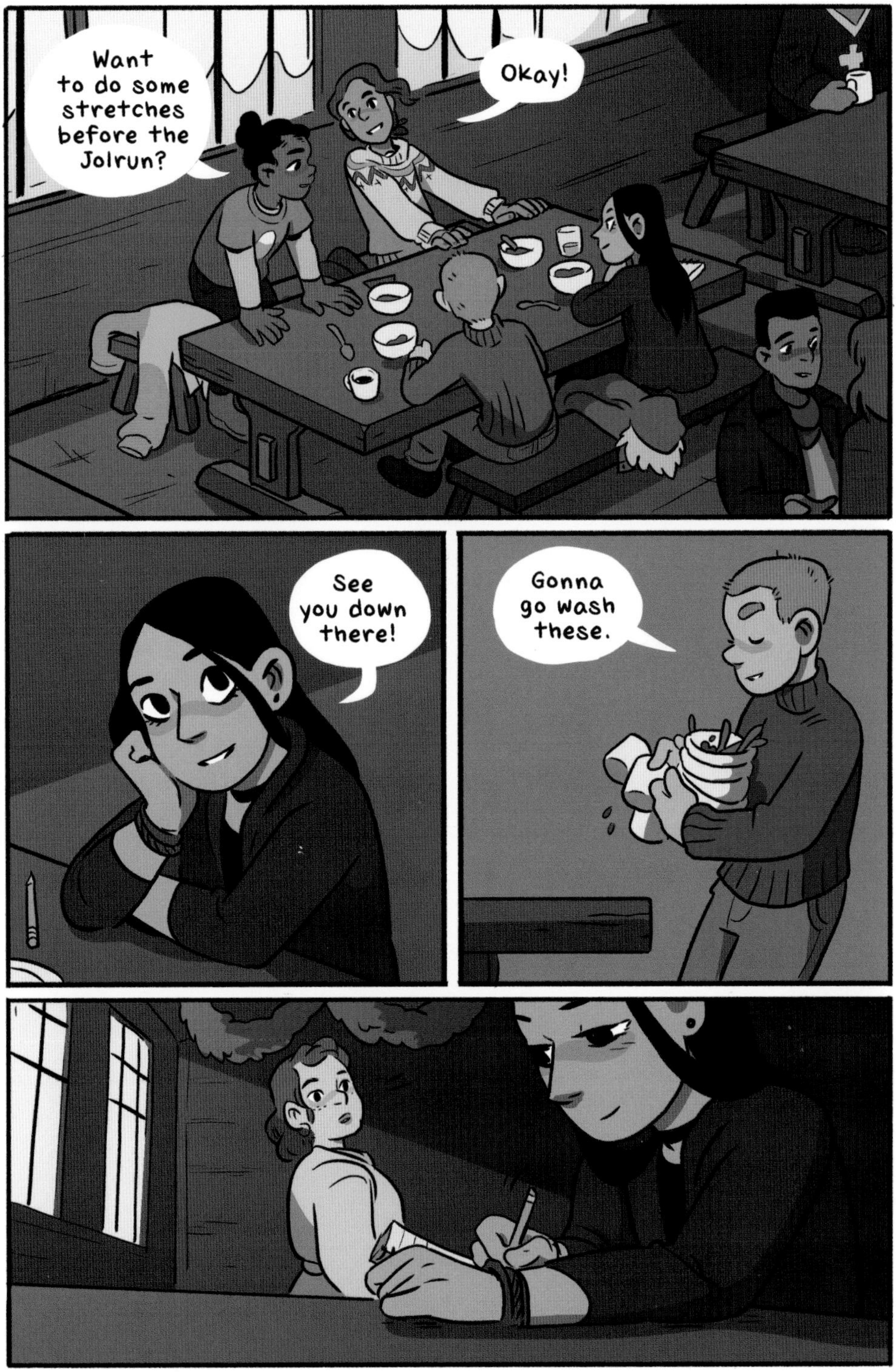

Want to do some stretches before the Jolrun?
Okay!
See you down there!
Gonna go wash these.

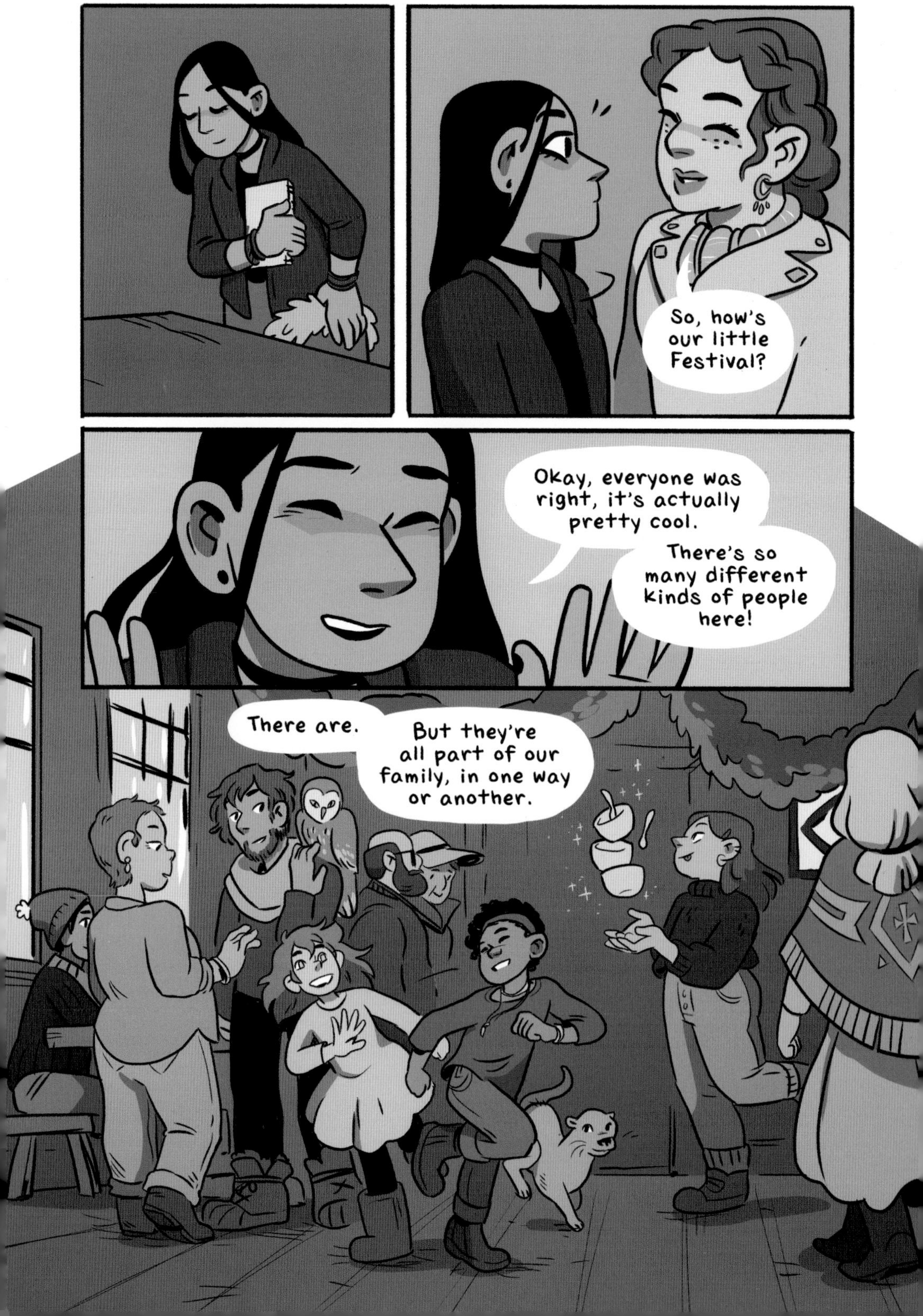
So, how's our little Festival?
Okay, everyone was right, it's actually pretty cool.
There's so many different kinds of people here!
There are.
But they're all part of our family, in one way or another.

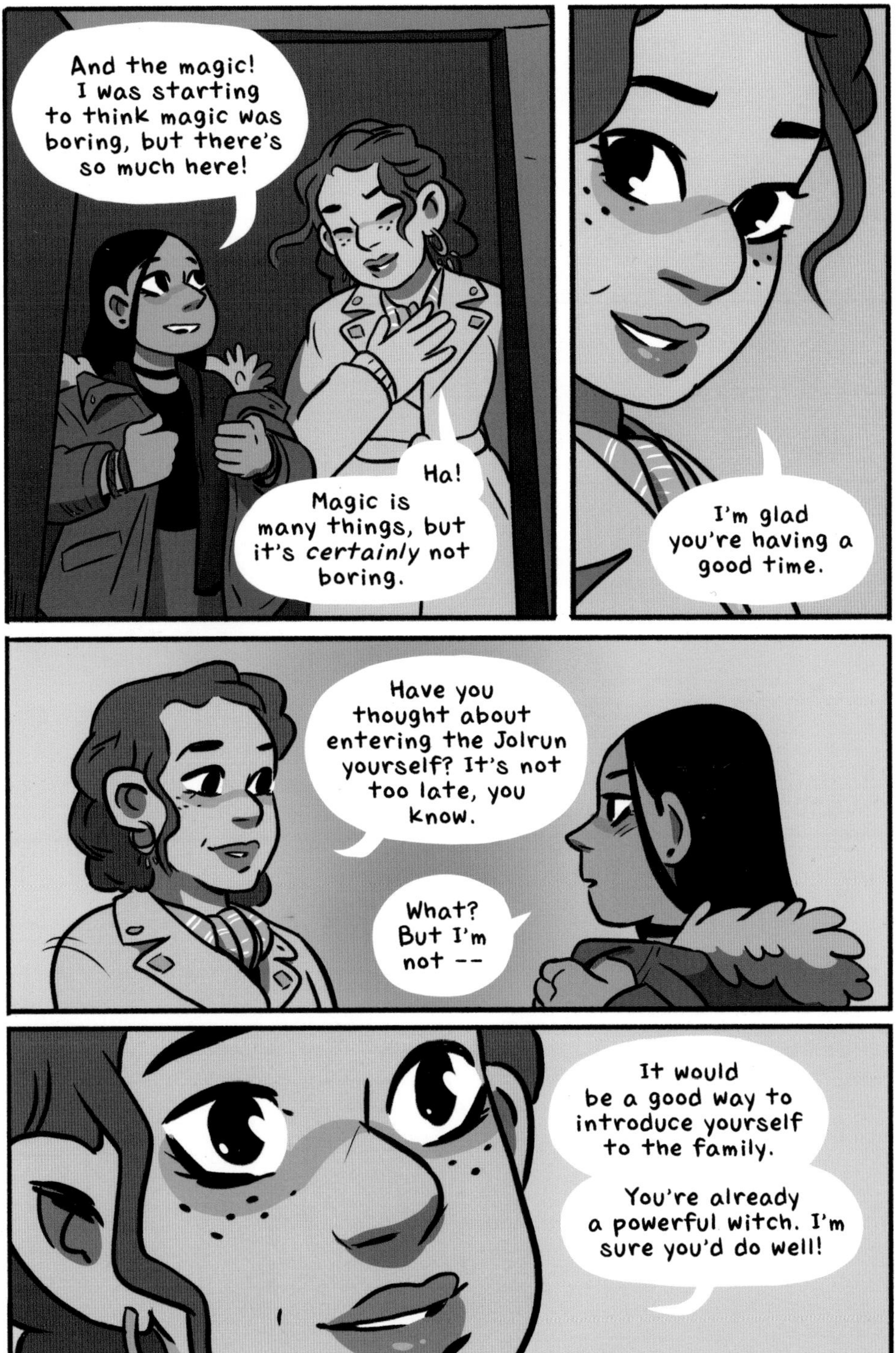
And the magic! I was starting to think magic was boring, but there's so much here!
Ha! Magic is many things, but it's *certainly* not boring.
I'm glad you're having a good time.
Have you thought about entering the Jolrun yourself? It's not too late, you know.
What? But I'm not --
It would be a good way to introduce yourself to the family.
You're already a powerful witch. I'm sure you'd do well!

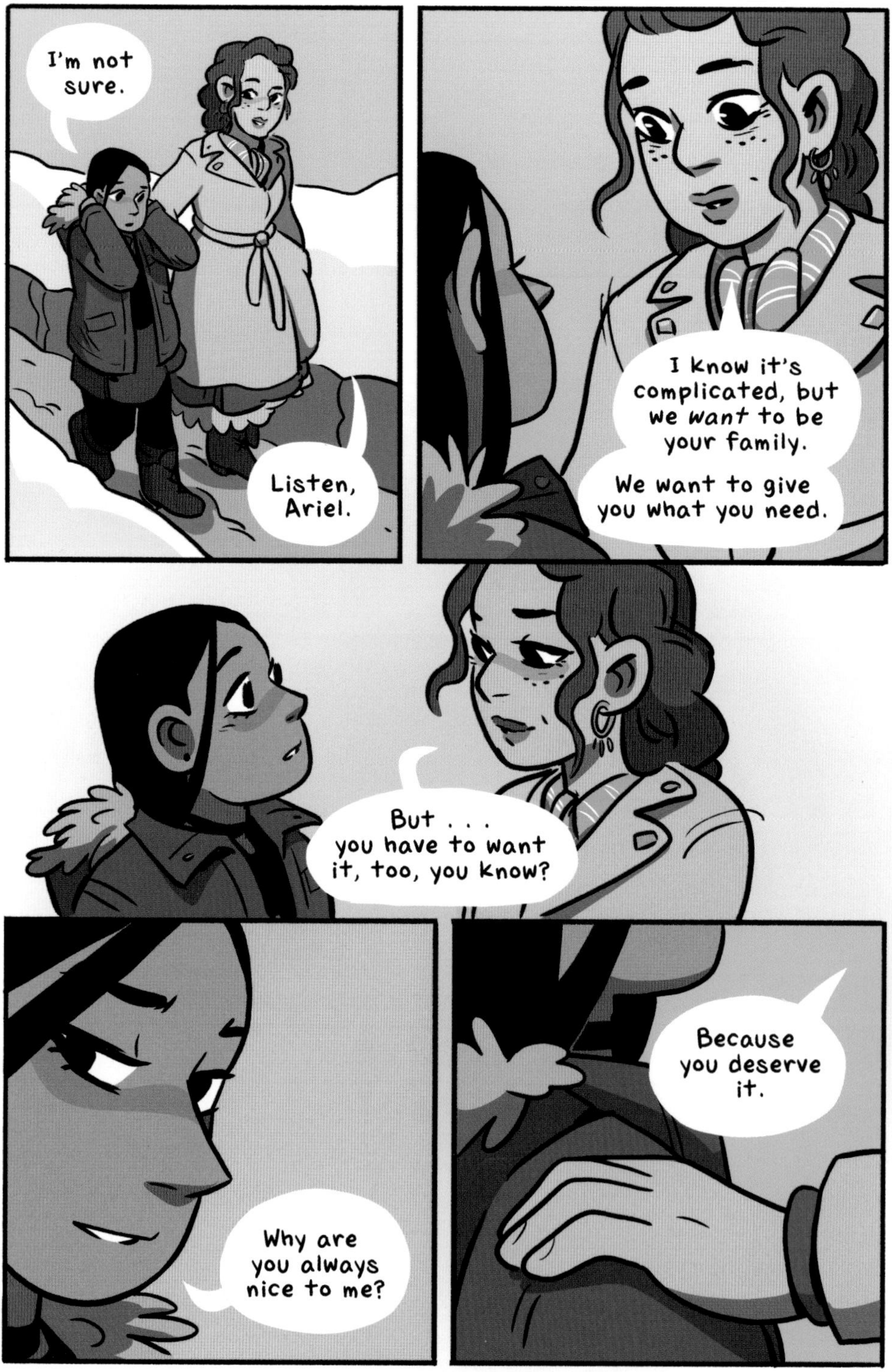

I'm not sure.
Listen, Ariel.
I know it's complicated, but we *want* to be your family.
We want to give you what you need.
But . . . you have to want it, too, you know?
Why are you always nice to me?
Because you deserve it.

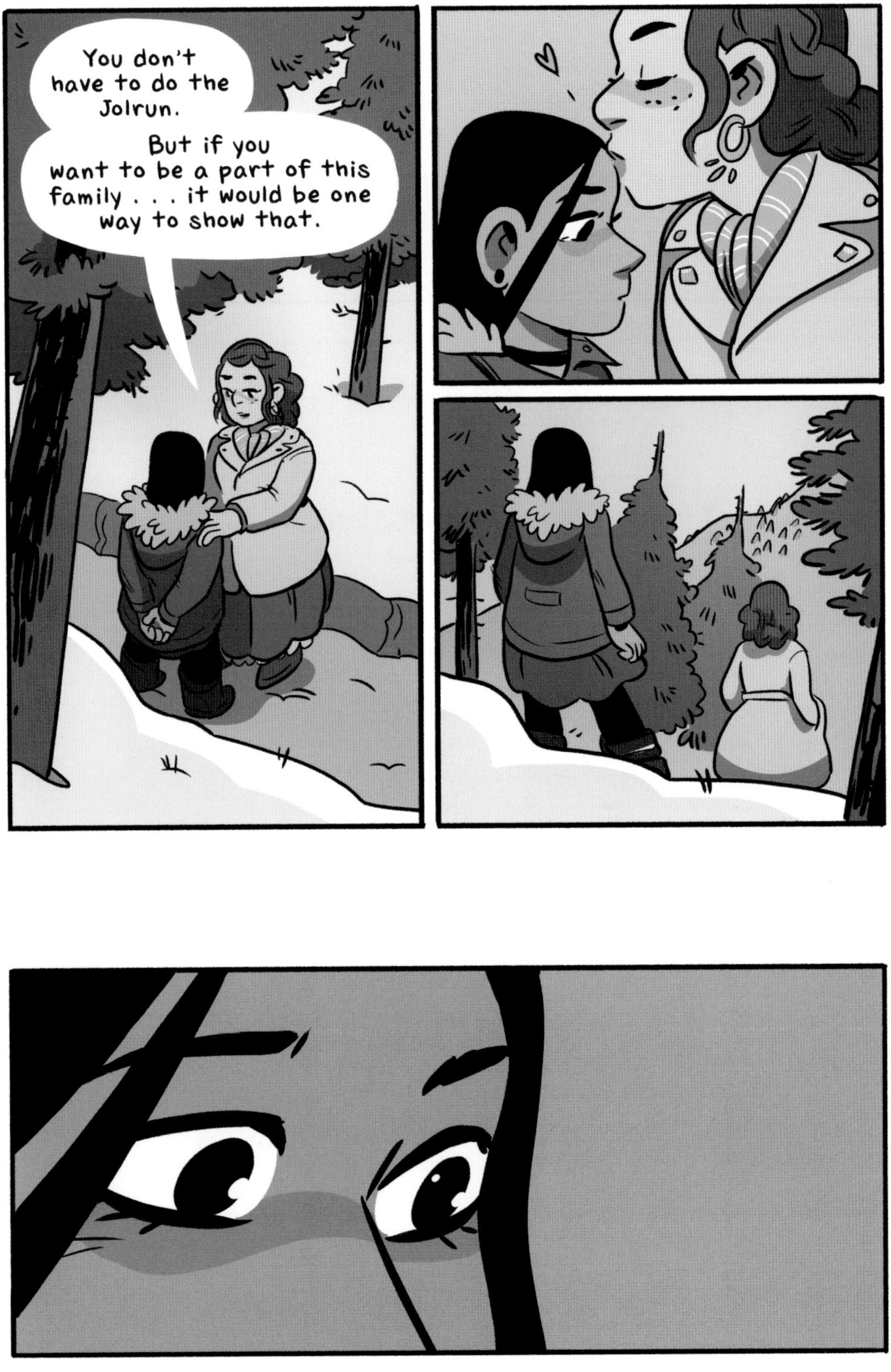
You don't have to do the Jolrun.
But if you want to be a part of this family . . . it would be one way to show that.

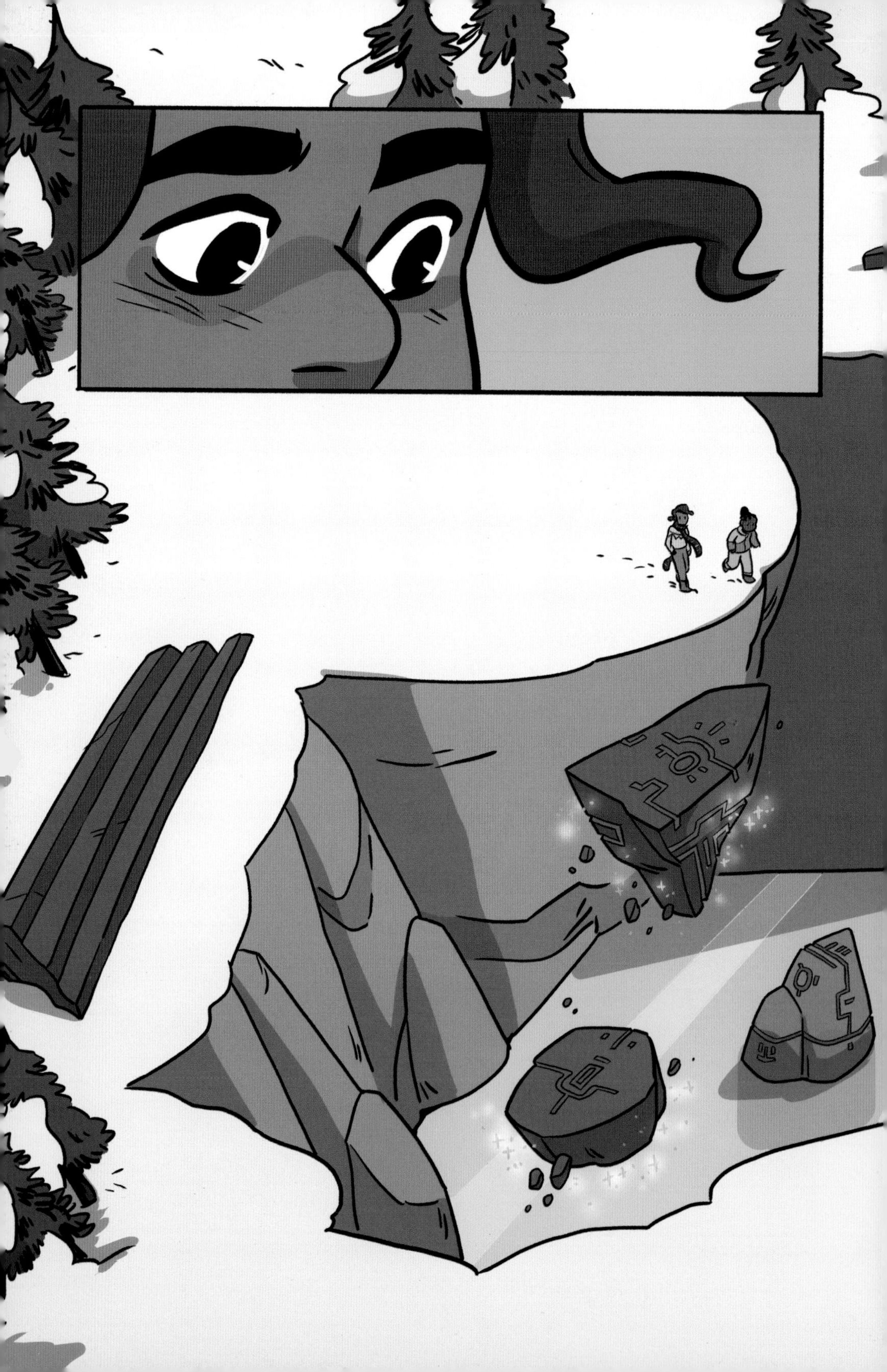

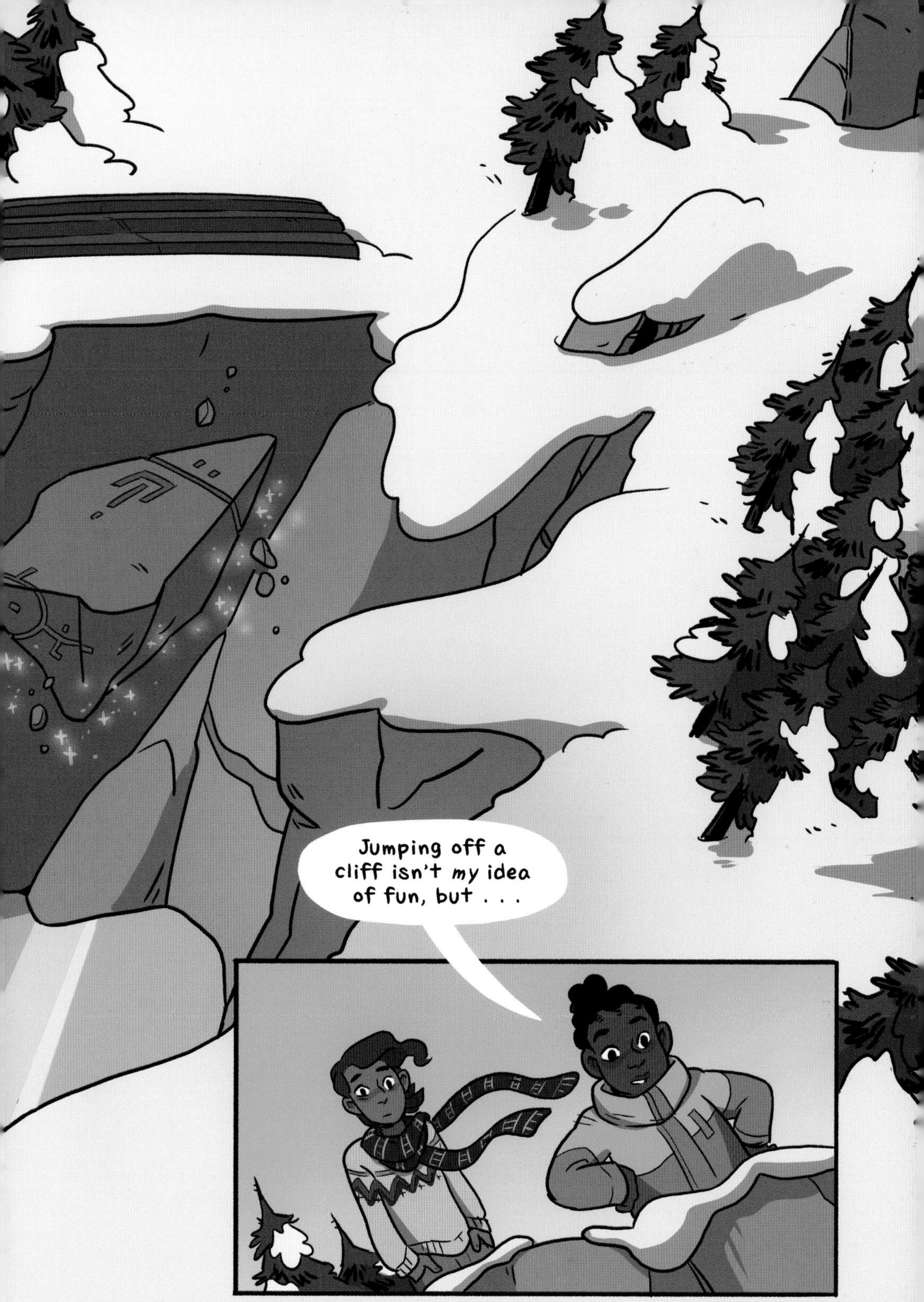
Jumping off a cliff isn't my idea of fun, but . . .

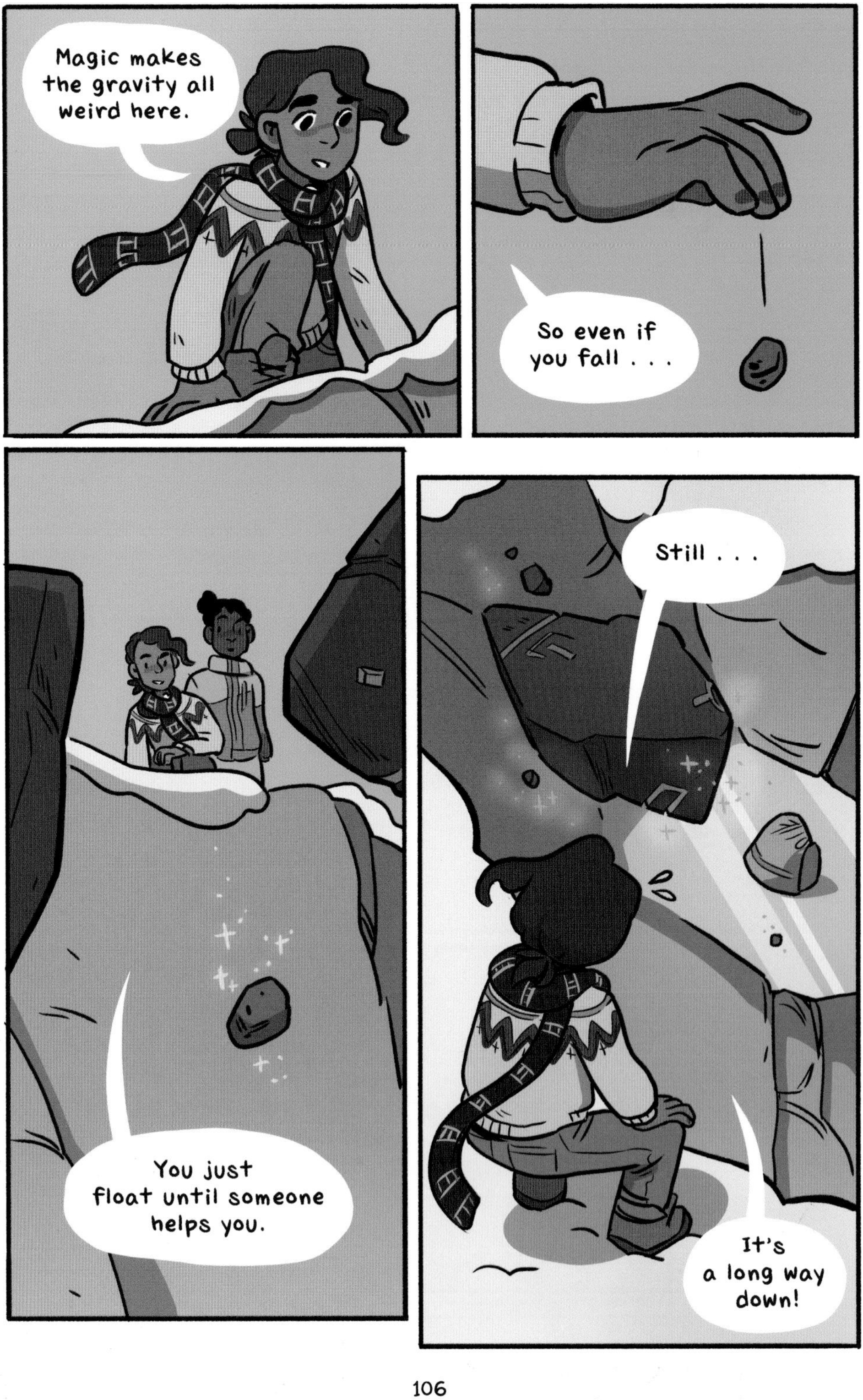
Magic makes the gravity all weird here.
So even if you fall . . .
You just float until someone helps you.
Still . . .
It's a long way down!

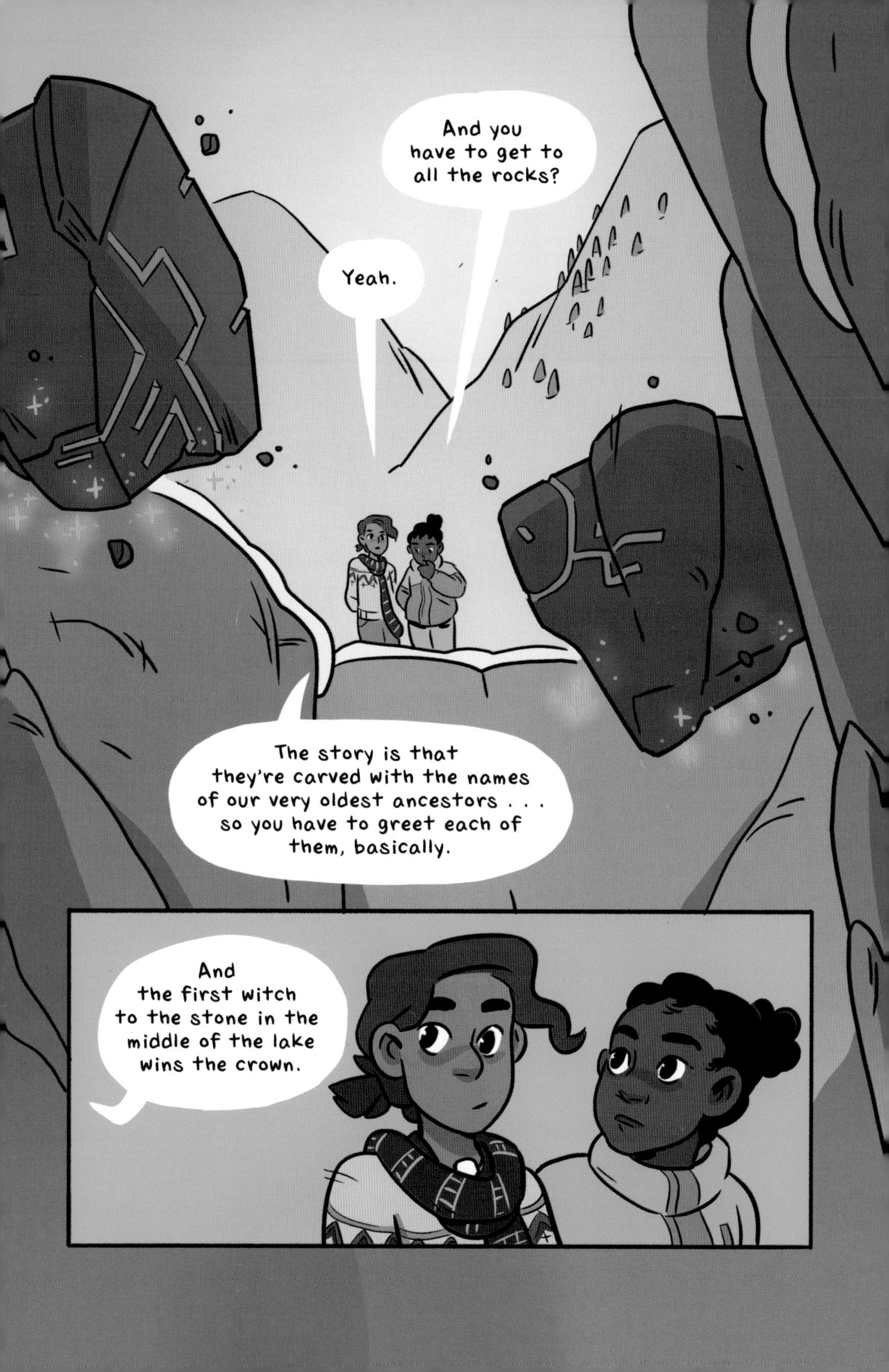
And you have to get to all the rocks?
Yeah.
The story is that they're carved with the names of our very oldest ancestors . . . so you have to greet each of them, basically.
And the first witch to the stone in the middle of the lake wins the crown.

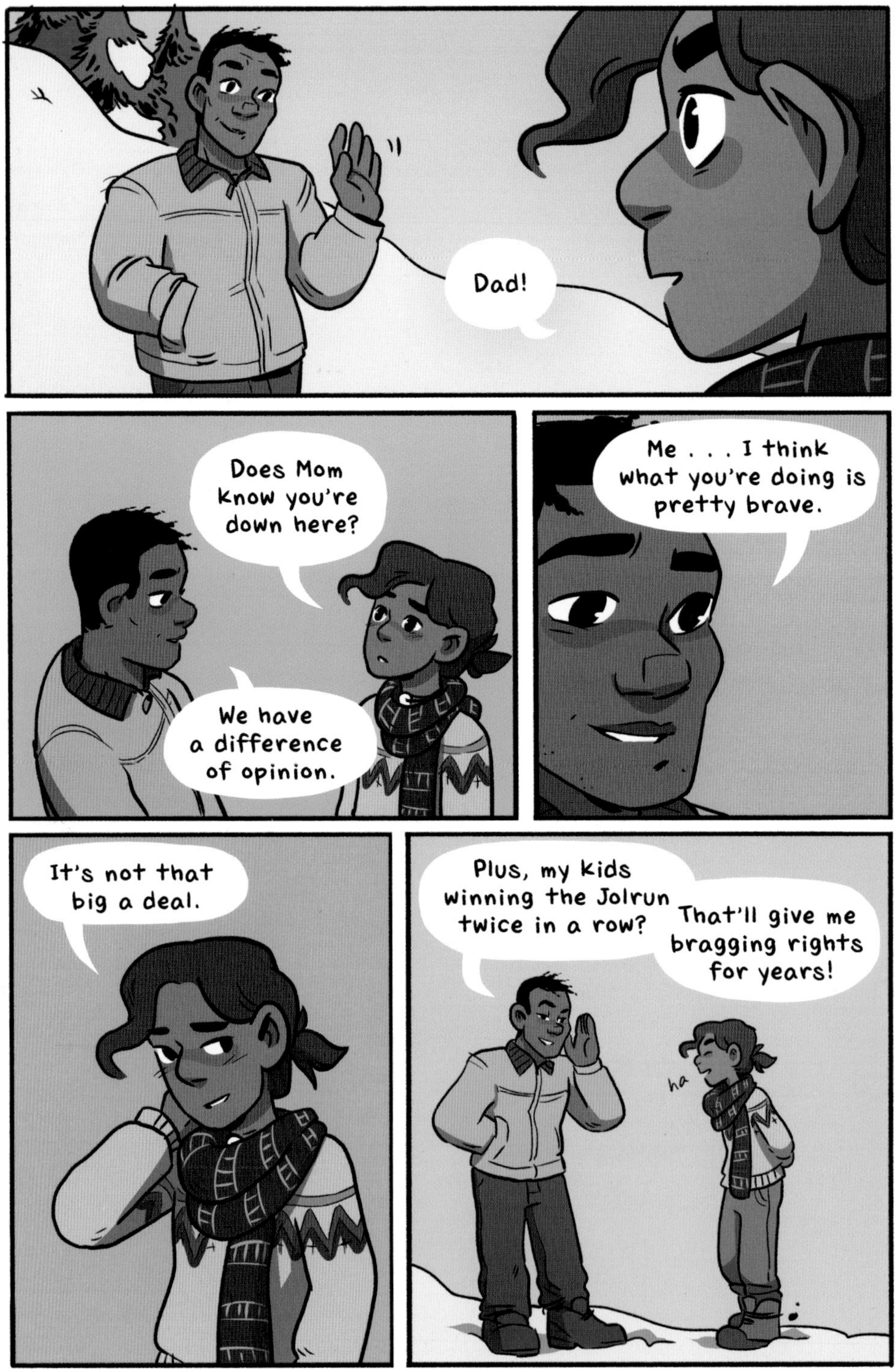
Dad!
Does Mom know you're down here?
We have a difference of opinion.
Me . . . I think what you're doing is pretty brave.
It's not that big a deal.
Plus, my kids winning the Jolrun twice in a row?
That'll give me bragging rights for years!
ha

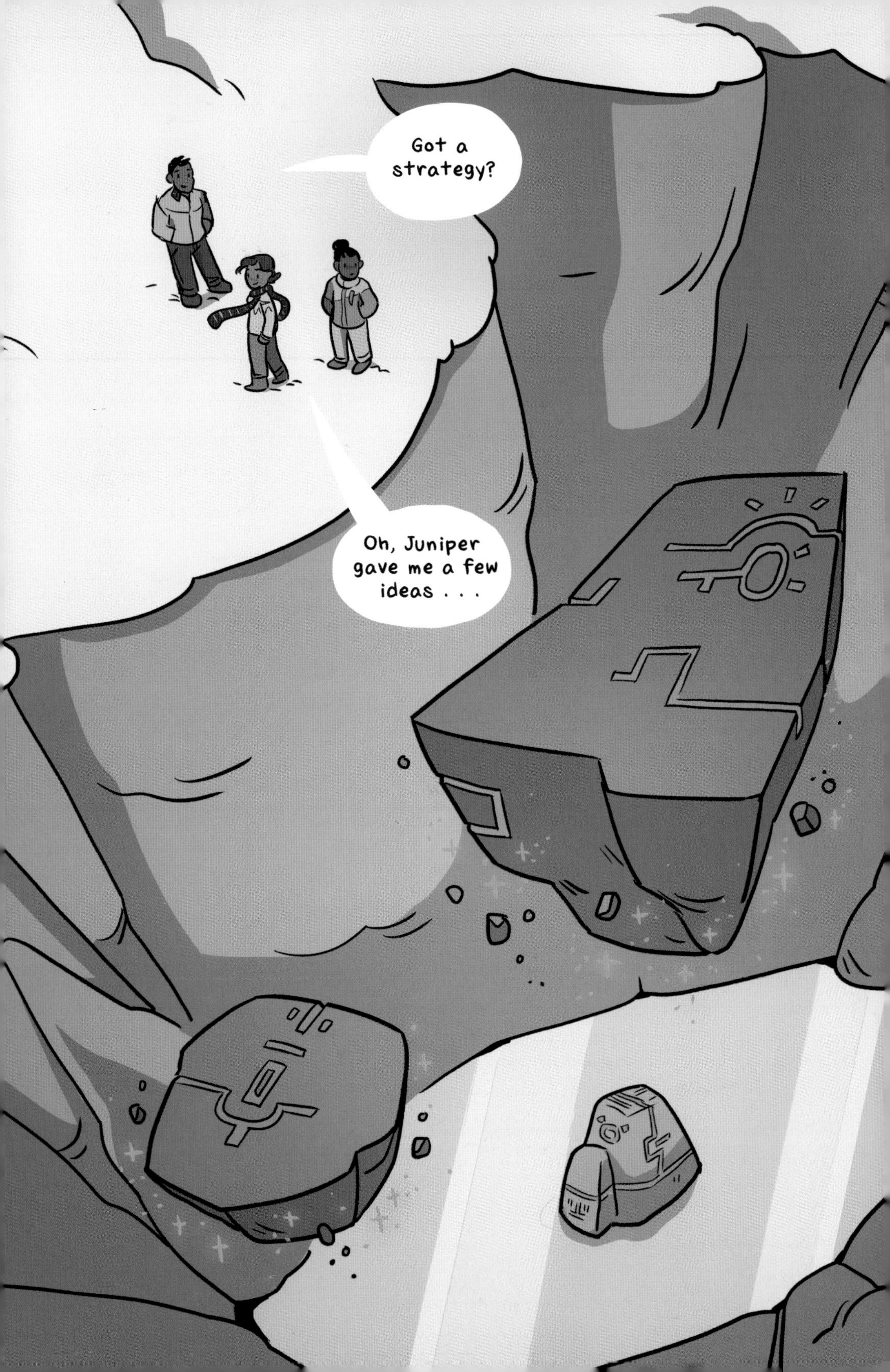
Got a strategy?
Oh, Juniper gave me a few ideas . . .

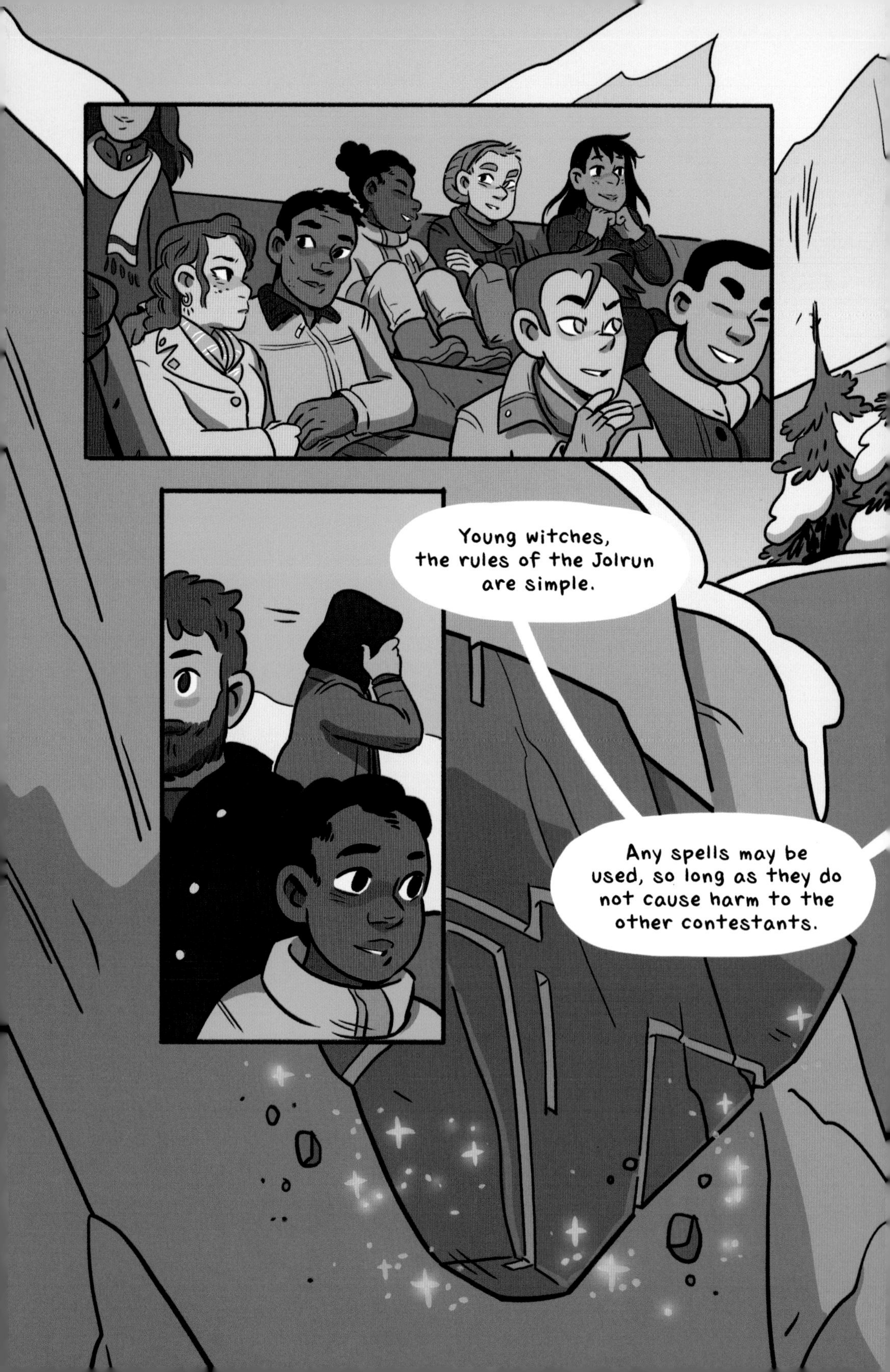
Young witches, the rules of the Jolrun are simple.
Any spells may be used, so long as they do not cause harm to the other contestants.

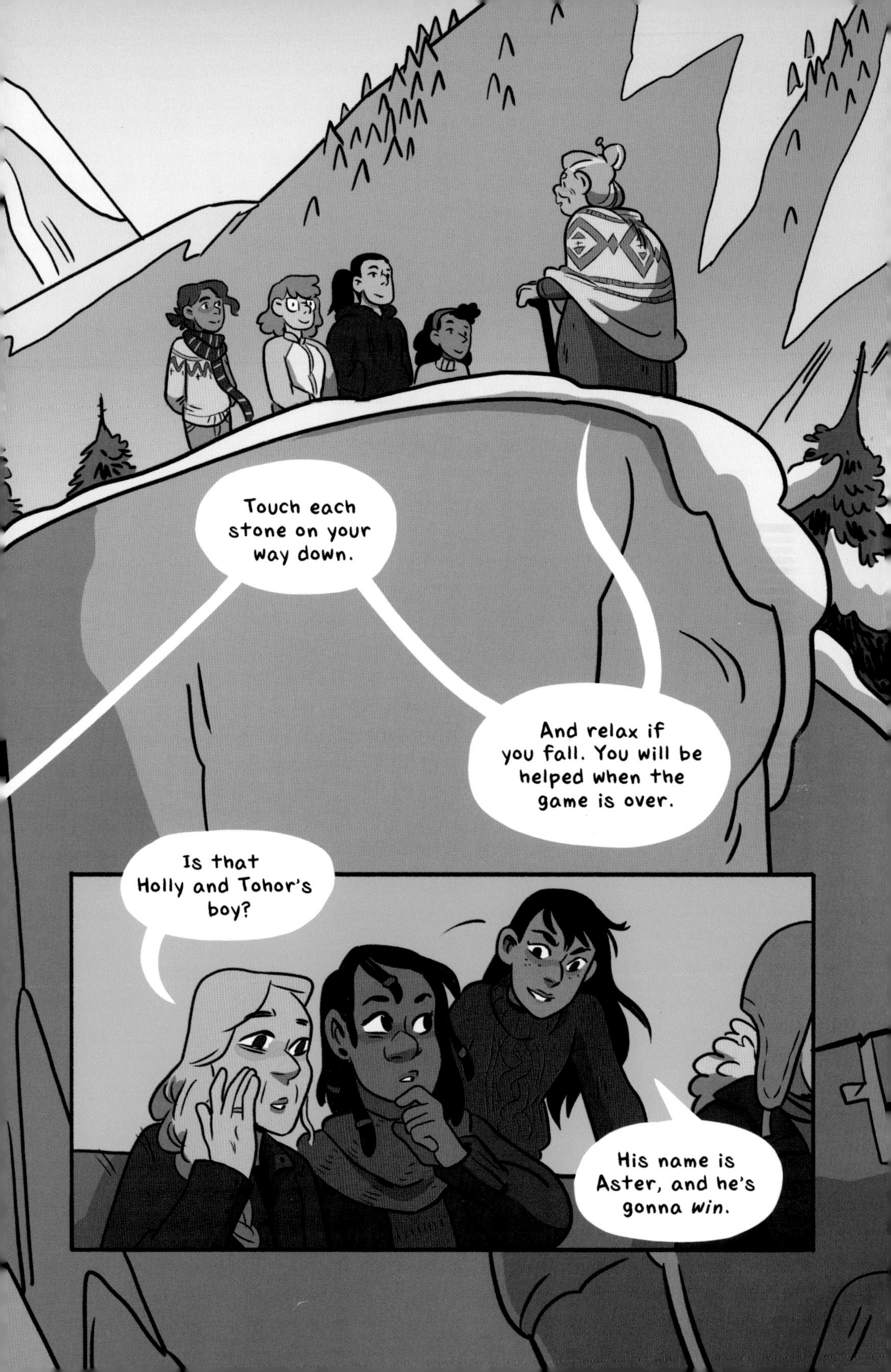
Touch each stone on your way down.
And relax if you fall. You will be helped when the game is over.
Is that Holly and Tohor's boy?
His name is Aster, and he's gonna *win*.

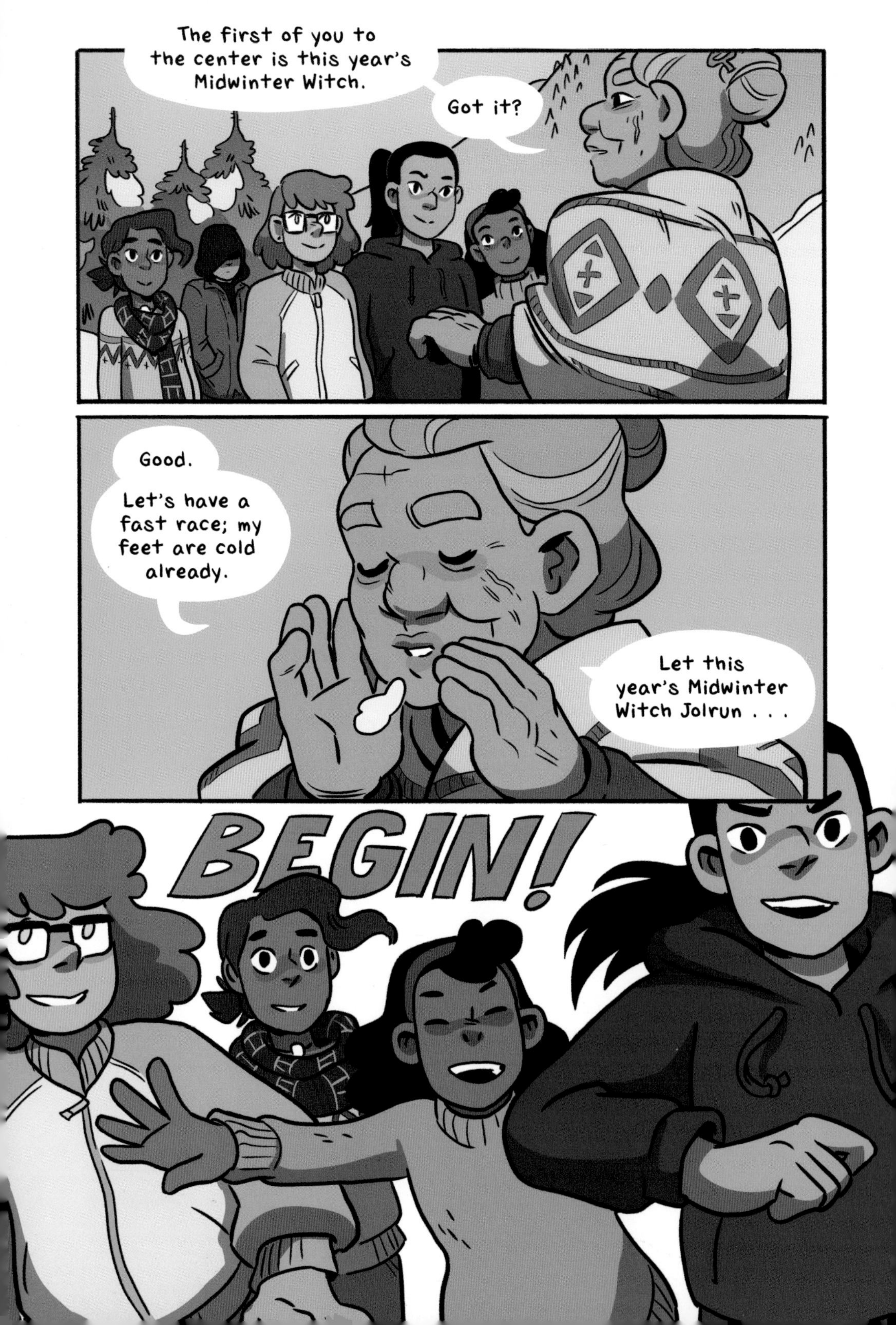
The first of you to the center is this year's Midwinter Witch.
Got it?
Good.
Let's have a fast race; my feet are cold already.
Let this year's Midwinter Witch Jolrun . . .
BEGIN!

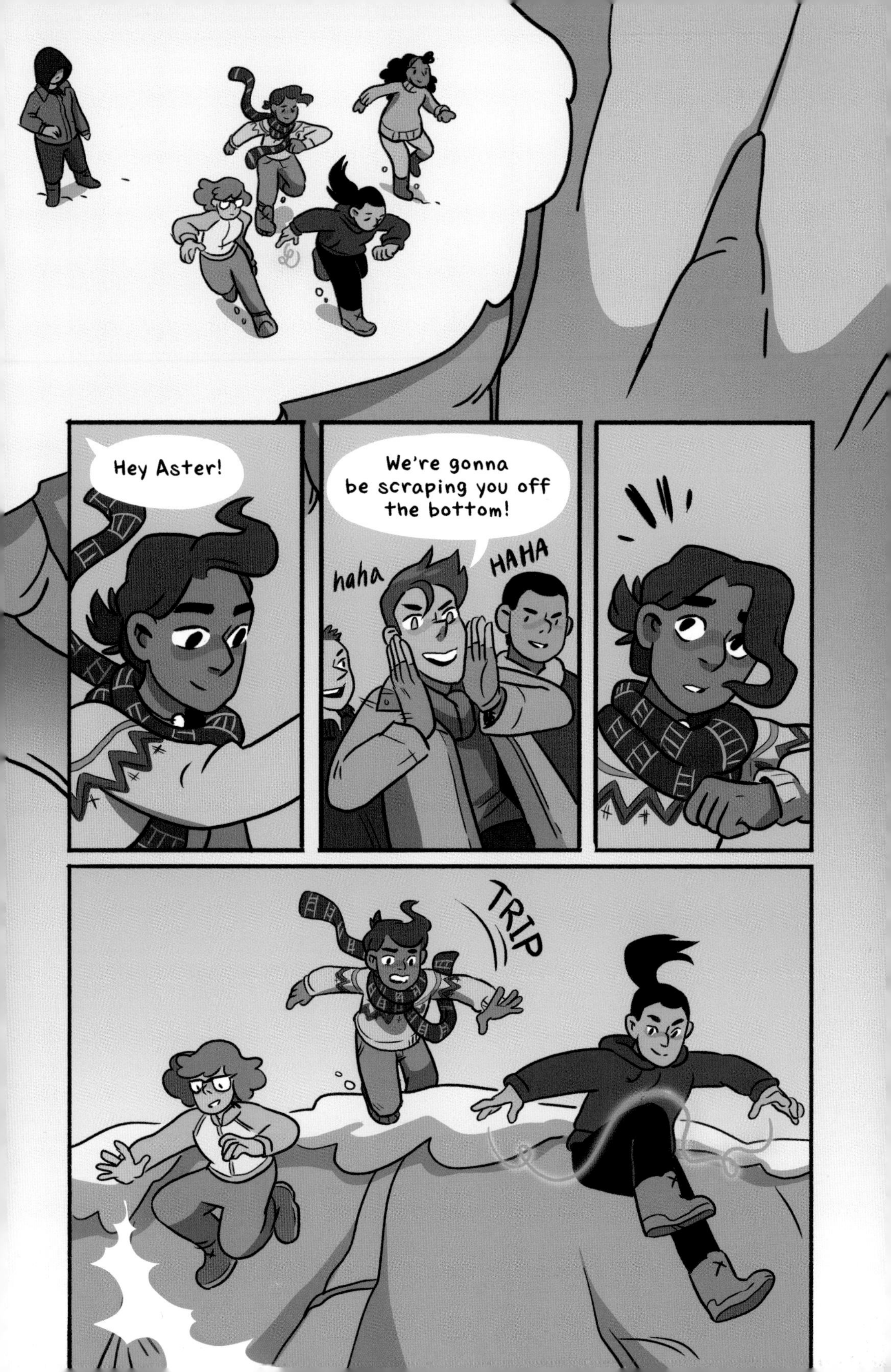
Hey Aster!
We're gonna be scraping you off the bottom!
haha
HAHA
TRIP

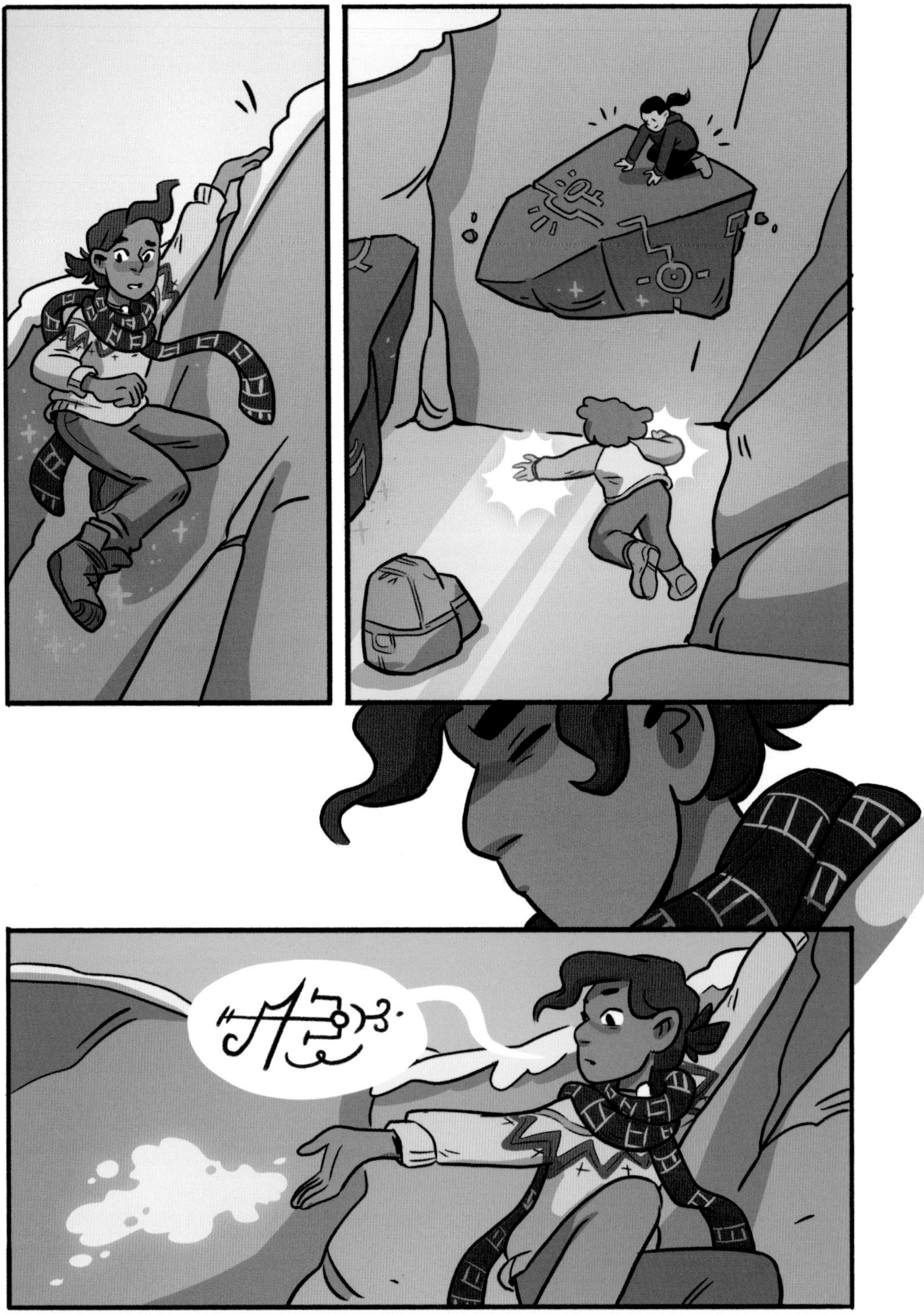

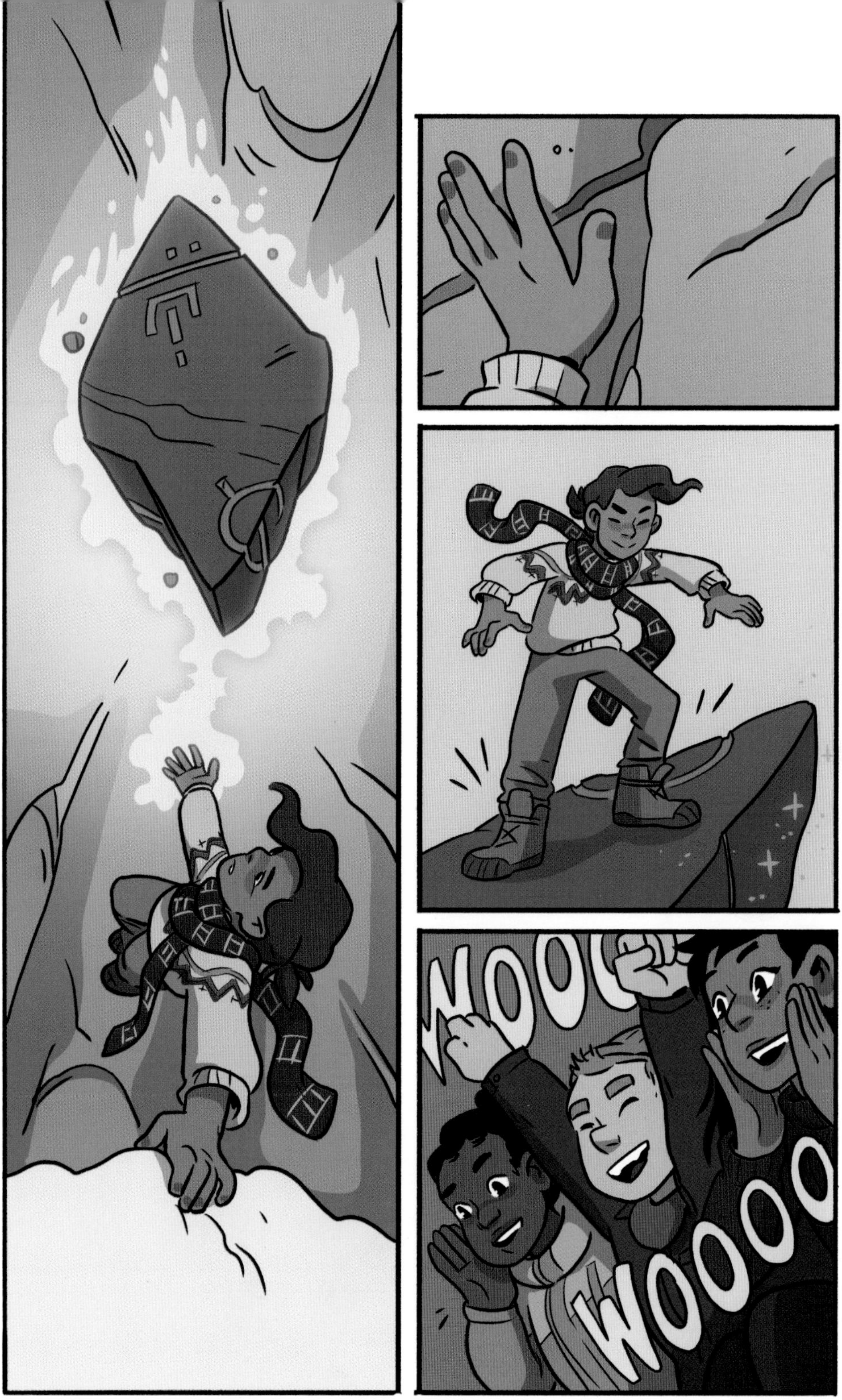
WOOO
WOOOO

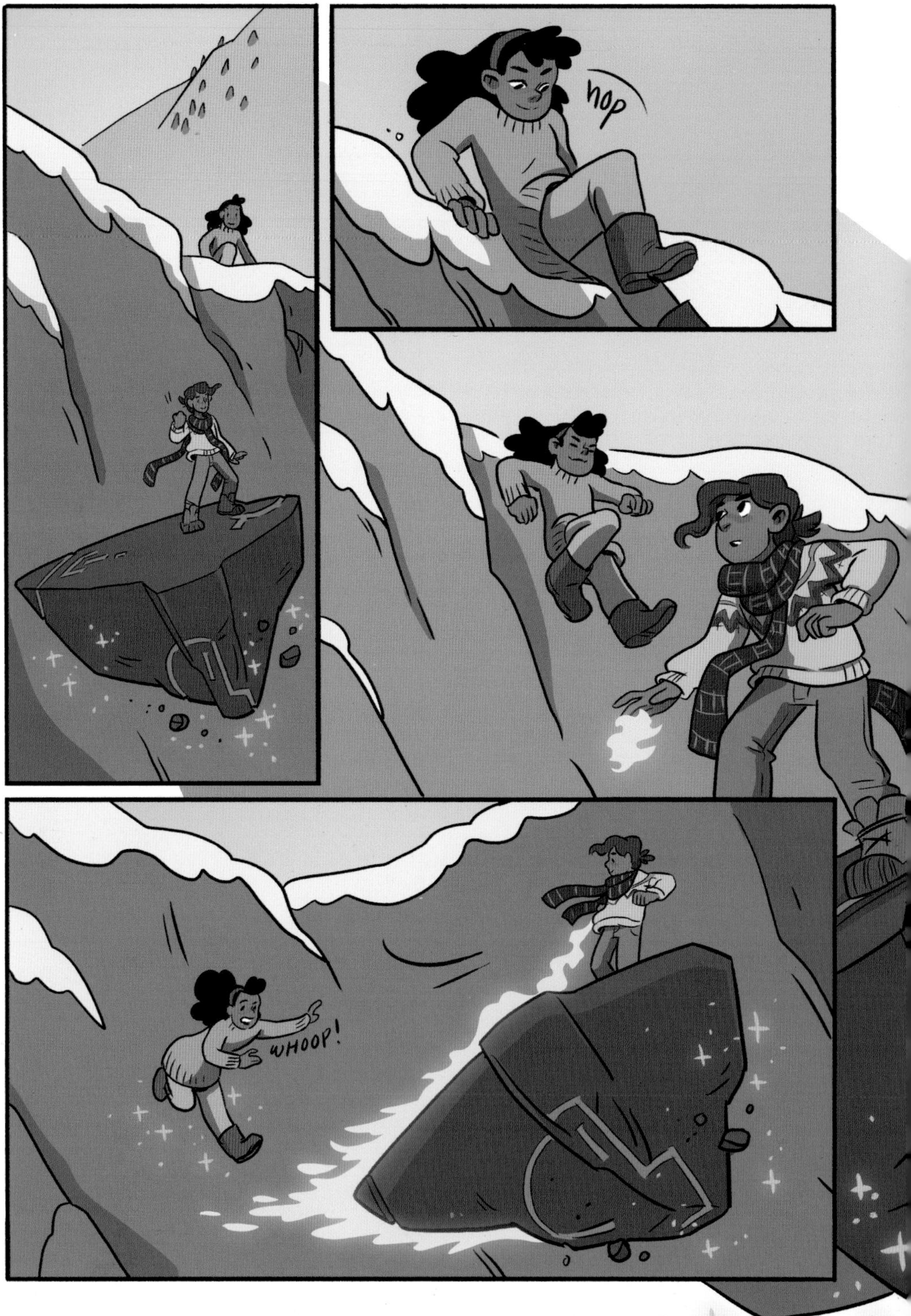
hop
WHOOP!

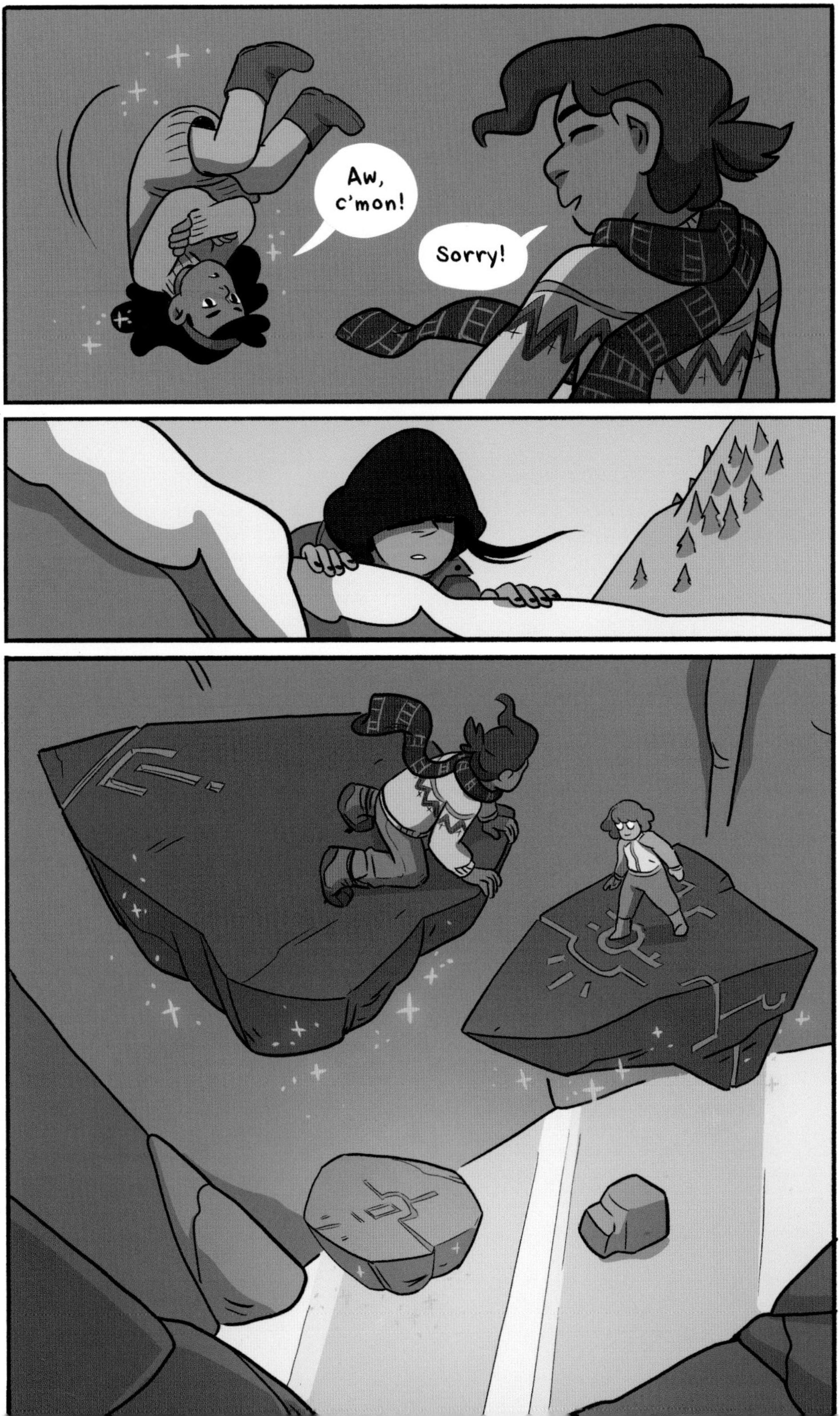
Aw, c'mon!
Sorry!

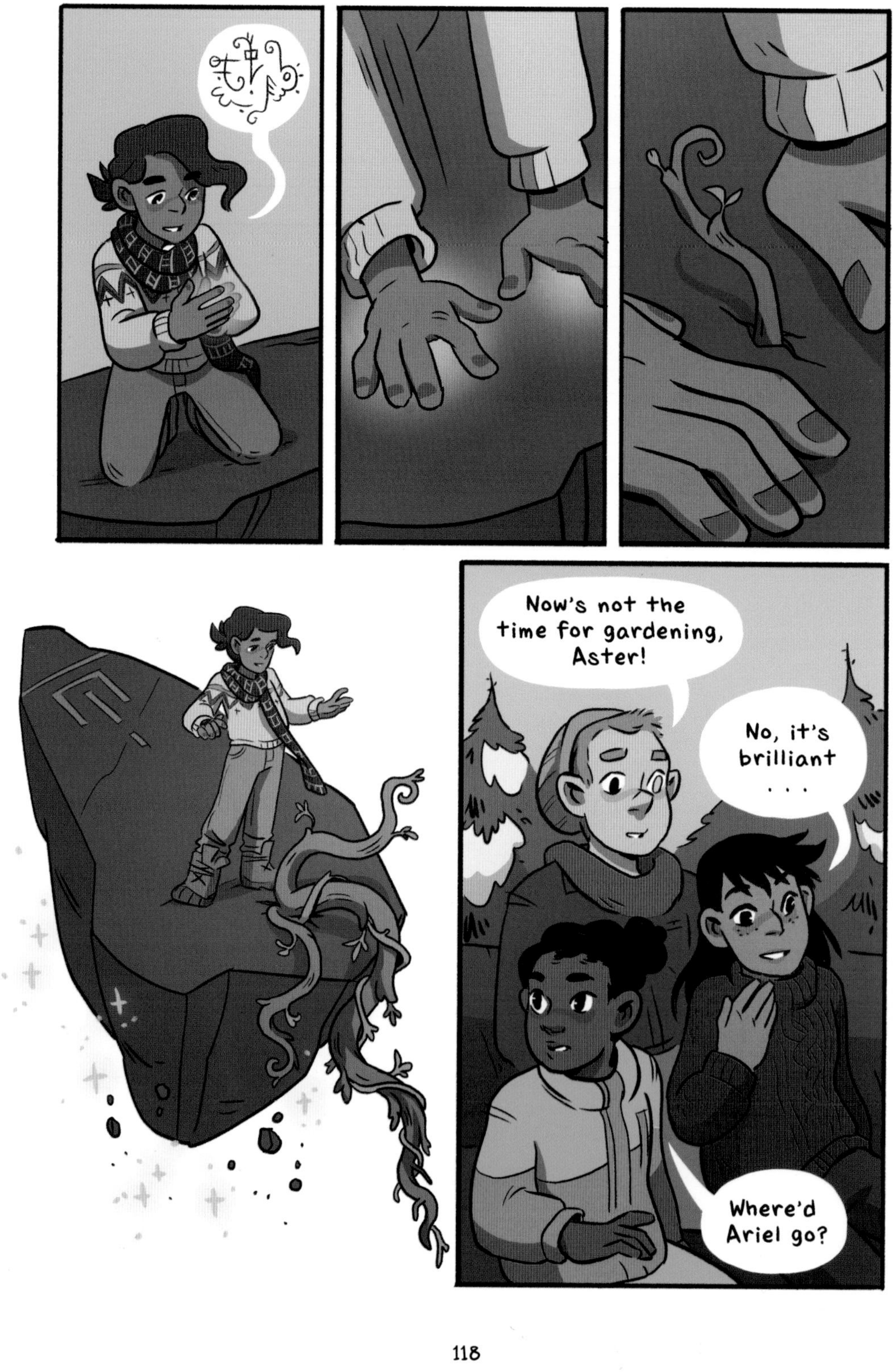
Now's not the time for gardening, Aster!
No, it's brilliant . . .
Where'd Ariel go?

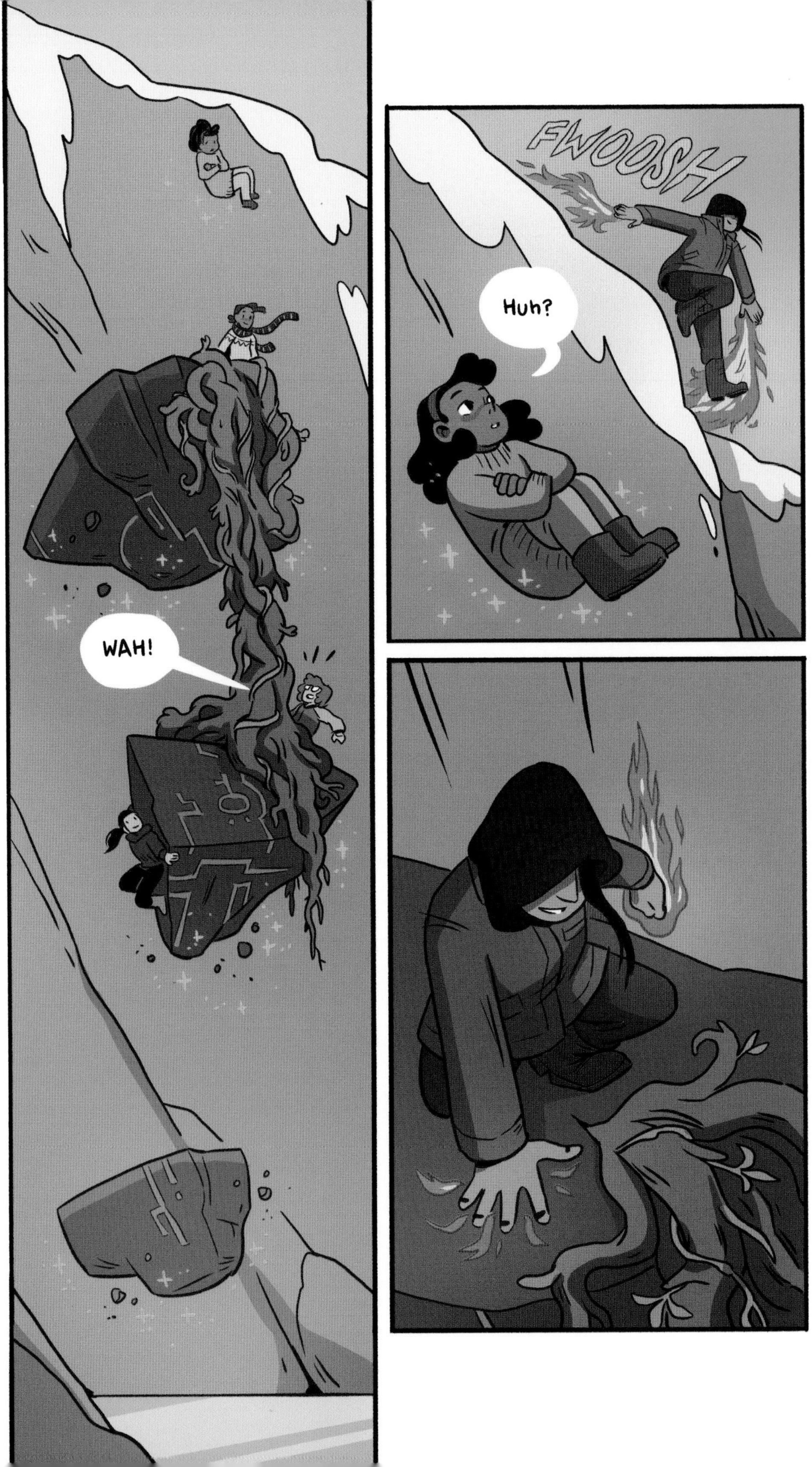

WAH!
FWOOSH
Huh?

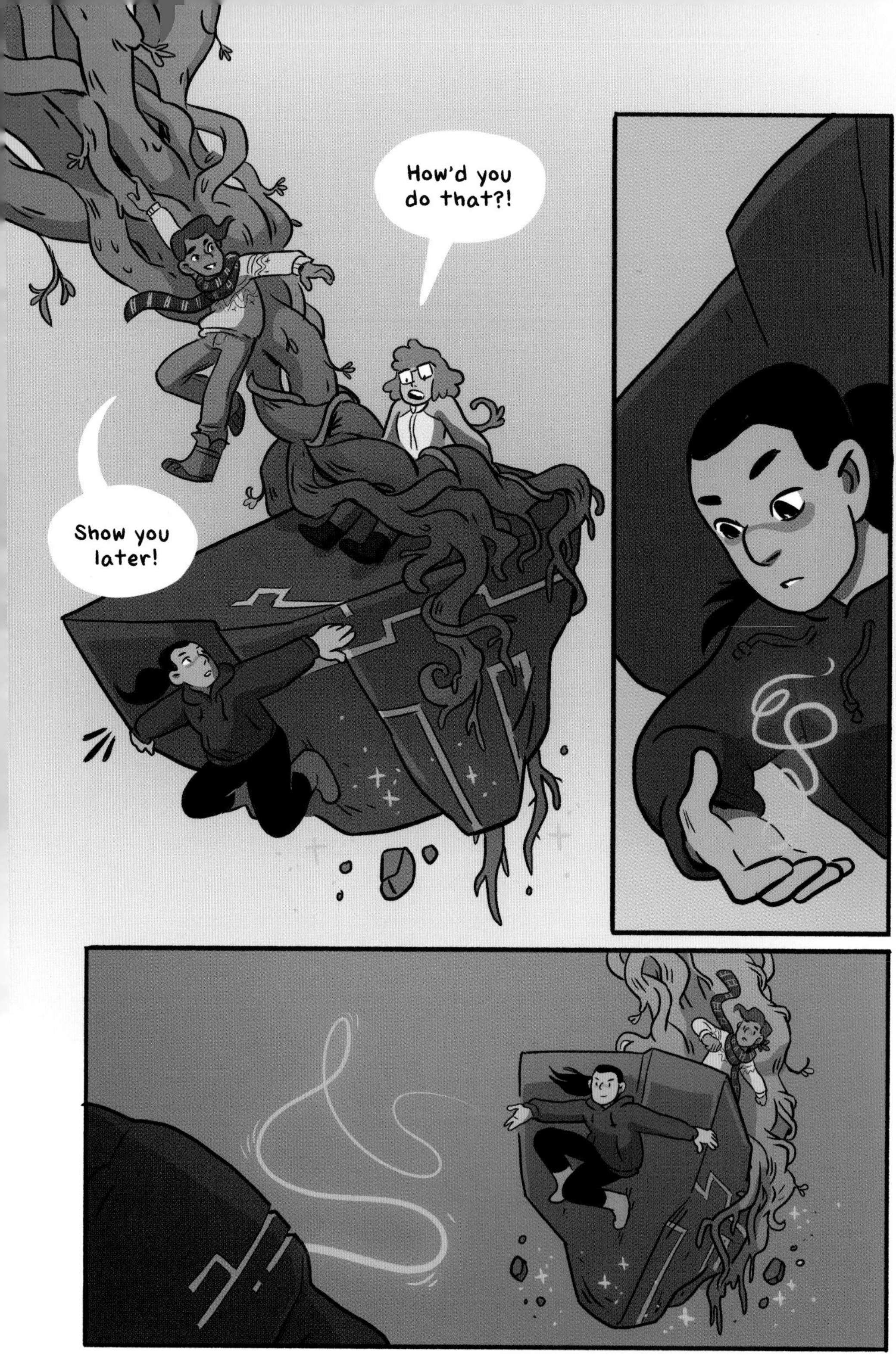
How'd you do that?!
Show you later!

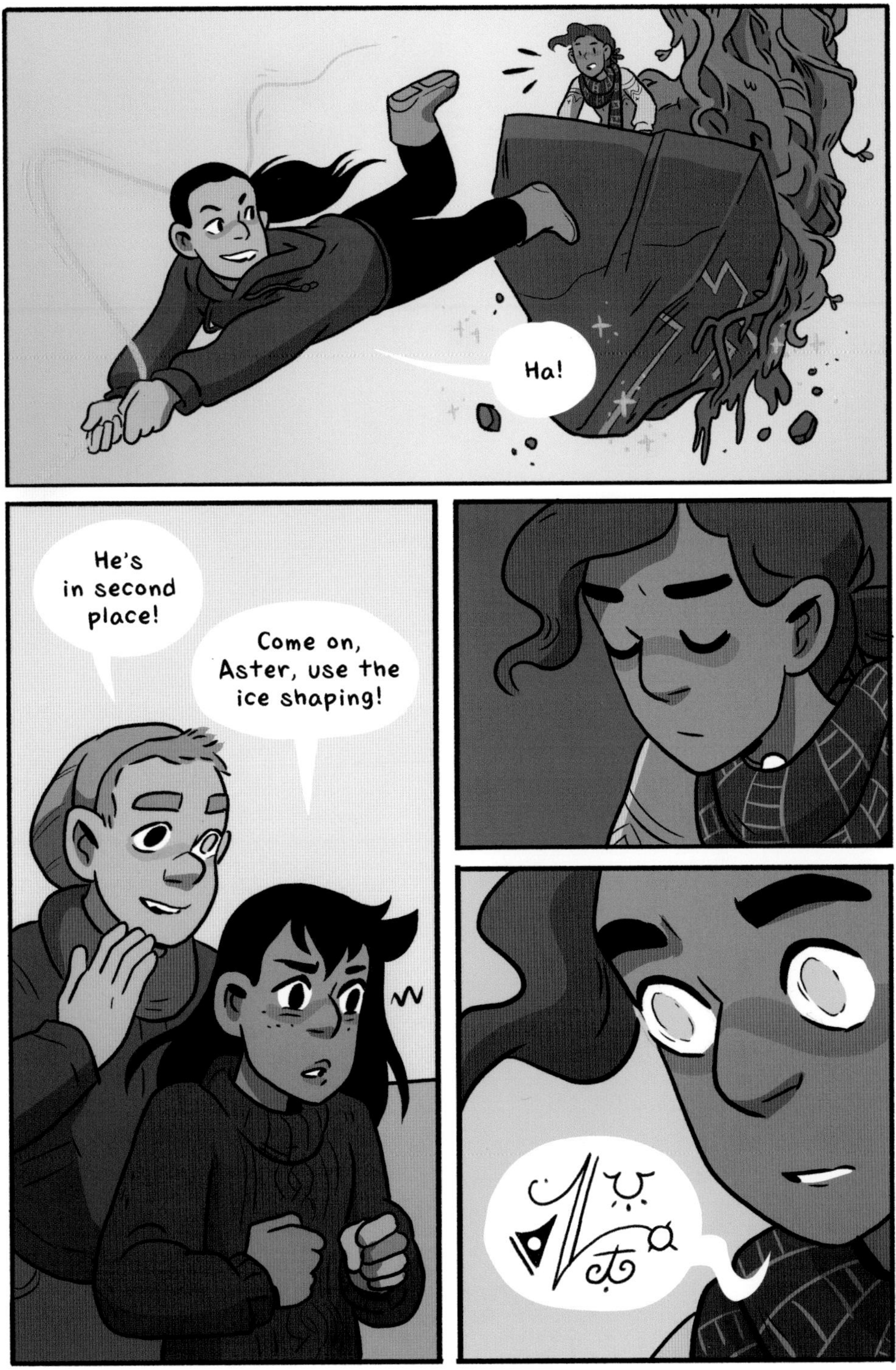
Ha!
He's in second place!
Come on, Aster, use the ice shaping!

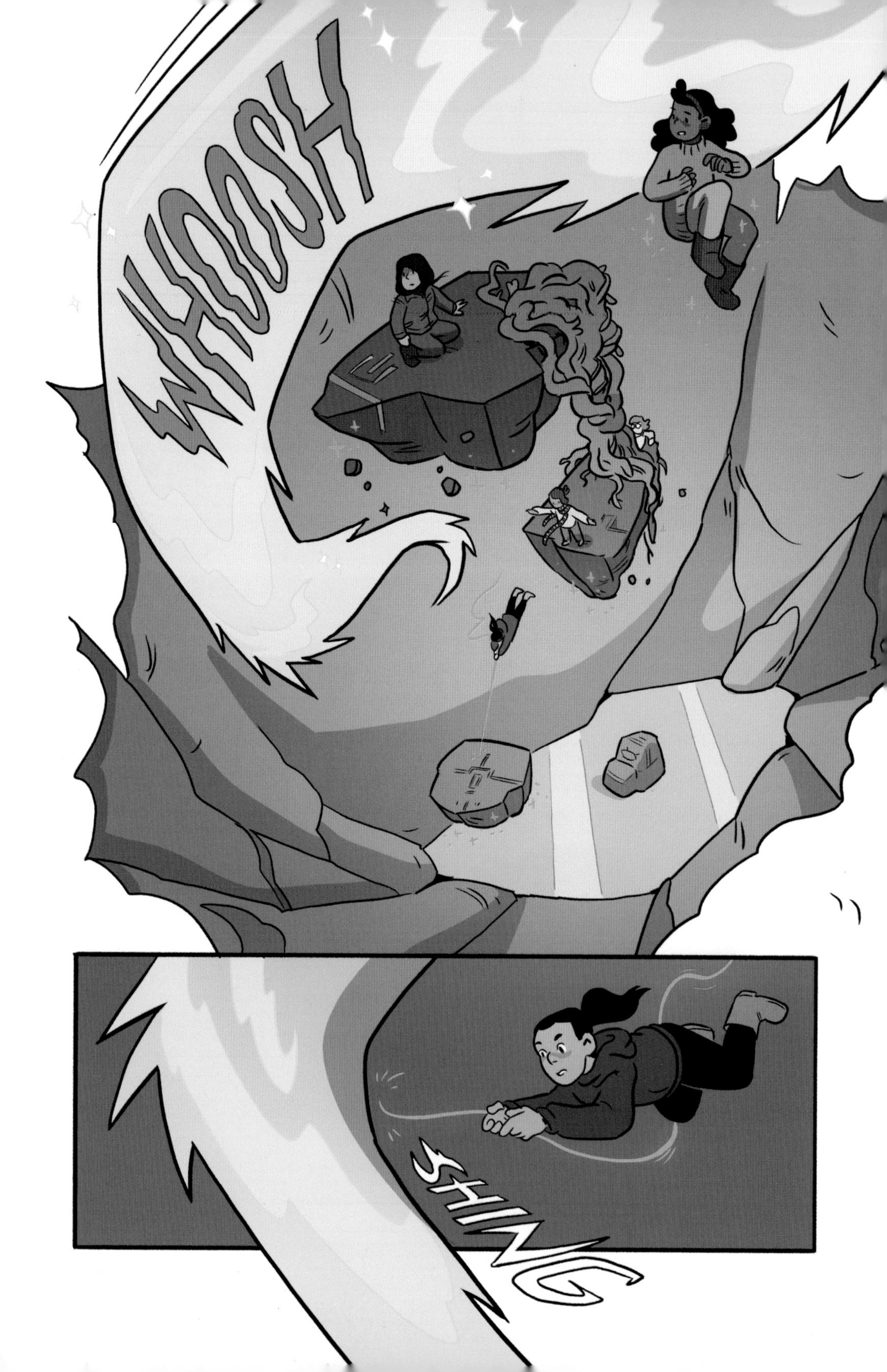
WHOOSH
SHING

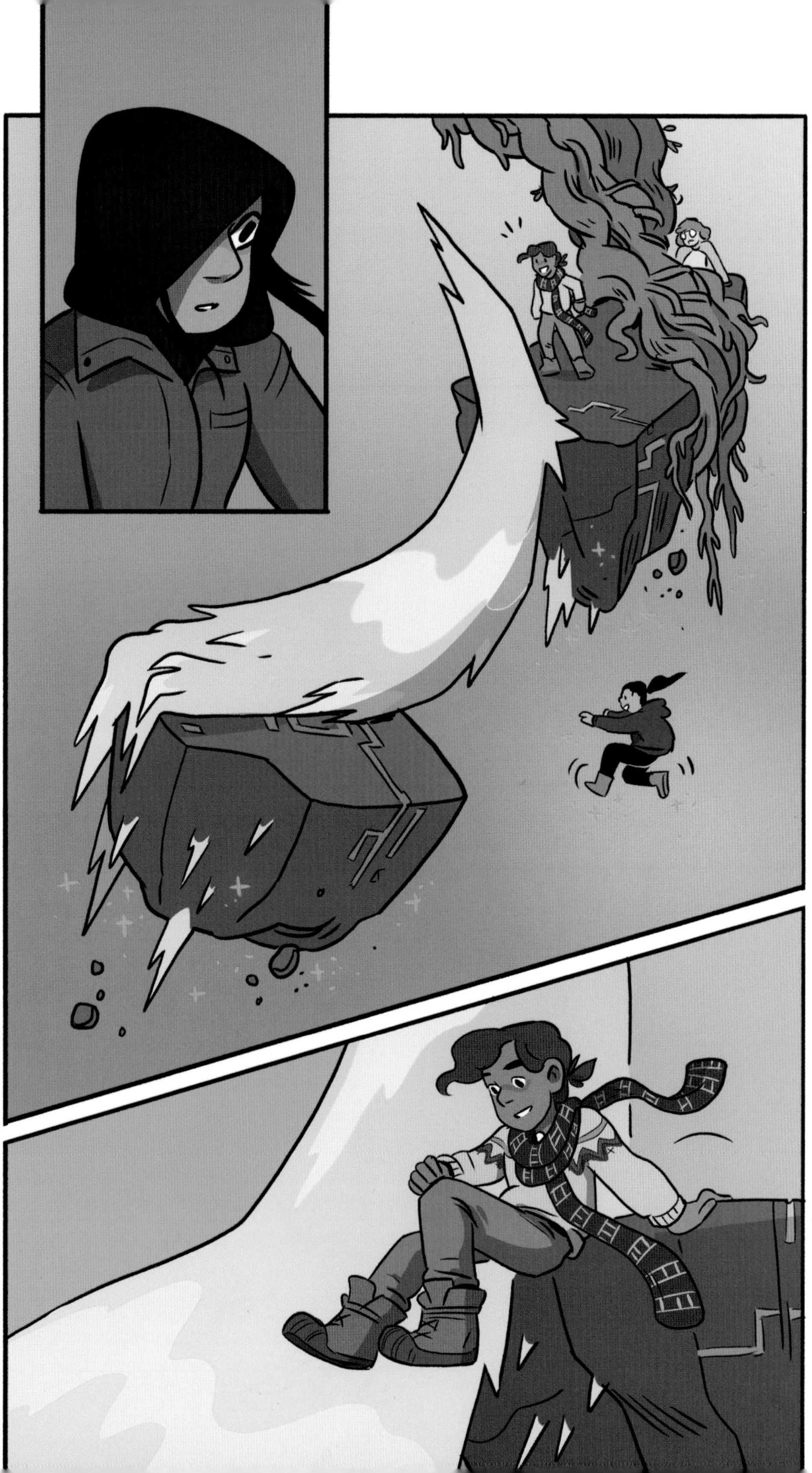

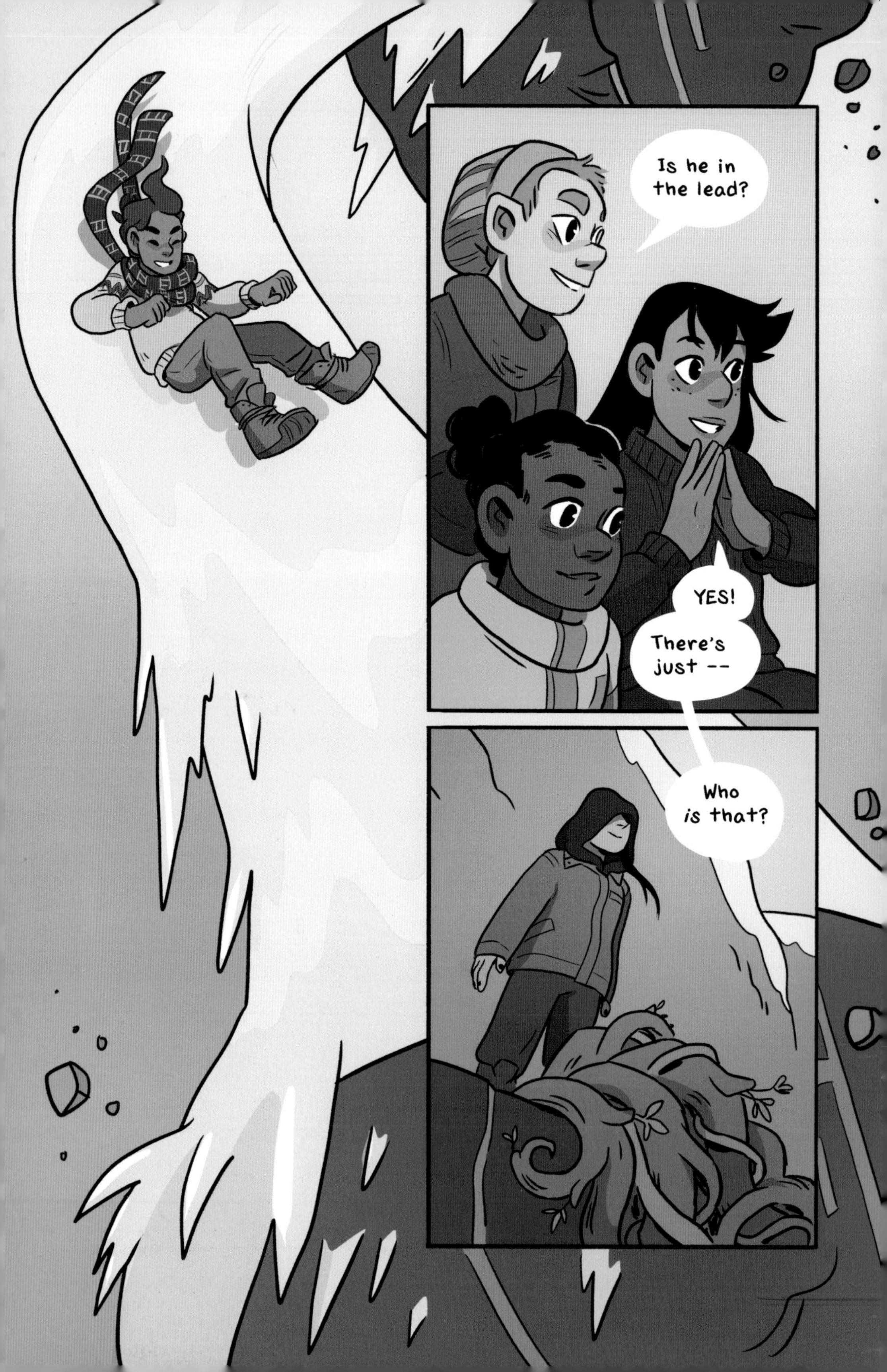
Is he in the lead?
YES!
There's just --
Who is that?

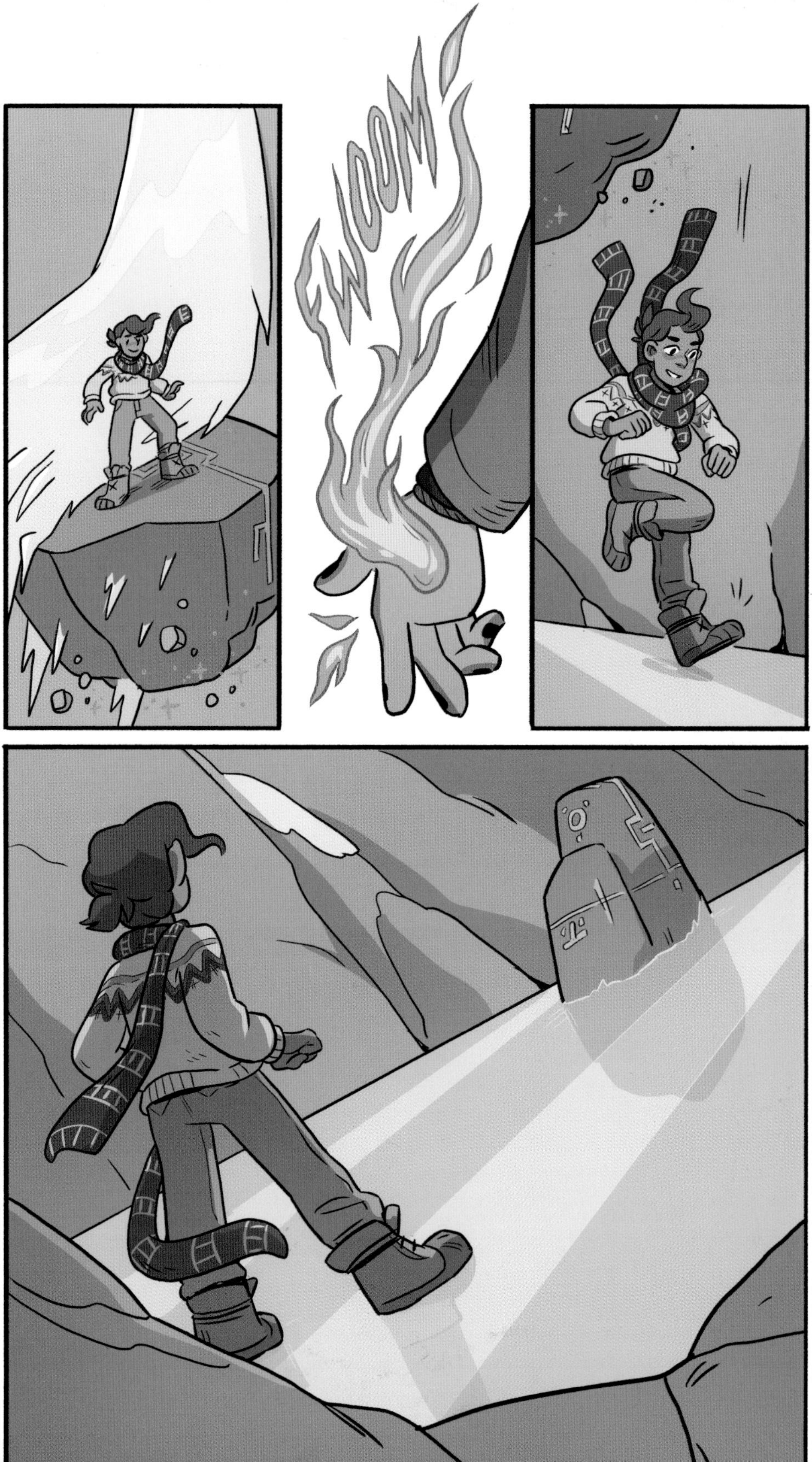
FWOOM!

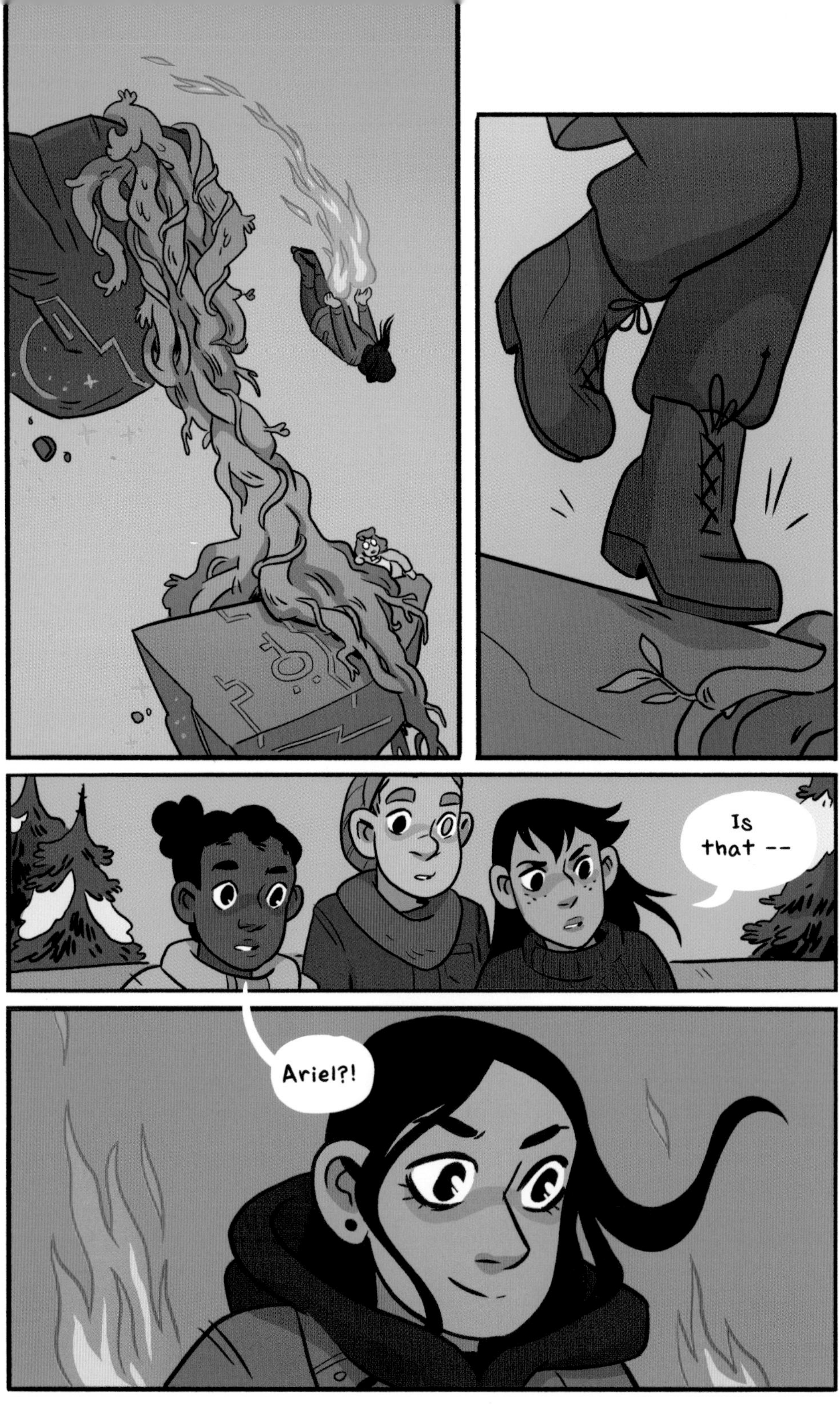
Is that --
Ariel?!

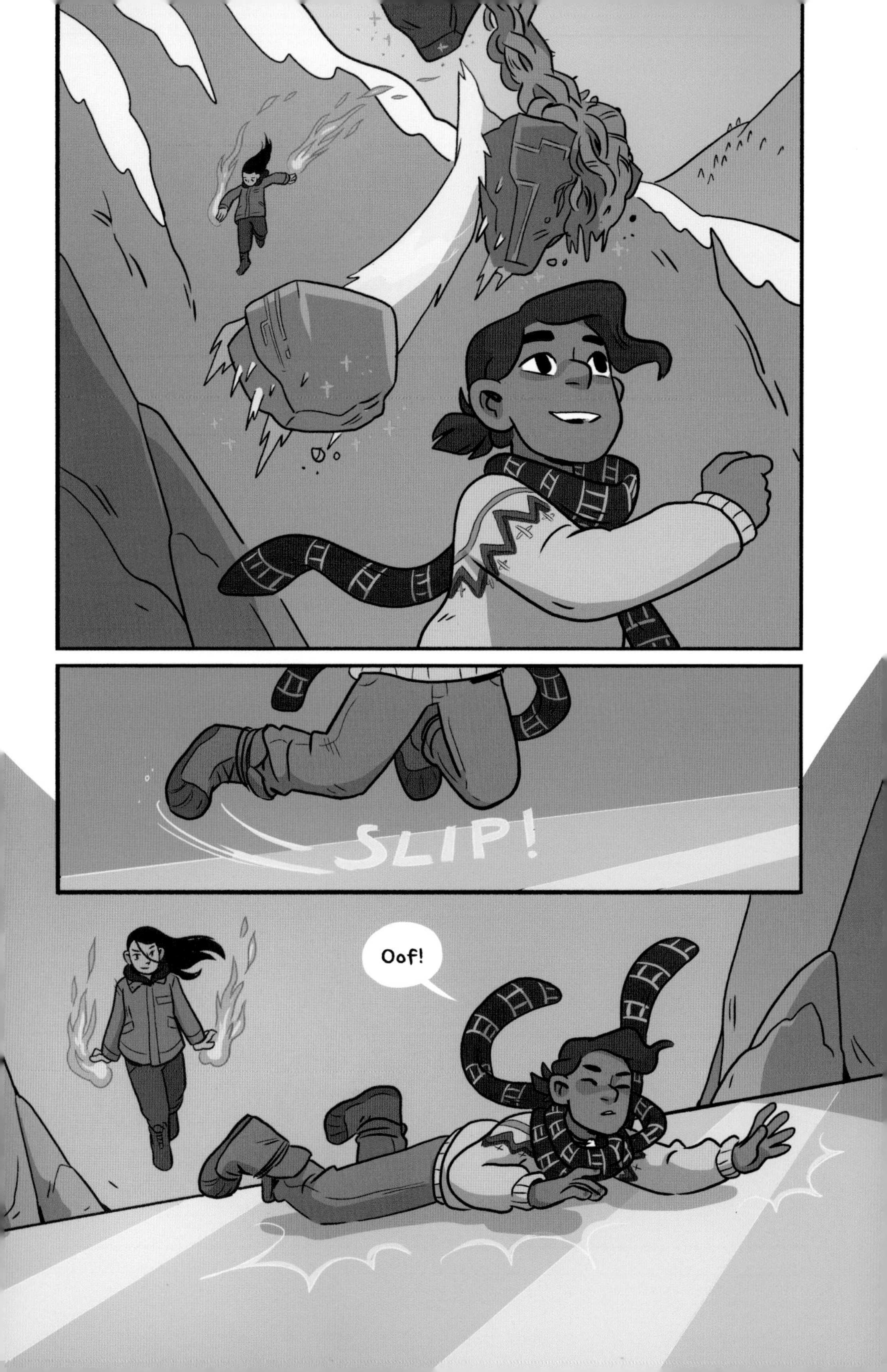
SLIP!
Oof!

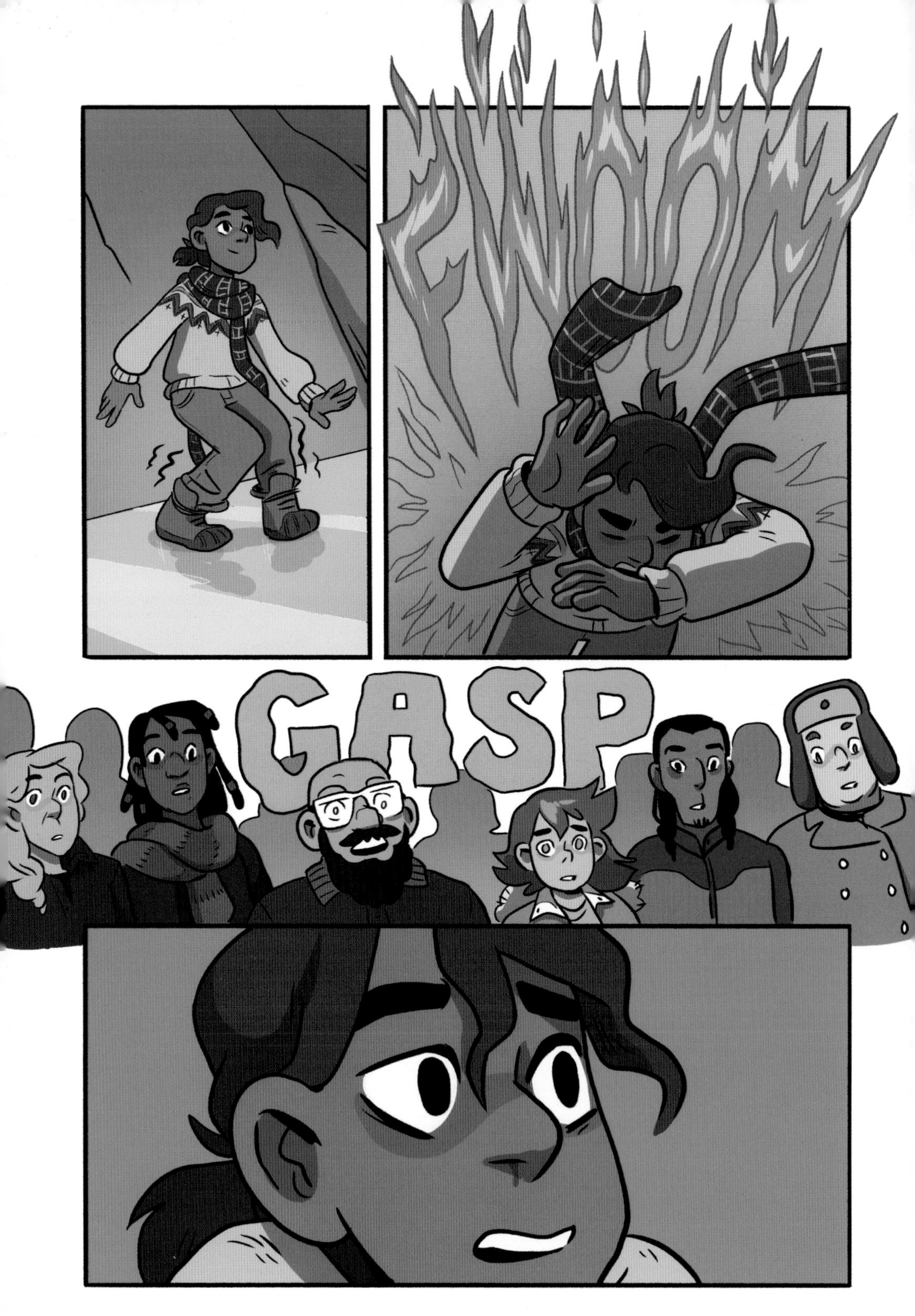
FWOOM
GASP

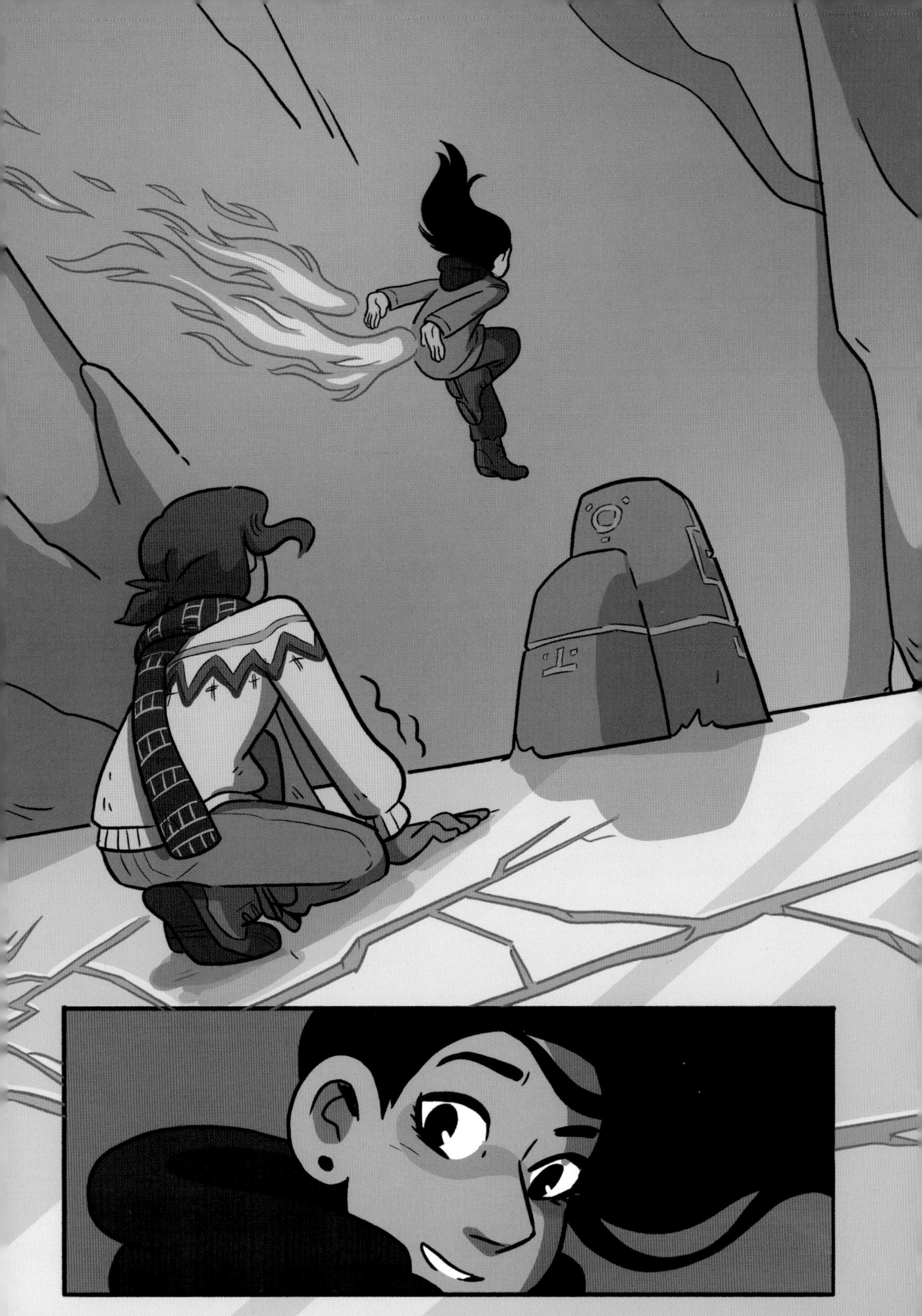

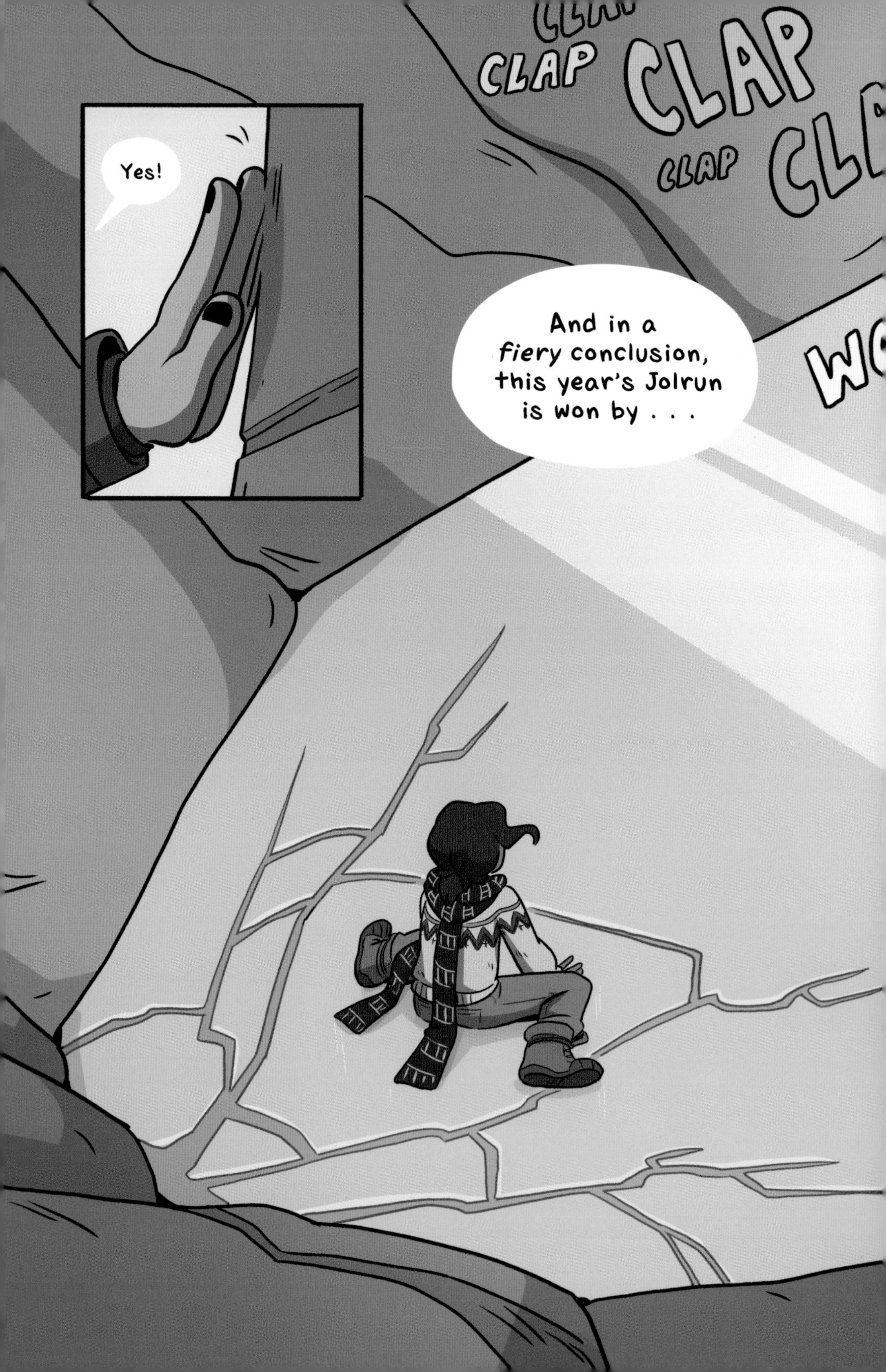
Yes!
CLAP CLAP
CLAP
And in a *fiery* conclusion, this year's Jolrun is won by . . .

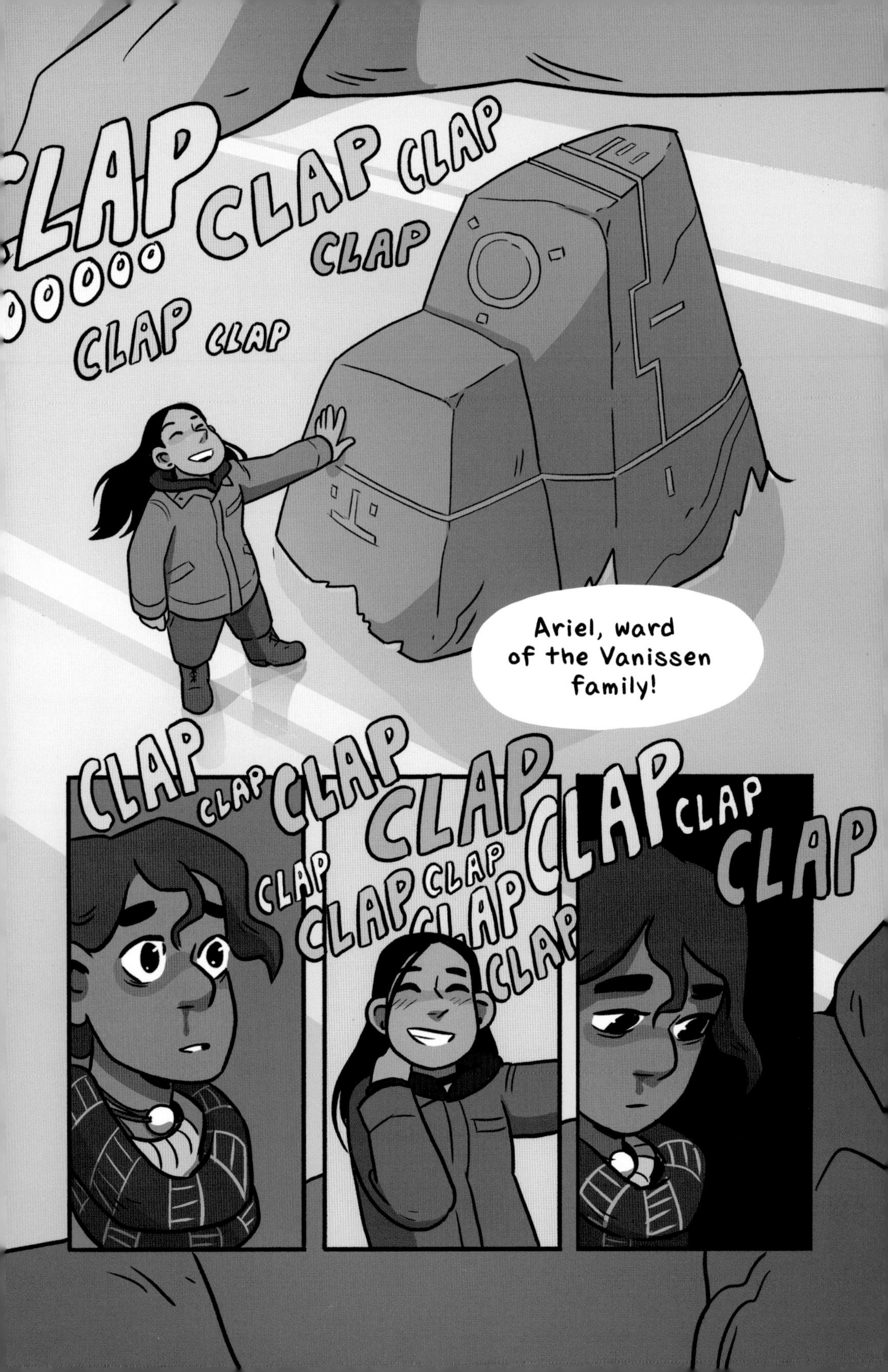
CLAP
OOOOOO
CLAP CLAP
CLAP
CLAP CLAP
Ariel, ward of the Vanissen family!
CLAP CLAP CLAP CLAP CLAP CLAP CLAP
CLAP CLAP CLAP CLAP CLAP CLAP CLAP

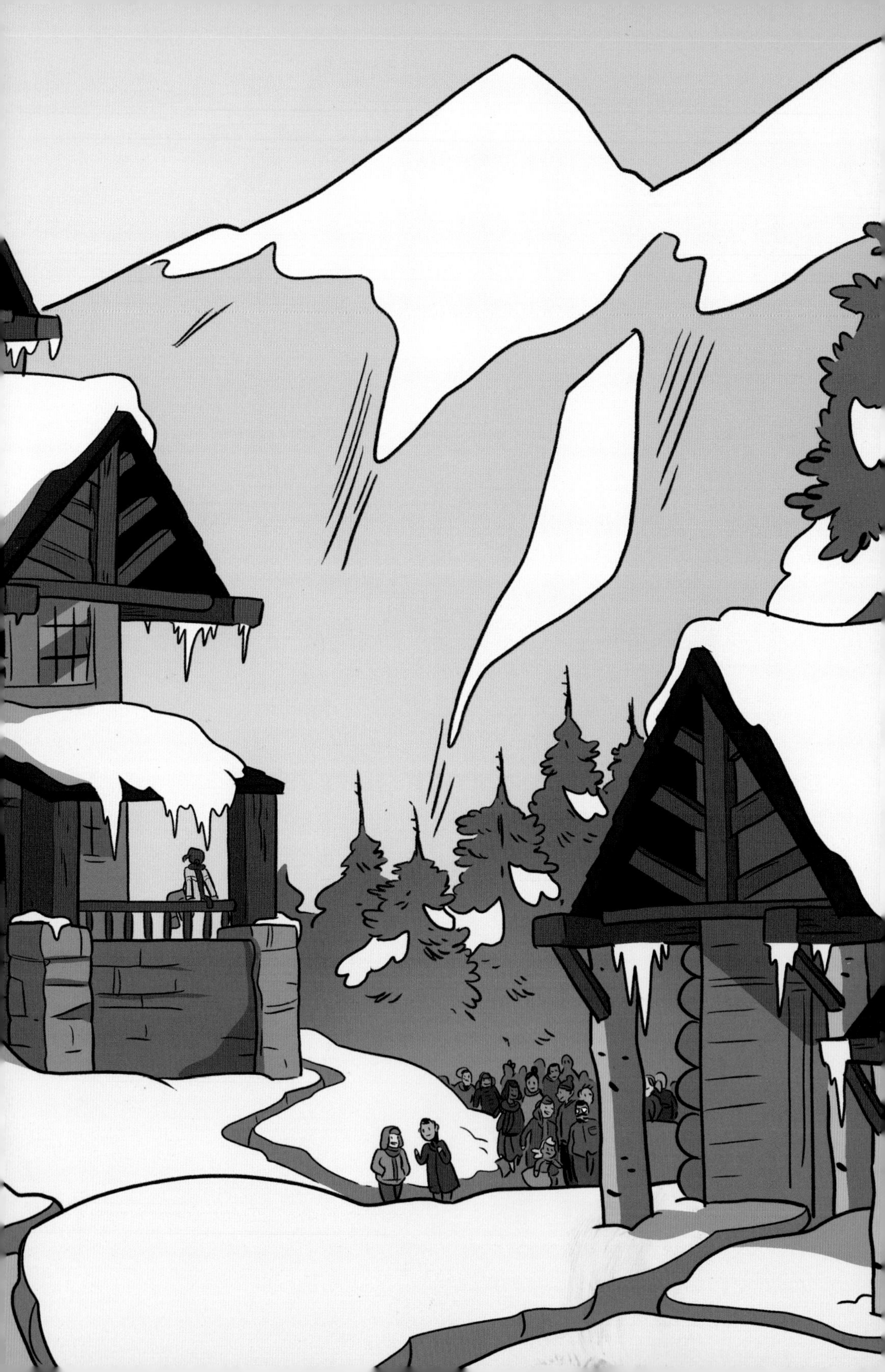

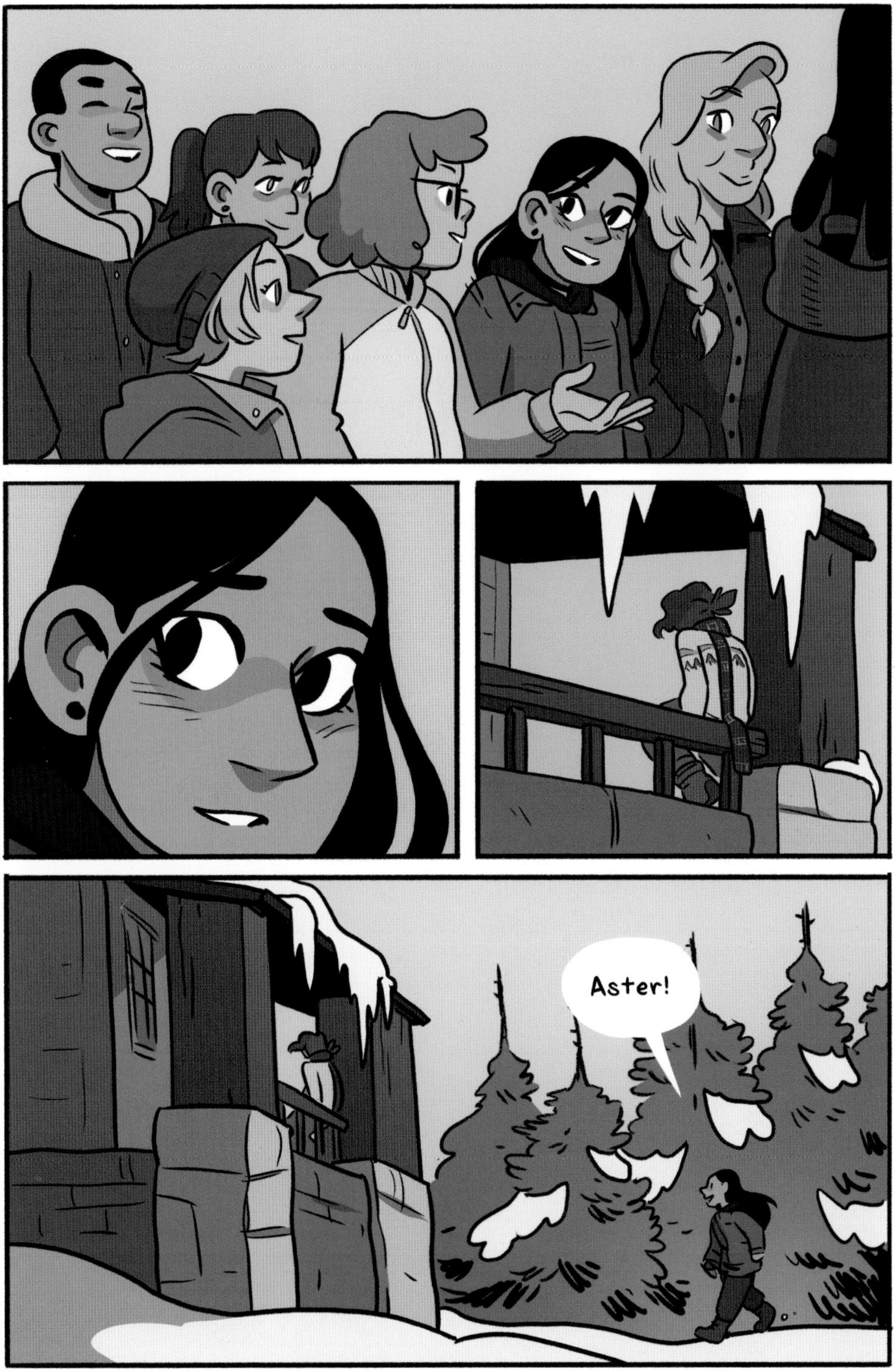
Aster!

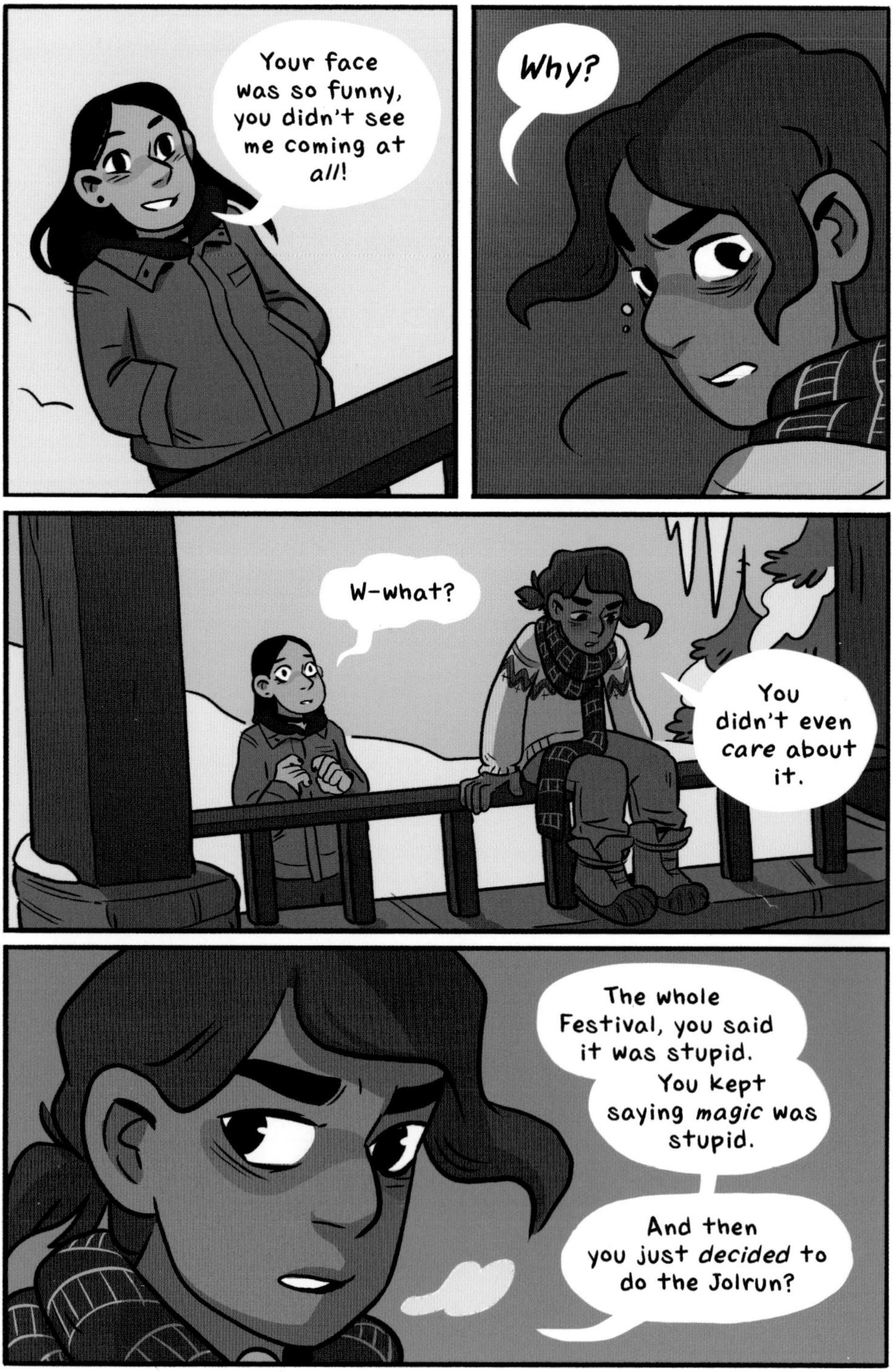
Your face was so funny, you didn't see me coming at *all*!
Why?
W-what?
You didn't even *care* about it.
The whole Festival, you said it was stupid.
You kept saying *magic* was stupid.
And then you just *decided* to do the Jolrun?

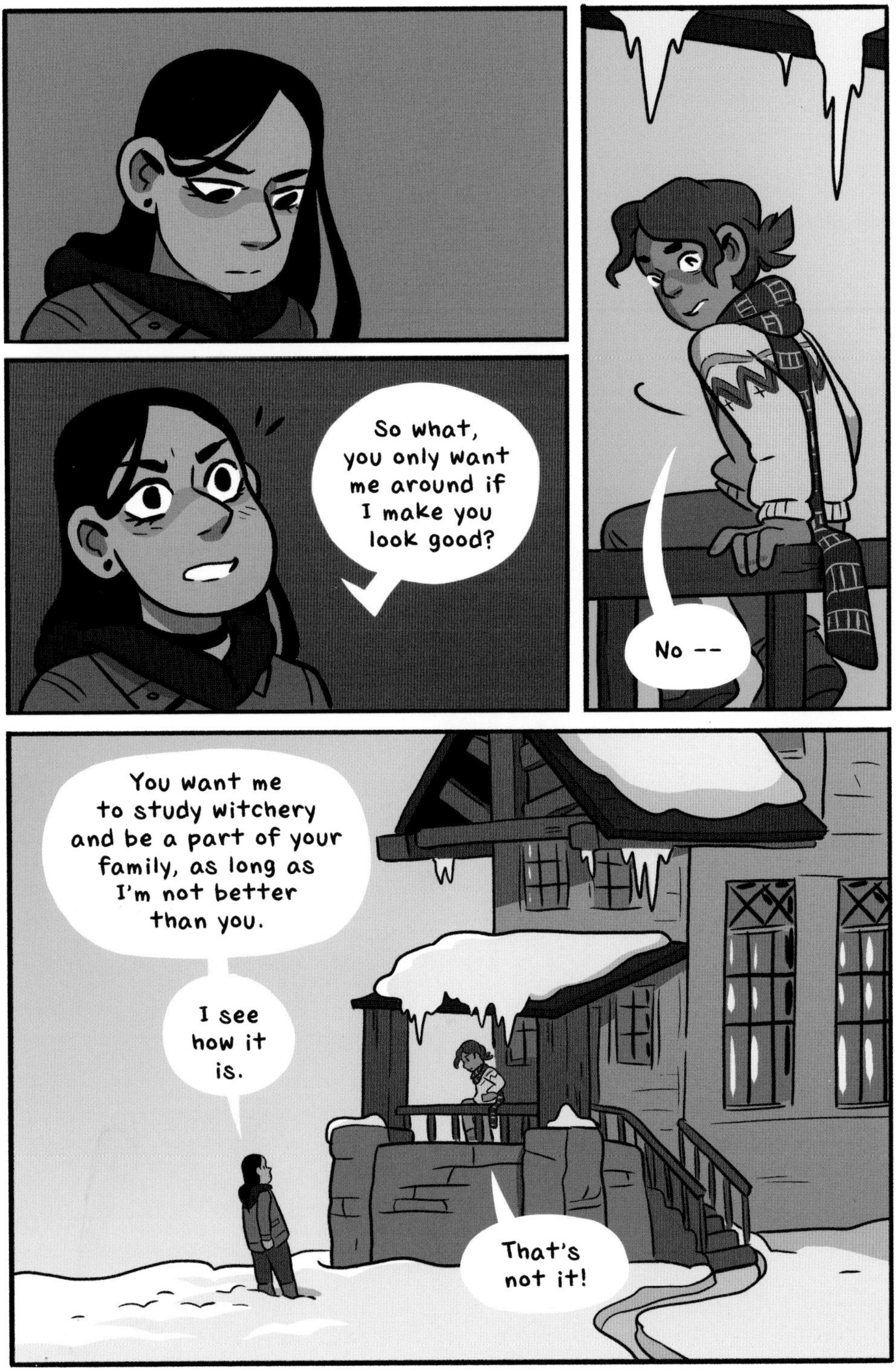
So what, you only want me around if I make you look good?
No --
You want me to study witchery and be a part of your family, as long as I'm not better than you.
I see how it is.
That's not it!

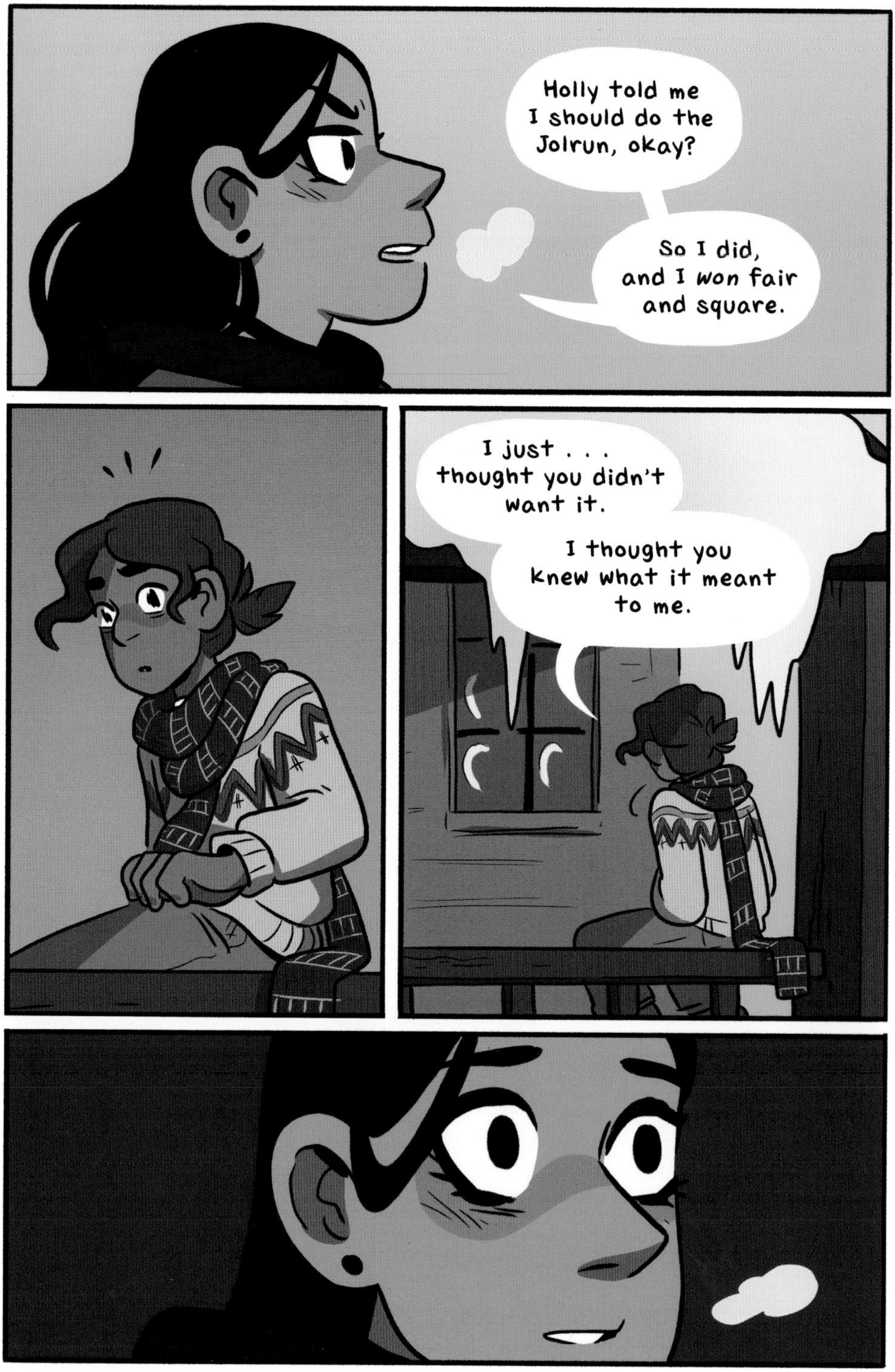
Holly told me I should do the Jolrun, okay?
So I did, and I *won* fair and square.
I just . . . thought you didn't want it.
I thought you knew what it meant to me.

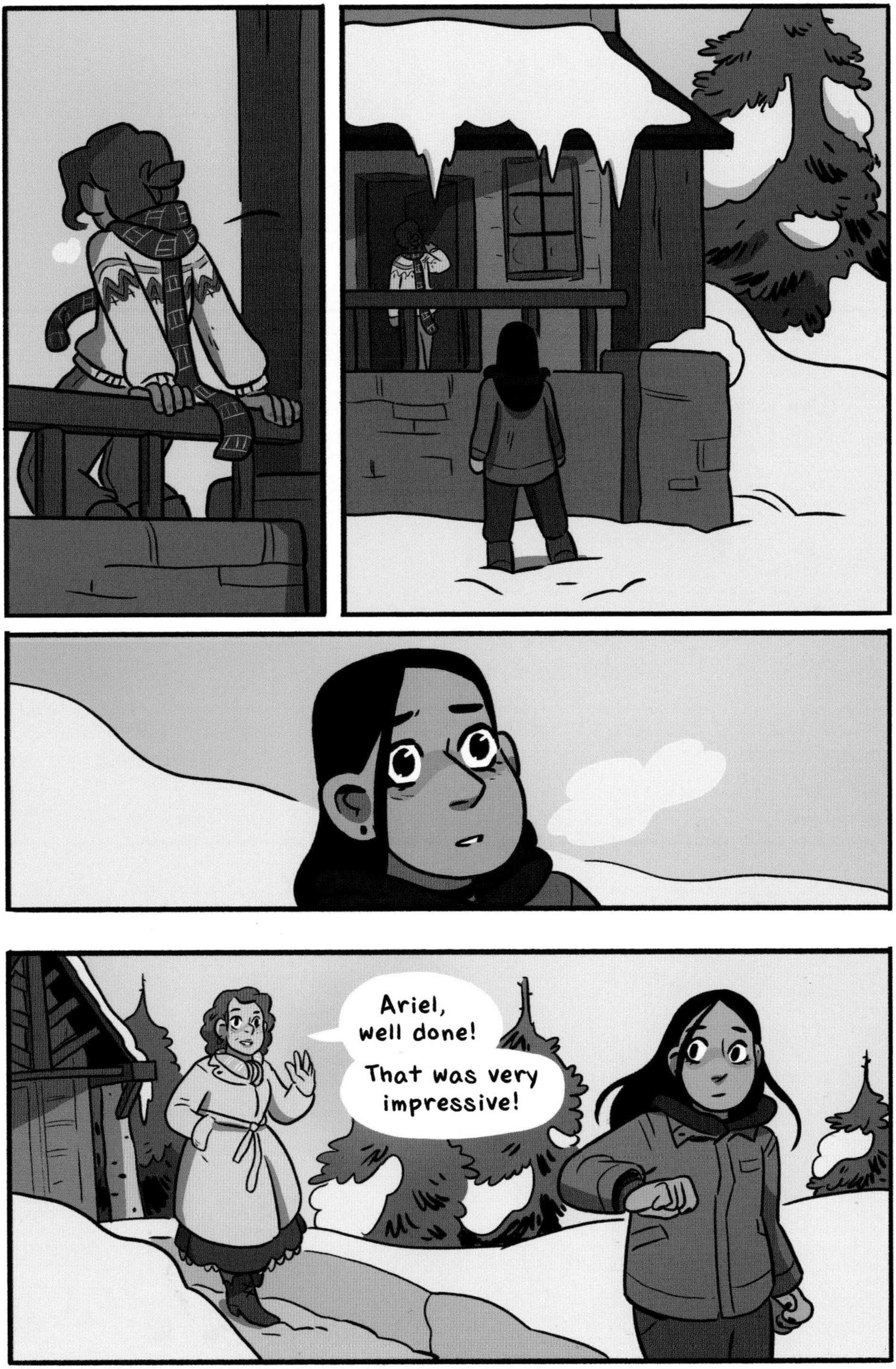
Ariel, well done!
That was very impressive!

What do you want?

What's wrong, sweetheart?

You're *not* my mom, Holly, so just *leave* me alone!

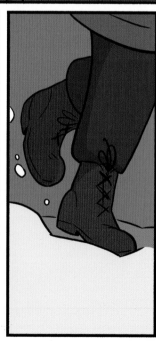

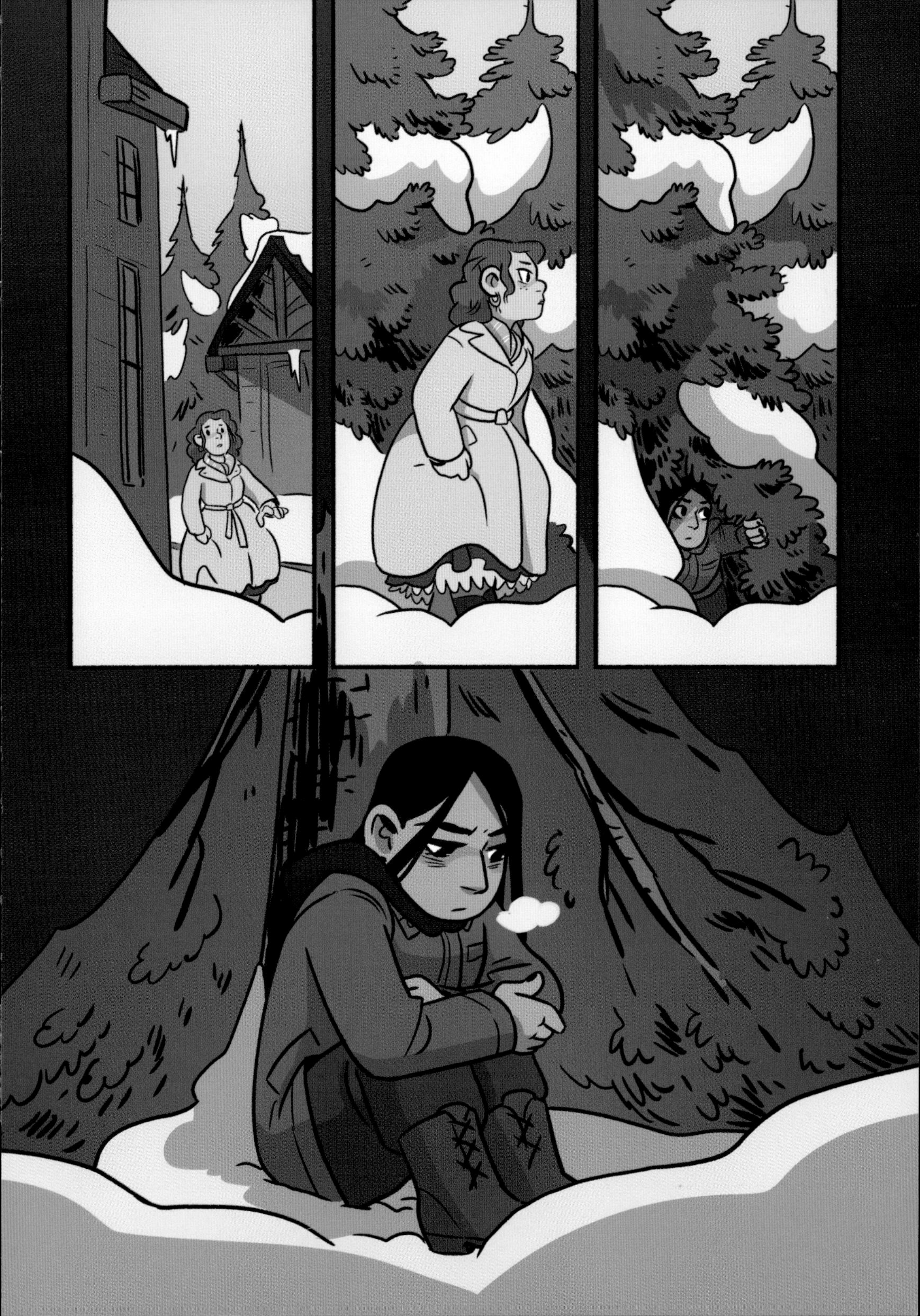

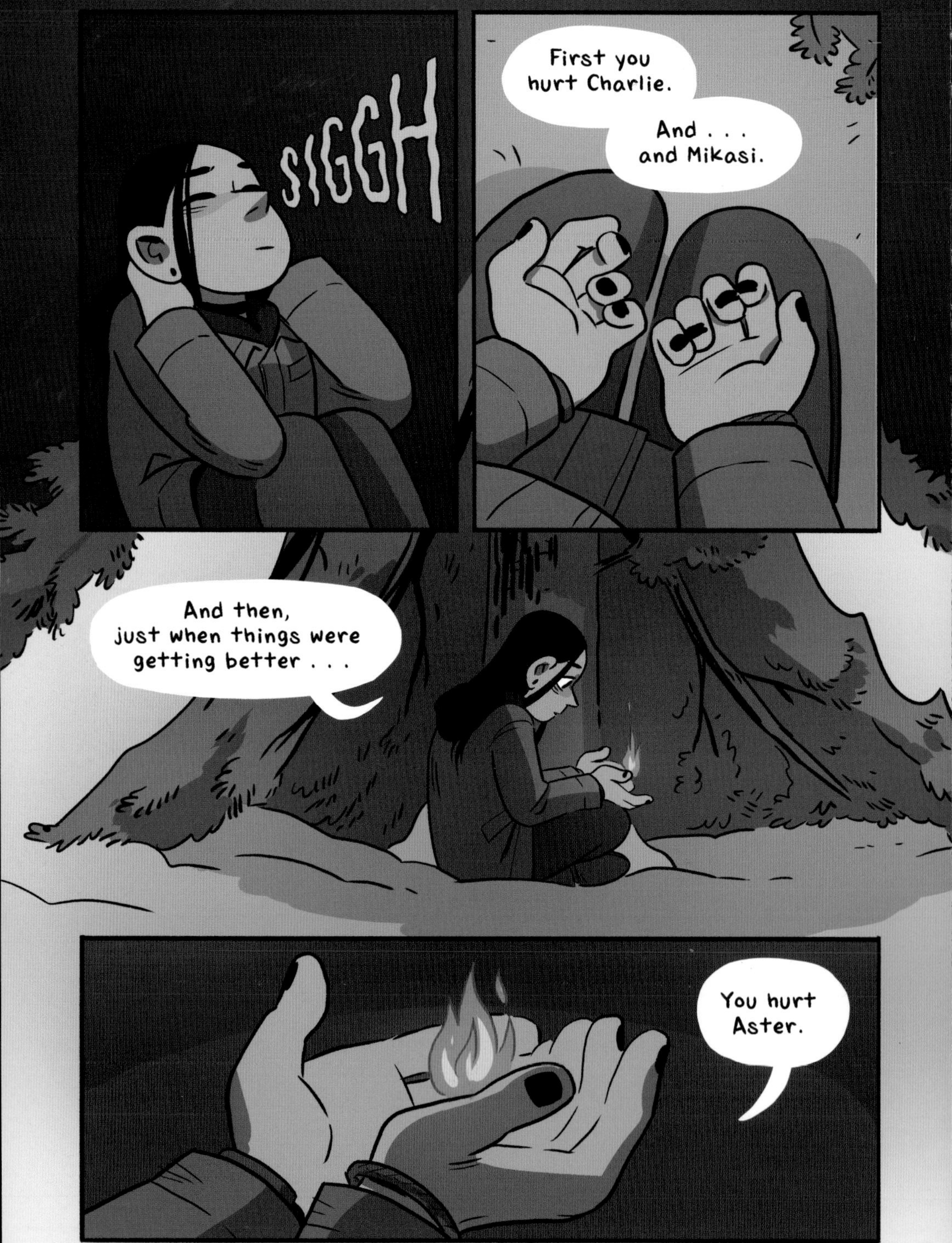
SIGGH
First you hurt Charlie.
And . . . and Mikasi.
And then, just when things were getting better . . .
You hurt Aster.

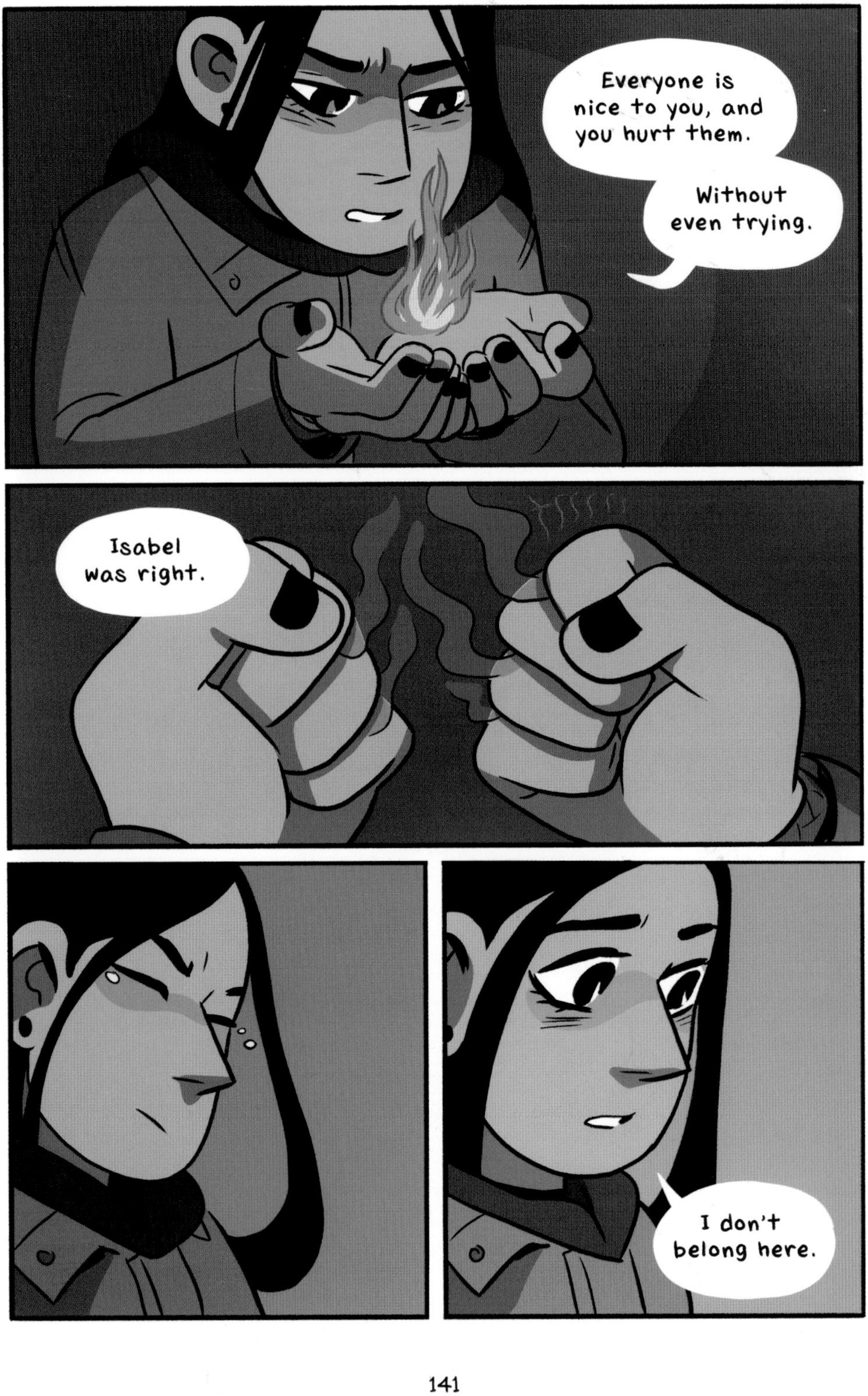
Everyone is nice to you, and you hurt them.
Without even trying.
Isabel was right.
I don't belong here.

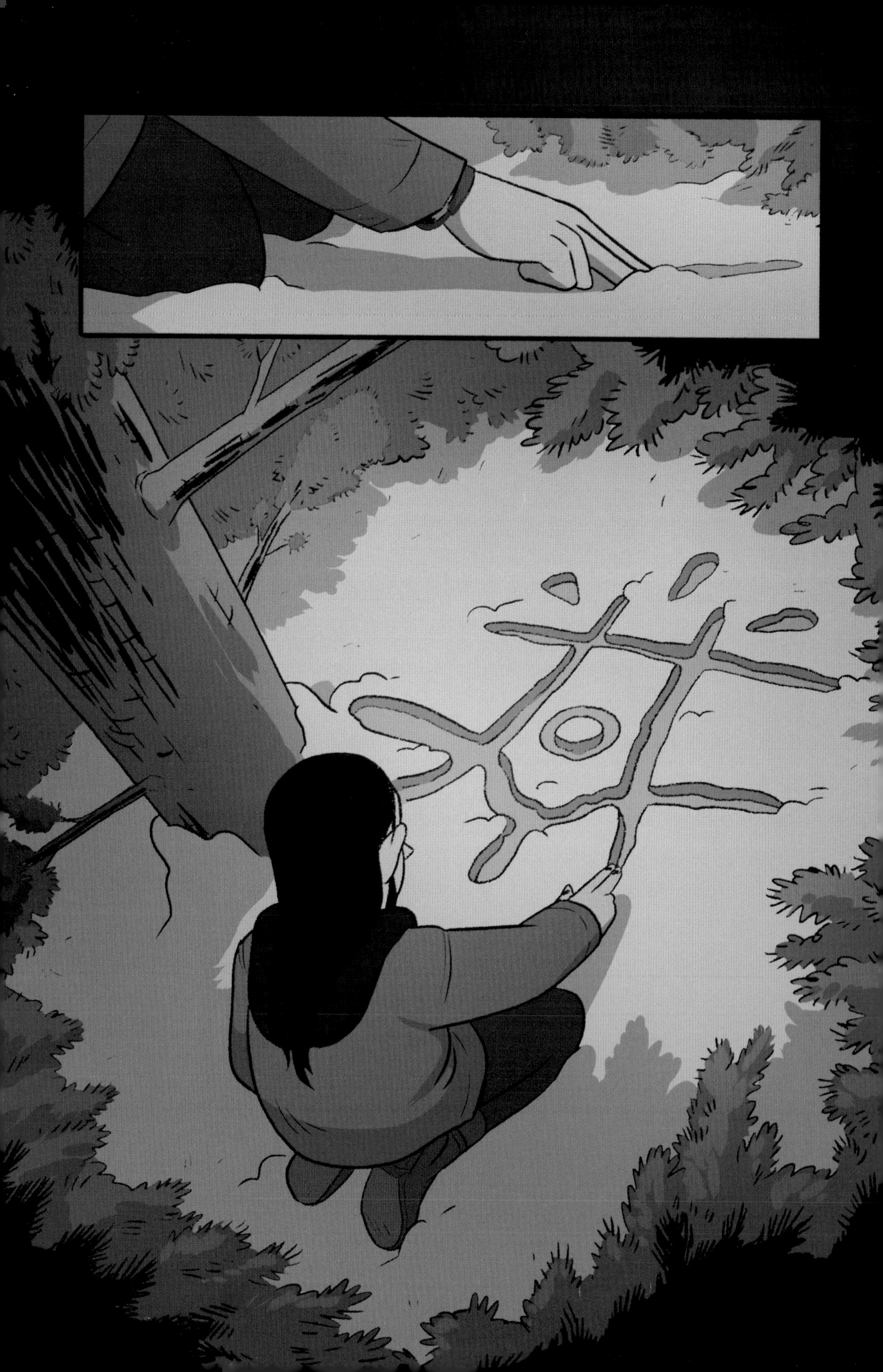

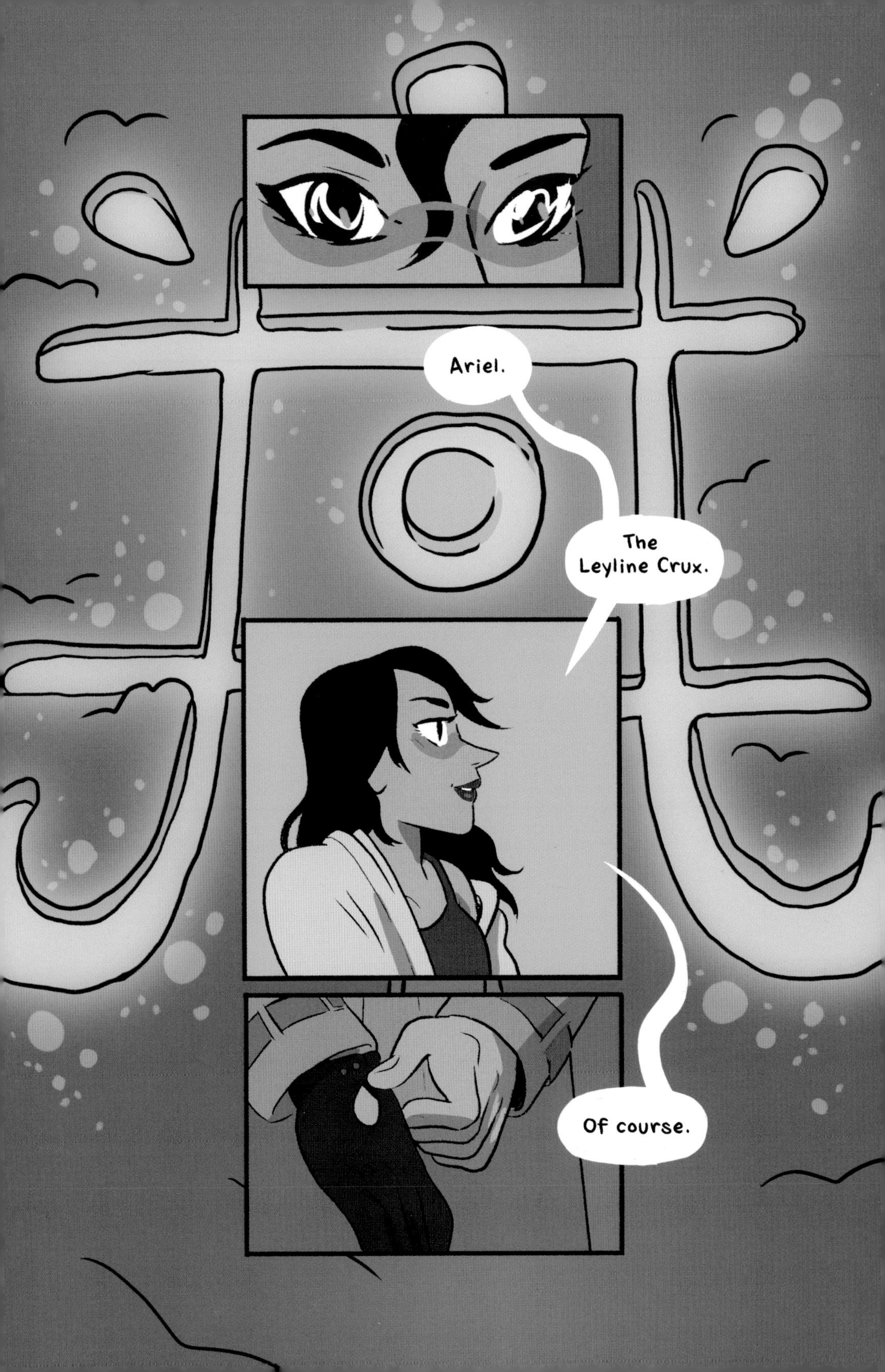
Ariel.
The Leyline Crux.
Of course.

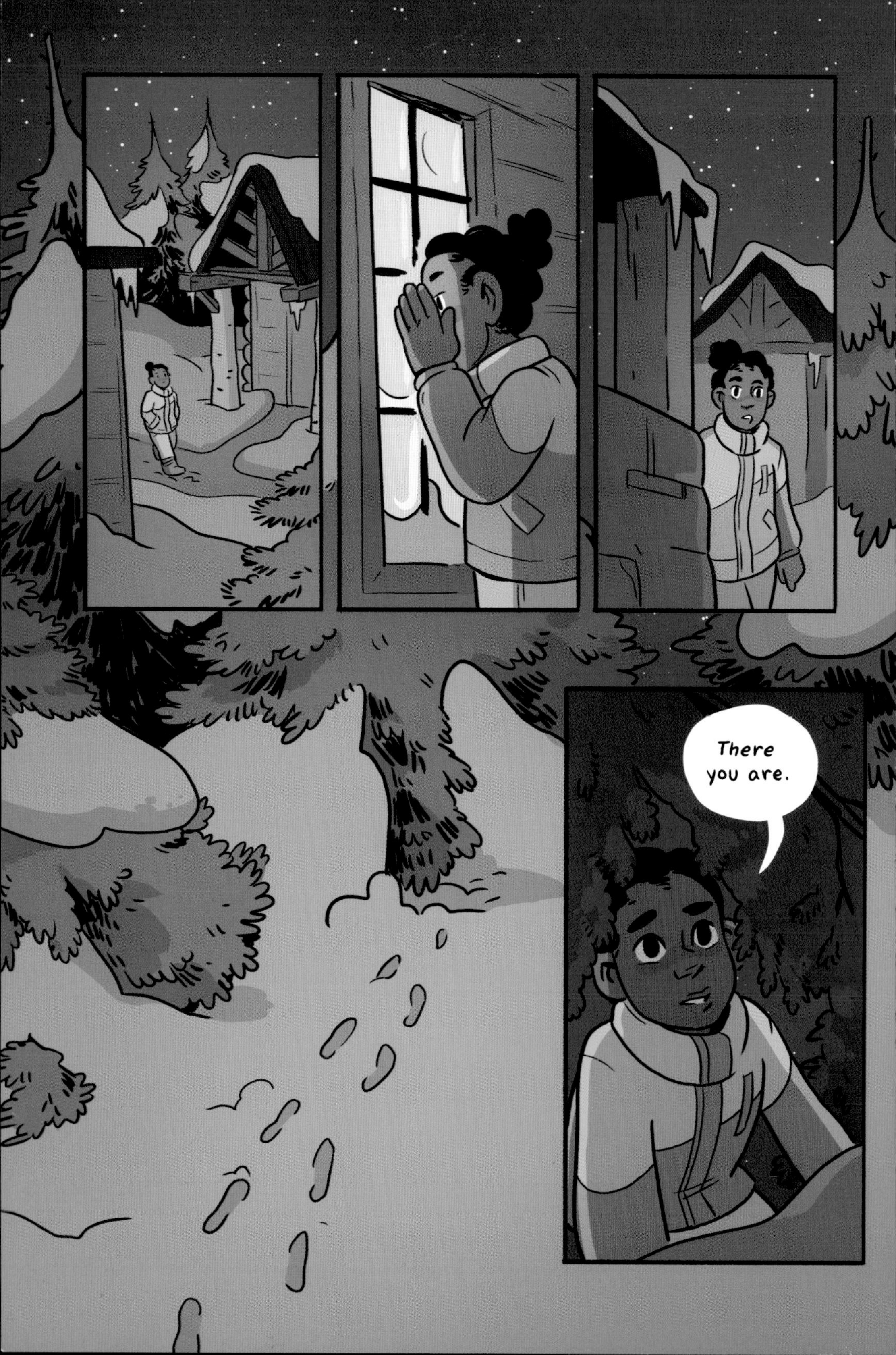
There you are.

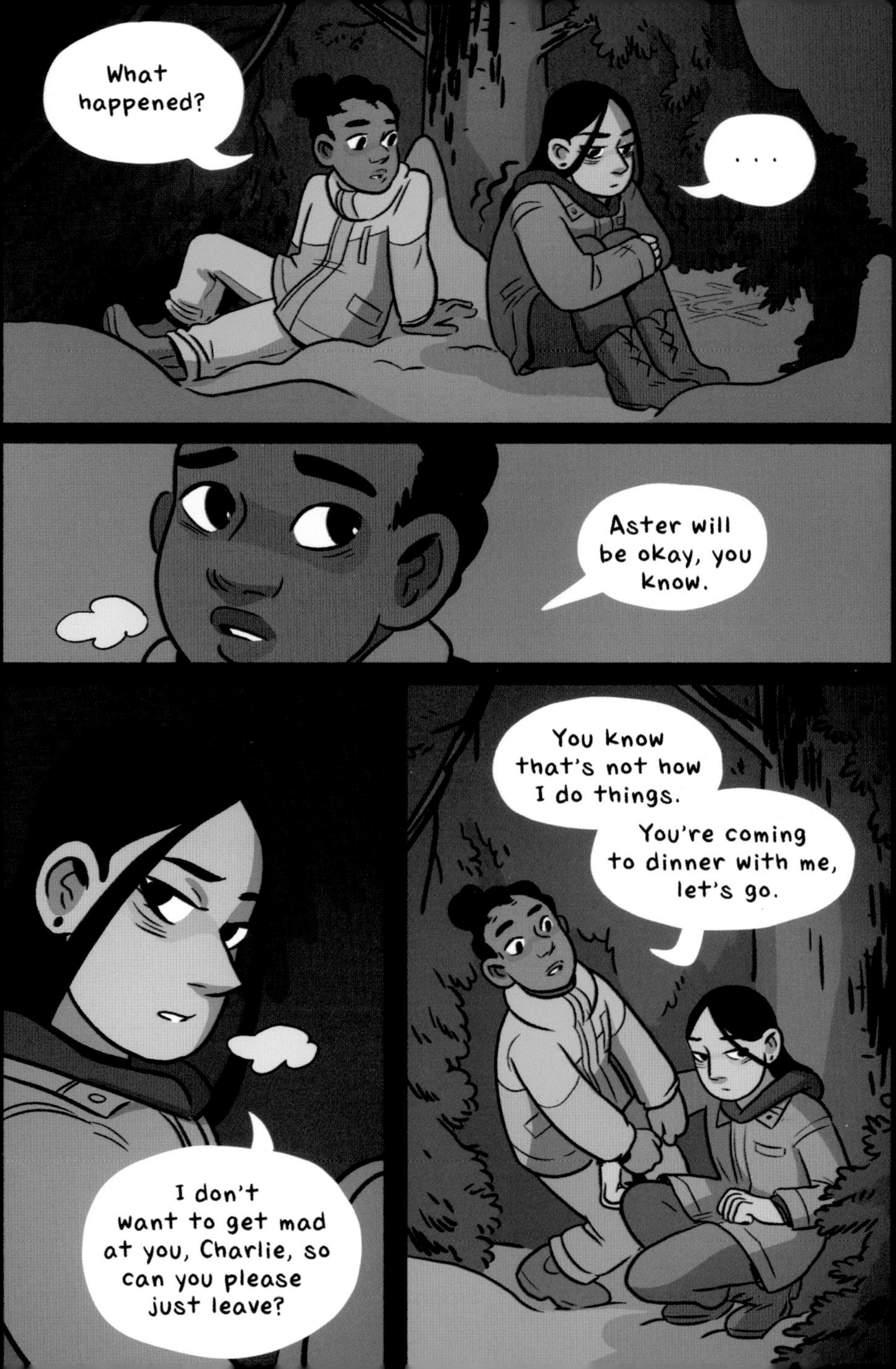
What happened?
. . .
Aster will be okay, you know.
I don't want to get mad at you, Charlie, so can you please just leave?
You know that's not how I do things.
You're coming to dinner with me, let's go.

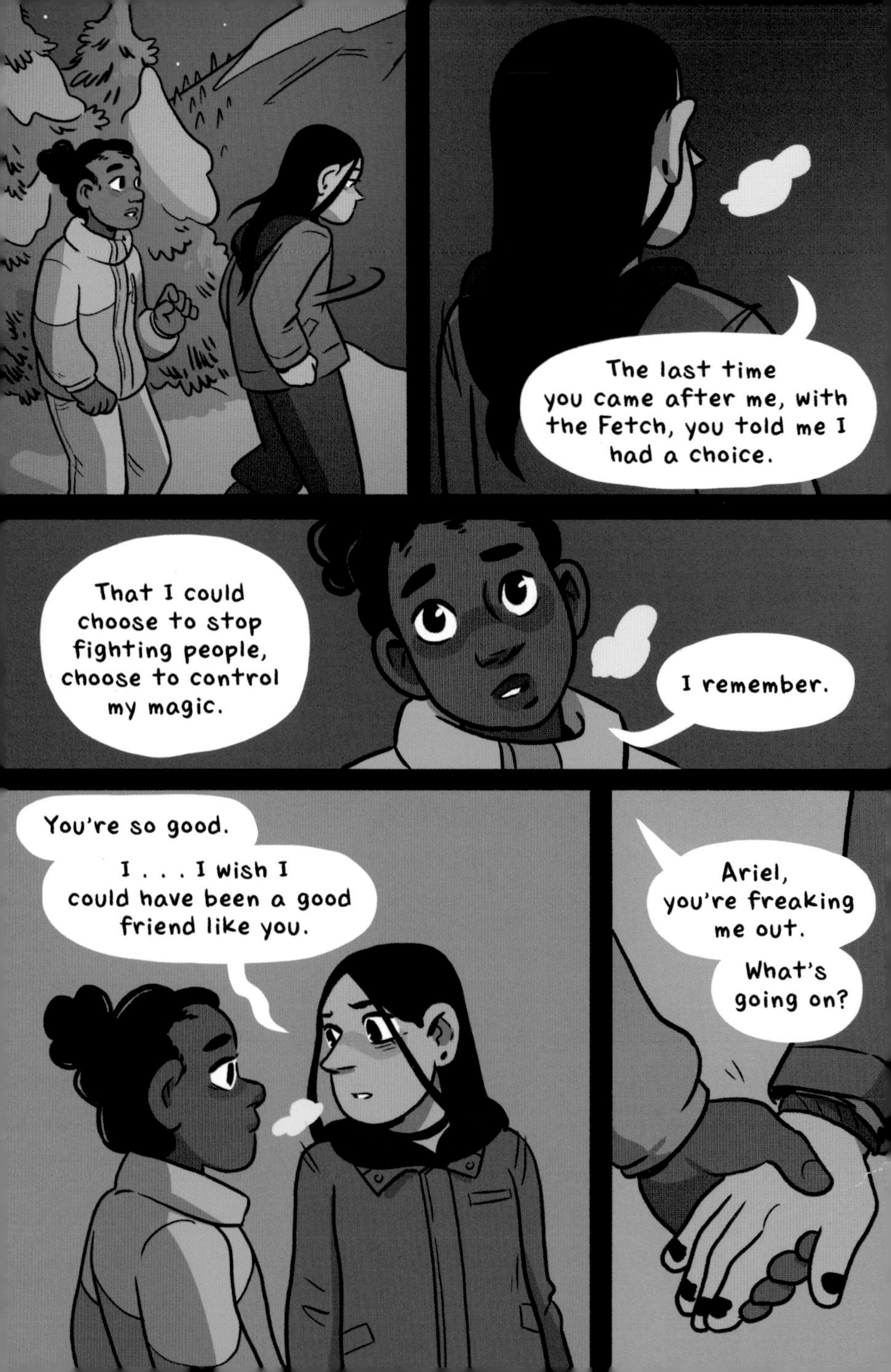
The last time you came after me, with the Fetch, you told me I had a choice.
That I could choose to stop fighting people, choose to control my magic.
I remember.
You're so good.
I . . . I wish I could have been a good friend like you.
Ariel, you're freaking me out.
What's going on?

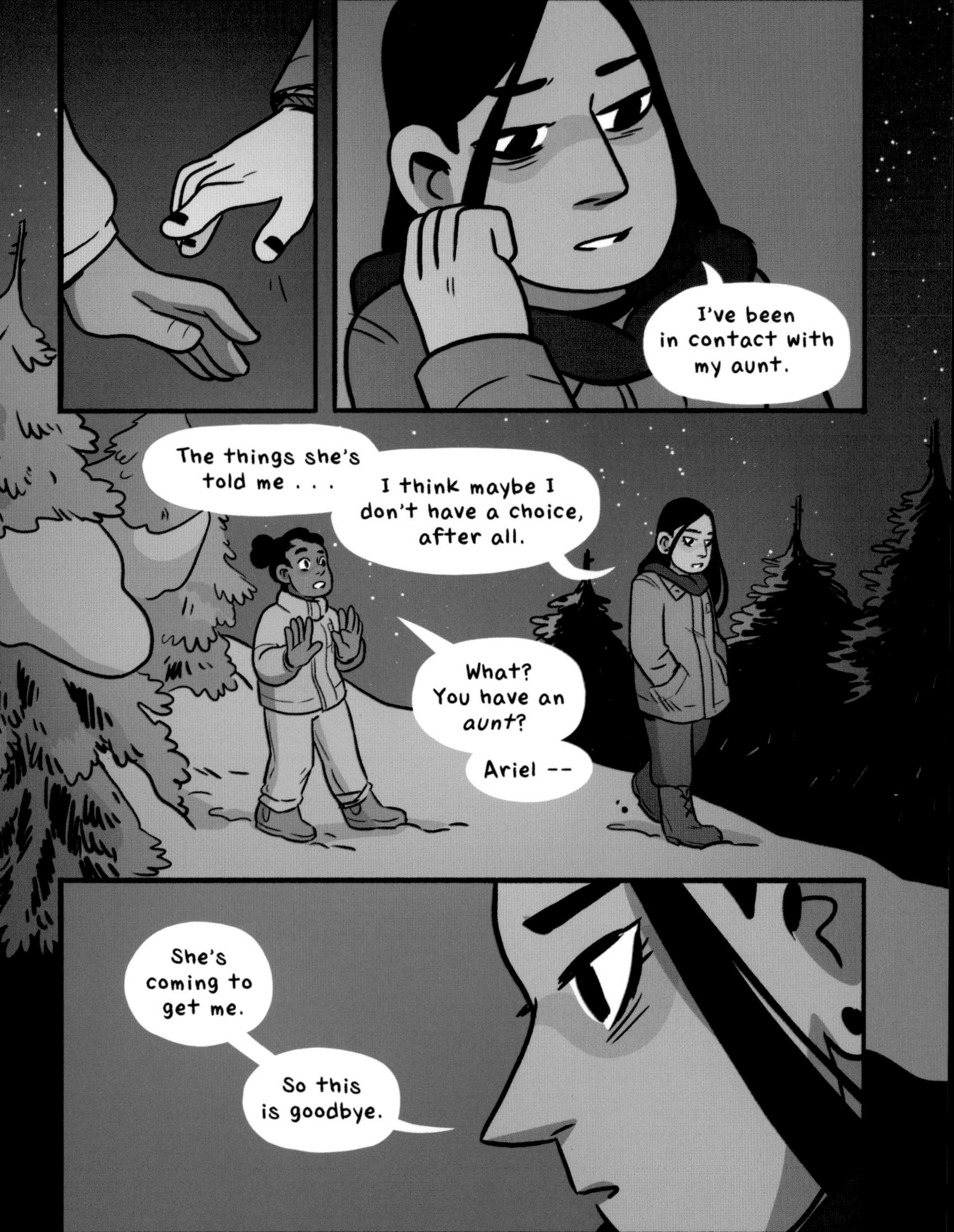
I've been in contact with my aunt.
The things she's told me . . .
I think maybe I don't have a choice, after all.
What? You have an *aunt*?
Ariel --
She's coming to get me.
So this is goodbye.

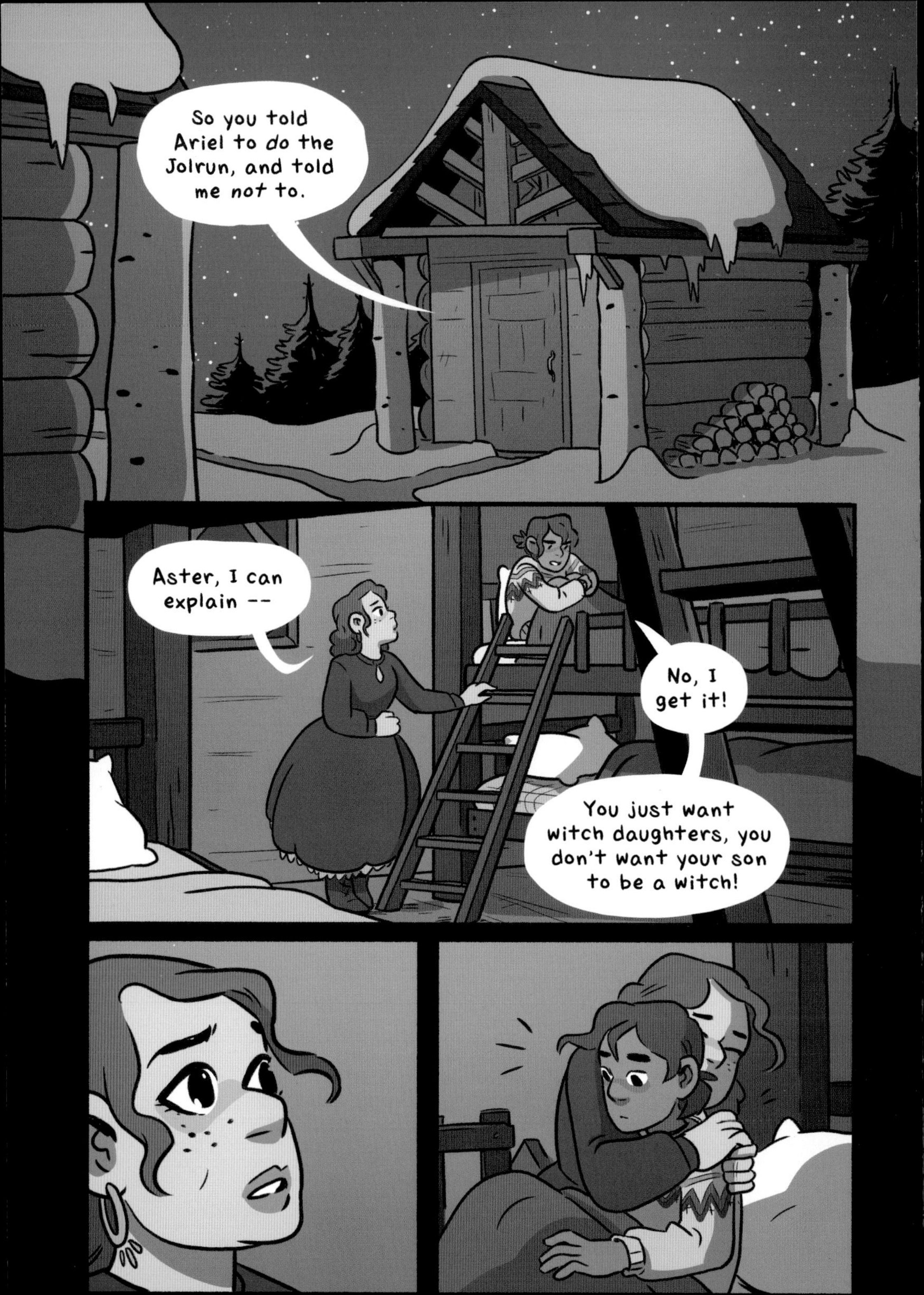
So you told Ariel to *do* the Jolrun, and told me *not* to.
Aster, I can explain --
No, I get it!
You just want witch daughters, you don't want your son to be a witch!

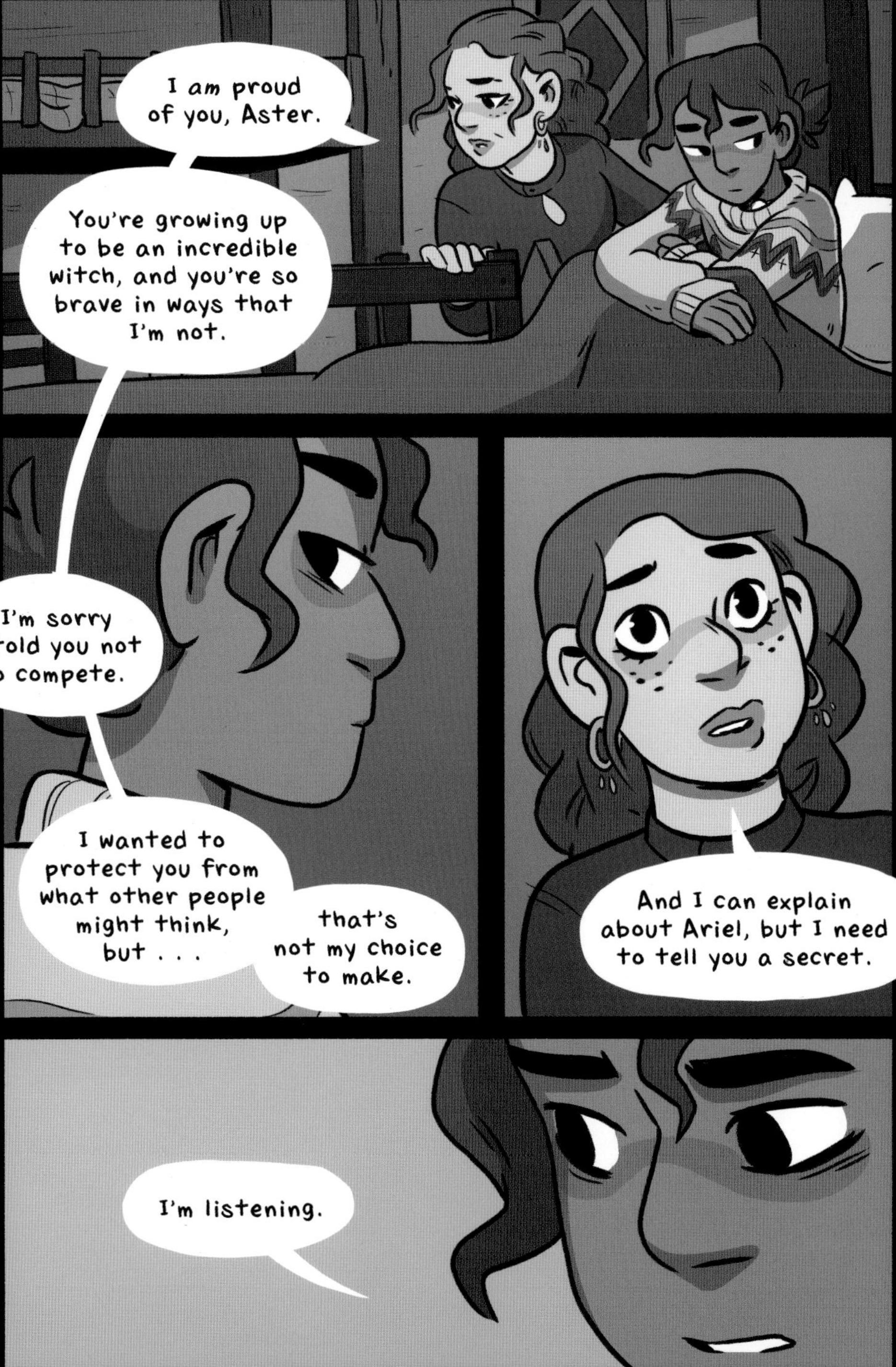
I am proud of you, Aster.
You're growing up to be an incredible witch, and you're so brave in ways that I'm not.
I'm sorry I told you not to compete.
I wanted to protect you from what other people might think, but . . .
that's not my choice to make.
And I can explain about Ariel, but I need to tell you a secret.
I'm listening.

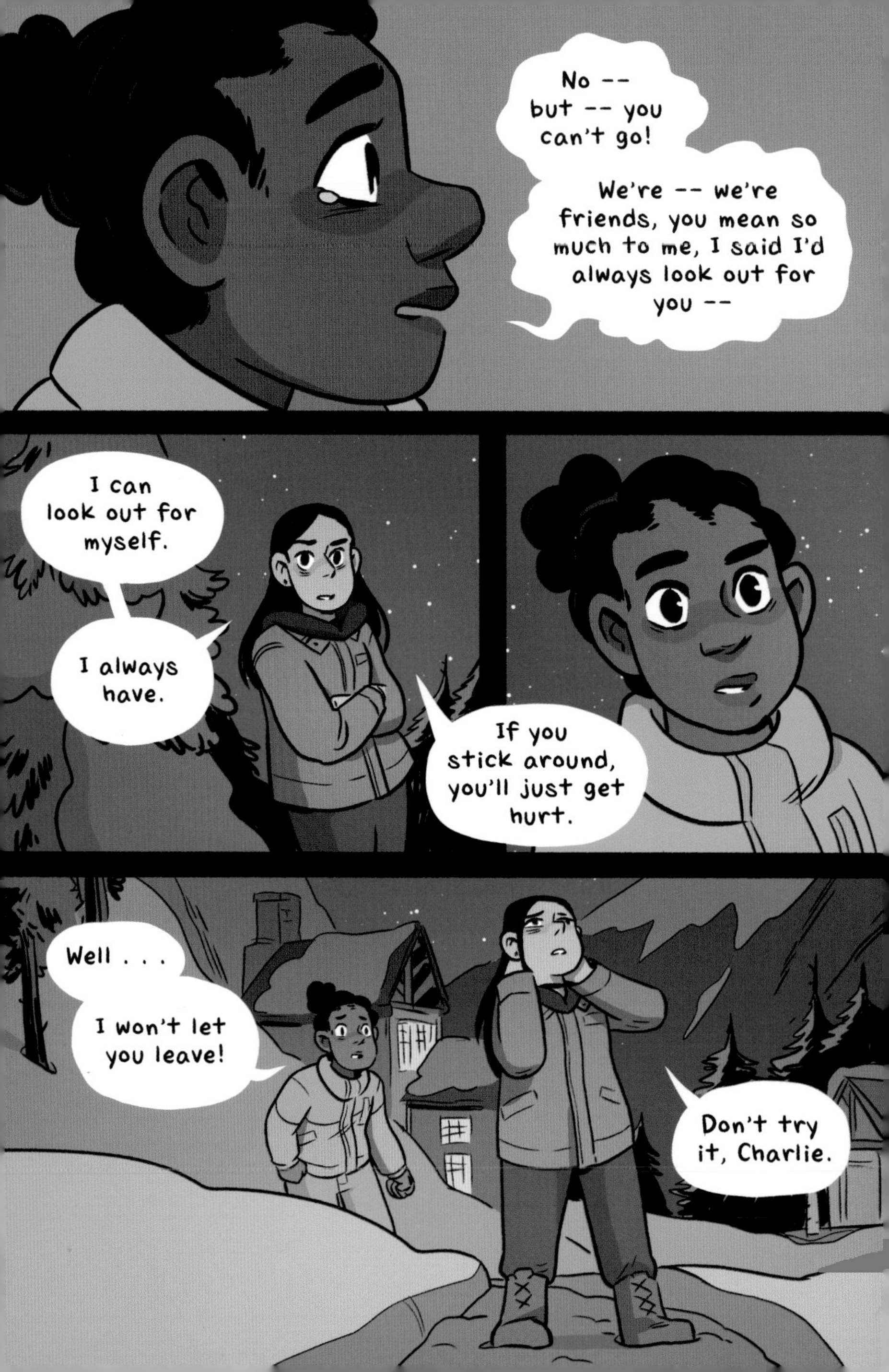
No -- but -- you can't go!
We're -- we're friends, you mean so much to me, I said I'd always look out for you --
I can look out for myself.
I always have.
If you stick around, you'll just get hurt.
Well . . .
I won't let you leave!
Don't try it, Charlie.

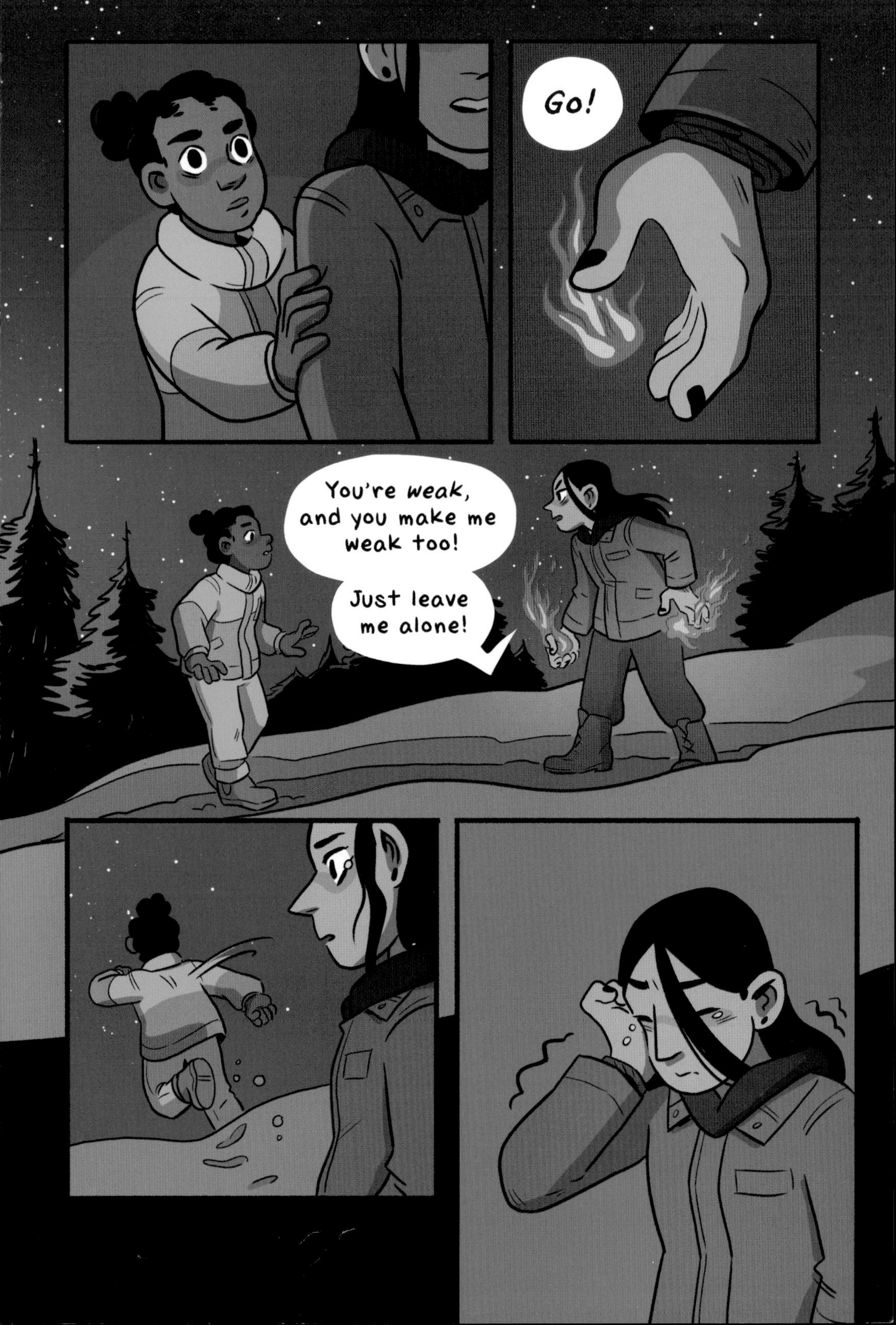
Go!
You're weak, and you make me weak too!
Just leave me alone!

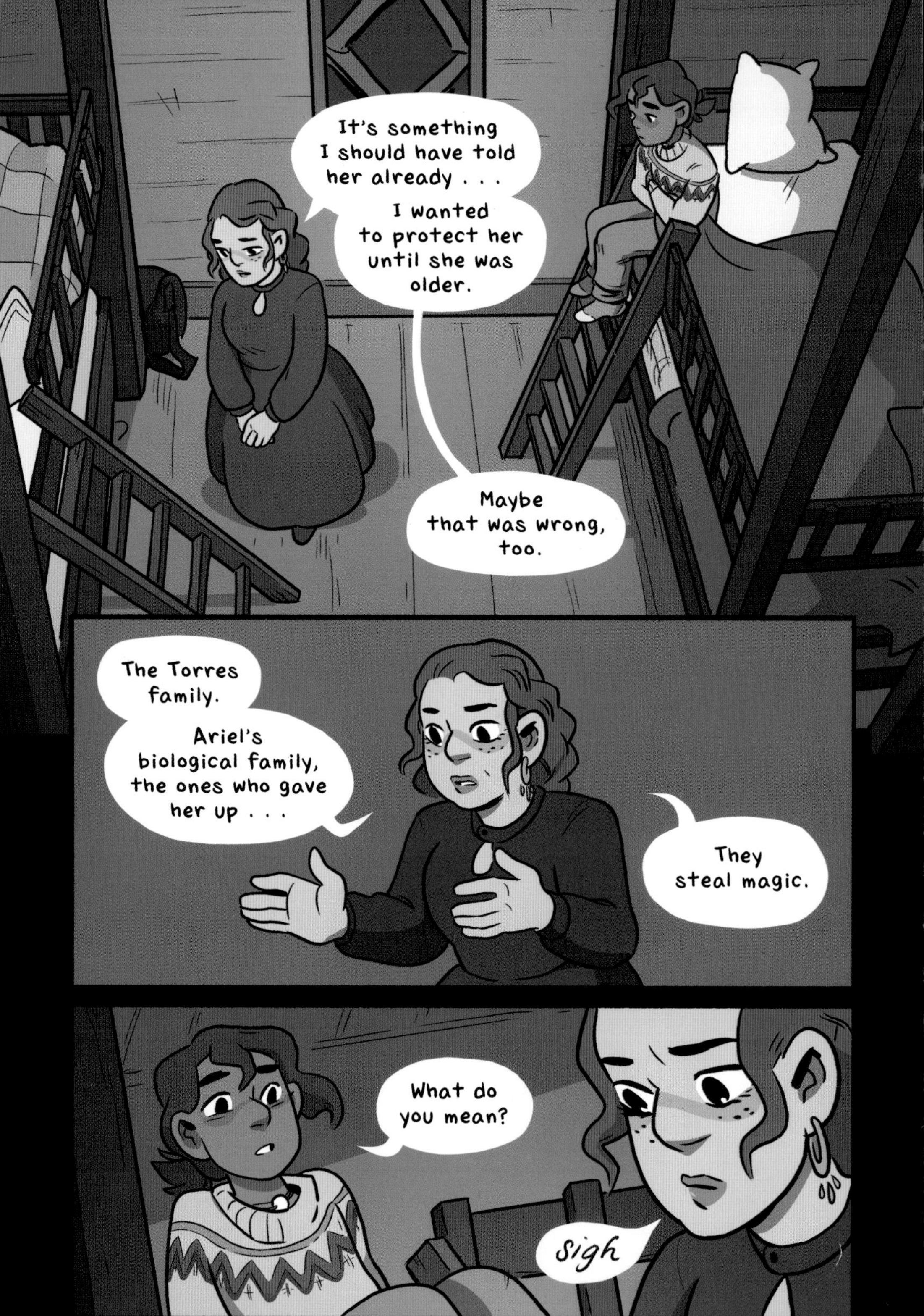
It's something I should have told her already . . .
I wanted to protect her until she was older.
Maybe that was wrong, too.
The Torres family.
Ariel's biological family, the ones who gave her up . . .
They steal magic.
What do you mean?
sigh

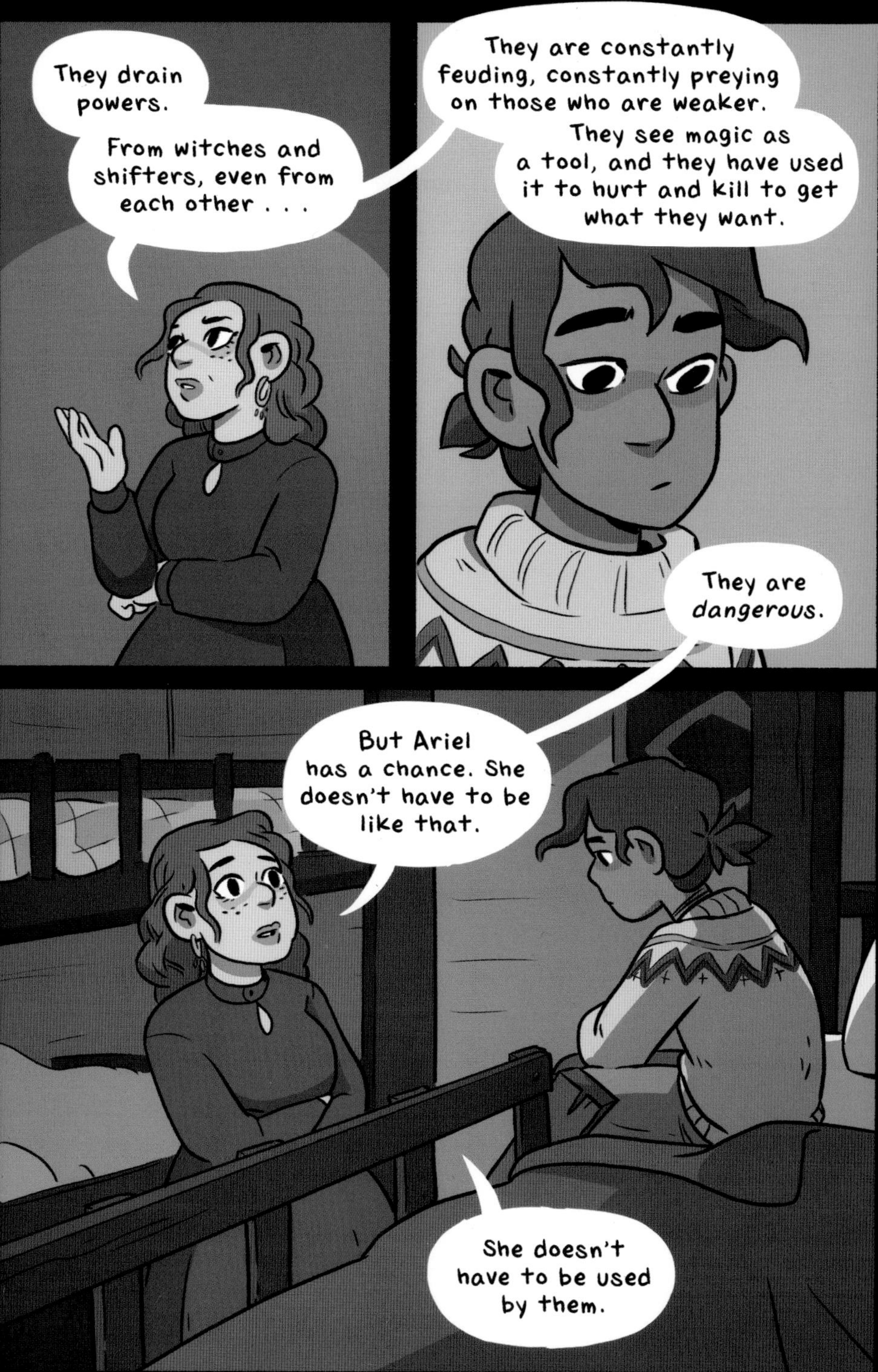
They drain powers.
From witches and shifters, even from each other . . .
They are constantly feuding, constantly preying on those who are weaker.
They see magic as a tool, and they have used it to hurt and kill to get what they want.
They are *dangerous.*
But Ariel has a chance. She doesn't have to be like that.
She doesn't have to be used by them.

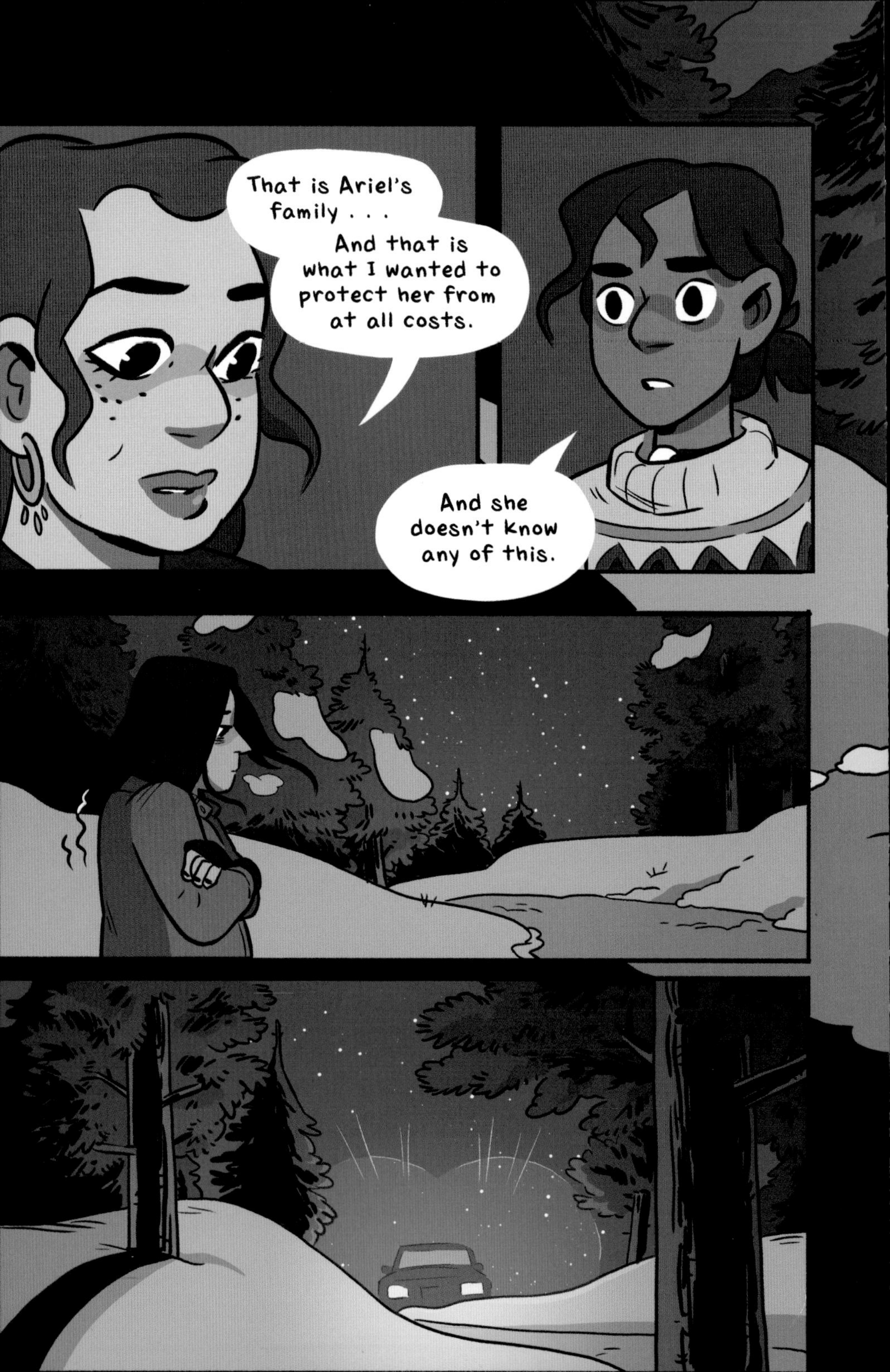

That is Ariel's family . . .
And that is what I wanted to protect her from at all costs.
And she doesn't know any of this.

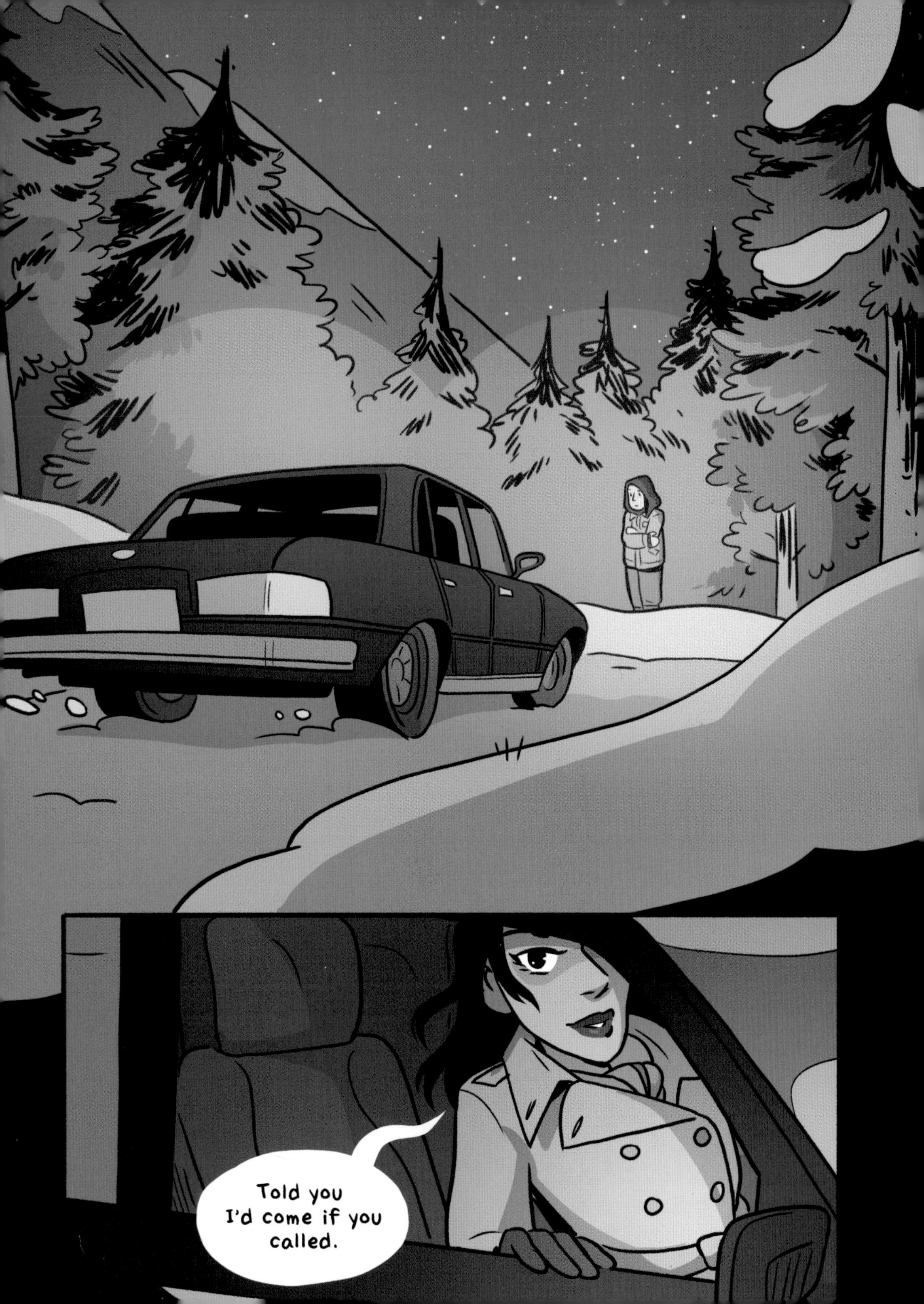
Told you I'd come if you called.

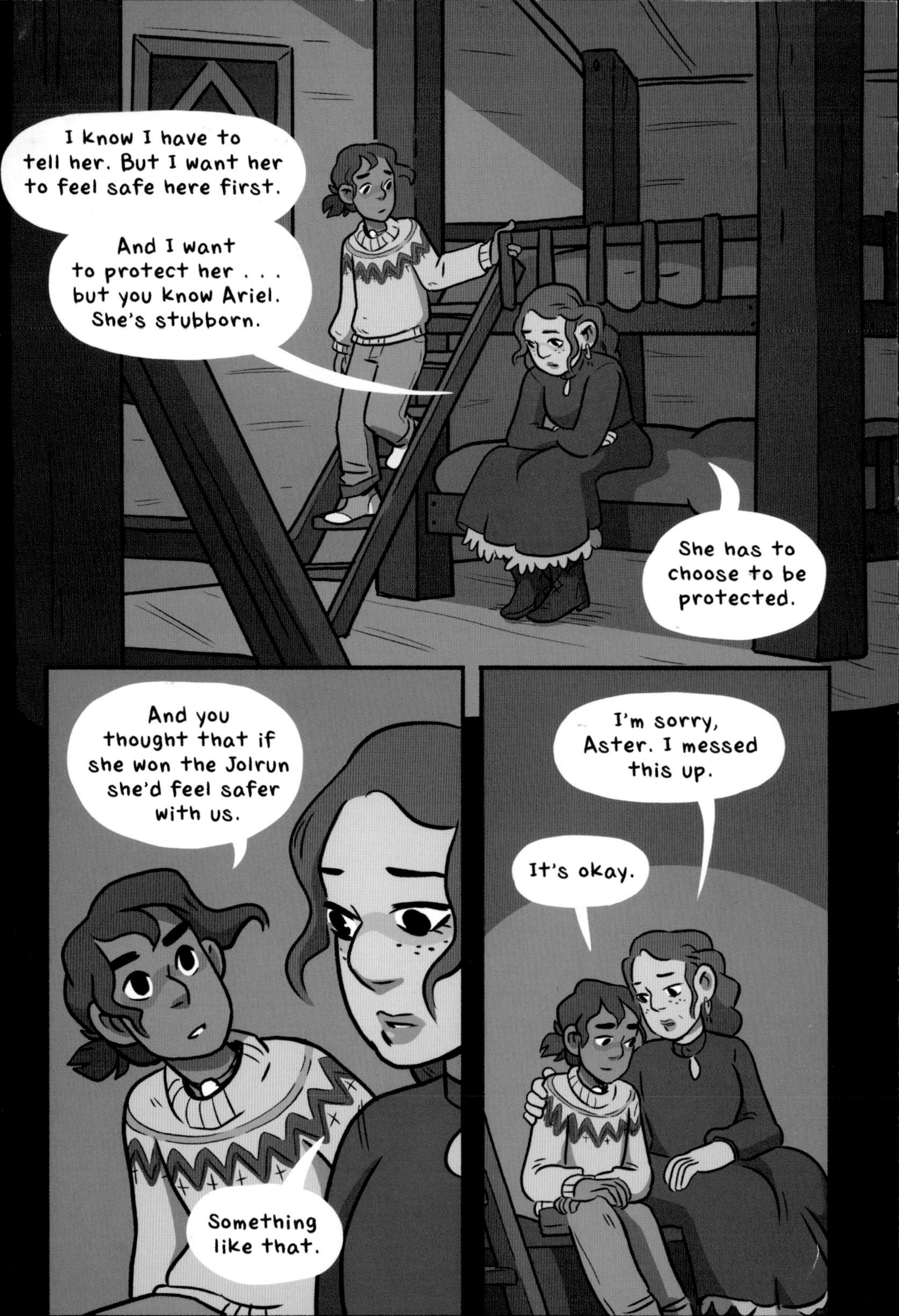
I know I have to tell her. But I want her to feel safe here first.
And I want to protect her . . . but you know Ariel. She's stubborn.
She has to choose to be protected.
And you thought that if she won the Jolrun she'd feel safer with us.
Something like that.
I'm sorry, Aster. I messed this up.
It's okay.

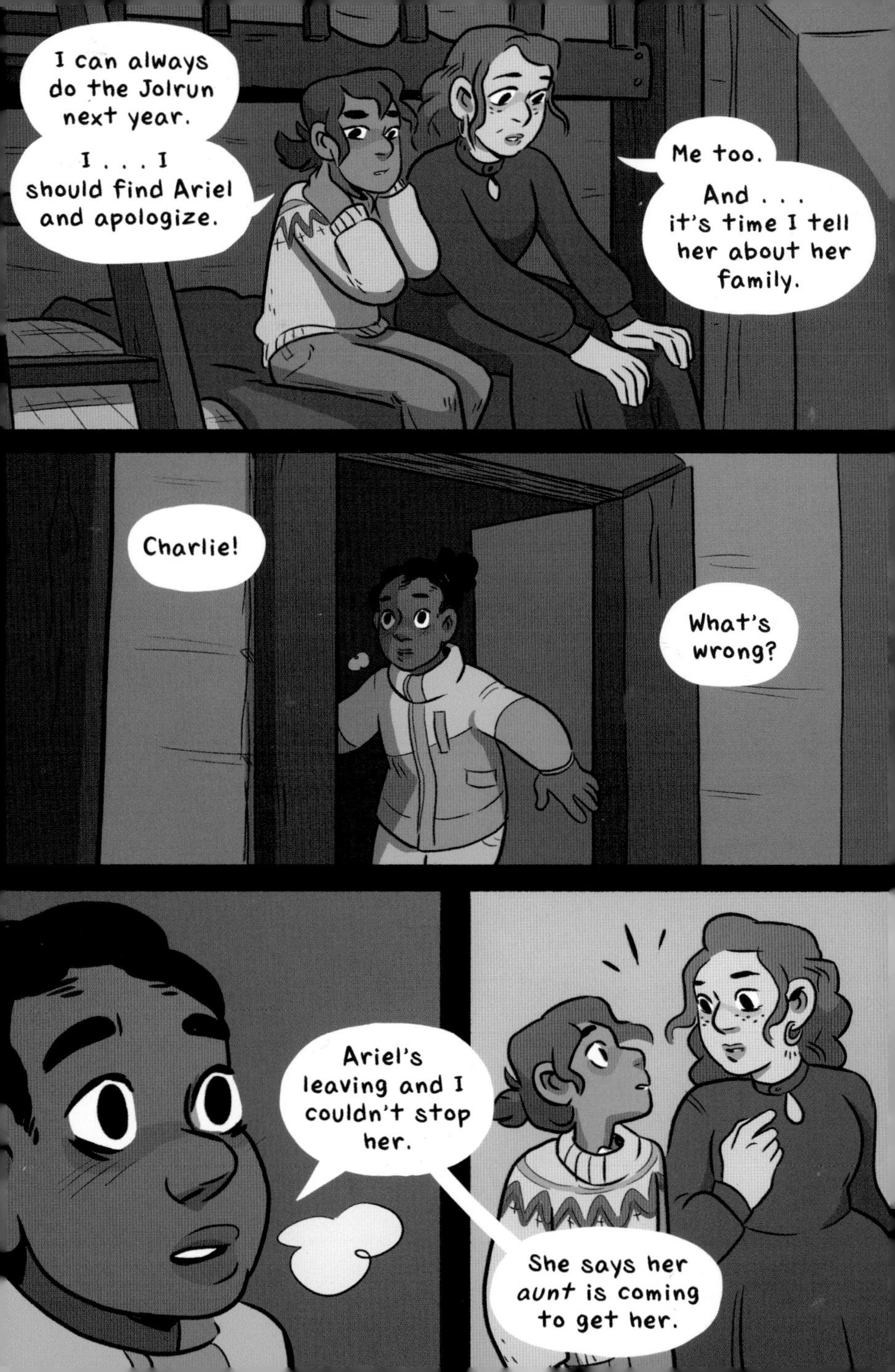
I can always do the Jolrun next year.
I . . . I should find Ariel and apologize.
Me too.
And . . . it's time I tell her about her family.
Charlie!
What's wrong?
Ariel's leaving and I couldn't stop her.
She says her *aunt* is coming to get her.

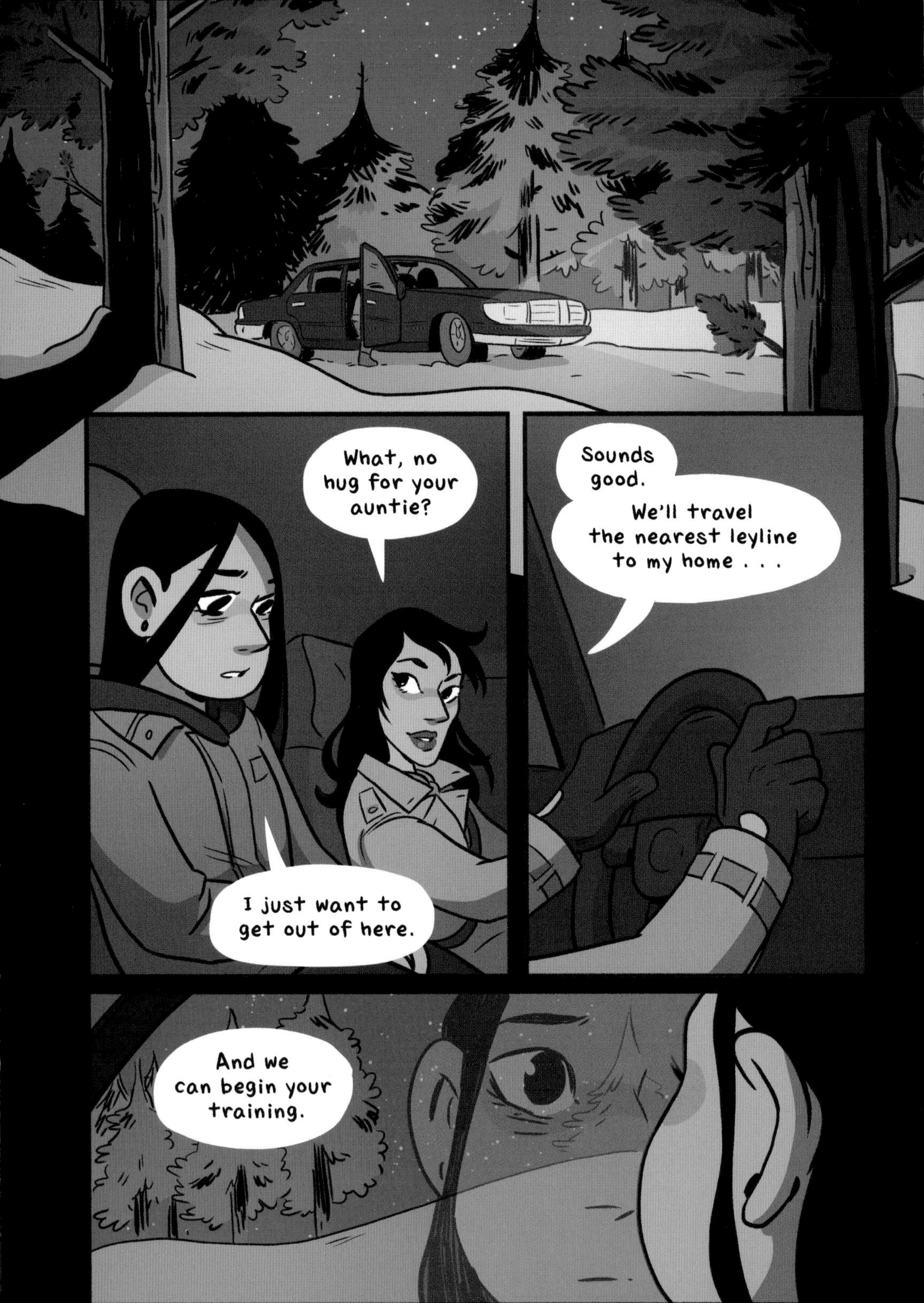
What, no hug for your auntie?
I just want to get out of here.
Sounds good.
We'll travel the nearest leyline to my home . . .
And we can begin your training.

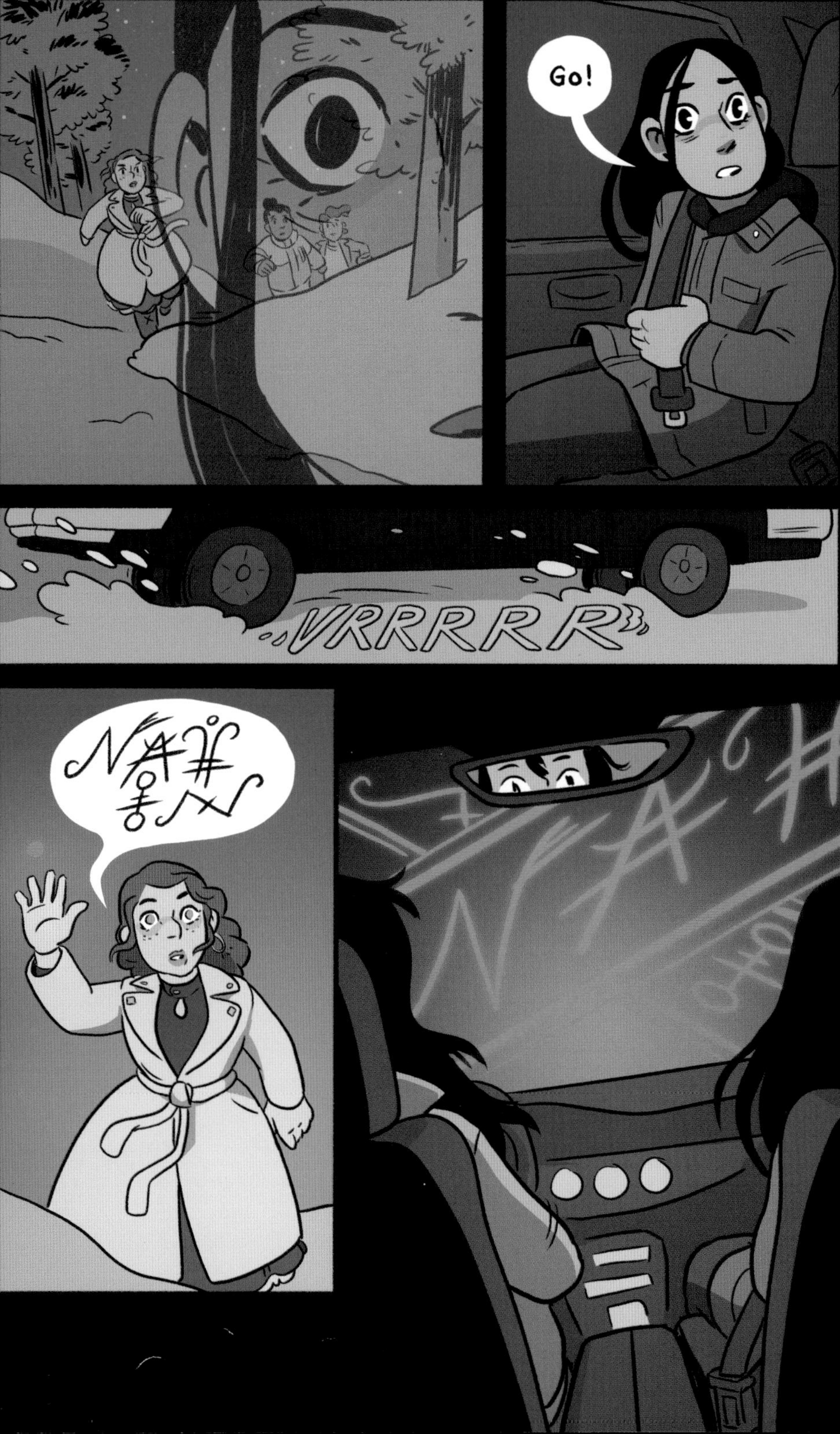
Go!
VRRRRR

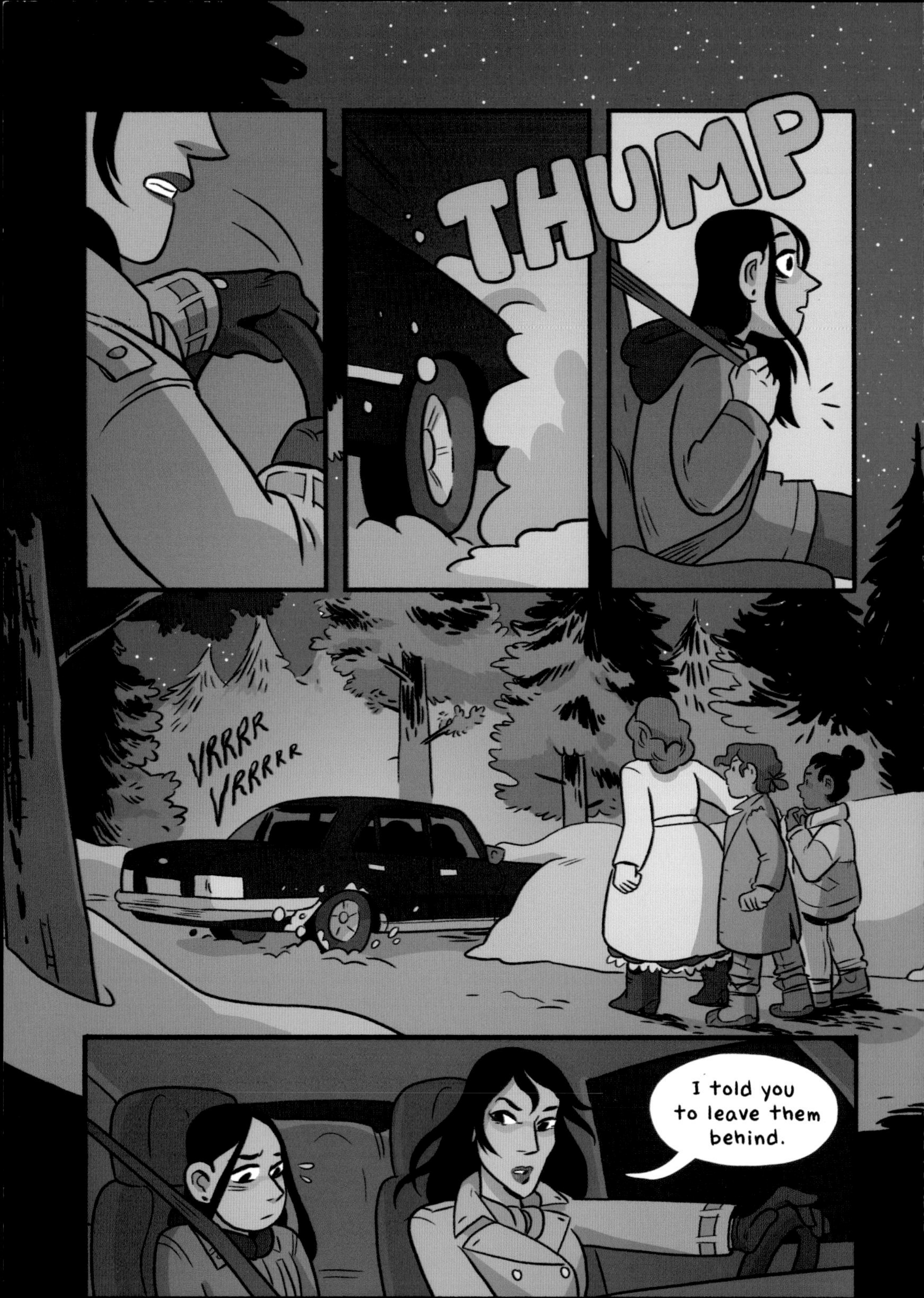
THUMP
VRRRR
VRRRRR
I told you to leave them behind.

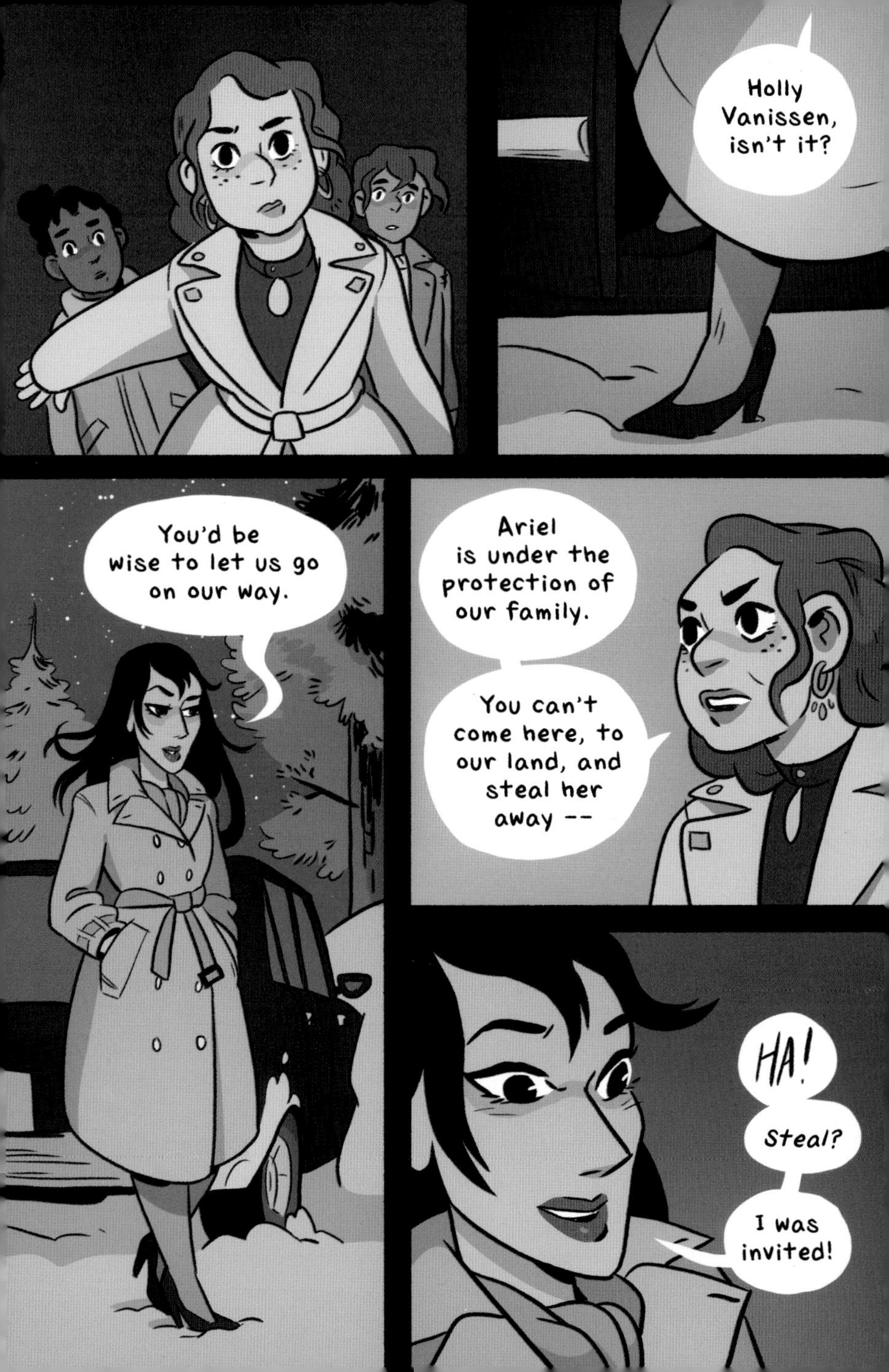
Holly Vanissen, isn't it?
You'd be wise to let us go on our way.
Ariel is under the protection of our family.
You can't come here, to our land, and steal her away --
HA!
Steal?
I was invited!

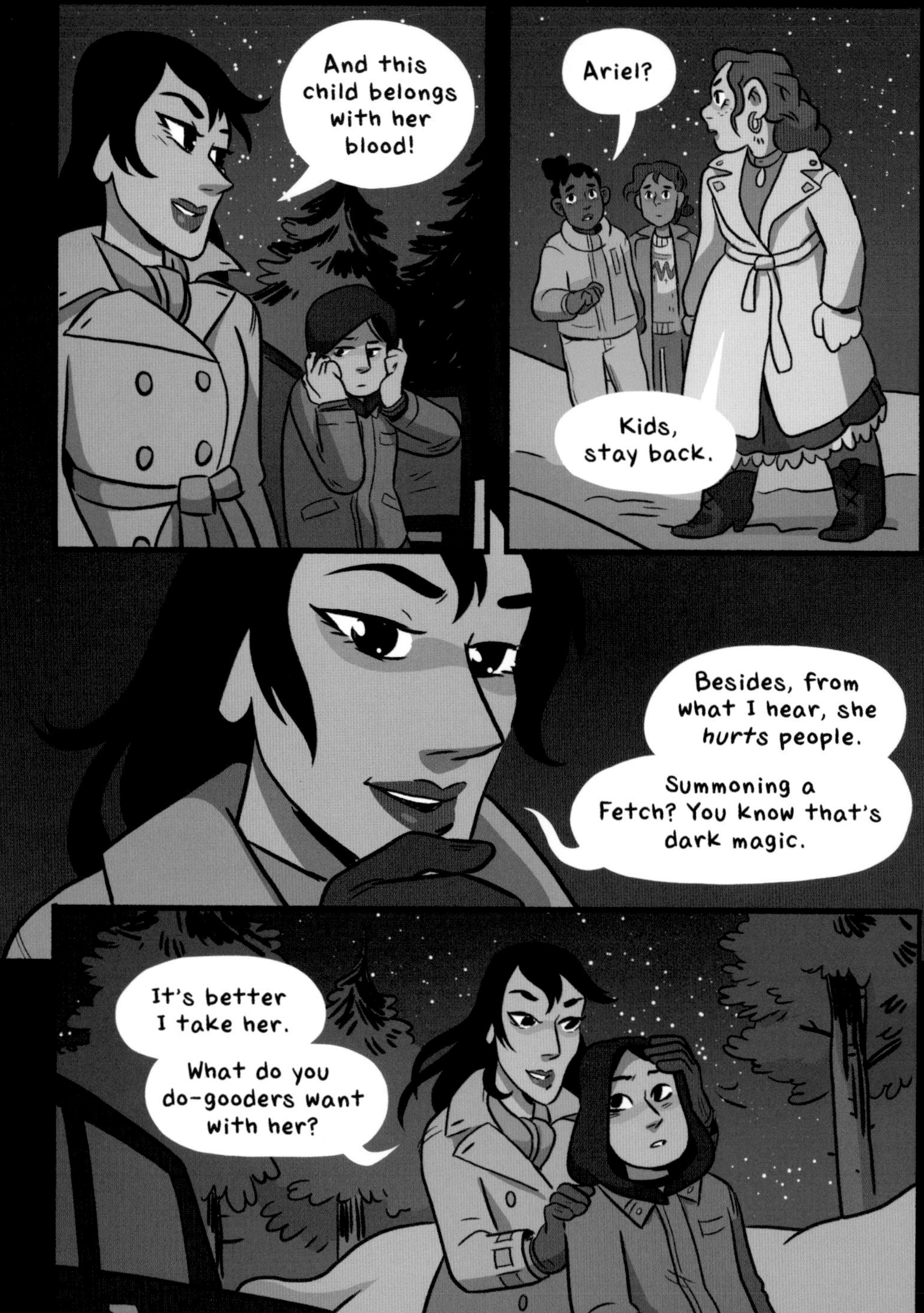

And this child belongs with her blood!
Ariel?
Kids, stay back.
Besides, from what I hear, she *hurts* people.
Summoning a Fetch? You know that's dark magic.
It's better I take her.
What do you do-gooders want with her?

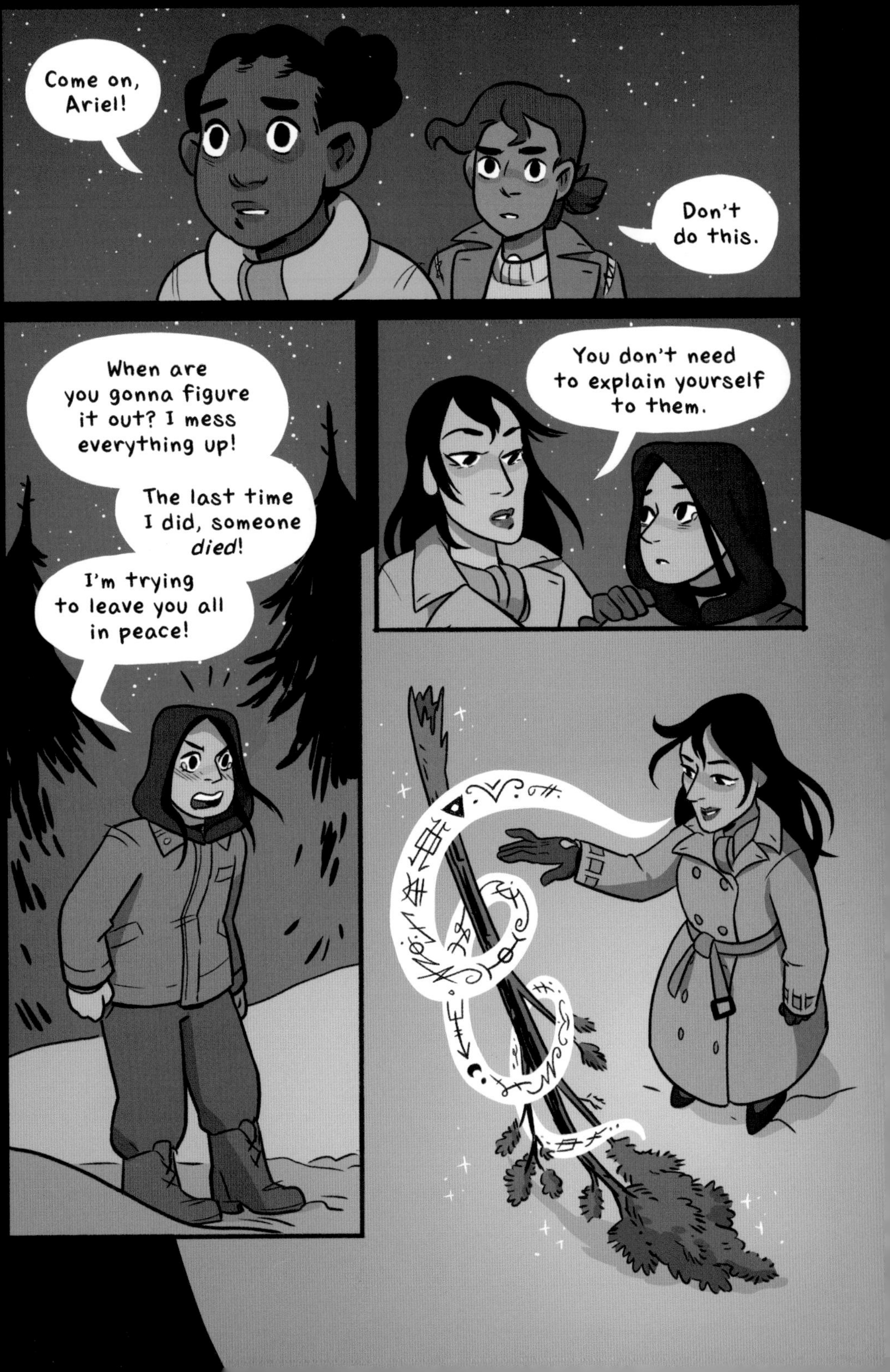
Come on, Ariel!
Don't do this.
When are you gonna figure it out? I mess everything up!
The last time I did, someone *died*!
I'm trying to leave you all in peace!
You don't need to explain yourself to them.

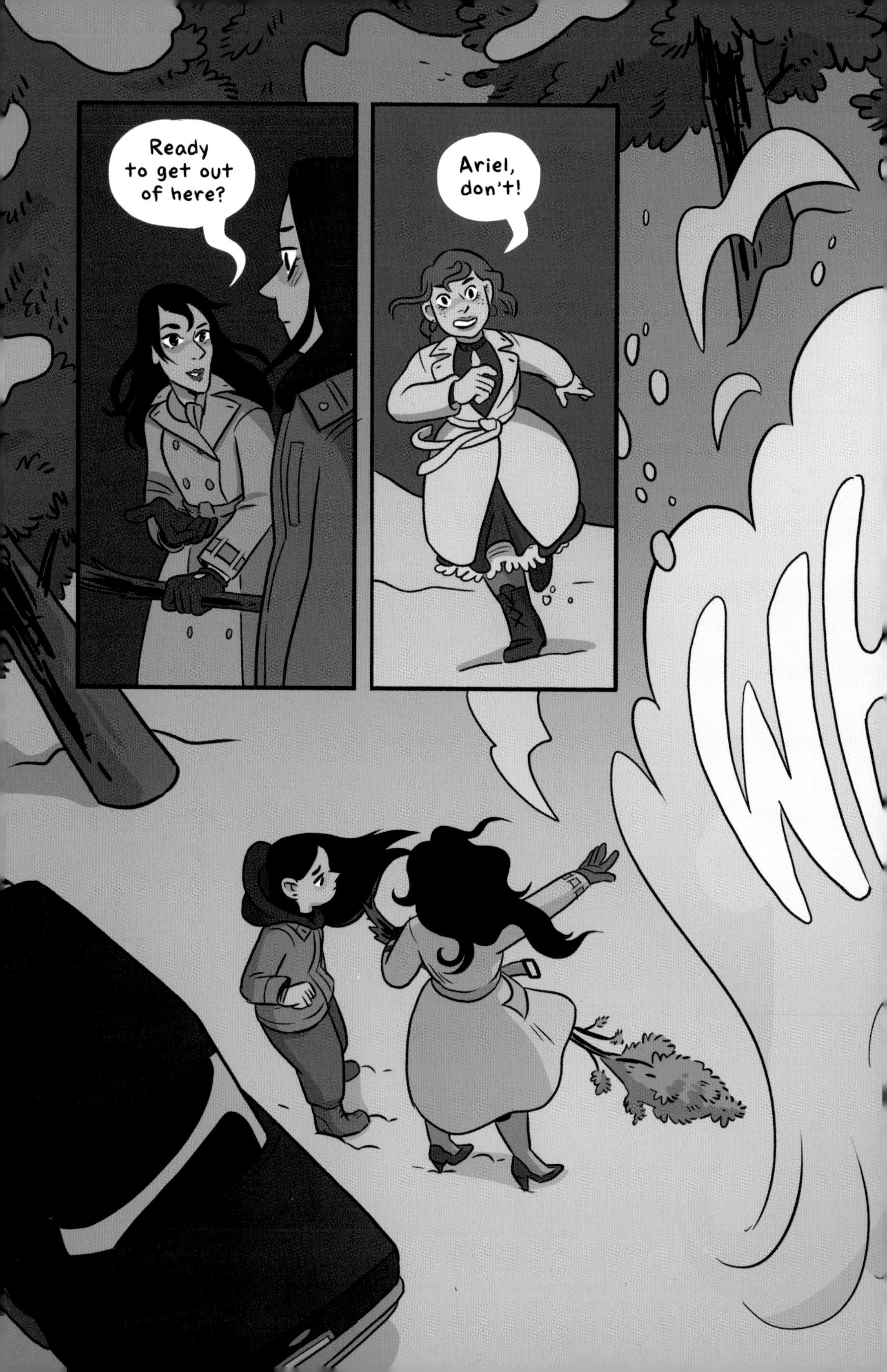
Ready to get out of here?
Ariel, don't!

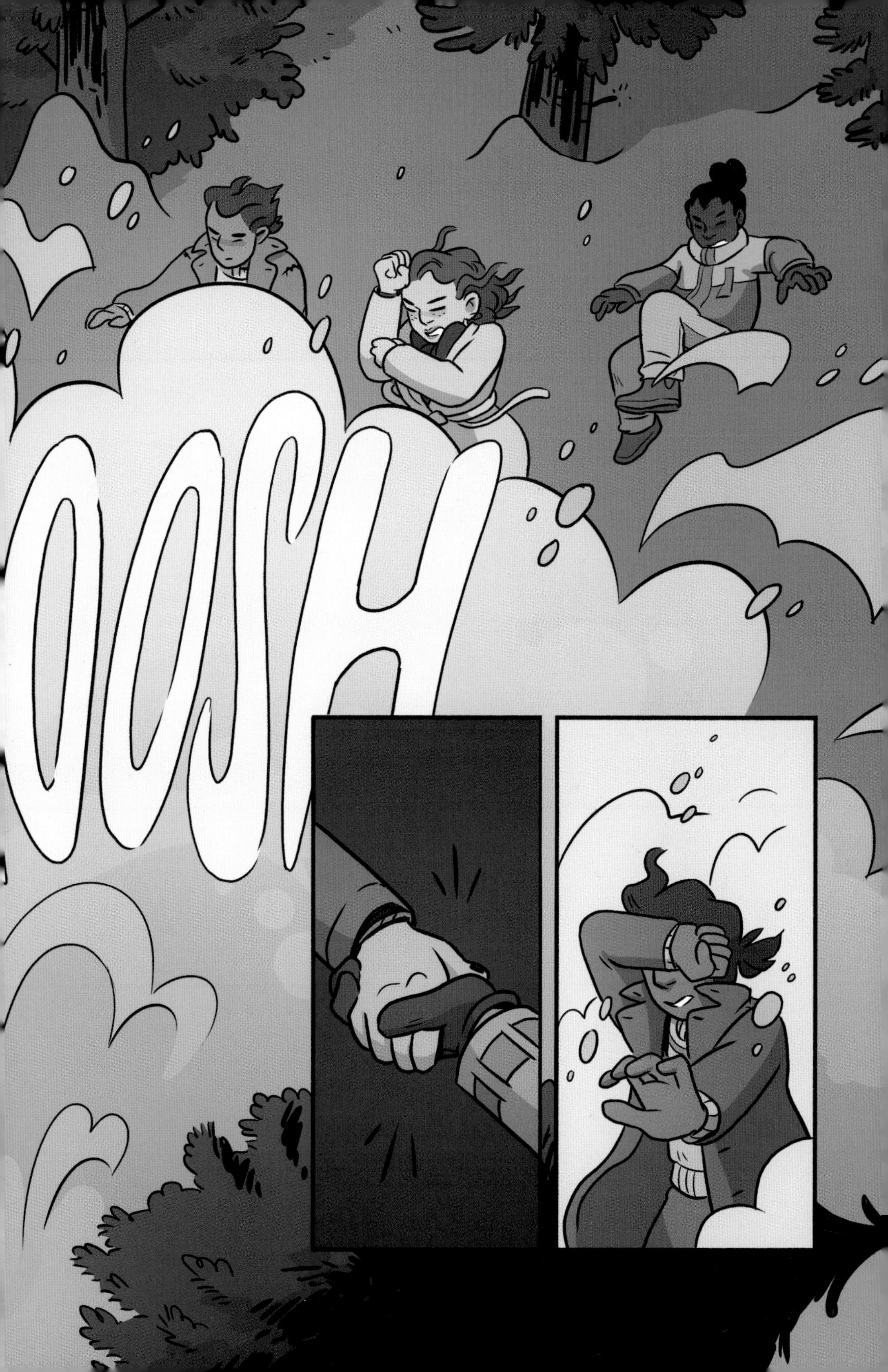
OOSH

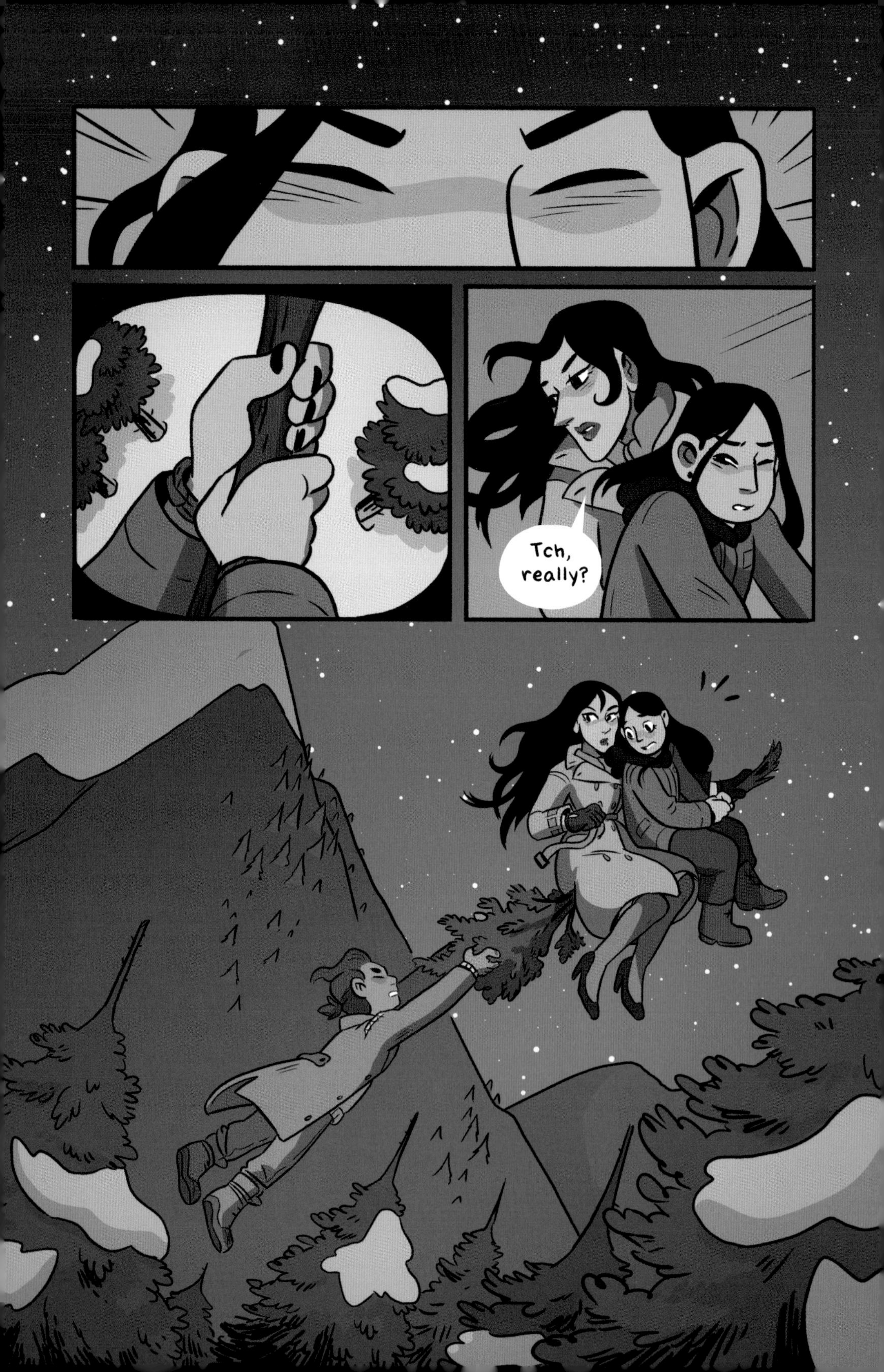
Tch, really?

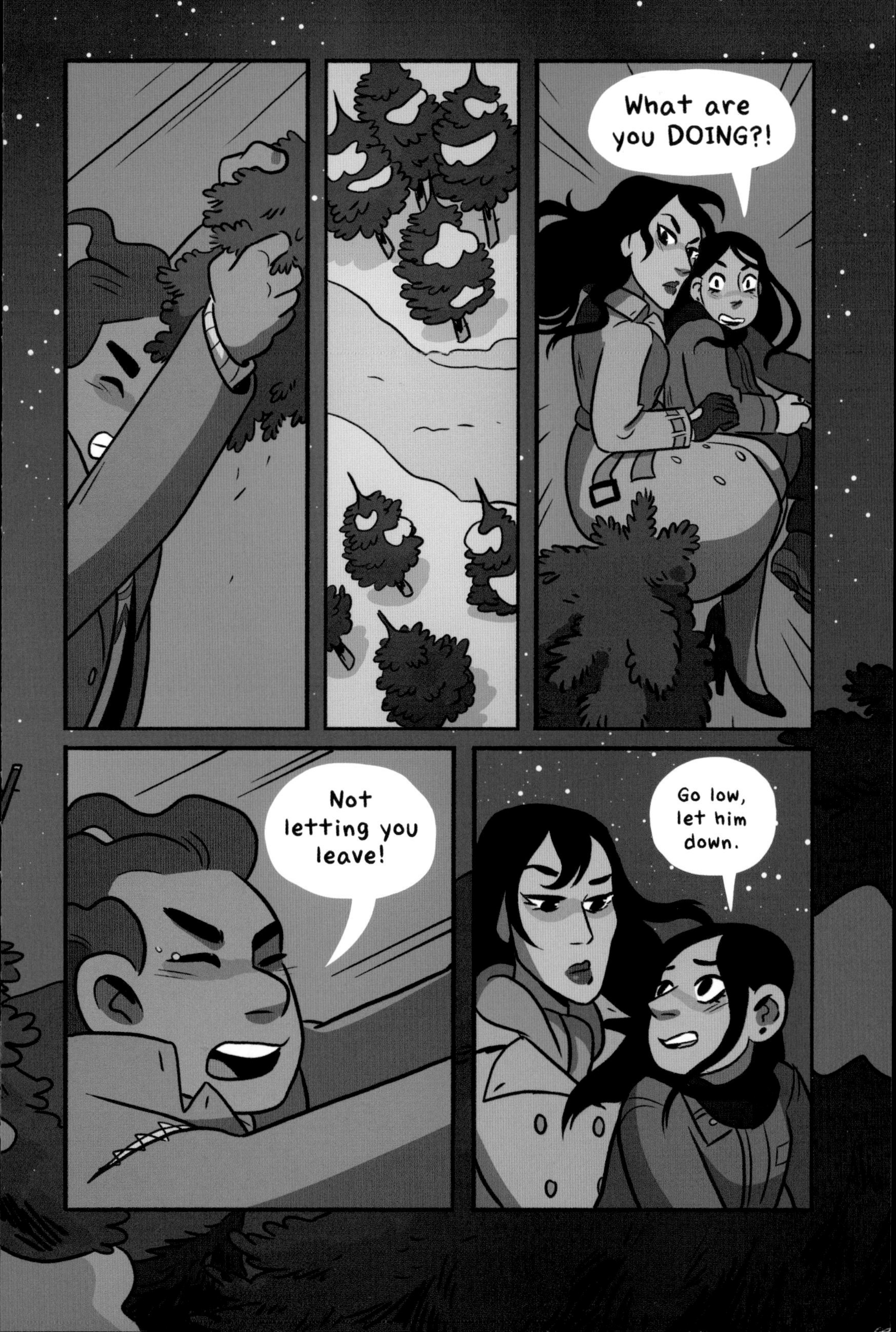
What are you DOING?!
Not letting you leave!
Go low, let him down.

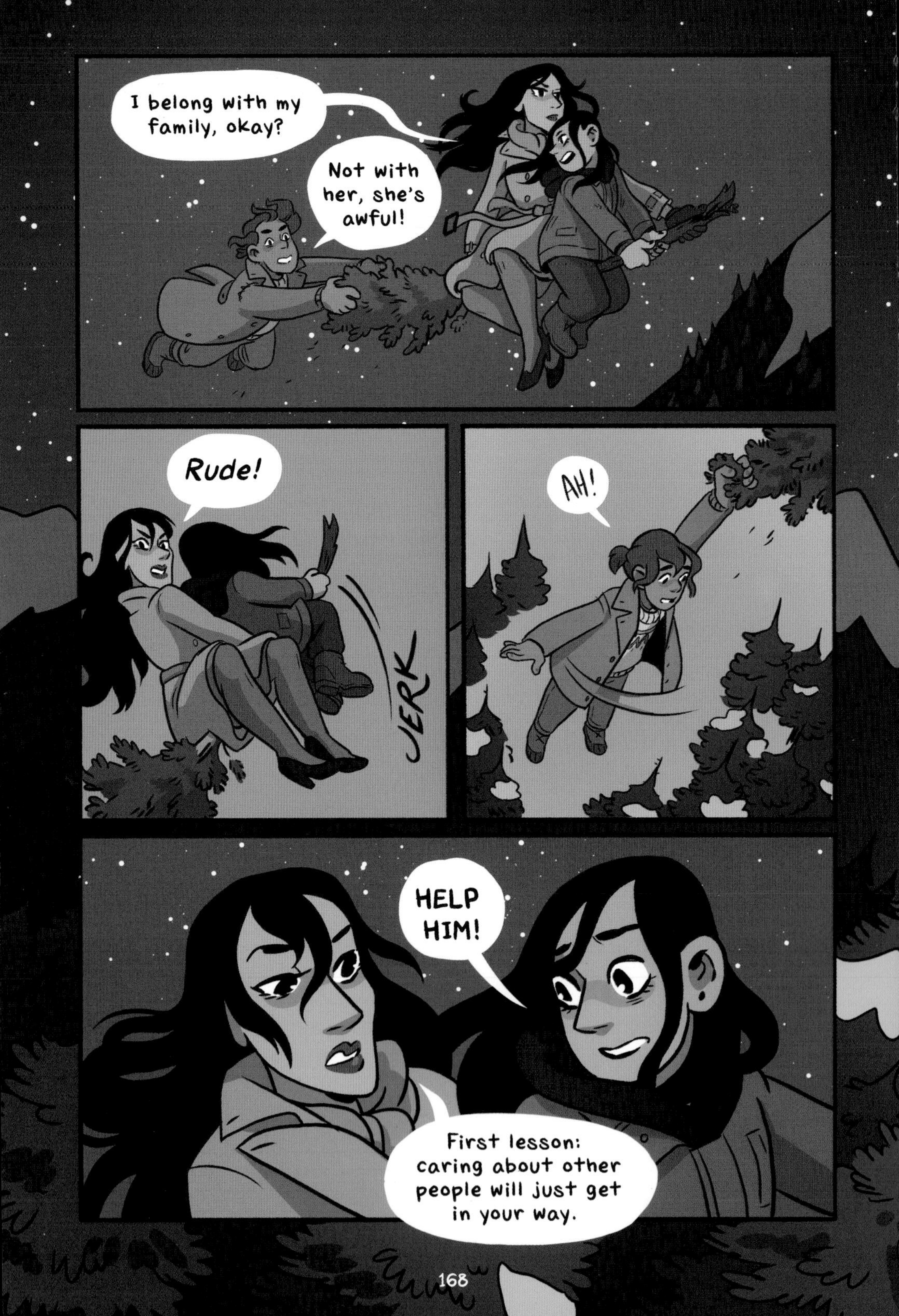
I belong with my family, okay?
Not with her, she's awful!
Rude!
JERK
AH!
HELP HIM!
First lesson: caring about other people will just get in your way.

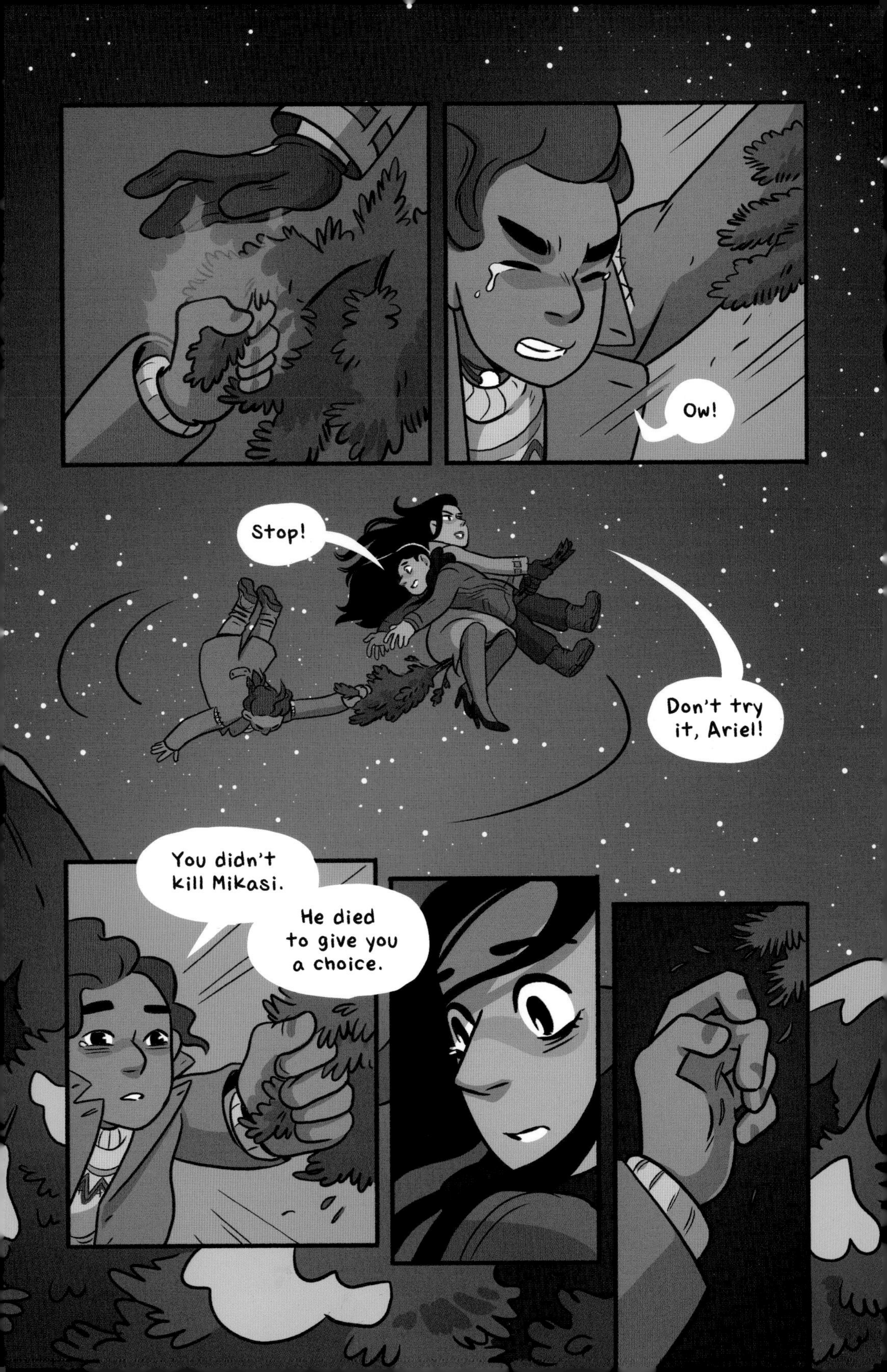
Ow!
Stop!
Don't try it, Ariel!
You didn't kill Mikasi.
He died to give you a choice.

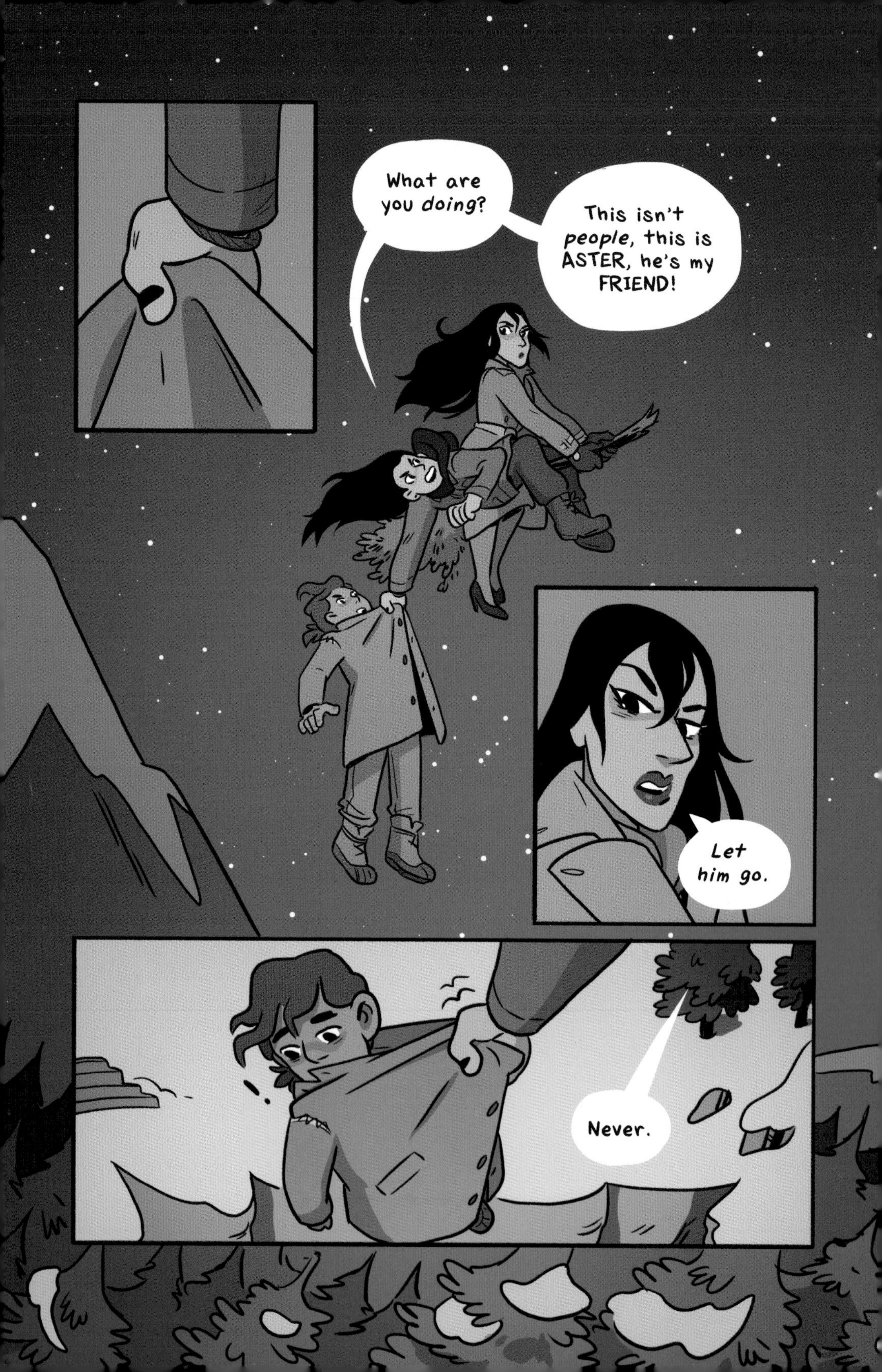
What are you *doing*?
This isn't *people*, this is ASTER, he's my FRIEND!
Let him go.
Never.

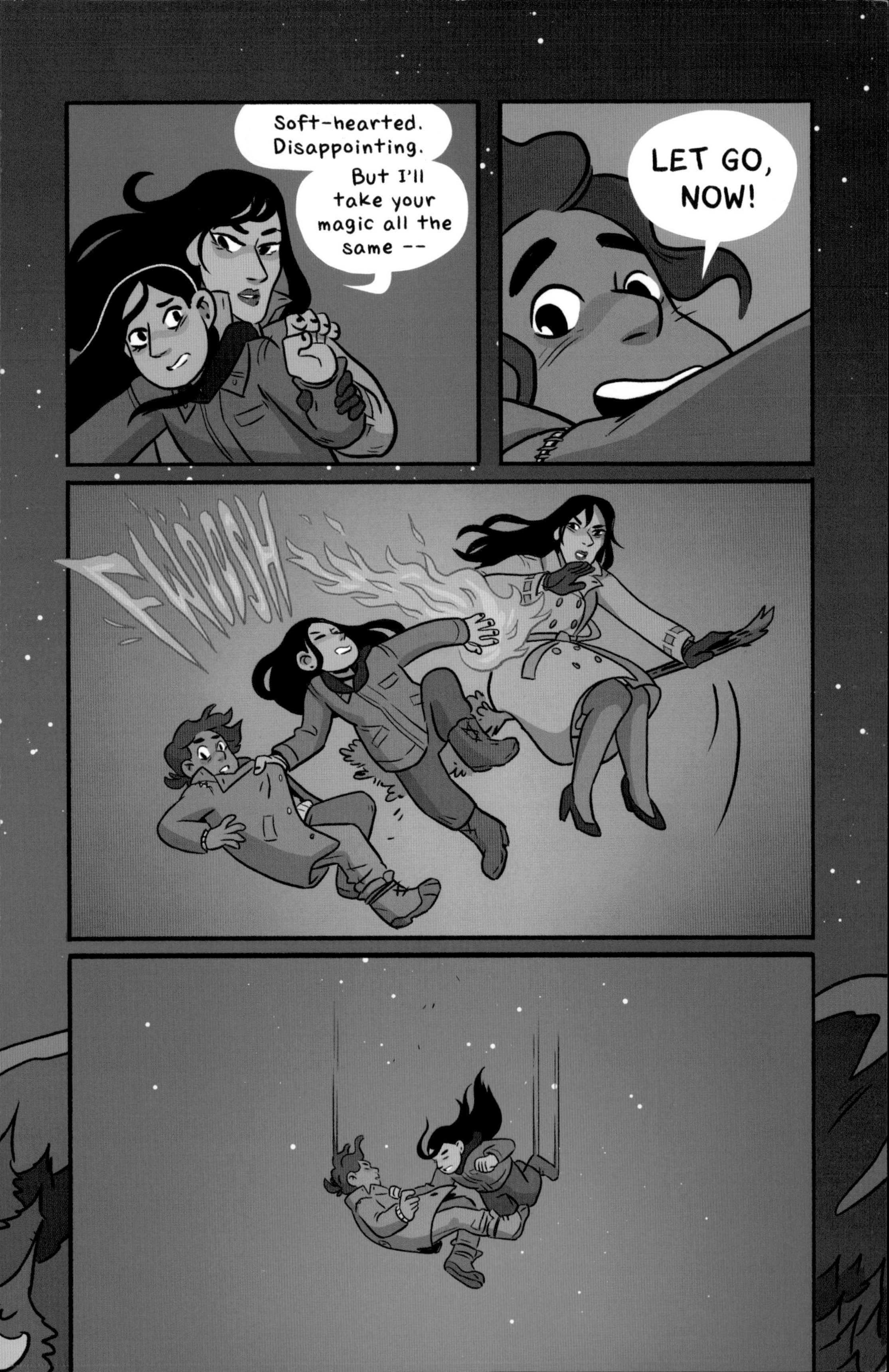
Soft-hearted. Disappointing.
But I'll take your magic all the same --
LET GO, NOW!
FWOOSH

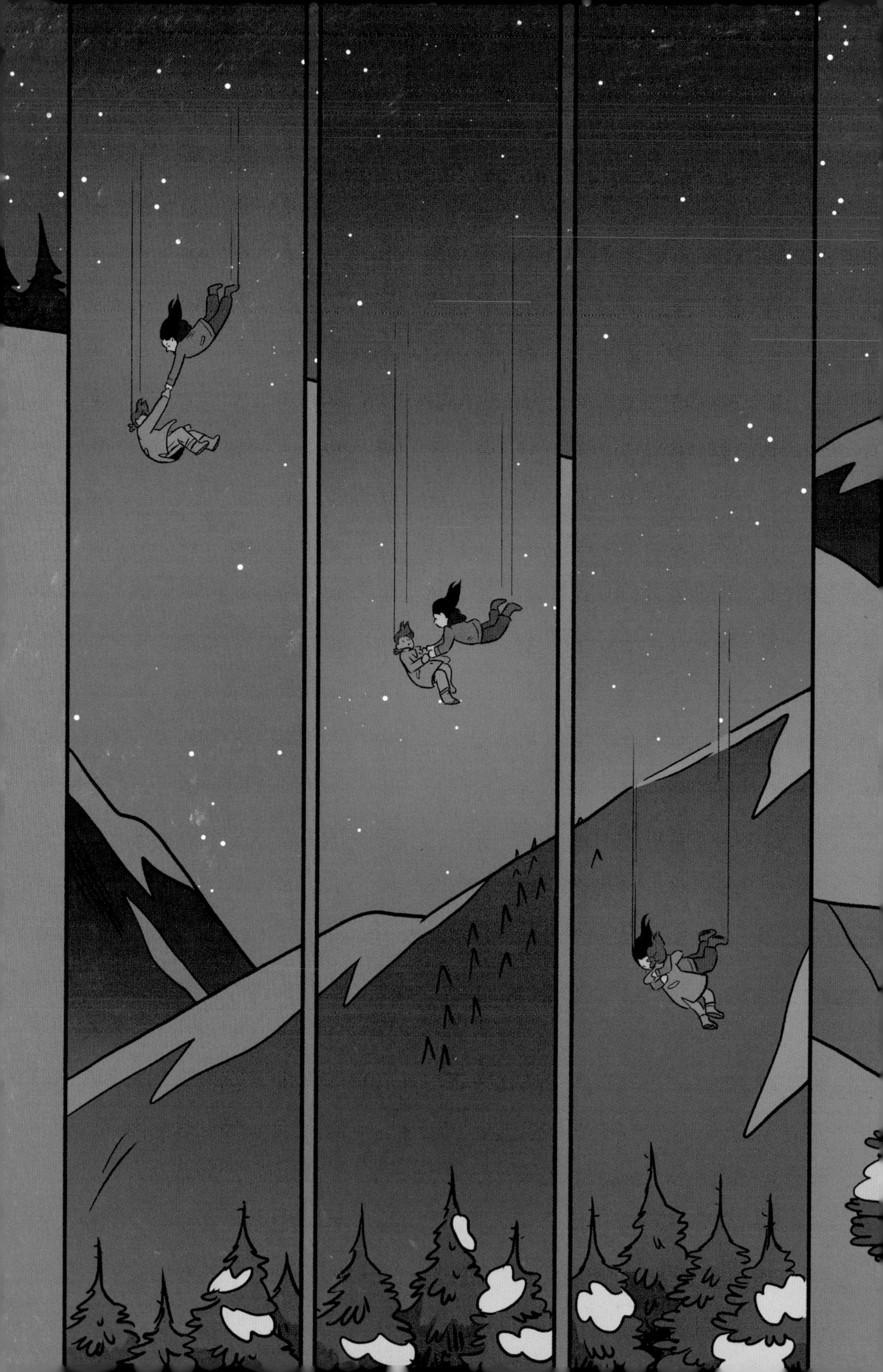

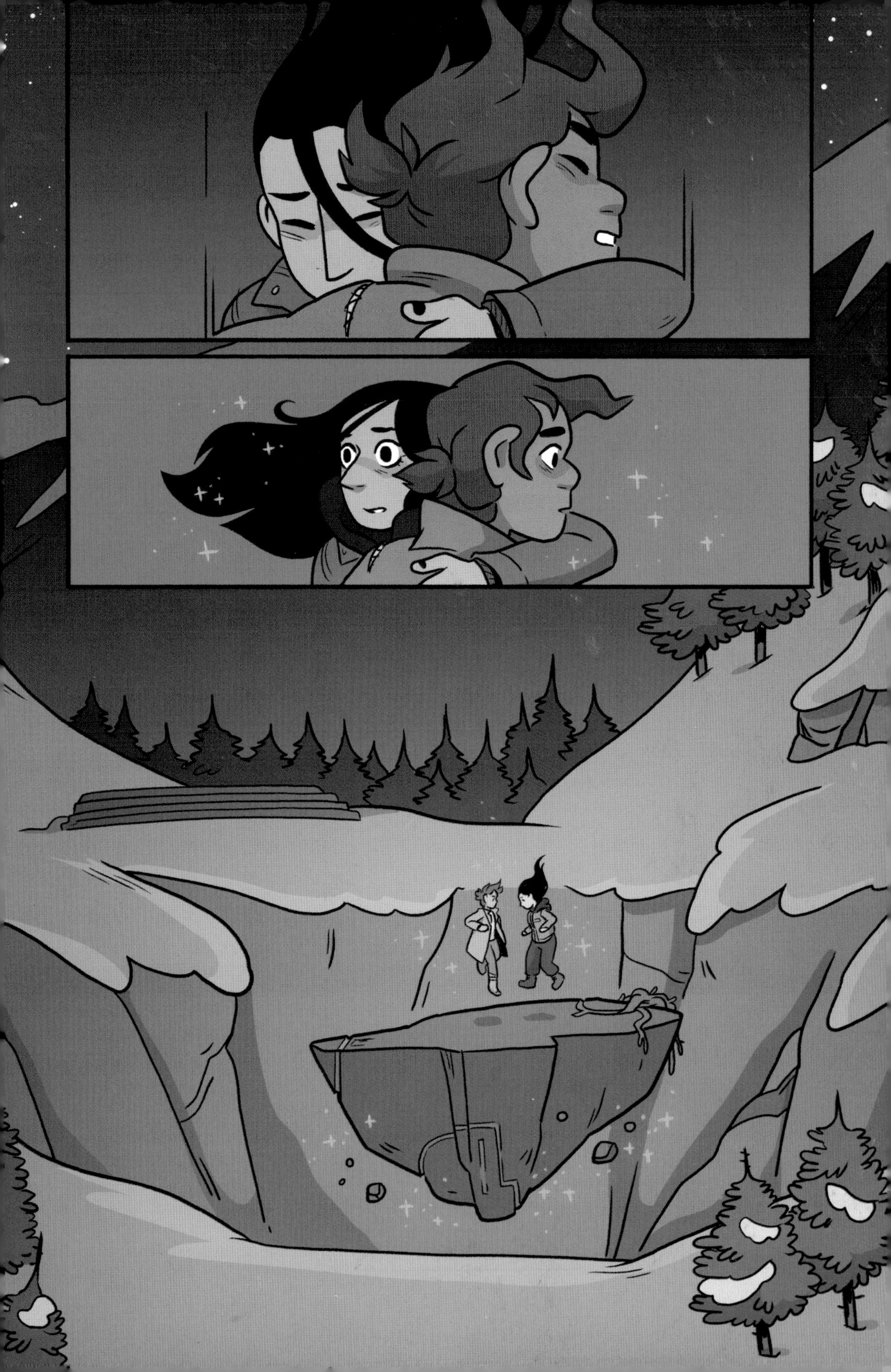

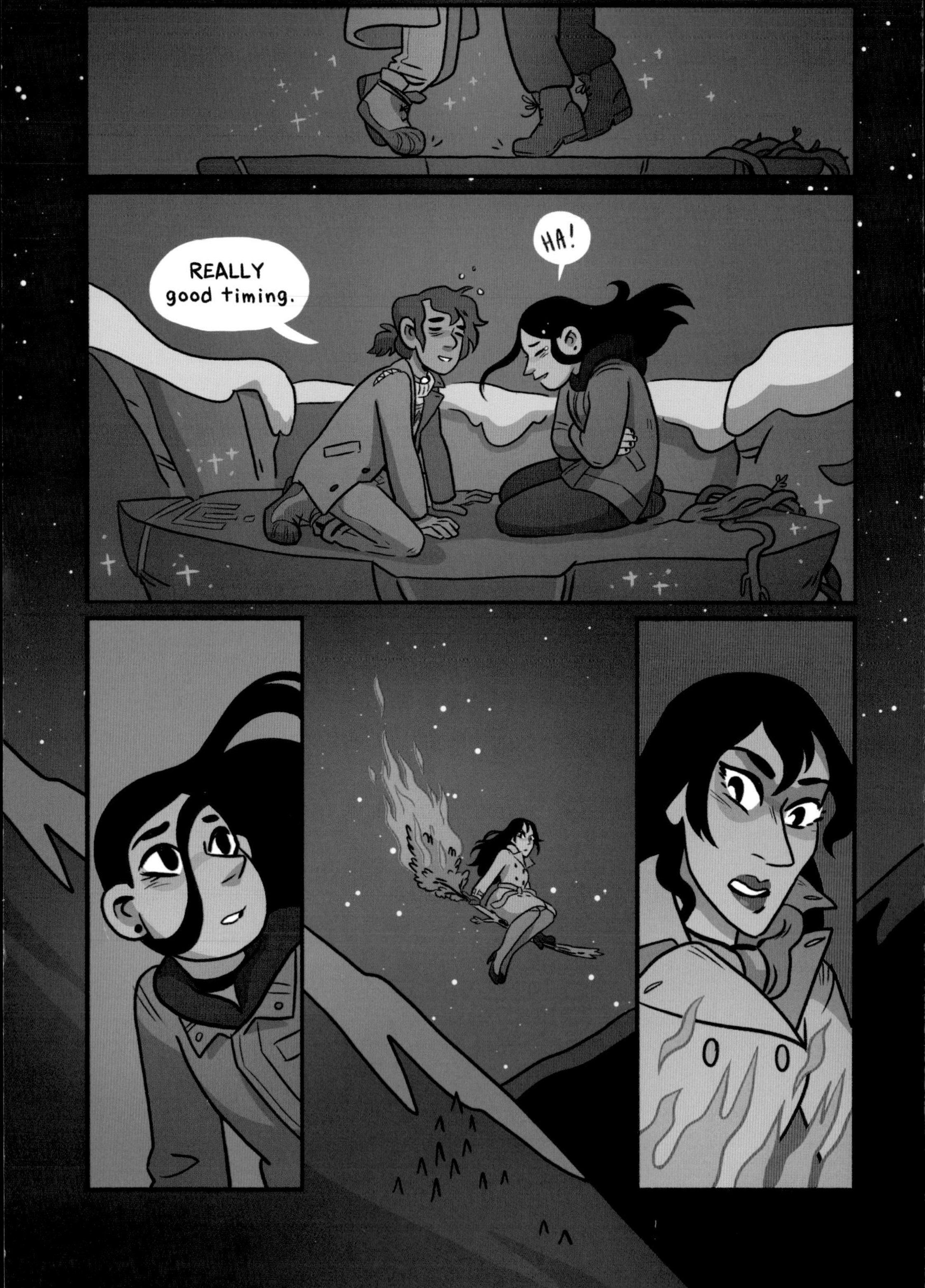
REALLY good timing.
HA!

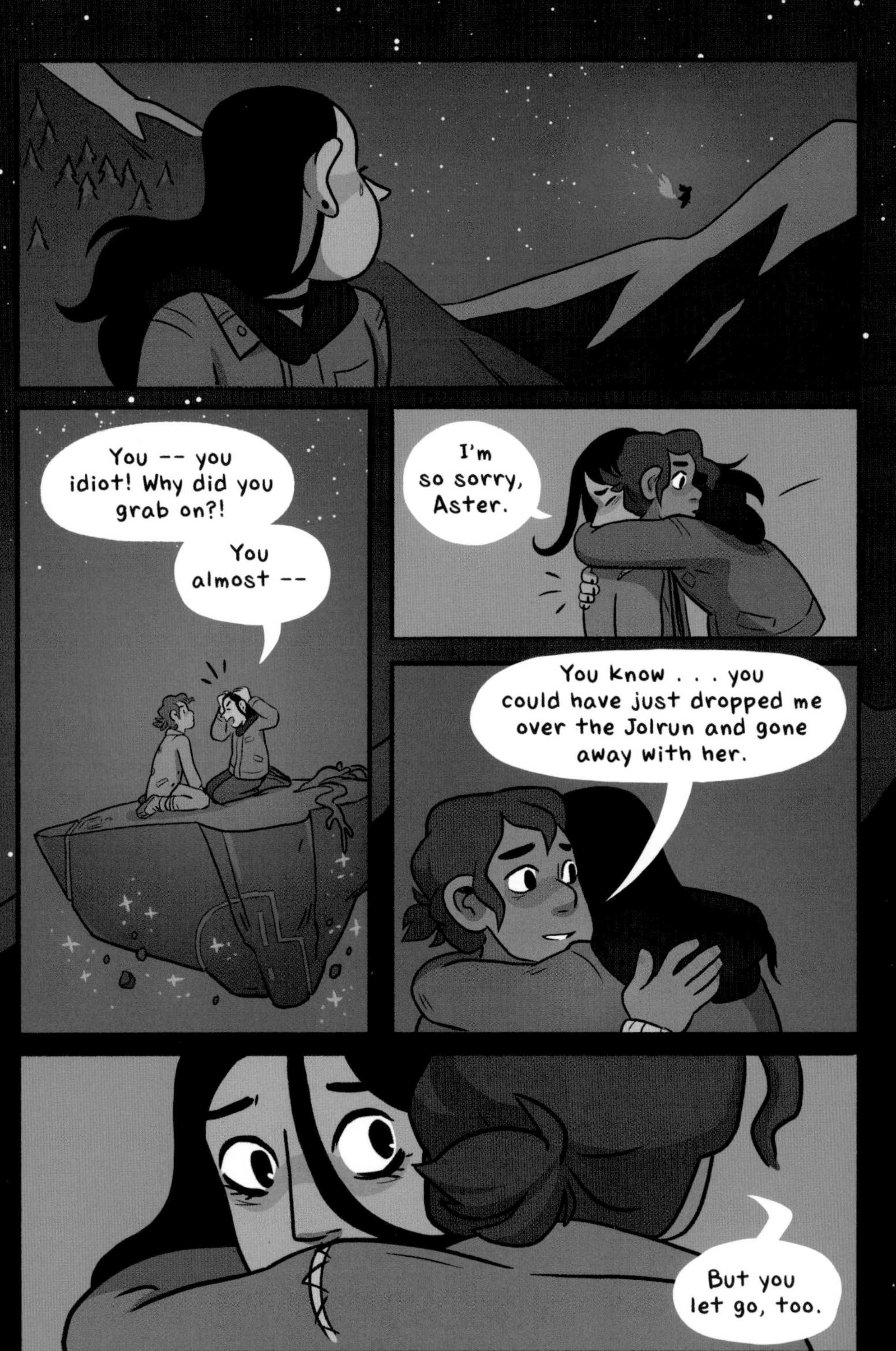

You -- you idiot! Why did you grab on?!
You almost --
I'm so sorry, Aster.
You know . . . you could have just dropped me over the Jolrun and gone away with her.
But you let go, too.

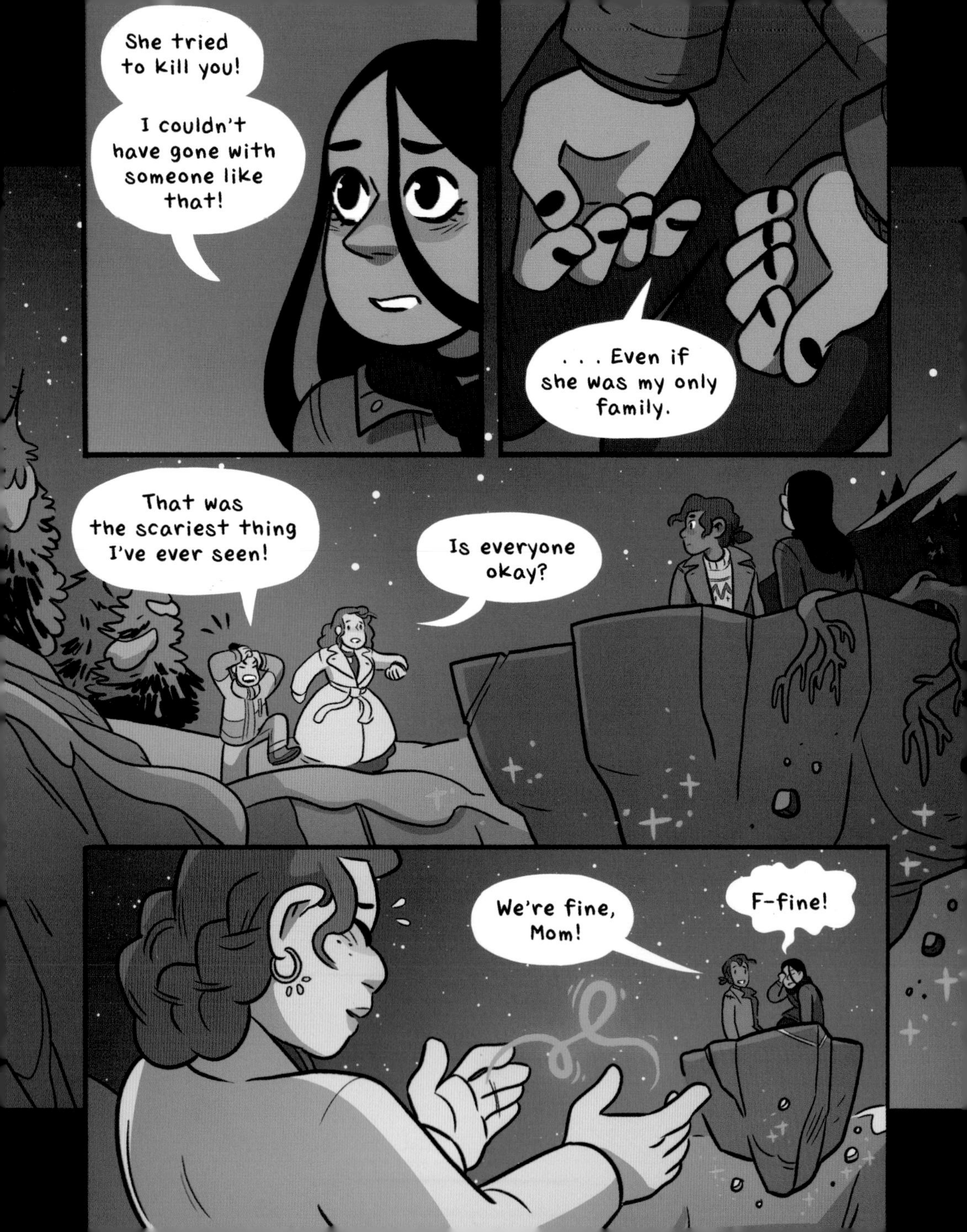
She tried to kill you!
I couldn't have gone with someone like that!
. . . Even if she was my only family.
That was the scariest thing I've ever seen!
Is everyone okay?
We're fine, Mom!
F-fine!

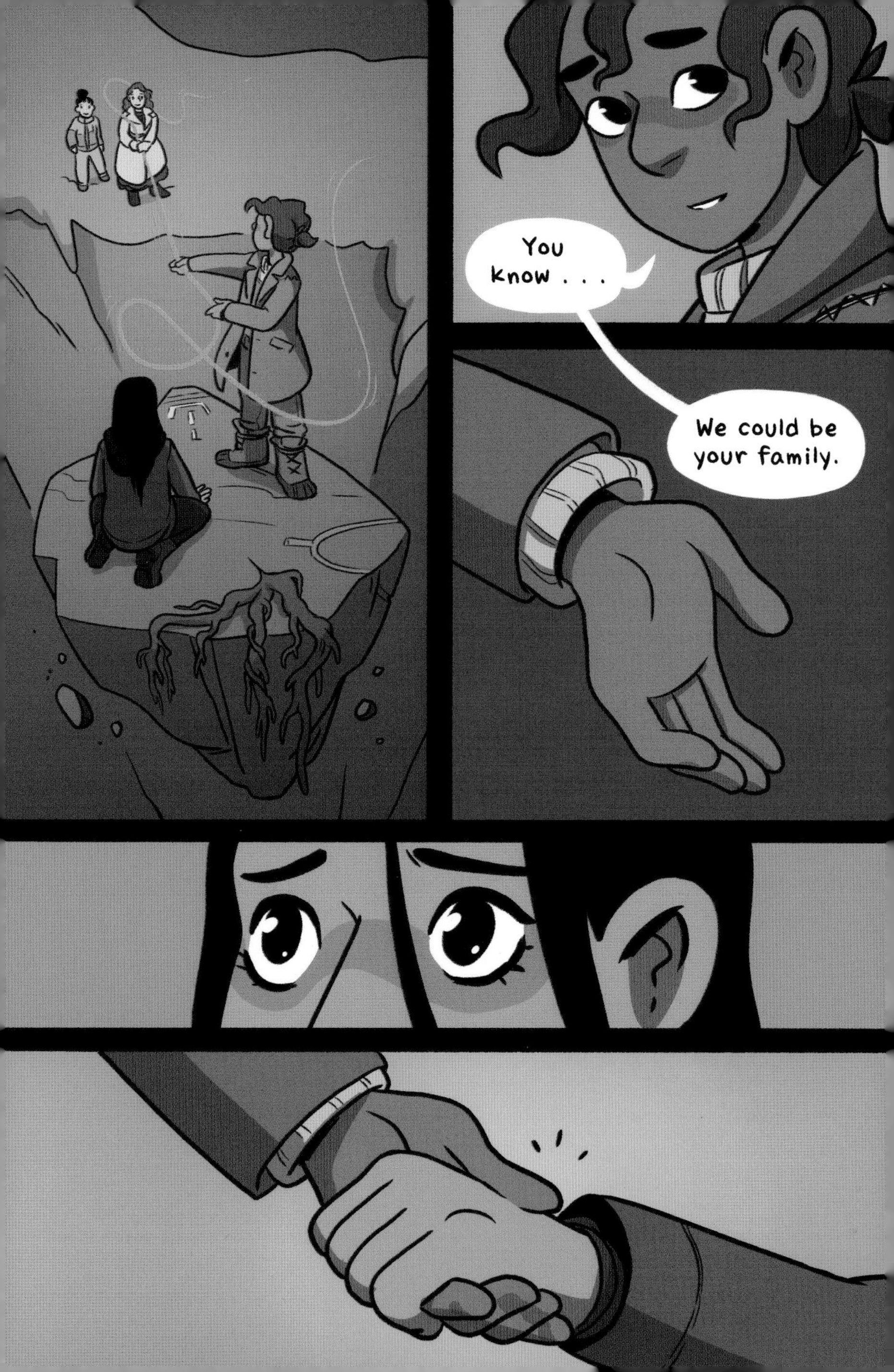
You know . . .
We could be your family.

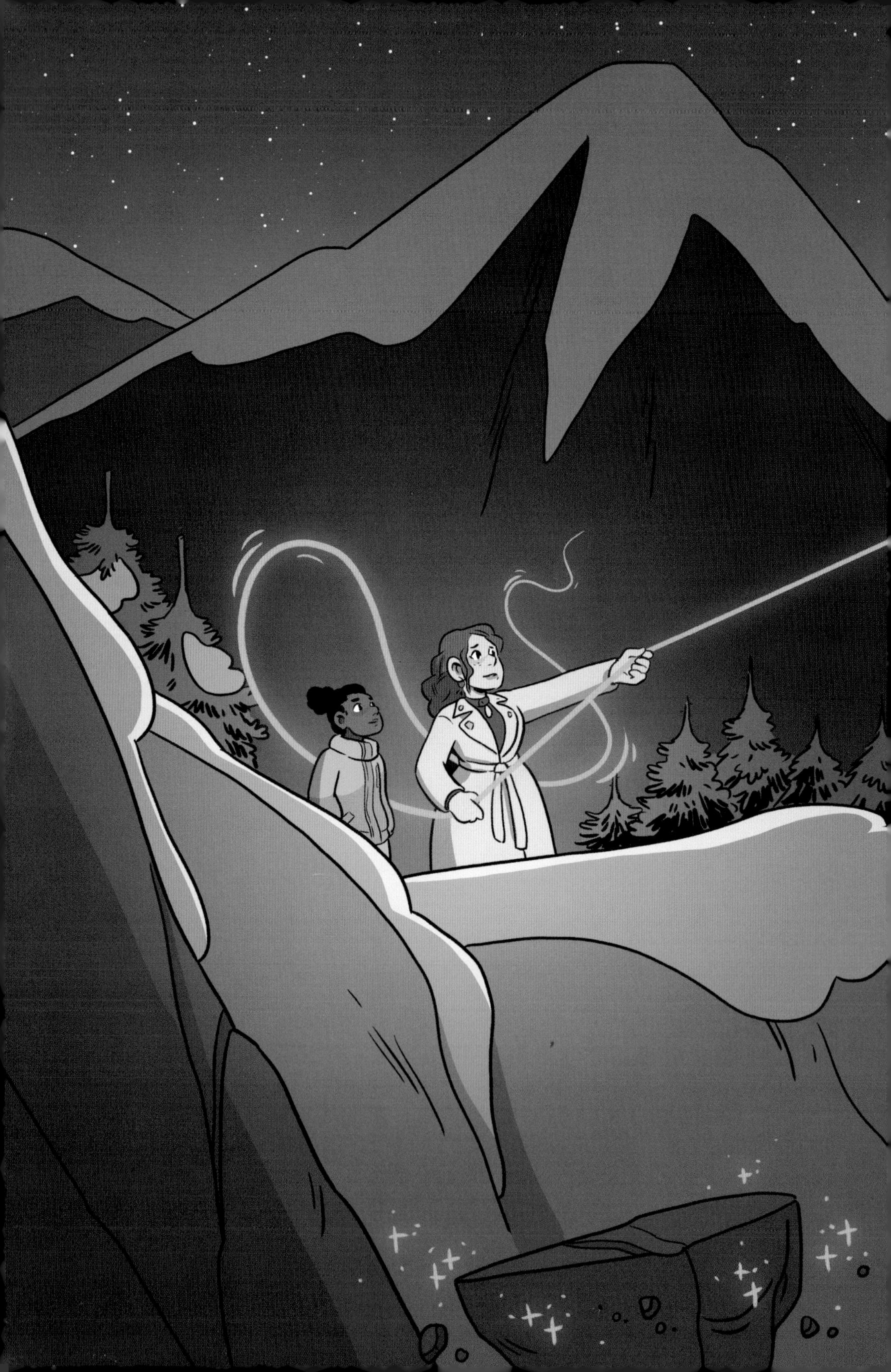

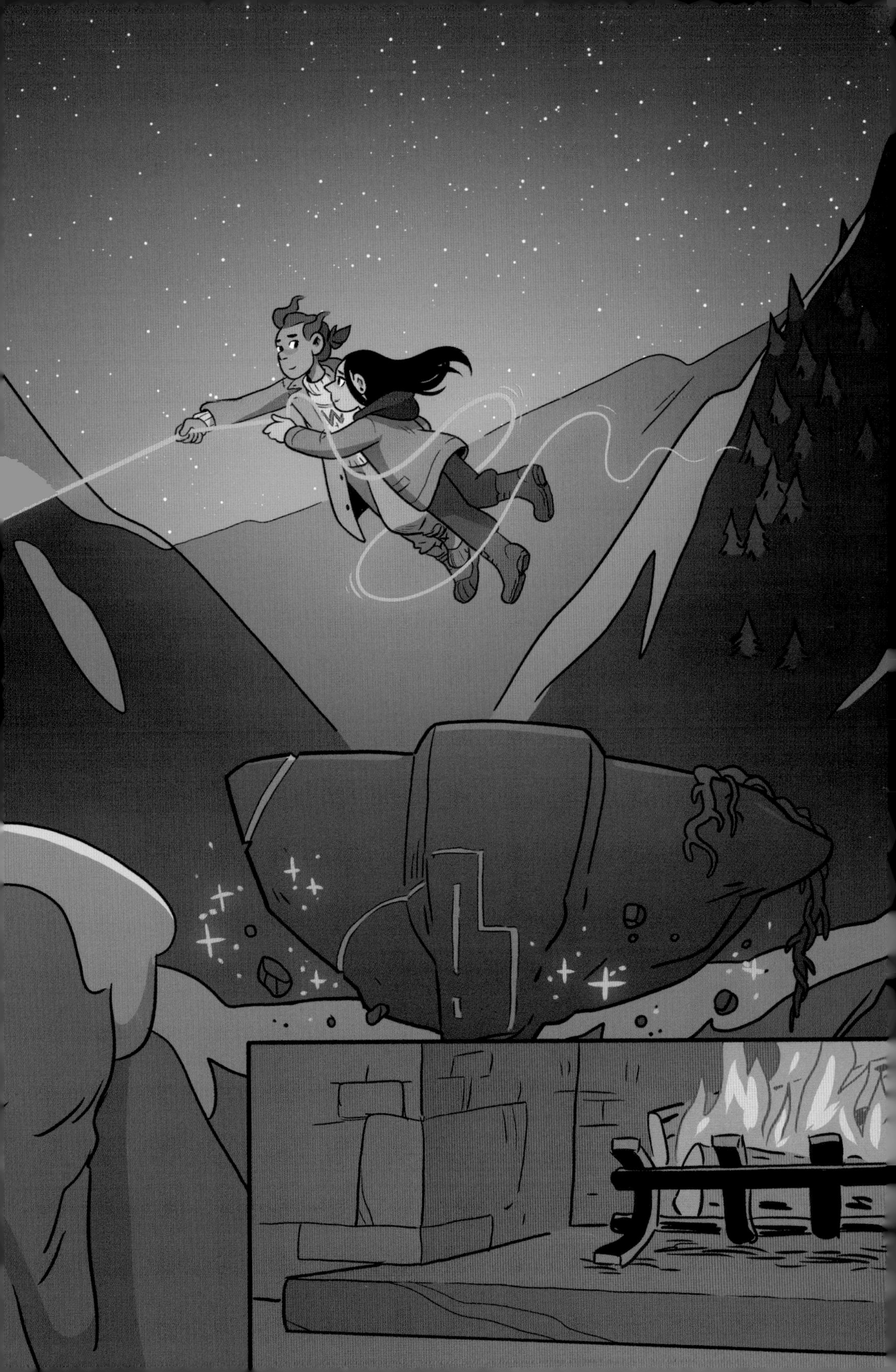

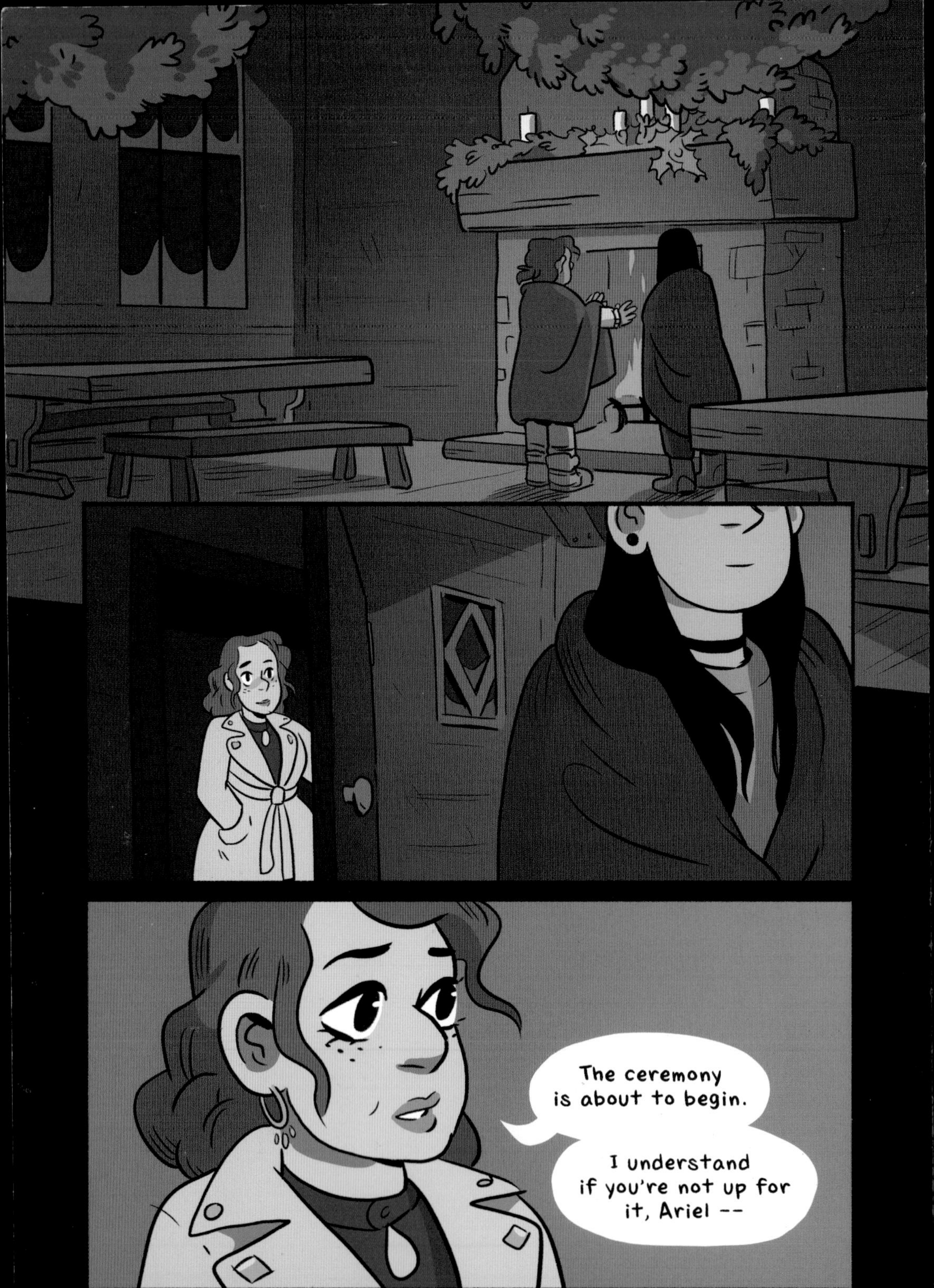
The ceremony is about to begin.
I understand if you're not up for it, Ariel --

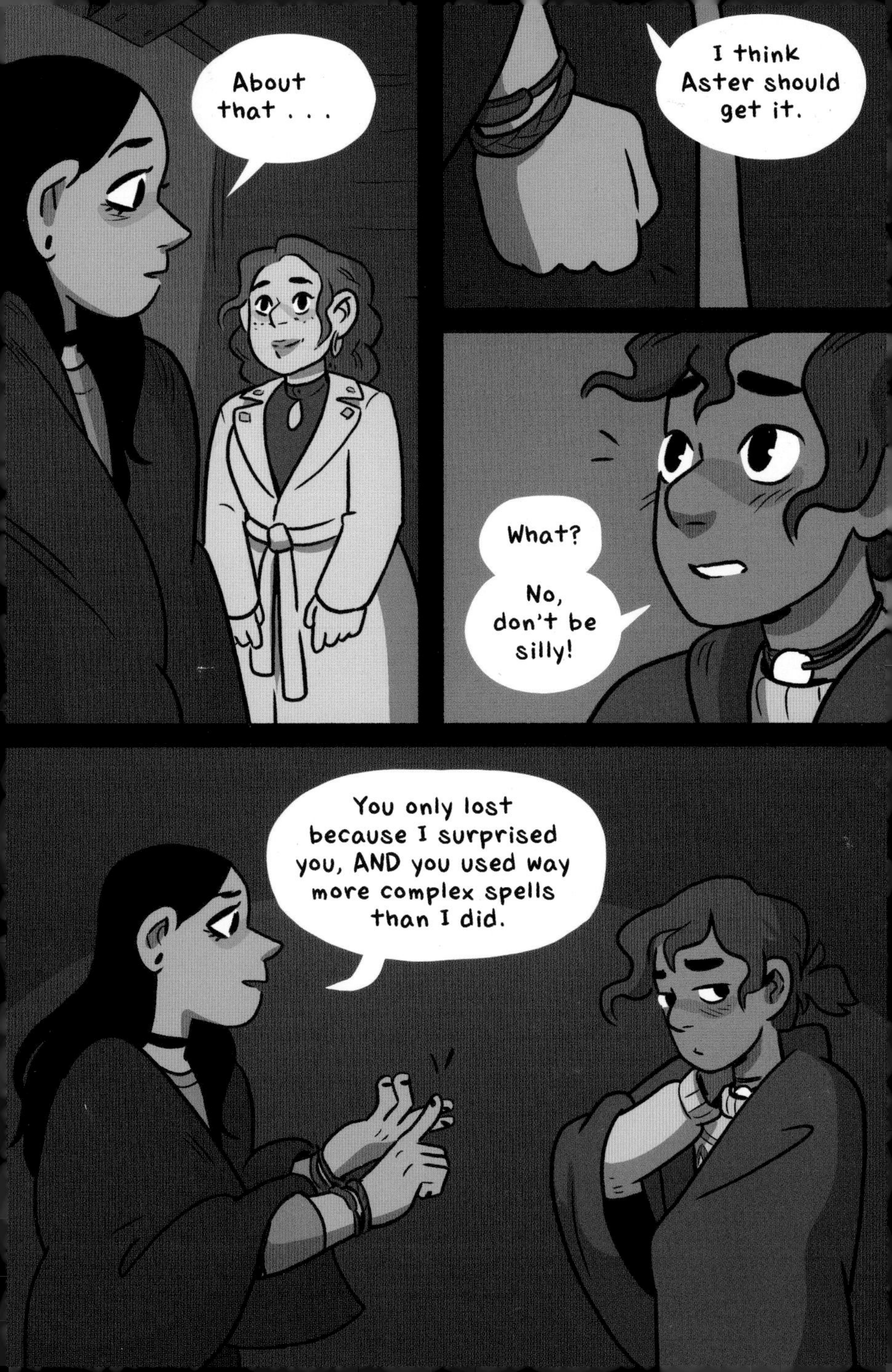
About that . . .
I think Aster should get it.
What?
No, don't be silly!
You only lost because I surprised you, AND you used way more complex spells than I did.

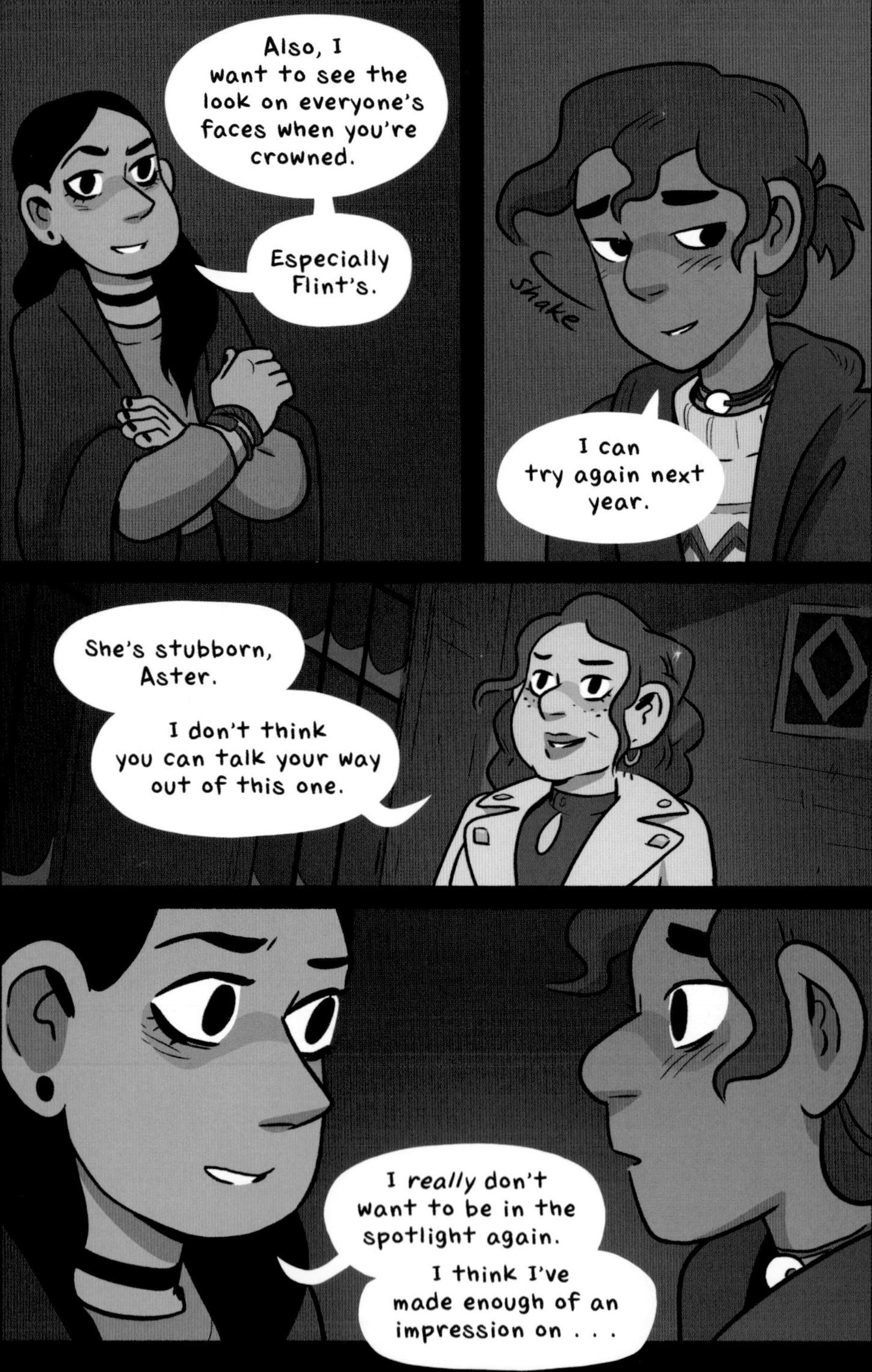
Also, I want to see the look on everyone's faces when you're crowned.
Especially Flint's.
Shake
I can try again next year.
She's stubborn, Aster.
I don't think you can talk your way out of this one.
I *really* don't want to be in the spotlight again.
I think I've made enough of an impression on . . .

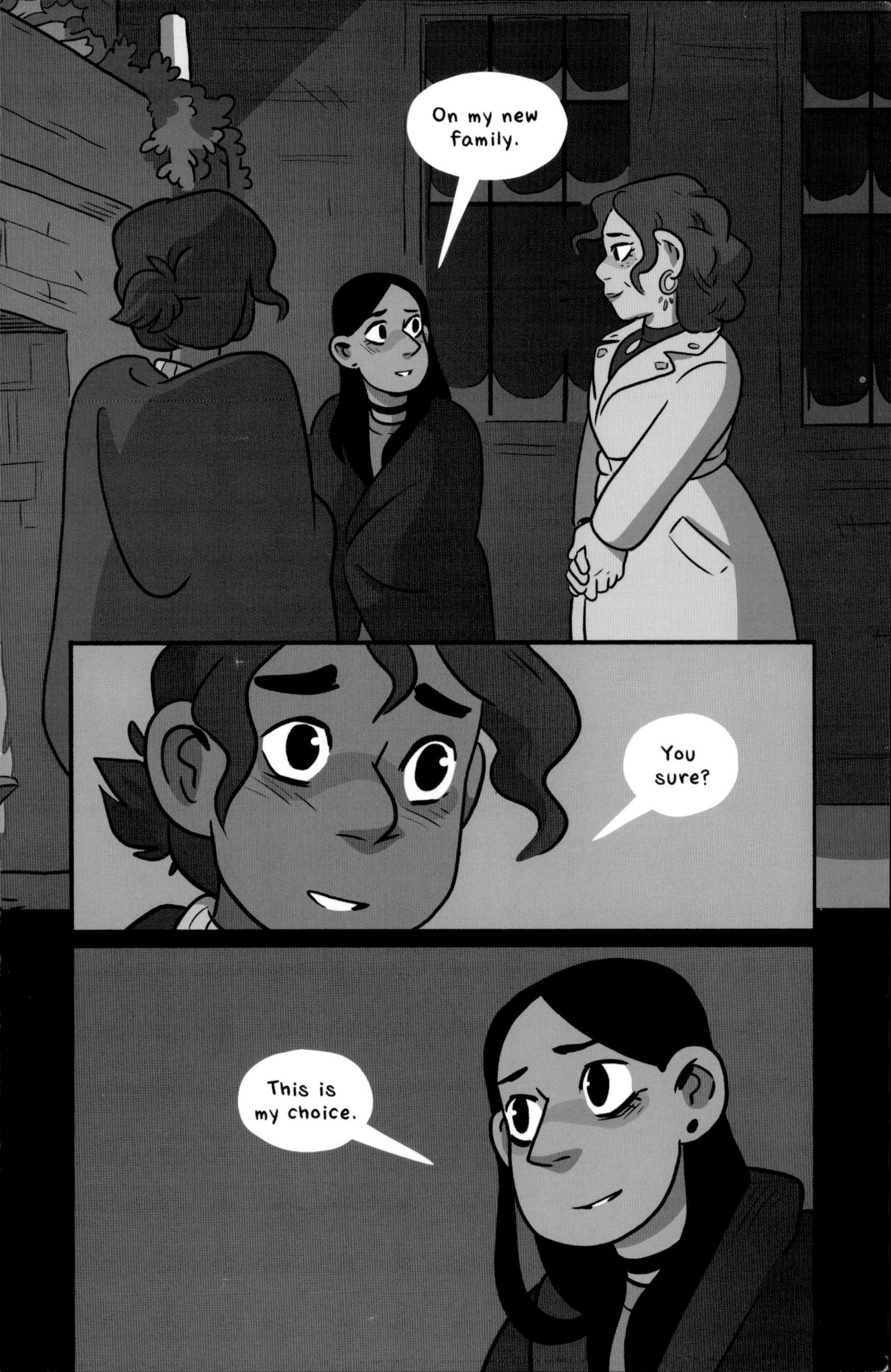
On my new family.
You sure?
This is my choice.

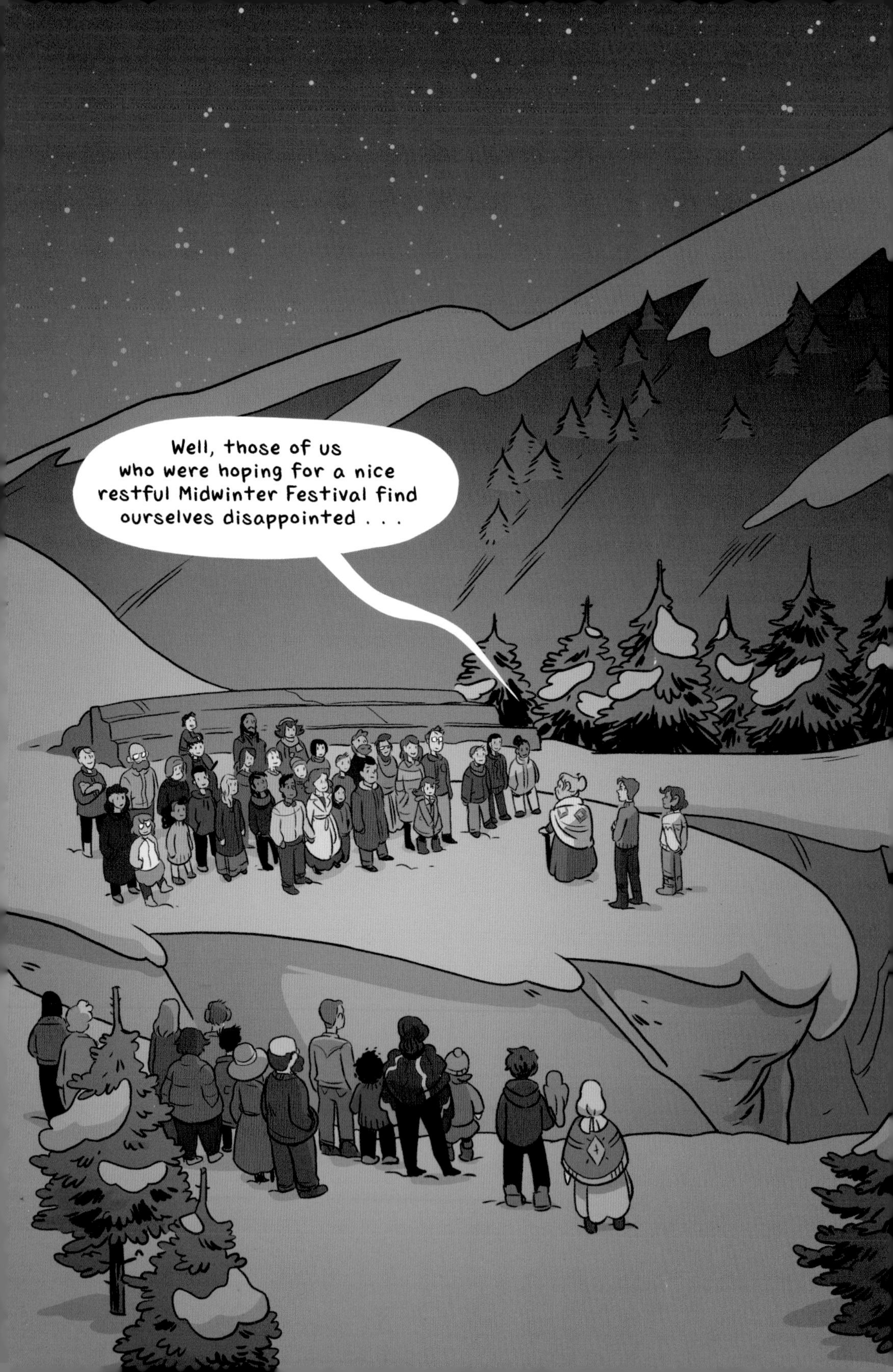
Well, those of us who were hoping for a nice restful Midwinter Festival find ourselves disappointed . . .

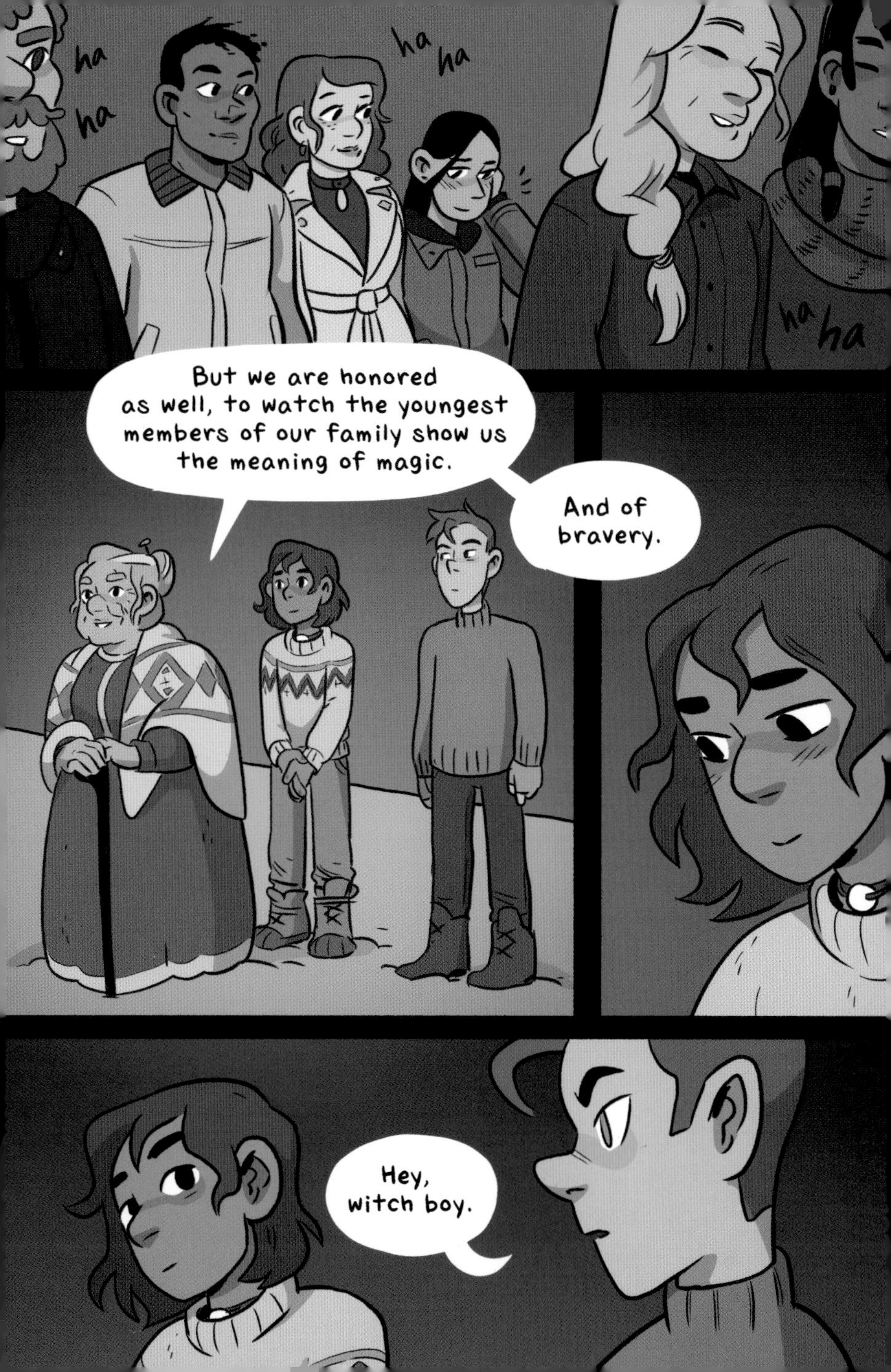
ha
ha
ha
ha
ha
ha
But we are honored as well, to watch the youngest members of our family show us the meaning of magic.
And of bravery.
Hey, witch boy.

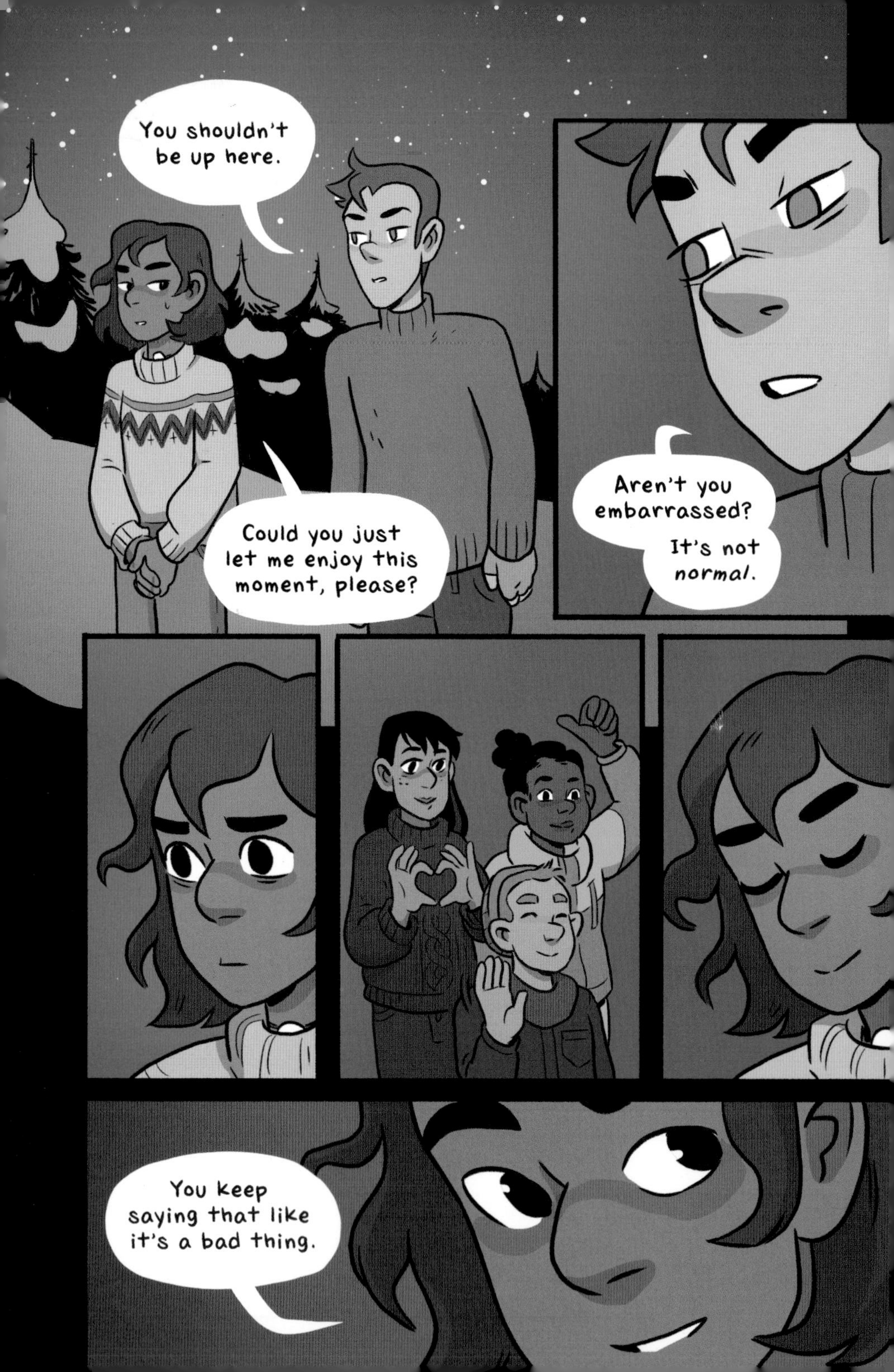

You shouldn't be up here.
Could you just let me enjoy this moment, please?
Aren't you embarrassed?
It's not *normal*.
You keep saying that like it's a bad thing.

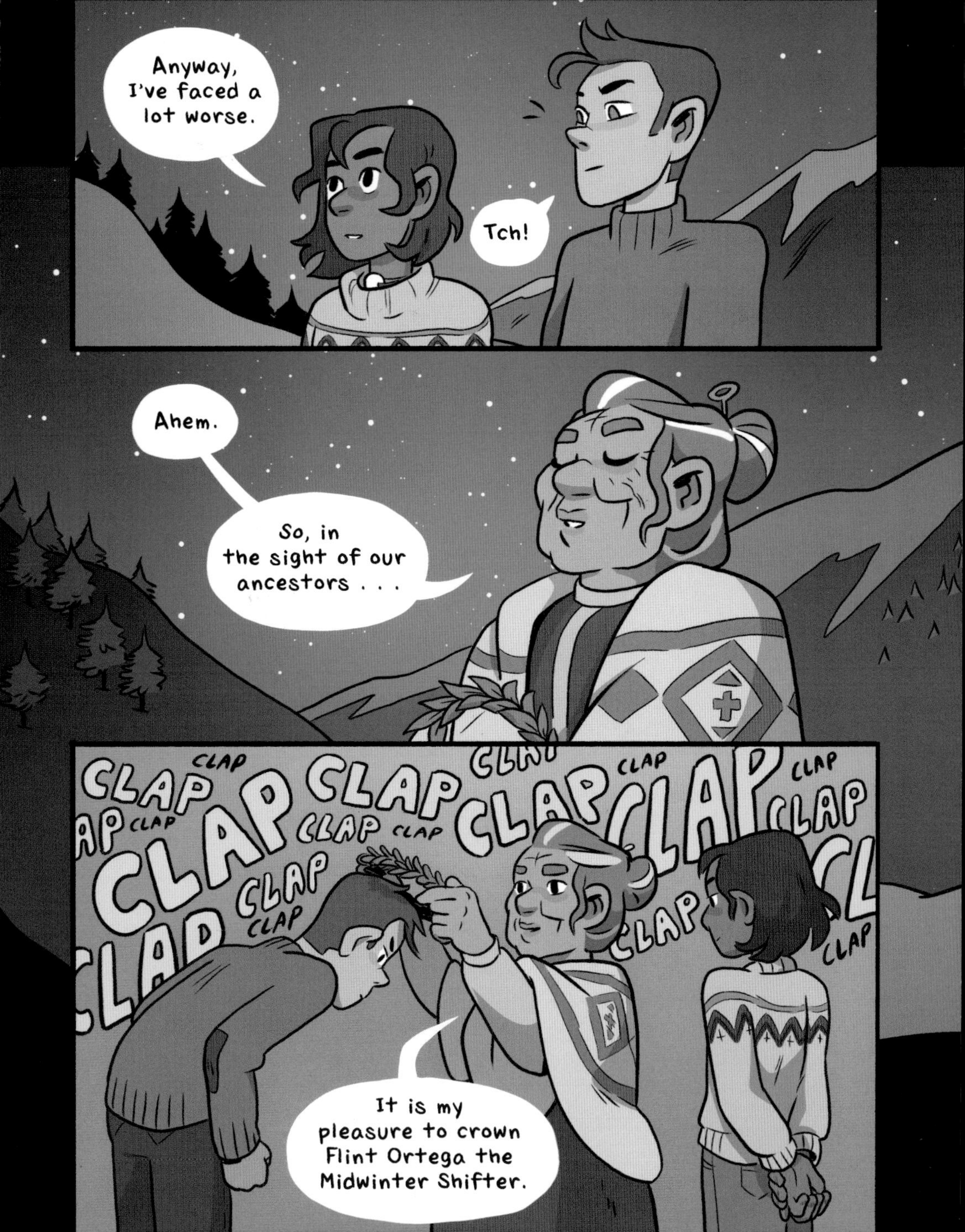
Anyway, I've faced a lot worse.
Tch!
Ahem.
So, in the sight of our ancestors . . .
CLAP CLAP CLAP CLAP CLAP CLAP CLAP CLAP CLAP CLAP CLAP CLAP CLAP
It is my pleasure to crown Flint Ortega the Midwinter Shifter.

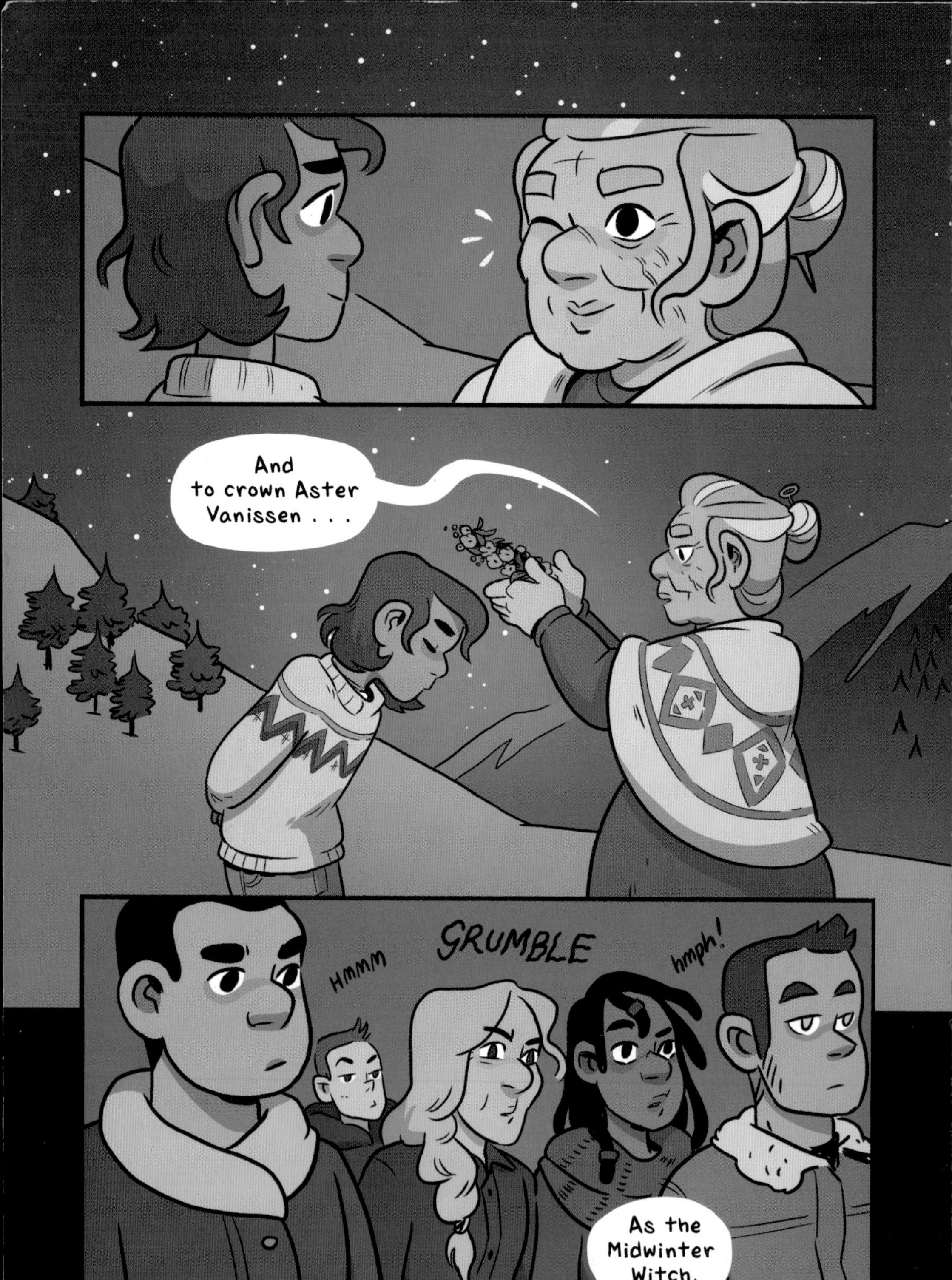
And to crown Aster Vanissen . . .
GRUMBLE
Hmmm
hmph!
As the Midwinter Witch.

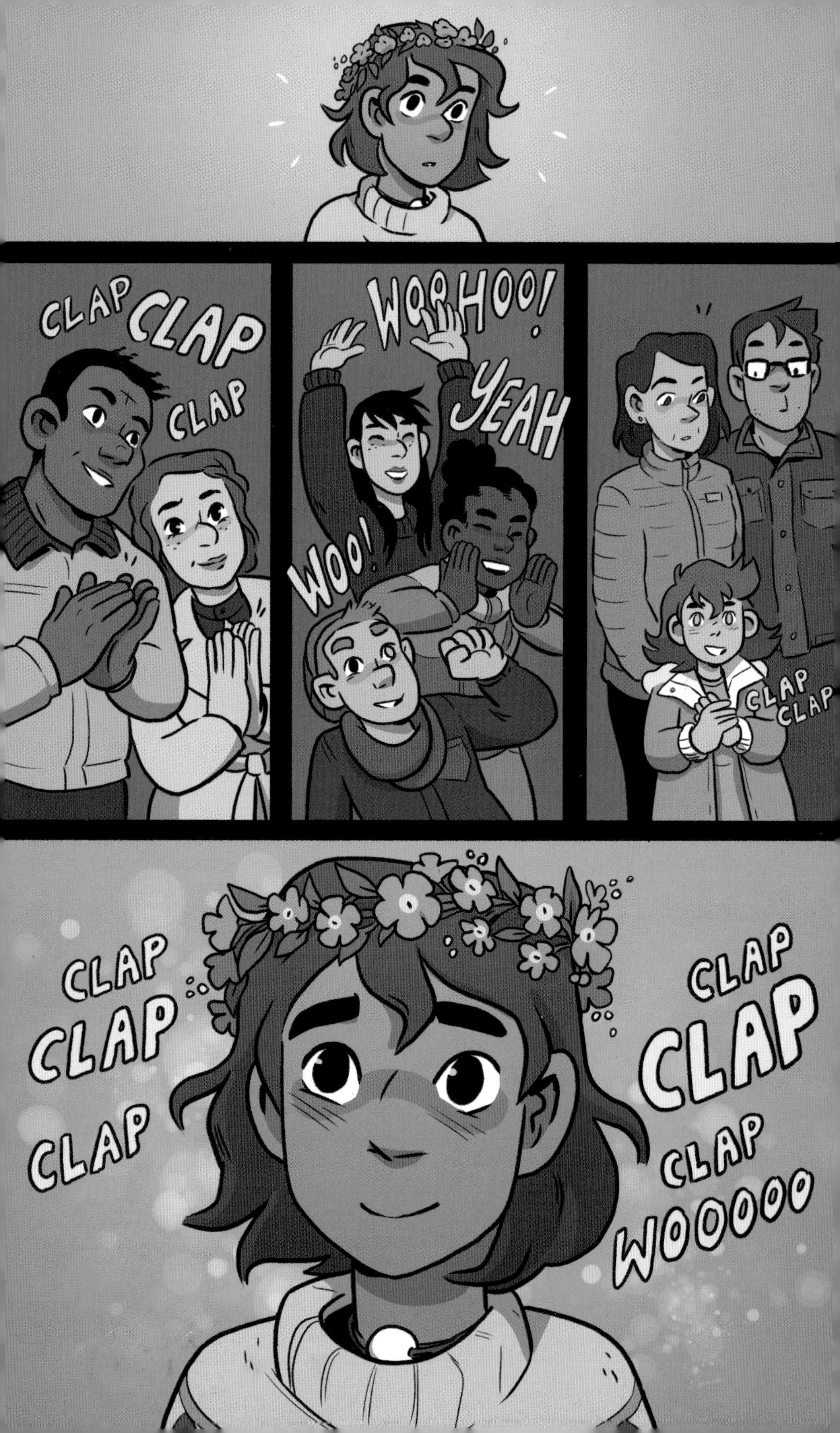
CLAP CLAP
CLAP
WOOHOO!
YEAH
WOO!
CLAP
CLAP
CLAP
CLAP
CLAP
CLAP
CLAP
CLAP
WOOOOO

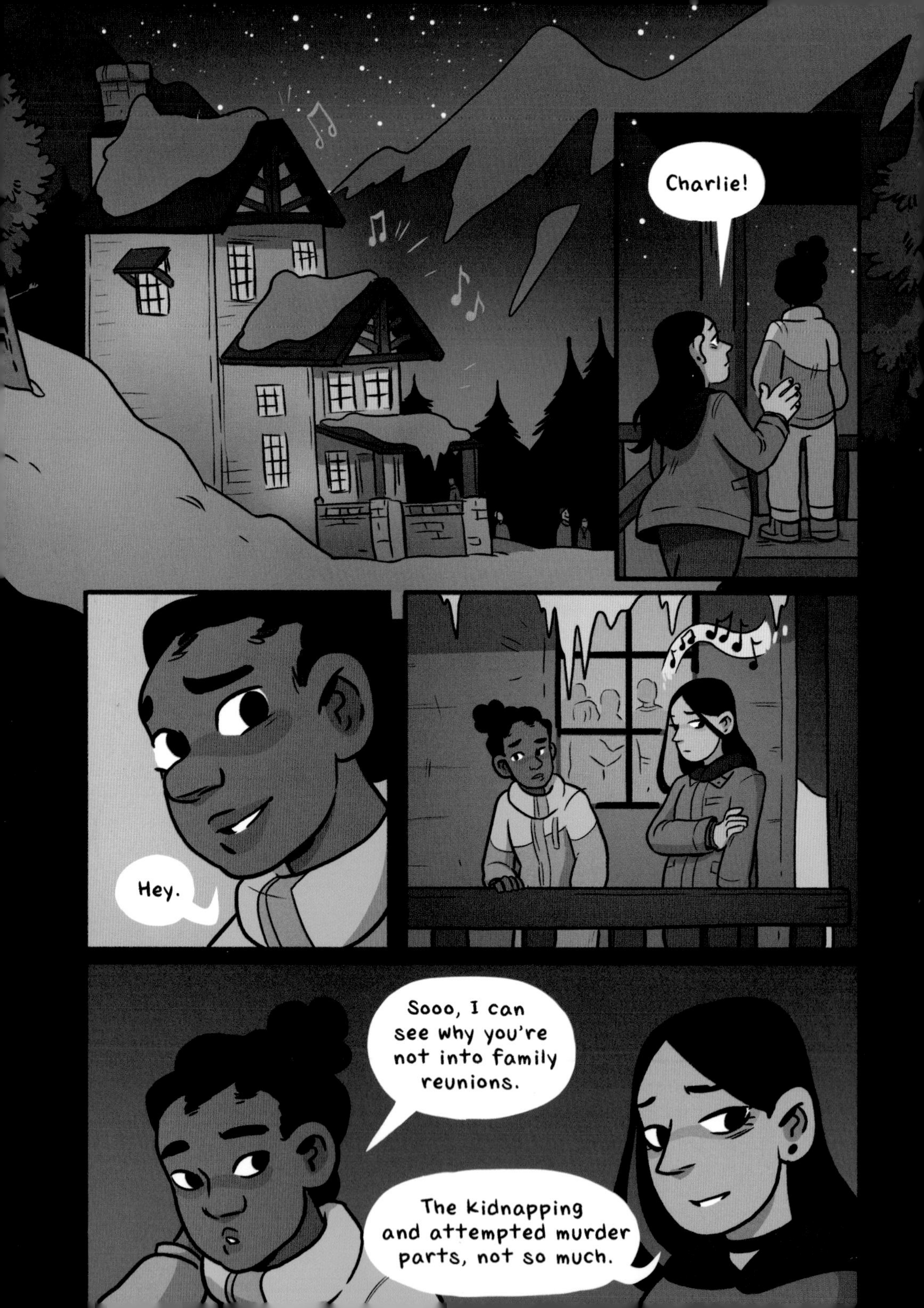
Charlie!
Hey.
Sooo, I can see why you're not into family reunions.
The kidnapping and attempted murder parts, not so much.

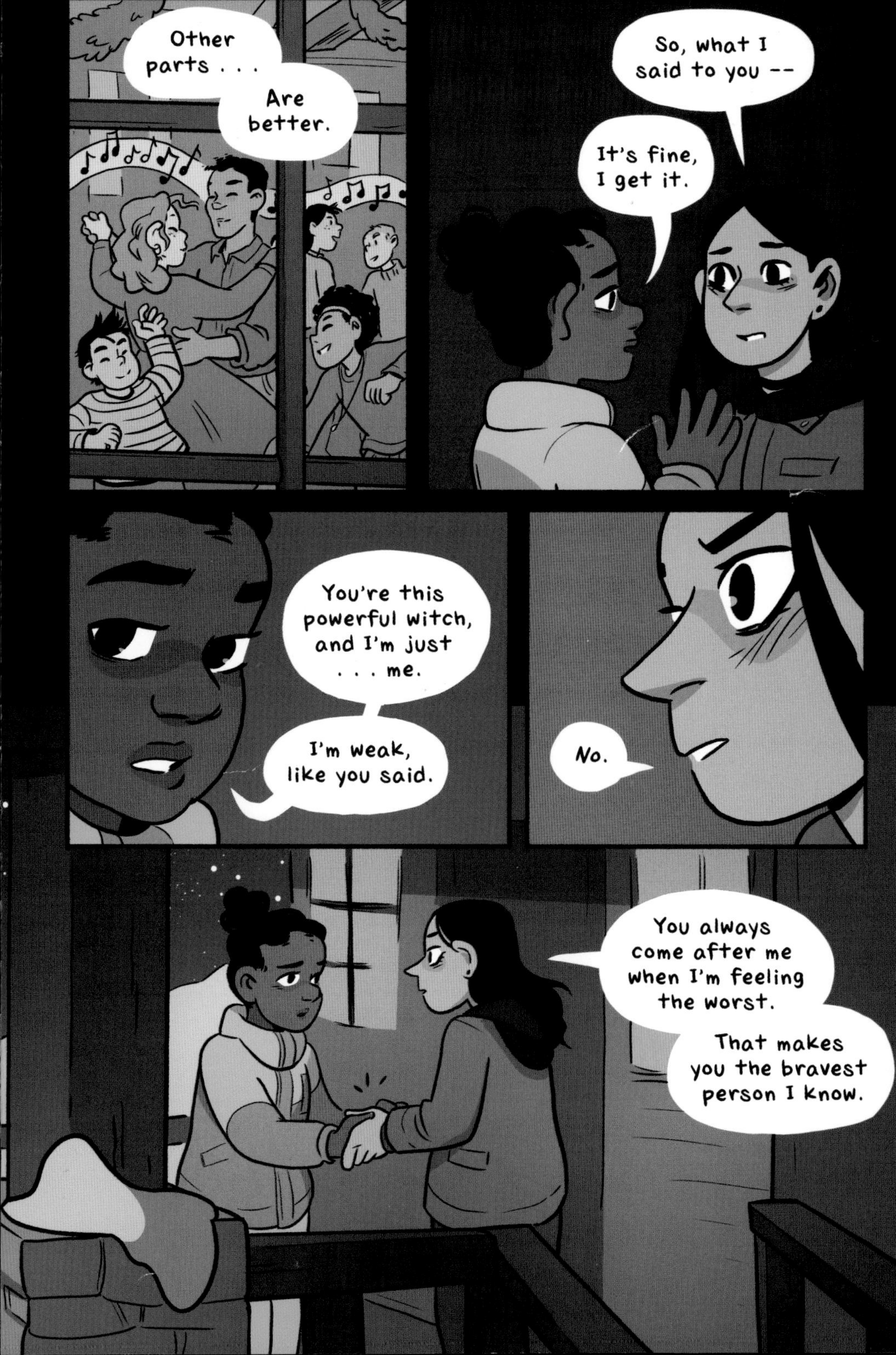
Other parts . . .
Are better.
So, what I said to you --
It's fine, I get it.
You're this powerful witch, and I'm just . . . me.
I'm weak, like you said.
No.
You always come after me when I'm feeling the worst.
That makes you the bravest person I know.

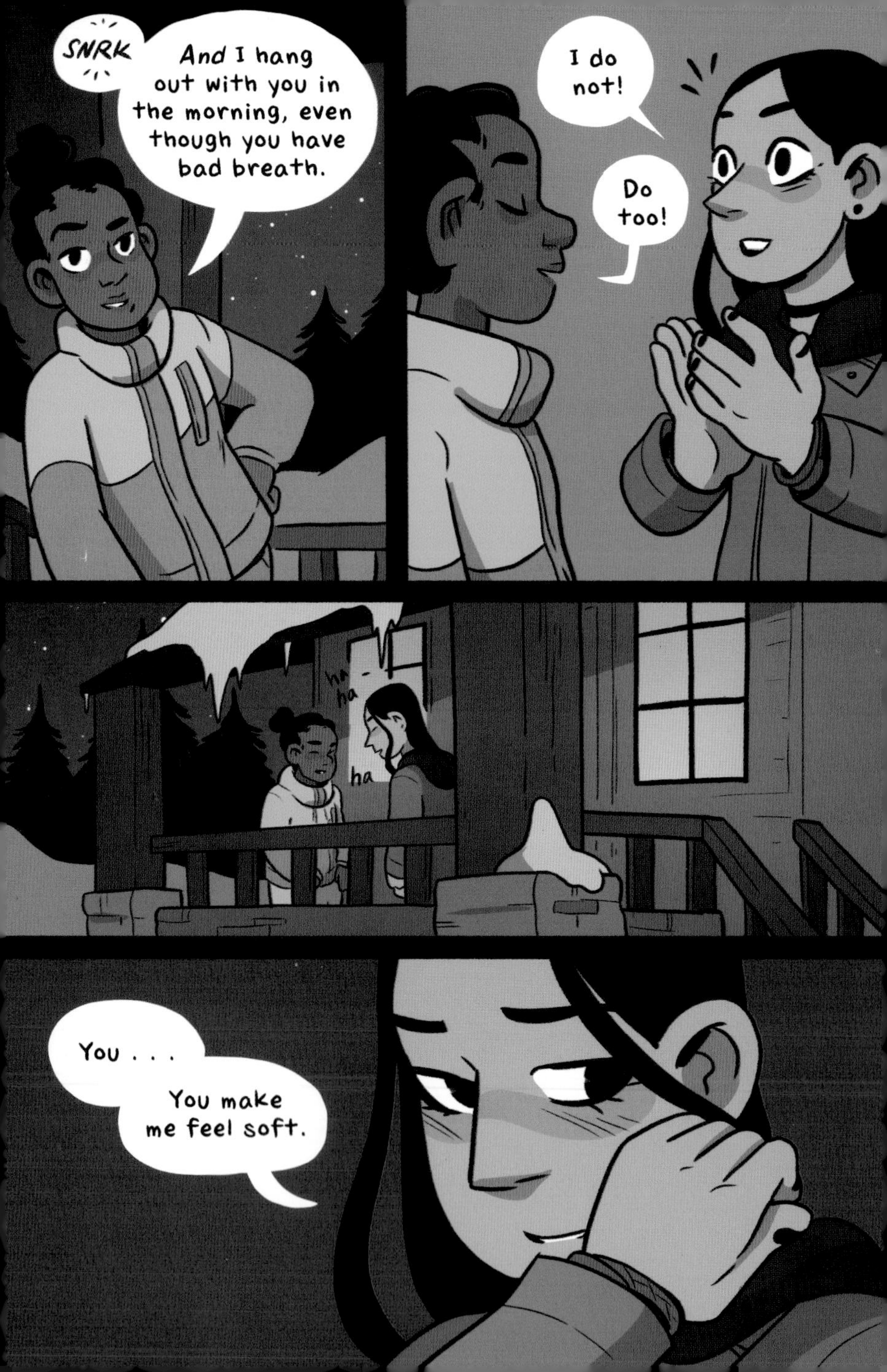
SNRK
And I hang out with you in the morning, even though you have bad breath.
I do not!
Do too!
ha ha
ha
You . . .
You make me feel soft.

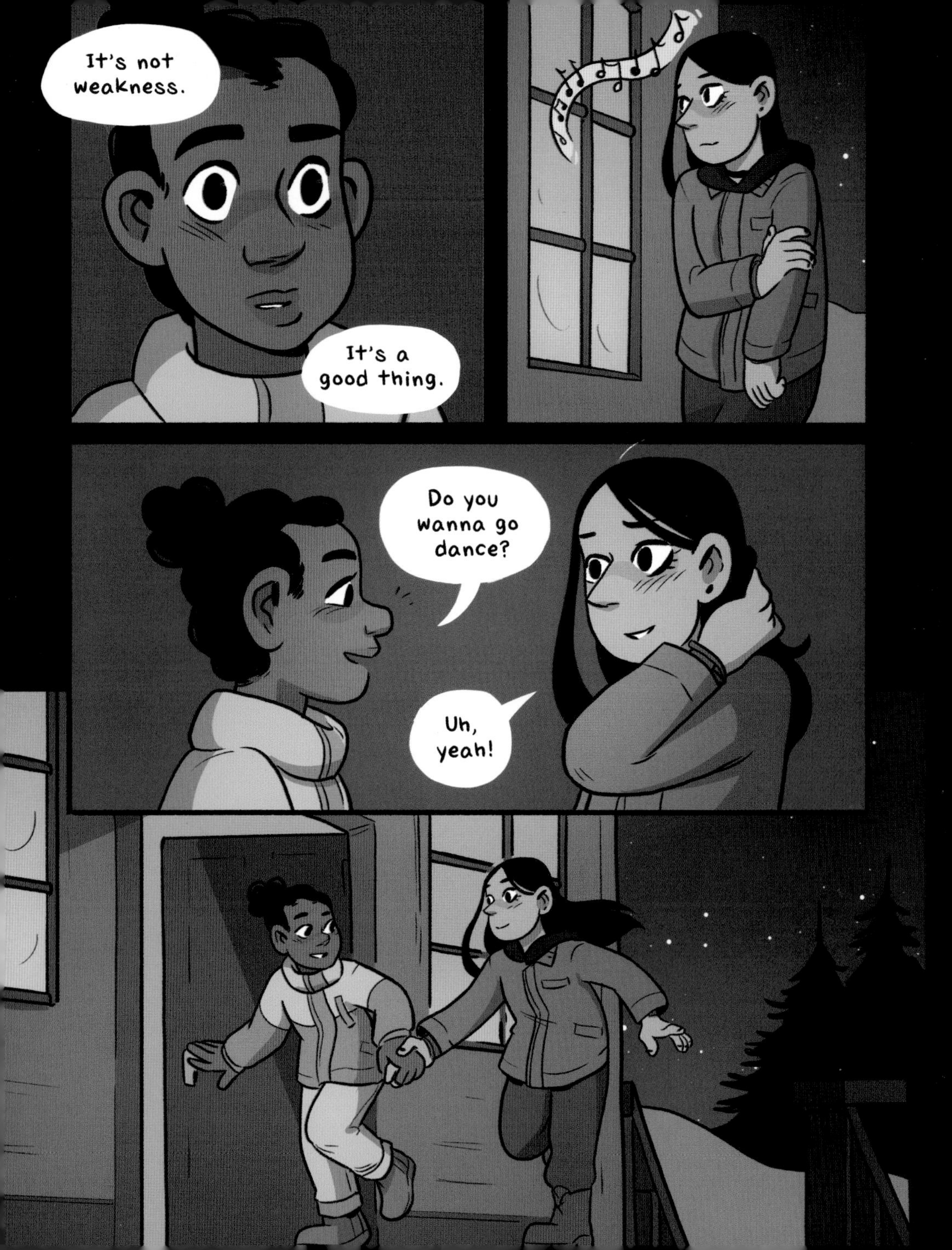
It's not weakness.
It's a good thing.
Do you wanna go dance?
Uh, yeah!

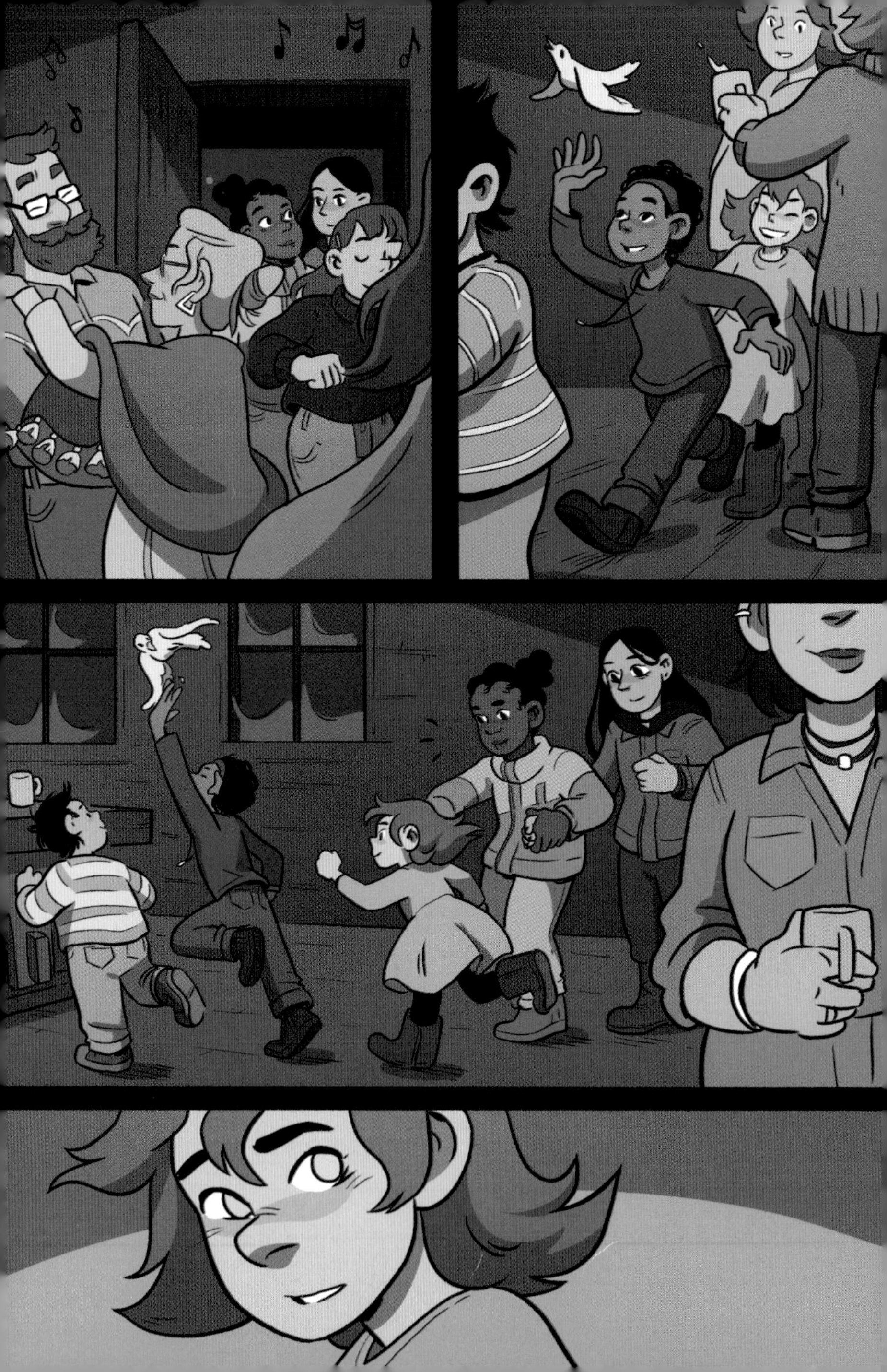

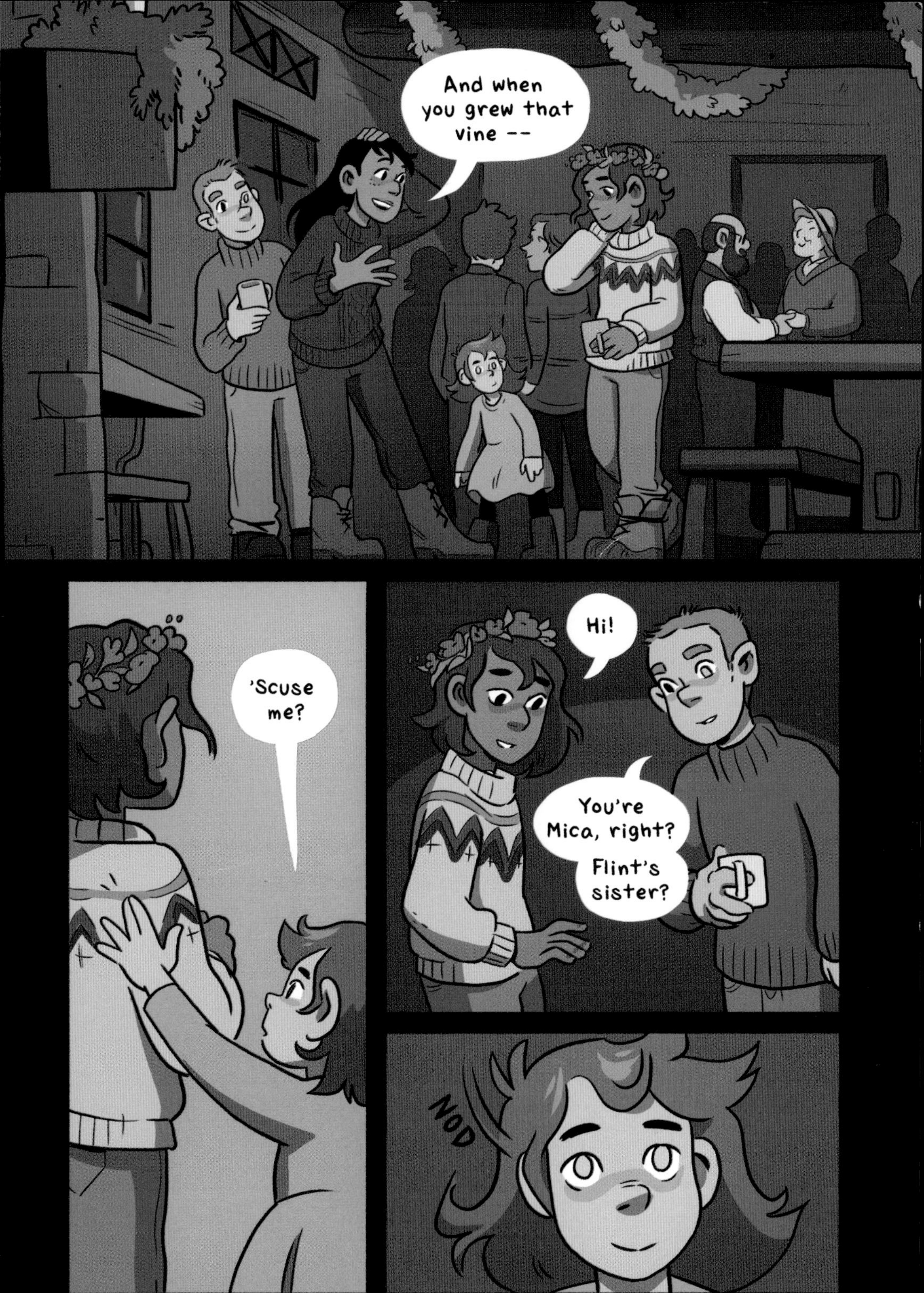
And when you grew that vine --
'Scuse me?
Hi!
You're Mica, right?
Flint's sister?
NOD

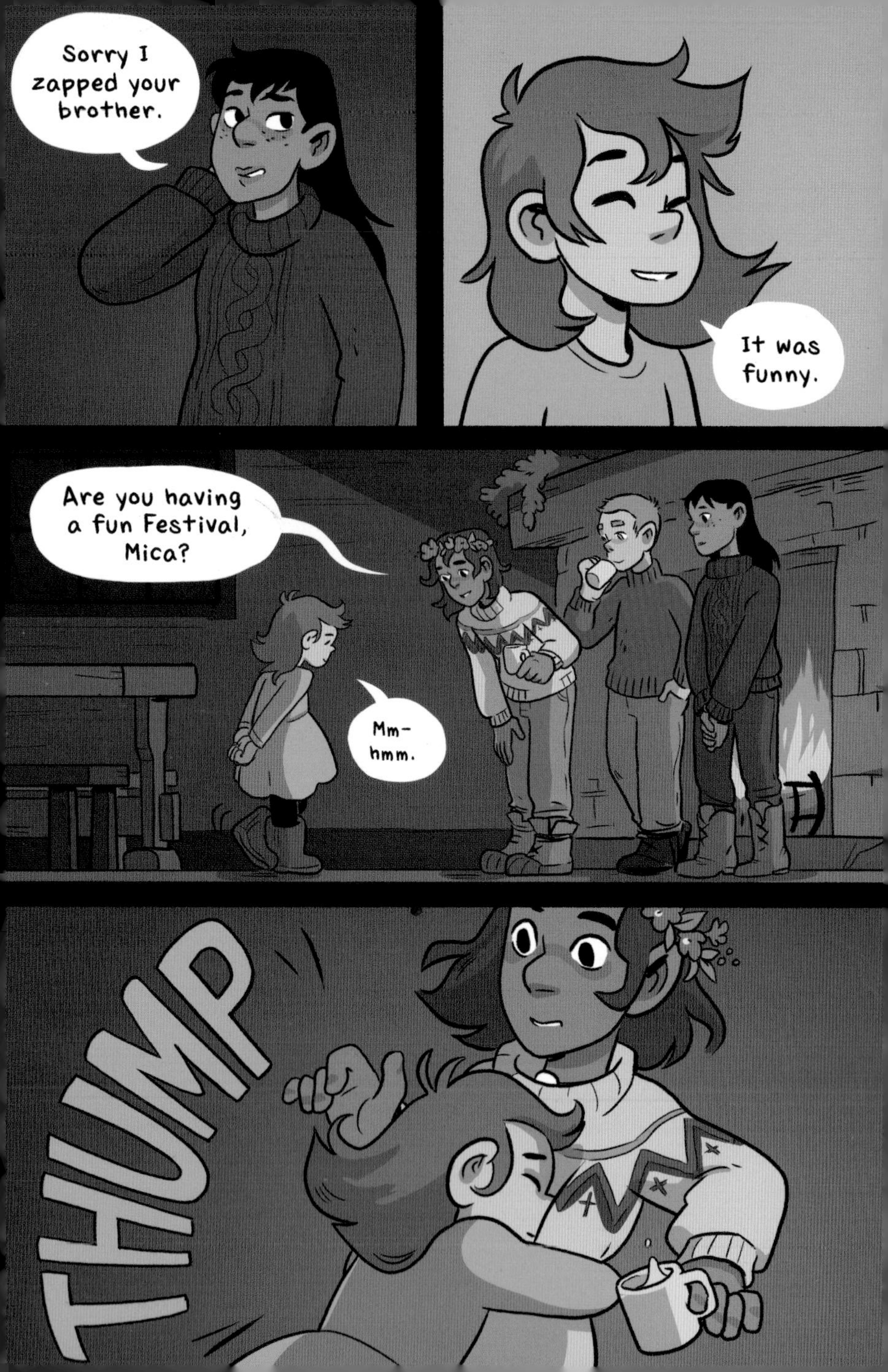

Sorry I zapped your brother.
It was funny.
Are you having a fun Festival, Mica?
Mm-hmm.
THUMP

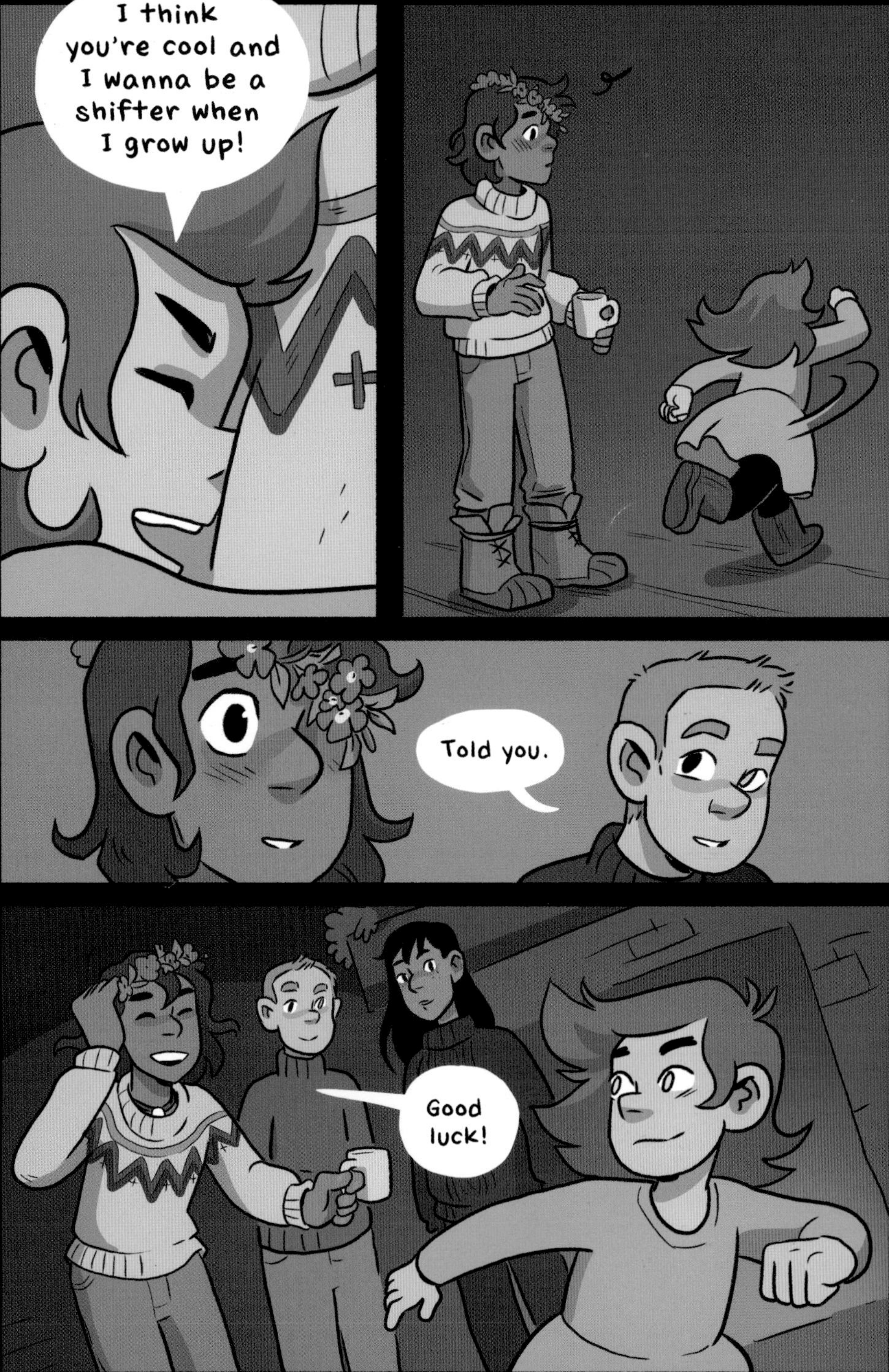
I think you're cool and I wanna be a shifter when I grow up!
Told you.
Good luck!

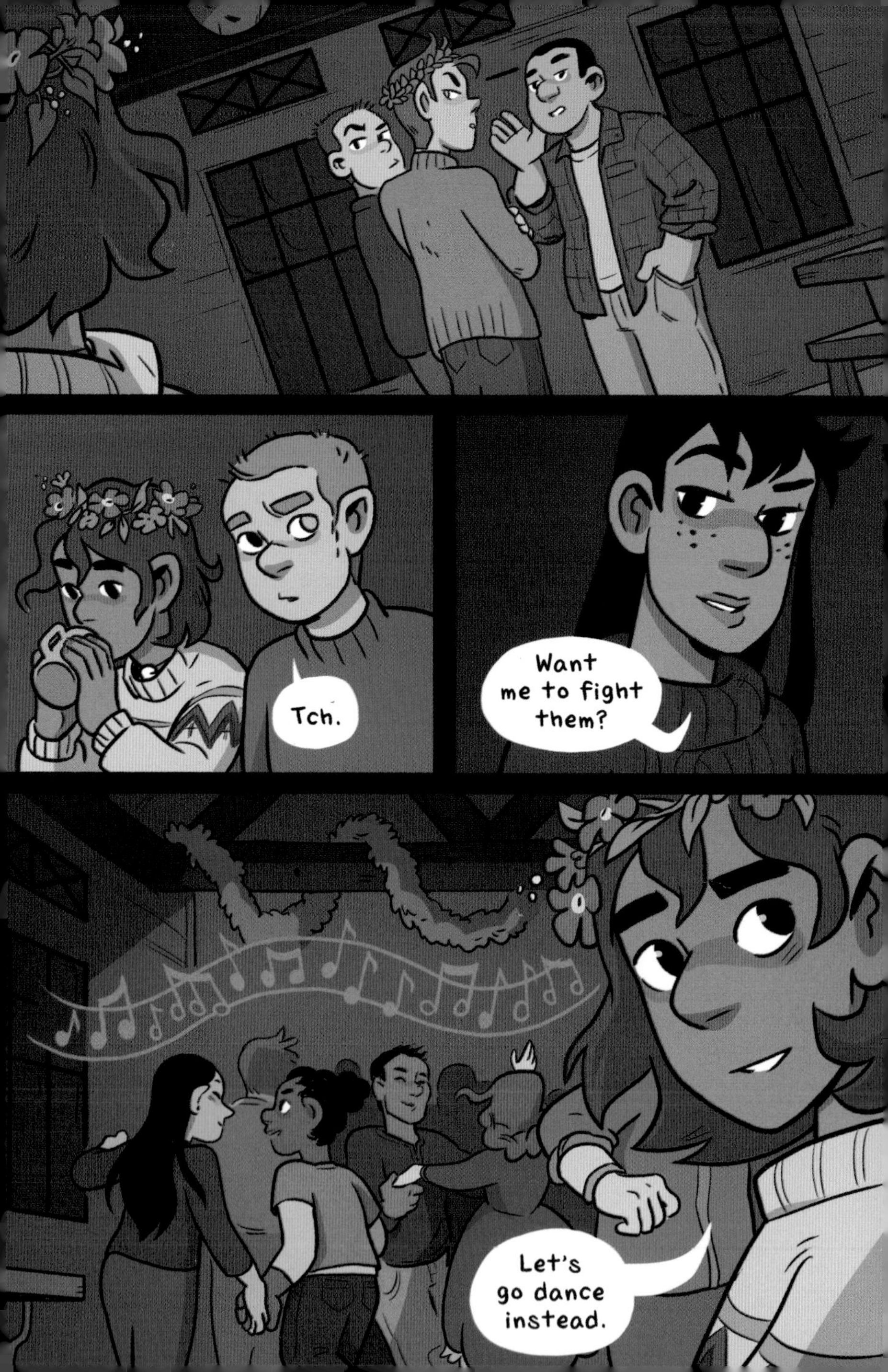
Tch.
Want me to fight them?
Let's go dance instead.

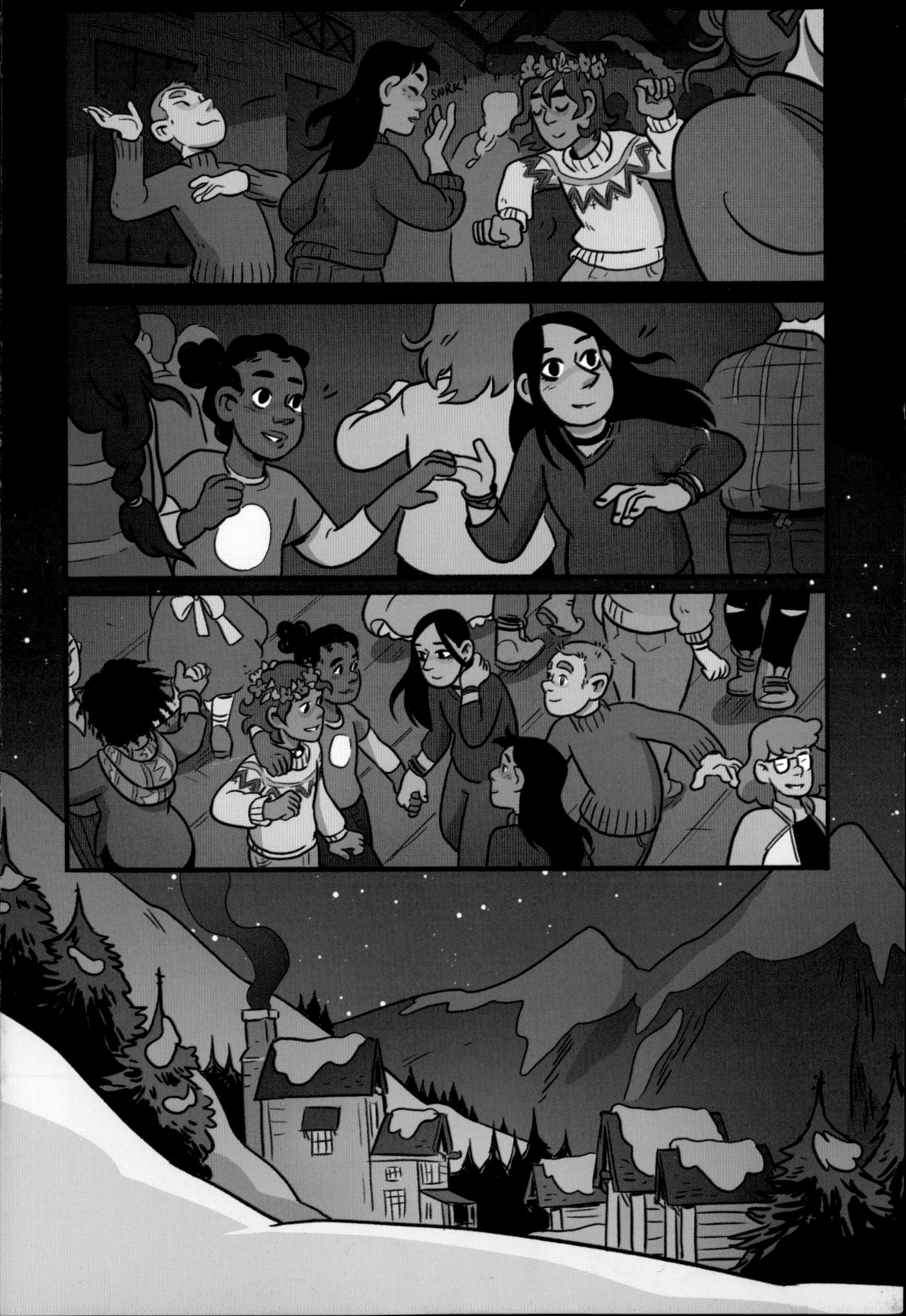
SNRK!

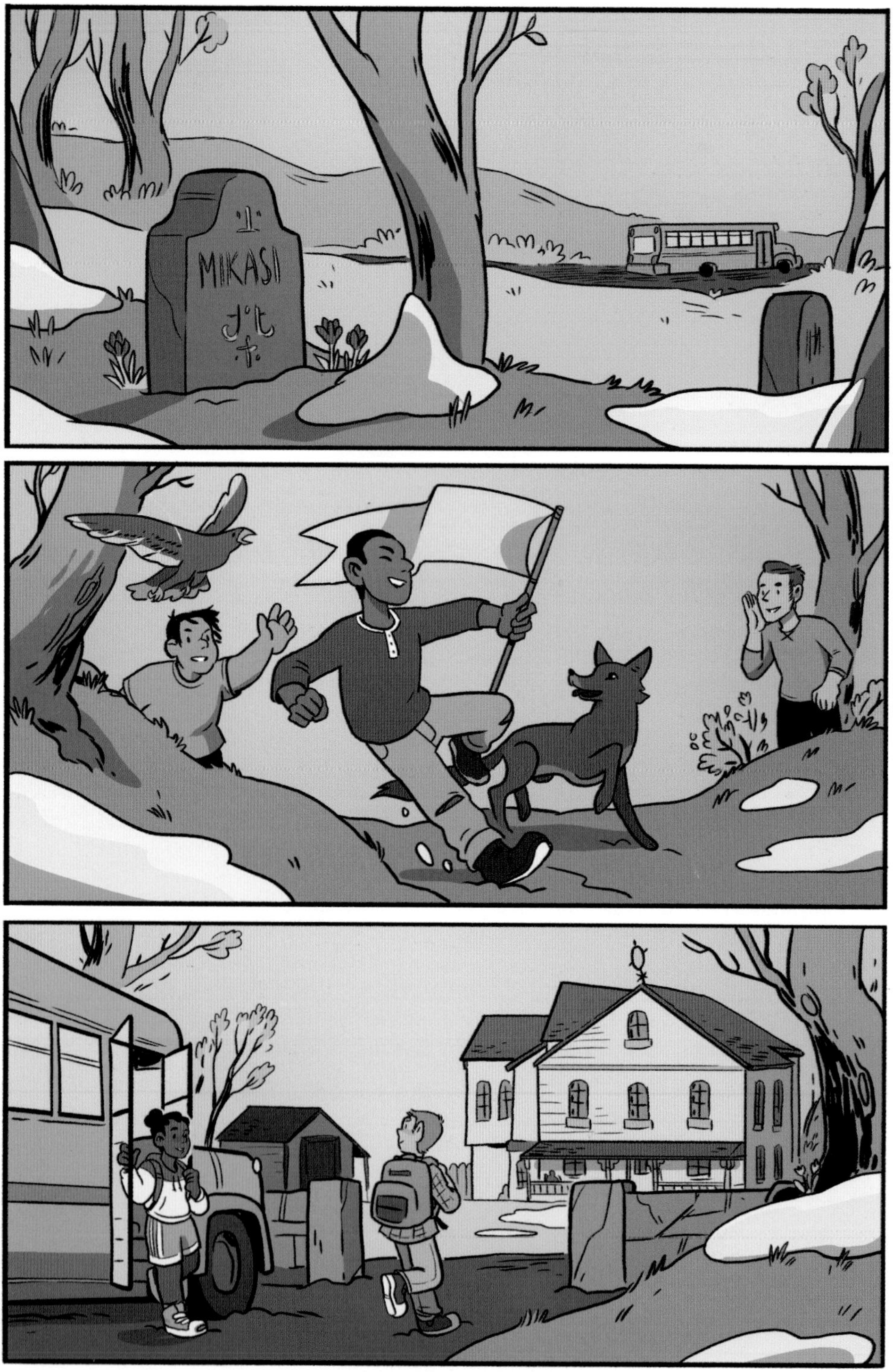
MIKASI

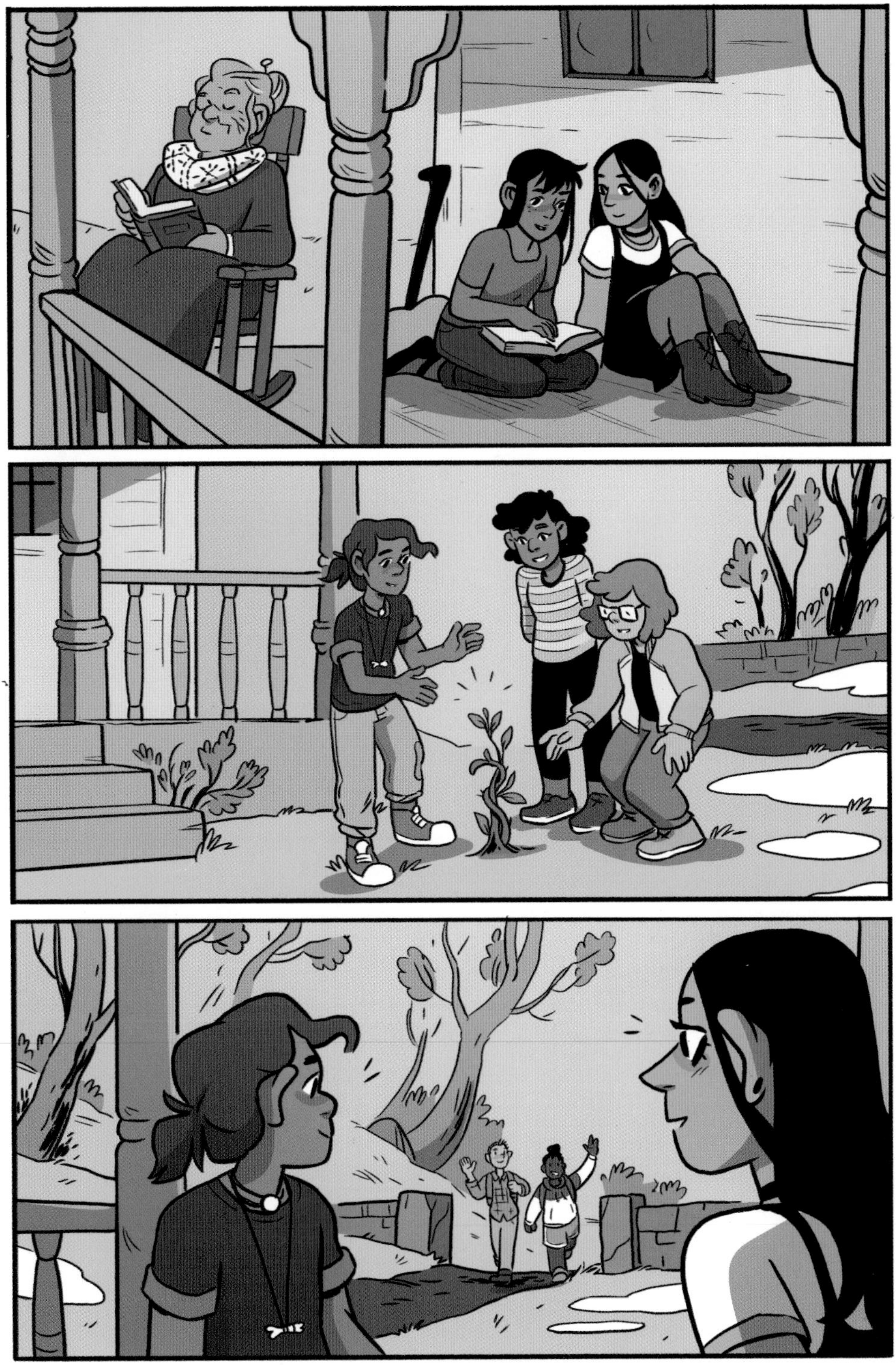

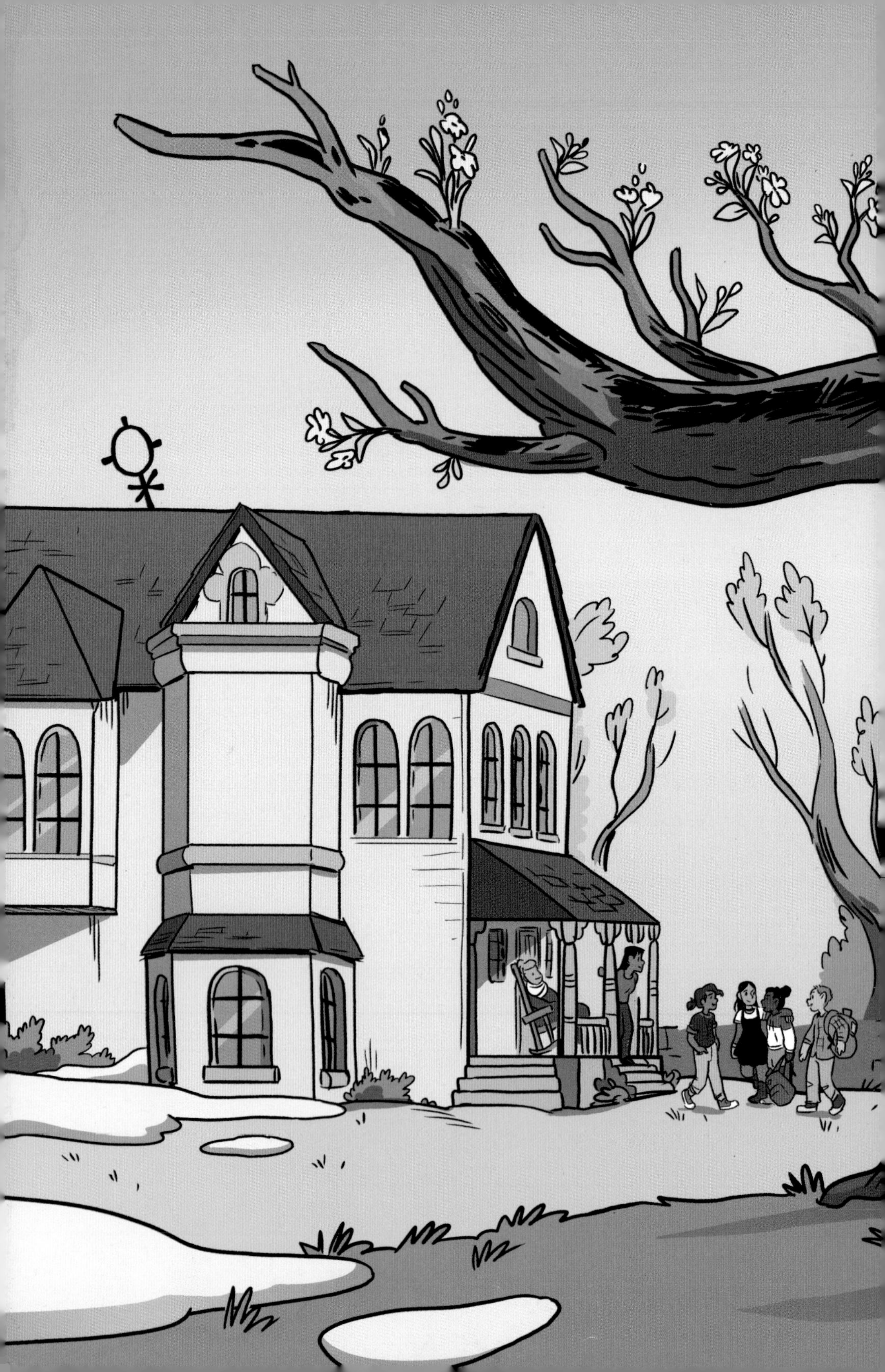

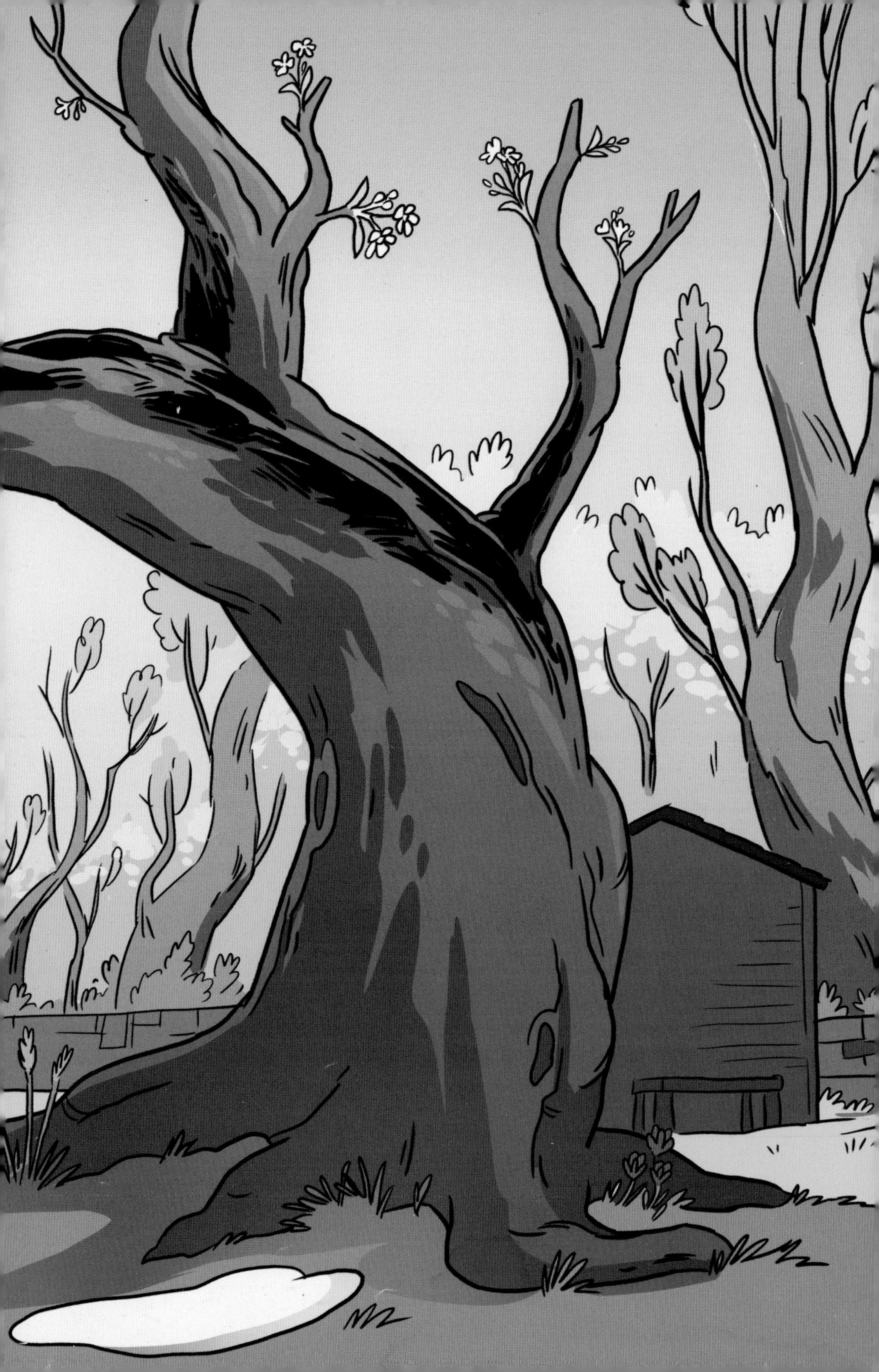

MOLLY KNOX OSTERTAG

is the author and illustrator of the acclaimed graphic novels *The Witch Boy* and *The Hidden Witch*, as well as the illustrator of several projects for older readers, including the webcomic *Strong Female Protagonist* by Brennan Lee Mulligan and *Shattered Warrior* by Sharon Shinn. She grew up in the forests of upstate New York and graduated in 2014 from the School of Visual Arts, where she studied cartooning and illustration. She currently lives in Los Angeles with her wife and several pets. You can find her online at mollyostertag.com.

MAARTA LAIHO spends her days and nights as a comic and graphic novel colorist, where her work includes Lumberjanes, Delver, and the Wings of Fire series. When she's not doing that, she can be found hoarding houseplants and talking to her cat. She lives in the woods of Maine.